AFTERLIFE
A CROSSBREED NOVEL

USA TODAY BESTSELLING AUTHOR
DANNIKA DARK

All Rights Reserved
Copyright © 2021 Dannika Dark
First Edition: 2021

First Print Edition
ISBN-13: 979-8719416-12-0

Formatting: Streetlight Graphics

No part of this book may be reproduced, distributed, or transmitted in any form or by any means, or stored in a database retrieval system, without the prior written permission of the author. You must not circulate this book in any format. Thank you for respecting the rights of the author.

This is a work of fiction. Any resemblance of characters to actual persons, living or dead, is purely coincidental.

Edited by Victory Editing and Red Adept.
Cover design by Dannika Dark. All stock purchased.

www.dannikadark.net
Fan page located on Facebook

Also By Dannika Dark:

THE MAGERI SERIES
Sterling
Twist
Impulse
Gravity
Shine
The Gift (Novella)

MAGERI WORLD
Risk

NOVELLAS
Closer

THE SEVEN SERIES
Seven Years
Six Months
Five Weeks
Four Days
Three Hours
Two Minutes
One Second
Winter Moon (Novella)

SEVEN WORLD
Charming

THE CROSSBREED SERIES
Keystone
Ravenheart
Deathtrap
Gaslight
Blackout
Nevermore
Moonstruck
Spellbound
Heartless
Afterlife

The difficulty in life is the choice.

– *George Moore*

Chapter 1

"Who wants cake?" Wyatt leaned out of the kitchen entryway and brandished a butcher knife.

Shepherd glowered at his partner, who stood beneath an archway of colorful balloons. "If you cut that cake, I'll cut out your heart."

"Easy there, Hannibal Lecter. I'm only having some fun."

I took the knife from his hand and replaced it with a plastic bag of uninflated balloons. "If you want to have fun, finish blowing these up." I set the knife on the long table behind Viktor's chair, which we normally used for alcohol. Today it was filled with plates of sugar cookies and a large bowl of fruit punch. Kira was busy preparing a birthday feast for Hunter, who turned six today.

Balloons outlined the doorways, plates with cartoon characters filled the table, and colorful streamers hung from the iron chandelier. I'd been to a few birthday parties in my time—more than these guys had—and was put in charge of buying party supplies. I could have let Shepherd do it all, but I'd needed the outing. It had only been a week since closing our last case, and while the paycheck should have been enough to satisfy me, I still felt unsettled after my burial. That gap in my memory gnawed away at my sanity each night, and when I'd tried calling the White Owl twice to speak to Houdini, he wasn't there. Even if he wasn't the one behind it, he might have seen something. The last thing I remember before waking up in a coffin was walking out of his club. After that… nothing.

Gem rolled around me and skidded to a stop. "Are you okay?"

I smiled at her outfit. "You look more festive than the decorations."

With her hip jutting out, she glanced down at her pink romper. "Do you think the skates match?"

Her roller skates shimmered like prisms and reflected light from every direction, the laces and wheels both pink.

"I almost chose the all-pink ones," she explained, "but that would be too much pink."

I gestured to her crystal necklace. "They match your jewelry."

Her violet eyes widened. "You're right! Oh, I adore celebrations. It's my first party. I don't mean the fancy balls we go to but a *real* birthday party with presents and balloons. It's better than television! Nobody better spike the punch. I want a big glass of it," she said, rolling away with a streamer tangled around one of her wheels.

Gem was the only one who had dressed up for the occasion. The rest of us looked ready for a street fight, especially Shepherd, who had a pack of cigarettes tucked inside the sleeve of his black T-shirt.

I finished taping the last inflated balloon to the back of my chair.

Christian waltzed in and dropped two giant handfuls of candy on Hunter's empty plate. "The sweets are from me."

A balloon escaped from Wyatt's lips and noisily deflated in an erratic pattern above the table before dropping to the floor. "Hold your ponies. Those are from *my* vending machine. Did you break into it again?"

Christian smiled wryly as he took a seat. "'Tis the thought that counts."

I sat next to him. "Why didn't you buy him a gift? It's not like you don't have any money."

Christian folded his arms. "We didn't have presents when I was growing up, and I turned out just fine."

Shepherd finished taping up the Happy Birthday sign on the far wall and wiped his brow. "Fucking hell, whose idea was this?"

"*Yours,*" we all chanted.

"I don't recall asking for all *this* bullshit," he grumbled, eyes darting between the decorations.

Secretly, Shepherd was enjoying the hell out of it. He'd gone out of his way to buy his son presents on the sly. Hunter had picked them out himself without knowing it on a recent shopping trip. This would be his first genuine birthday party, and we aimed to make it memorable. We knew Patrick Bane, the cruel bastard, had never done anything special for the boy.

I couldn't help but wonder how Shepherd was handling this momentous day. It wasn't just Hunter's birthday but also the day of his wife's death and one he had thought was his son's death. Those tragic events traumatized him physically and mentally. He'd only recounted the story once, but the scars covering his hands, arms, and chest were a constant reminder. Shepherd must have dwelled on that tragedy every June 2, but today would mark the first time it would mean something entirely different.

"A monkey could do better than that," Shepherd growled, pushing Wyatt aside. "Let me handle it before you mess everything up." Shepherd removed three inflated balloons from the archway and repositioned them in a way that didn't make any difference.

Christian leaned back in his chair and rested his hand on my thigh. We quietly watched the team scurry about to get the finishing touches in order.

Blue rushed into the room, her feather earrings fluttering behind her and a bag in hand. "Sorry I'm late. Do you guys need help with anything?"

Cookie crumbs fell from Wyatt's mouth as he gobbled up one of the treats. "Ask the warden."

Still winded, Blue leaned over Hunter's chair and noticed the presents. "I wanted to get him a bow and arrow, but Shep said no."

"Damn right I said no," he parroted from the doorway.

She shook her head. "He's the right age for it. Anyhow, I got him something better."

Shepherd finished adjusting the last balloon and returned to the table. "Better not be an axe."

"Modern toys don't make sense to me," she said. "I know a guy who makes hand-carved toys, and I asked him to design little people and a horse. Kids should be spirited away by their imagination, not electronics."

Wyatt strutted to his chair and sat. "I don't know what you've got against my gift."

She threw him a sharp look. "A Nincompoop?"

"*Nintendo*. And it's vintage."

Gem rolled out from the kitchen and whispered, "She's making spaghetti and meatballs."

"Why are you whispering?" Wyatt asked.

Gem grimaced. "Because I don't think she's using beef for the meatballs."

Wyatt shrugged. "Maybe it's squirrel."

Gem wrinkled her nose and shuddered, which made Wyatt laugh.

Shepherd smacked the back of Wyatt's head, knocking off his slouchy cap. Then he took his seat between Wyatt and Gem. "The meatballs are ground pork and Italian sausage. It's an old recipe that… well, it's good." He stared at the mountain of gifts, which were mostly from him. "Where's Claude?"

"He's the lookout," I said. "I sent him to let us know when they're on their way down. Someone should call Viktor in here before the party starts."

"He's still on a business call," Christian informed me, and I sensed something in his tone.

I twisted in my chair to look at the gifts lined up against the wall. They were identical in length and size, each wrapped in a different colored paper. Two long ones were leaning in the corner beside a wider package. "What the hell is all that?"

"A bookshelf," Gem said. "It's from Claude."

I snorted. "He wrapped each individual shelf? That should be exciting. Too bad we can't take pictures of the kid's face when he tears away the paper and finds a plank of wood."

Gem giggled while clutching her crystal pendant. "Claude likes to be funny. It's going to be a project for them to assemble together. You know how boys like to bond over tools. I think he bought it to hold all the new toys."

Shepherd scratched his whiskery jaw, his dark eyes pensive. "I didn't think about a shelf. Good idea."

Gem slapped the table with her palms. "I'm so excited I can hardly stand it!"

Wyatt leaned back, hand over his stomach. "I'm so hungry I can hardly stand it."

"I need a smoke," Shepherd complained.

Gem poked his shoulder. "Don't you dare stink up this room with your cigarettes. It smells heavenly right now. Like cake, frosting, cookies, and—"

"Rubber," Wyatt added, sniffing his tattooed fingers.

Niko entered the room with a basket of freshly cut peonies. "I hope these will suffice. I'm not able to see their blooms, but they smelled good enough to pick."

Blue collected the basket. "Thanks, amigo. They're perfect. I'll go put them in a vase."

Everyone quietly grinned at Niko's unicorn shirt, all except Gem. Her knowing smile made me wonder if Niko had told her that he knew about the team's little prank on his wardrobe.

"So what are we supposed to do when he walks in?" Wyatt tucked his chin in his palm. "Jump out and scare him?"

Gem worried her bottom lip. "Maybe we should play some music. I've got Spice Girls on my phone."

Shepherd shook his head. "He wouldn't like all that noise."

"So we just sit here?" Christian shifted in his seat. "Sounds like a grand idea. Someone pour me a glass of wine."

"No alcohol," Gem said, touching up her pink lipstick. "You can't drink at a child's birthday party."

"Speak for yourself," Christian murmured.

I had to smile. A kid's birthday party was the last place a fanghole like Christian would be. Then again, Keystone wasn't exactly the *Brady Bunch*. Shepherd had no choice but to assume a fatherly role, and in many ways, he reminded me of Crush with his unorthodox method of child-rearing. A man with no experience, trying to do the best he could without screwing it all up. If anything, Hunter's presence was a diversion from all the hardcore stuff we dealt with on a daily basis. He served as a constant reminder of what we were fighting for—so little guys like him would have a better world to live in.

Claude whooshed into the room so fast that he dislodged a balloon from the wall and sent it flying. "Get ready. They're coming," he said quietly.

Blue returned from the kitchen and set the vase of flowers near me.

We all rose from the table when Switch entered the room and winked just seconds before Hunter dawdled in behind him.

The second Hunter noticed the decorations, his jaw dropped, and his eyes rounded. *Damn. Why didn't we yell out* surprise? Instead, I began singing the "Happy Birthday" song. The others joined in.

Except Christian. He just added silly sound effects between the lyrics, which made Shepherd give him a thorny look.

Hunter clutched Switch's hand and marveled at the streamers, balloons, and the pile of wrapped presents.

After the song ended, we clapped and whistled.

Shepherd approached Hunter and held out his hand. "Come on, little man. You're six years old today. This is the day you were born, and we're having a big party."

Wyatt pointed at the table behind Viktor's chair. "You want a cookie?"

"Not yet," Shepherd barked, leading Hunter to his chair.

Hunter excitedly sat down on his folded legs so he could see everything. Sometimes I caught a strong resemblance to Shepherd in his features. Though Shepherd kept his hair short, I imagined it would be wild like Hunter's if he grew it out. But Hunter must have inherited his big blue eyes from his mother.

Shepherd moved the candy and plate aside and slid a box in front of him, which earned a great big hug from Hunter. He didn't seem to know what it was, only that it was pretty.

Shepherd started to tear the paper, and Hunter jerked the box away from him. "You gotta see what's inside. This is all for you. Go on. Tear it open."

After admiring the printed balloons on the wrapping paper, Hunter slowly peeled it away, taking an excruciating amount of time to open his gift.

Wyatt stole a seat. "Hurry up, kid. I'm growing roots over here."

When Hunter finally got the last bit of paper off and opened the box, his eyes lit up.

"That's the one you liked." Shepherd puffed out his chest. His grin was almost sinister and unnatural, but he was clearly proud of himself.

Hunter clutched the stuffed black cat and gave it a tight squeeze. Shepherd slid another box in front of him, and everyone took their seats and watched him slowly tear open the paper as if it might trigger a bomb to go off. Inside that one, a dinosaur that roared. The next gift was a Barbie. Seeing what Hunter picked out was about as pure as it got. Prior to staying with us, this kid had lived a sheltered life with no television or playmates.

When he opened a bag filled with rubber balls, we didn't think Shepherd would be able to get him to stop throwing them around the room. But the gift-opening ceremony wasn't over yet.

Switch collected all the torn paper and ribbons and cleared the table without a complaint, his long hair seeming to draw attention to his handsome yet animalistic features. He wasn't good at hiding his thoughts. This wasn't a conventional home for children, and I often saw the concern on his face. But not today. Before taking out the trash bag filled with wrappings, he stuck a blue bow on Hunter's head.

Hunter smiled from ear to ear as he dug through a bag of socks. All of them were predominantly pink but with different designs and patterns.

Niko reached out to touch the gift. "These are from me. Blue helped me pick the right color. Do you like them?" While Hunter didn't answer, Niko nodded as he looked in his direction. Niko could understand Hunter in a way the rest of us couldn't by simply reading his light.

"I'm pleased," he said. "Shall we tell Kira we're ready to eat?"

Viktor finally strode into the room. "We cannot eat until we have cake! Always dessert first on birthday." He took the bow off Hunter's head and rumpled his hair. "You are big boy today. Happy birthday," he said, repeating it in Russian. "I see you have many gifts. Open your hands."

Hunter splayed his fingers and looked up at him.

"Nyet. Cup them together like you are holding water." When Viktor reached in his pocket, it jingled, and he dropped several coins into Hunter's hands.

I leaned over the table to see.

"These are special coins. Very old. You should keep them in a special box. Do you have a box to put important things in?"

Hunter shook his head.

"You do now," Switch said, returning from the kitchen and holding out a wooden box. He opened the lid, and Hunter dropped the change inside.

When the box closed, Hunter placed it on the table and ran his fingers over the wolf carved on the lid.

"That was nice of you," Gem said.

Switch put his hands in his pockets and shrugged. "Can't have coins without a place to put them. When Viktor told me what he was giving him, I thought about a box I had as a kid. I used to put all my treasures in there, which amounted to nothing more than rocks, a watch face, a map of all the places I wanted to visit, an arrowhead I found once while digging in the yard, and a pack of gum."

I jerked my head back. "Gum?"

"Yeah. They discontinued it, so I saved my last pack."

"Some brands last for years," Wyatt said, twirling a fork between his fingers. "Have you ever tried the stuff made from whale blubber? It's the best."

Christian hooked his arm over the corner of his chair. "Do you know what happens to whales when they're trapped?"

I pinched his leg. "*Not at this party,*" I hissed. Christian didn't come with a filter, especially when it came to random animal facts that might repulse others.

He clenched his jaw and glowered at Wyatt before steering his gaze to the kitchen entryway.

Kira floated in with a three-tier cake that was the most colorful creation I'd ever seen. She had masterfully used rainbow stripes over the blue icing, and it looked like a professional cake you would order.

"I showed her a magazine," Gem said with a deliberate nod.

Shepherd rushed to help Kira, no doubt fearing she would drop the tray. The six candles lit on top were precariously close to setting her kerchief on fire. When they reached the table, they gingerly set the cake in front of Hunter, the flames dancing, wax dripping down the candles.

Wyatt began singing "Happy Birthday" again, and even though we'd already been through this, we joined in for an encore. This time, we were loud.

Shepherd held his spot behind Hunter's chair and quietly watched. It was near sunset, and Kira hadn't lit the lanterns or chandelier, so the six bright candles illuminated Hunter's enthralled face.

Claude folded his arms over the back of a chair. "Go on, little one. Make a wish and blow them out. If you wait too long, the cake will melt."

Hunter tilted his head up and looked at Shepherd, who pressed his lips tightly together. When his father nodded in approval, Hunter leaned forward and blew out two candles. Shepherd's eyes glistened as Hunter struggled before snuffing them all out.

His victory received a thunderous applause of palms slapping against the table.

"Finally! We can eat," Wyatt exclaimed.

Hunter plugged his nose and waved away the smoke.

While Kira pulled the candles out of the cake, Viktor circled the table to his chair and briefly glanced at the snacks behind him, no doubt wondering where his wine collection had gone.

"We're not drinking tonight," I informed him, watching Shepherd hack through the beautiful cake.

Instead, Viktor filled a crystal glass with punch and took his seat.

With a stuffed cat on his lap and toys within reach, Hunter nibbled his dessert and then fed cake to his dinosaur. He tried putting one of Blue's carved figures into his box, but it wouldn't fit. Shepherd dragged his chair next to his boy, his elbow on the table and his fist tucked against his cheek as he watched Hunter delight in all his goodies.

"Was your phone call a job offer?" I asked Viktor hopefully.

"That was… personal call." A smile touched his lips. "I've made plans to dine with the enchanting Miss Parrish."

"Lenore?" Had I been eating, I would have choked on my food. "Do you normally go out to dinner with your associates to talk business?"

"This is not work related, and she is the one who invited me."

Christian's chair scraped against the floor as he scooted back and got up.

Gem walked around the table to hand Viktor his cake and then set a plate in front of me. "You have a date, Viktor? Do tell."

Blue scooted over to Christian's chair. "Isn't that a conflict of interest to have a personal relationship with someone who contracts work for us?"

Christian returned from the punch bowl and handed me a glass. "Perhaps you should find yourself a lass who will let you wear the pants. That one is all trousers."

Gem frowned as she sat in her chair. "Since when are men the only ones allowed to ask someone out? That's an archaic ritual with no purpose except to assert that women should have no power over what happens in their lives. Good for you, Viktor."

"Women complain that chivalry is dead." Wyatt licked icing off his fork. "But the minute you go old school with chivalry, they call you a chauvinistic asshole."

"Maybe that's because you *are* an asshole," Blue retorted. "Ever thought of that?"

He swallowed his bite. "All I'm saying is that women never ask me out, so I'm the one doing all the work."

"That doesn't help prove your case," Blue countered.

"Whatever you say, bird lady. If a woman's pretty, I let her know it. But I treat them with respect. Ask Claude."

"It's true," Claude said from across the table. "Wyatt speaks to females with respect. It's what he does with his eyeballs that I have an issue with."

"I don't know what you're talking about." Wyatt shoveled a large bite into his mouth.

"Aye, you don't have any control over your leering ways," Christian agreed. "Those eyeballs of yours would incinerate if splashed with holy water."

"Can we change the subject?" Gem snatched a candy ring from the table and put it on her finger. Instead of eating it, she admired it as if it were a real ruby.

We kept the conversation light and let Hunter play with all his toys for about an hour before Kira served spaghetti and meatballs. Because it was a special occasion, she and Switch stayed in the room, though they chose to sit in one of the booths. Normally they ate at a different time so they wouldn't overhear sensitive discussions we had about work.

I wasn't sure where Wyatt put it all, but after gobbling up ten cookies, he enjoyed two helpings of dinner. Hunter nibbled on everything, but he was too excited to sit still and eat his entire dinner. I'd given him a giant bottle of bubbles—which he blew on everyone—and a kite. I figured since we had plenty of land behind the mansion, a kite would give Shepherd some father-and-son time with him.

"You seem a million miles away," Christian said, his arm around me, his chair scooted close.

I stared at the empty plates and cake crumbs on the table, listening to everyone in the gathering room as Hunter played with his new toys. "I'm just tired."

"Nightmares?"

I shut my eyes. The nightmares used to be about Fletcher

chaining me to a wall, but now those dreams mingled with darkness, a coffin, and suffocation. "I think I just need a new mattress."

"Don't be fibbing. I haven't brought up your burial since that night, but if you want to talk about it, I'm your man. I've been there. I've done that."

I tugged on his fingers that rested over my shoulder. "Talking about it doesn't make it go away. It doesn't make me feel better. What *would* make me feel better is finding the person who did it."

"And what would you do? Spoon out their eyes?"

I flicked his palm. "I want to know *why* they did it. If they're getting back at me for something, if I know this person…"

Christian sighed melodically. "You're too young to appreciate patience. You can't let something like this consume your every thought, or you'll never enjoy your life. Put all those emotions stirring inside you on the back burner."

I smiled. "That's such a human thing to say."

"Would you rather I suggest you dismember their corpse in a wood chipper and feed it to wild boars?"

"How did I find such a romantic?"

He kissed my head. "I'll never feed you to the hogs."

Switch swaggered over, flipped Wyatt's chair around, and straddled it. "Do the lovebirds have plans today?"

"You're a wanker," Christian said.

Switch gave him a bored look. "News flash—I don't give a shit what you think. I'm not here to impress you."

"Mission accomplished."

Switch addressed me with a look. "Going to see your old man?"

"I hadn't planned on it. Why?"

Switch rubbed his chin against his arm and looked at the empty cookie tray. "Just wondering."

"What's wrong?"

He shrugged and averted his wolfish eyes, which went against his nature. Switch wasn't supposed to meddle in my work or personal life, but something was bugging him, and apparently he couldn't help himself.

"Switch, I've got a knife in my boot. If you don't tell me what's going on, I'll add two more ornaments to my Christmas tree."

His gaze darted to the gathering room and then back to me. "I don't know for sure. I'm not around the local packs as much as I used to be, but I drove out there yesterday, and something's off."

"Off how?"

"My father had a few important people over, including Crush. When I walked in the door, they got real quiet and gave me the look."

"What look?"

"The look Keystone gives me when I accidentally walk in on deep discussions."

I folded my arms on the table. "Why would my father be involved in Shifter business?"

Christian snorted. "Why *wouldn't* he be? Your da has a gift of inserting himself where he doesn't belong."

When Switch sat up straight, his chair creaked. "If there's anywhere Crush belongs, it's in the middle of pack business. Well, at least with the packs in that area. They're family. Anyhow, just thought you might want to pay him a friendly visit." Switch stood and flipped the chair around. "They don't tell me much about pack business anymore. Not since..." He rapped his knuckles against the table. "I need to put together some study guides. See ya."

I watched Switch strut out of the room with a rock star stride that must have beckoned the ladies... up until they learned about his sketchy past. From my understanding about Shifters, the protection that came with belonging to a pack was paramount, but none of that mattered now since he couldn't settle down and mate until his time at Keystone was up.

What mess has my father tangled himself up in?

I scooted back my chair. "I'm heading out."

"Have a nice ride."

That was Christian's way of not inviting himself. Just as well. Whenever he and my father were in the same room, they were like two sticks of dynamite with a short fuse.

I swung my leg over Christian and straddled him.

"*Mmm*, I like that," he said, his voice low and sexy.

I gave him a feather-soft kiss and then nipped his bottom lip. Before his erection reached full capacity, I broke the kiss and nuzzled into the crook of his neck. His pulse ticked against my lips but didn't tempt me. My thoughts were elsewhere. "I might be home late. Keep the bed warm?"

"You think I want to hang around here with the loons? Perhaps I'll go out for a pint."

When I licked his neck, Christian hissed and jumped in his seat as if a snake had bitten him.

"If you keep that up, Precious, I'll take you right here on this table."

We both turned our heads when Claude forcefully cleared his throat. He glared at us through one of the archways in the divider wall like a judge about to sentence a criminal.

"Why don't you shove a fecking cookie up your nose, Chitah?"

It wasn't as if Hunter was anywhere near us or within earshot, but Claude couldn't help reacting to emotional scents.

With that, I stood and briefly touched the onyx ring on Christian's finger. He centered his eyes on my ruby necklace, and it felt as though we were claiming each other with that quiet exchange.

I stretched away. "If you go out, behave yourself, Mr. Poe."

"Always do, Precious. Always do."

Chapter 2

WHEN I PULLED MY TRUCK into my father's driveway, the trailer porch light switched on. I honked my horn, a sound he was familiar with since this was his old truck. It was either that or risk him charging outside with a shotgun pointed at me.

Crush leaned on the railing while I parked. "You got mud on your truck."

I slammed the door and rounded the front. "It's old, like you. It's gonna get dirty."

Crush chuckled. "Don't I know it."

When I reached the top of the steps, he wrapped me up in a bear hug.

"I missed you, Cookie."

I squeezed him hard and let go. "It's barely been a week."

He folded his arms over the Harley logo on his tattered, oil-stained T-shirt. "You're not still wound up about that little errand, are you?"

Crush still didn't think giving me a necklace with a hidden camera on my last mission had been a big deal even though that little stunt could have gotten him killed or blown my cover.

Walking past him, I glared. "The next time Viktor asks you for a little favor, say no." Once inside the small trailer, I waited by the round kitchen table on my left and stared at an empty TV dinner tray. Nothing left but a few brownie crumbs, chicken bones, and a puddle of grease. "Tell me you're not back to eating that crap."

"I'm too damn tired to cook when I get home. Fruit spoils in a day. That shit will last in my freezer for thirty years." He lifted the plastic tray and dropped it into the trash. "Quit judging my life."

I pulled out a vinyl chair and sat. "You could at least buy one of those roasted chickens. They have premade dinners at the grocery store. Containers filled with salad, beans, soups—healthy stuff."

"I had chicken tonight. That's healthy."

"You do realize that's nothing but grease and sugar."

"Isn't that what fathers are made of?"

"You're practically pickled."

He rummaged around in a drawer. "Don't give me that sass."

There was no point in trying to change his bad habits, but I kept hoping that maybe one day he would listen.

I stared at the muted television in the living room and recognized *The Honeymooners* playing. Crush liked watching old shows—especially comedies. It seemed like just yesterday I was living here. Everything was the same, and yet so much time had passed. Of all the enemies I'd fought over the years, time was the most elusive and cruel. I twirled a large skull ring in the center of the table before cleaning off the motor oil with a paper napkin.

Crush returned to the table with two bottles of orange soda. "Feel free to tell me all about your last assignment. The whole damn city knows about it now. Well, they don't know about you specifically, but I might have bragged to one or two of my buddies."

The ring swallowed up my finger. "You can't talk about my job to anyone, not even people you trust."

After sipping his bubbly drink, he set down the bottle and pulled the elastic band out of his grey goatee. "You looking for a place to crash for a while? Trouble in paradise?"

I sat back. "Don't look so hopeful. No, everything's fine with Christian."

He flicked the bottle cap across the room, showing his disappointment.

"I'm actually here about you."

The creases in his brow deepened. "If this is some kind of fried-chicken intervention, you can get back in that muddy-ass truck of yours and roll on outta here."

"Rumor has it that something's going down, and you're in the middle of it."

His blue eyes narrowed before he nodded in understanding. "I'm not sure which is bigger—Switch's mouth or his imagination."

"Cut the shit. I can tell something's going on. You've got that look."

He belted out a laugh. "What look?"

"You'd be the worst poker player with your tells. Like the way you're scratching the back of your neck and avoiding eye contact. And now you're rubbing under your eye to stop scratching your neck."

"Dammit, Raven. Maybe I got fleas."

This time I laughed. "Still the same old bulldog."

"I'll drink to that."

We clinked our bottles before taking a sip.

"So spill it. I'm going to find out one way or the other. You know I don't want you involved in dangerous shit. Self-care means managing your cholesterol, eating healthy, avoiding stress, and not getting yourself killed."

He sniffed. "You're just mad because I told Wizard and his boys to take a hike. I don't want their wolves pissing around my property, babysitting me like I'm a fragile fucking human. It's bad enough they did all the repairs."

I snorted. "Bad enough? They saved your home from collapsing on you or burning down. You shouldn't have done that. I have a dangerous job, and I like knowing you're safe. Having a wolf on the property isn't the worst thing that could happen to you."

He arched his brow while holding the bottle to his lips. "Since when did you become the parent?"

"Quit steering the conversation and tell me what you're up to. You can trust me."

"Jesus, girl. I know that." Crush got up, peered out the window behind me, and closed the short curtains. Then he ambled into the kitchen, opened the freezer, and took out a gallon of ice cream. He set it down between us and offered me a serving spoon.

"You *do* realize they sell this in pint size."

"Not this brand of pistachio. Just the fancy, expensive shit. That's how they rip you off." When he pushed his spoon in and tried to pull out a scoop, the handle bent. After straightening it, he shoveled the ice cream into his mouth.

I tapped my spoon against the edge of the carton, waiting for the condensation to crystallize and the ice cream to soften. "Are you in trouble again?"

He sighed. "It's not about me. Funny you came by, because I was gonna call you."

"About what?"

He locked his fingers together, his rough hands clean but the cuticles stained with grease. "Shifters are dying, and the packs don't know what to make of it. The local Council hired bounty hunters, but this isn't their area of expertise."

I scooped a shaving of the ice cream even though I didn't like the flavor. "Did they reach out to the higher authority for help?"

"Let's just say that after the recent bust, the packs aren't feeling too confident about working with that side of the law. Besides, the higher authority expects them to handle their own shit. They barely tolerate giving Shifters land. You can't blame the packs for not trusting any of those people." Crush waved a hand dismissively. "I guess you already know how many of them were involved in the fighting rings. Shifters don't take that shit lightly. I got buddies who were once slaves. Some were kept in animal form for decades while serving their master. Anyhow, there's no way in hell they're involving the higher authority. The trust level is nonexistent until some of those fuckers prove themselves. They've got a lot of relationships to rebuild."

I set down my spoon and rested my arm on the table. "So why are you involved?"

"Little girl, I'm involved in all the shit that goes down around here."

I narrowed my eyes. "I'm sure that's true, but why are you *really* involved?"

He dug in for a big helping this time. After taking a purposeful bite, he studied the spoon. "I might have dropped your name as someone who can help."

I chuckled. "If they don't want the higher authority involved, what makes you think they want me? They think I'm a Mage, and my kind used to keep their kind as slaves. Remember?"

"They trust me, and that includes you by default. They've known you since you were a little girl. My buddy Ren is impressed with your work. You saved Shifters, and that's something they won't forget. Ren wanted to know if this was something in your wheelhouse, but hell, I'm not even sure what all you do. He wants to know what's involved and how much it'll cost."

I stared at the spilled drops of ice cream on the table. Viktor didn't work exclusively with the higher authority. Granted, that was where the big money came from, but we did other jobs. People might not know our names or faces, but the right ones knew about Keystone. Viktor was already passing out smaller assignments. Would he let me form a small group to check this out?

"You're not in any danger, are you?"

Crush wiped his mouth on the back of his arm and sank the spoon into the center of the ice cream. "Shifters are dying, but it was a few dead alphas that got everyone's attention."

My eyebrows reached for my hairline. "I thought Packmasters were strong and well guarded by their pack."

"I didn't say they were Packmasters. And it's not all alphas. Some women, some children. We don't have all the details."

"Why not?"

"Because it's not just wolves. Some of the other animal groups don't like comparing notes, so we only know what we've heard. Shifters don't report deaths to the Council. It's not protocol."

"But you think someone's killing them?"

Crush studied the tattoos on his left arm. "It's just speculation. Better than the alternative."

"Which is?"

"A disease. I think Ren just wants to cover all bases. Even if it's a virus, *someone* had to cook it up in a lab. If it's contagious, I don't know what the fuck they'll do. The higher authority will probably quarantine all Shifters."

I stood up and went to wash my spoon in the sink. "I'm not really sure what I can do. This might be out of my scope."

"I'm asking as a favor."

It got real quiet, and I returned to my seat.

Crush put the lid back on the carton of ice cream. "I just want them to know that I did everything in my power to help, and you're my everything. Only a few Packmasters know about it, and they're not going public. They don't want to start a panic before they've looked into it. Maybe it's nothing. Ren will talk to Viktor, but I think he wants to sit down with you first and see what you think. He doesn't want anyone else involved; that's why he's not going to Viktor first."

"It doesn't work like that. I won't do a job without Viktor's permission, and I sure as hell won't work it alone."

"He won't want a Vamp on the case."

"That's not up to him." I folded my arms. "He'll just have to get over it if he wants my help. We have partners for a reason—we look out for each other."

"I know," he said, waving his hand. "I don't like the peckerhead, but only a fool goes into danger alone."

I tapped my chin. "Hmm. Like that time loan sharks were coming after you?"

He gave me an indignant look that we both knew I didn't deserve, but that was Crush. He always had to be the exception to the rule, always had to protect his pride. But his grit was exactly why I was still alive. Crush had given me all the tools I needed to survive in this world even though he didn't know at the time that I would lead a less than normal life.

"Do you have his number?" I asked.

"I'll set up a meeting."

"Maybe you better not. If you involve yourself and this turns out to be something, I don't want you in the middle of it. You're all alone out here."

He swung his arm and pointed at a shotgun mounted on the living room wall. "See that? A man with a gun is never alone."

"Jesus. You should be a billboard for one of those gun shows."

He wiped an ice cream stain from his Harley shirt. "I live in a sketchy area of town and run with Shifters. I'd be an idiot not to be packing. If I'd been a banker living in some middle-class neighborhood, I might have raised you differently."

"Bankers get robbed."

"Yeah, but they have alarm systems, gates, dogs, multiple exits if there's a break-in…"

I stood up and circled behind him, crossing my arms around his neck. "That's why you should stop eating all that fried food. If someone busts through the front door when you're sleeping, how are you gonna squeeze your spare tire through these tiny windows? You won't have time to get in the closet and load your guns."

He patted my arms. "That's why I keep a machete."

"I'll see what Ren has to say, but my hands are tied if Viktor puts me on another case."

Crush shifted in his chair to look up at me. "That's all he wants. Just someone to check it out. I couldn't think of anyone better for the job than my baby girl."

I could only imagine how much my father had been bragging about me after the recent bust with the cage fights. But Viktor might not accept the case, so I'd have to tread carefully with how much commitment I gave Ren.

"I'm heading out," I said, still hugging him from behind. "Do you need anything? Food? Fruit juice? A stress test?"

"Get your ass outta here before I swat you."

I kissed his head and smiled. "Empty threats."

He stood to face me and put his hands on his hips. "I still have that paddle that used to hang on the wall."

I belted out a laugh. "The only time you ever took that showpiece off the wall was during a party when Wild Bill backed his truck into your bike."

He frowned. "How the hell do you know that? You were

supposed to be inside sleeping. I didn't let you roam around at that age during our parties."

"I had a ringside seat through the windows."

Crush stared at me long and hard. "What else did you see?"

"Dogs. I always thought your friends brought over their pets. Now I know better."

"They weren't supposed to shift around you. That was always the rule."

"I never saw them do it. If I had, I probably would have just remembered it as a dream or my imagination." I gripped the back of the vinyl chair when a thought sprang to mind. "Why don't you get a roommate?"

Crush reached out for the door and swung it open. "Time for you to go, little girl."

Chapter 3

After towel drying her hair, Blue stepped out of the bathroom and padded down the empty hallway. The stone floors chilled the soles of her feet but nothing like they did in the winter months. She could have chosen a room with an attached bathroom, but when Viktor had shown her the corner room, she'd fallen in love with the light. One set of windows faced west, providing a sweeping view of every sunset. As long as Blue could see the sky, her falcon was at peace.

Once inside her room, she glimpsed herself in the standing mirror to her left. She backed up a step and took a longer look. From the side, nothing looked unusual. Men had often admired her full breasts and lips, but Blue never considered those features the source of her femininity. It was her formidable stance, the depth in her eyes, and the power she exuded each time she wielded her tomahawk. Those qualities, in her view, defined her as a woman.

As she pivoted on her heel and stared at her reflection head-on, that confidence waned. Vanity had nothing to do with it, although a small part of her resented those scars for the way men looked at her differently. She had never liked the attention, but eyes once filled with desire now looked upon her with revulsion when they noticed even a fragment of the scars. Sometimes she wanted to rip off her shirt and show them everything. A smile touched her lips at the thought of grown men fainting at the sight of her.

Male Shifters often kept their scars to remind them of a victorious battle or a life saved. Most of those men weren't half the warrior she was.

Blue had spent endless hours staring at her reflection since the attack. It was the only way to get used to the change and accept what the fates had given her. At least her falcon was still flawless. The feathers overlapped the marks, which were smaller on her animal.

She opened her armoire, looking for her red dress. She loved the wide hood and bell sleeves that gave it a medieval appearance. It wasn't really hers—she found it in the armoire when she first joined Keystone, as if it had been waiting for her. Whether it was left behind or Viktor had put it there, she claimed it as her own. That and a blue cloak were small things that helped her detach from the outside world, so she enjoyed putting them on at night, after their work was done. Everyone needed a ritual.

The dress wasn't there.

She let the towel drop to the floor and reentered the hall. Even though Wyatt's office and some of her teammate's bedrooms were on the same floor, no one ever wandered to her corner of the mansion. Not that she cared. When Blue reached the balustrade, she swung her legs over and jumped. She hated the weight of her body in human form as it fell, but she and her animal were in sync, and seconds later, Blue felt the familiar rush of sliding out of her body as her falcon emerged. Her outstretched arms shrank and transformed to beautiful wings, powering her upward for a moment before she swooped to the first floor and down the hall. On its own, her falcon could get lost in the maze of hallways, but Blue was able to communicate her desires and steer her animal in the right direction. Of course, all animals had free will, and there was no predicting if they would listen or not. But since Blue let her falcon out regularly, they maintained a symbiotic relationship.

How she *loved* the freeing sensation of flight. Land Shifters bragged about running at high speeds or taking down large prey. Few appreciated avian Shifters for anything but a lookout. They had never experienced the thrill of ascending to the clouds where the only sound was the wind against your wings. The world beneath became smaller. People were insignificant specks that vanished into the vast landscape.

Her falcon flapped its wings, pushing down air and propelling her through a long hallway that cut through the mansion. When she reached the foyer, she veered right and swooped over Wyatt's head.

"Hey! Watch it, ladybird!"

Blue's falcon perched atop a statue. Many were intimidated by her gaze, including Wyatt, who hustled up the stairs without looking back. Blue relayed her desires to her bird, and within seconds, they took flight. Her falcon dove at Wyatt and snatched the slouchy beanie right off his head.

"*Son of a ghost.* Give that back!"

She flew toward the winged statue near the door and dropped the hat on its head before heading down the east hall toward a painting. When she made a sharp left down the outer hall, she glided by a long row of beautiful stained glass windows.

Blue spotted her dress by the door where she'd gone out the previous night. Sometimes she got it on the way back in, but last night, Blue's falcon wanted to perch on the rooftop for hours. Afterward, she'd flown through her open bedroom window and gone directly to sleep.

Up ahead, Viktor was admiring himself in a mirror.

He raised his arm. "Blue, if I could have a moment."

Blue soared past him. When she reached the side exit, she landed on the floor next to the pile of fabric and morphed. Without skipping a beat, she slipped the dress over her head from a kneeling position and stood.

Viktor hadn't pried his eyes away from his reflection.

Flipping her hair out from the collar, she strode toward him. "We didn't see you at dinner tonight. Are you securing a big case?"

"Nyet." He grumbled something in Russian and finally turned toward her. "I cannot straighten tie. Why must these be so complicated? Can you fix?"

She approached him and undid the knot. Ties weren't really Viktor's style. He exuded casual sophistication—usually chinos with pressed shirts and cardigans. Blue slowly adjusted the length of the necktie, something she'd learned to do since they occasionally went to formal parties, and the men in the house were hopeless. "I don't think I've seen you wear a tie to a business meeting."

"Not meeting. My date with Miss Parrish is this evening. I would have bought a tailor-made suit if it wasn't on such short notice."

Was Lenore worthy of a man like Viktor? "Maybe you should wear the clothes that you like. Be yourself."

"Fancy restaurants require fancy clothes. I must look good." His cheeks flushed. "Is this acceptable?"

Acceptable? Viktor was the definition of handsome. Seasoned by the years, his silver hair, often combed back, was peppered with dark grey. He kept in shape—just the right amount of definition in his arms and torso. And there was something about the way Viktor looked at a person that made them feel noticed. Men like Viktor possessed a quality that couldn't be taught: charisma.

"Miss Parrish is a lucky woman" was all she could say.

Viktor stroked his short beard, neatly groomed on the sides and longer around the chin and mouth. Aftershave wafted off him, and she noticed a bloody piece of toilet paper stuck to his neck.

After adjusting his tie, she reached up and removed the toilet paper, flicking it to the floor. "A man like you doesn't need to slice his jugular to impress a woman. Your reputation precedes you."

He cupped her cheek in his hand, and she warmed. "What would I do without my Blue?"

She stepped back. "Do you really think it's wise for people like us to pursue relationships? Gem's boyfriend lost his head. And if Raven and Christian split, it'll get ugly no matter what they say now. I always assumed you wanted us to keep any relationships we had with outsiders casual."

"In this job, it is for the best. But there comes a point when I cannot rule your lives, and I cannot predict my own path. Miss Parrish is an exception—she is not an outsider. She is privy to our secrets." He turned to the mirror and admired Blue's handiwork. "I do not think this will flourish into a romance. I am not deserving of a woman such as her."

Blue considered Lenore's beauty. While she didn't think much of her personality, there was no denying Lenore's attractiveness. Flaxen hair, a slim physique, money, class… and the *flawless* skin of a Vampire. "Any woman would be lucky to have you at their side. Don't let her intimidate you. Beautiful women have a way of doing that, and just because she asked you out, don't think that *she's* the one who has the upper hand." Blue stood behind him and brushed lint off the back of his jacket. "Look at what you've built, and all without the help of a pack. People respect you, Viktor. You can have any woman you want." She gazed at him through the mirror. "Just be careful."

Blue wanted to warn him that Lenore had the power to charm him with a look, but Viktor obviously knew the risks of dating a Vampire. *Why, of all Breeds, did it have to be a Vampire? Does he not want the loyal companionship of a wolf?*

She folded her arms. "Any new jobs for Niko and me?"

He turned around and fiddled with his cuffs. "Perhaps I might need a scout. I have not yet reviewed the details."

Blue clenched her fists but quelled the frustration in her tone. "I'm more than just my bird, Viktor. Any assignments that I can work in human form?"

"I have nothing. If you are bored, go relic hunting at the pawnshops or help Wyatt with side work." Viktor blew out a shaky breath, obviously distracted by his evening plans. "Well? How do I look?"

"Like a million bucks."

Viktor glanced at his watch. "I must hurry." He turned away and quickened his pace as he put distance between them. "Spasibo!"

Blue strolled to the back of the mansion and glided through the shadows, her long dress swishing at her feet. Most of the halls were identical—stone floors and walls, gorgeous arched ceilings that were expertly crafted, the only light provided by candles. Keystone was like stepping back in time, and the mansion was built to last. Blue wasn't easily spooked, but sometimes in the late evening, it felt as if the ghosts of her past were hiding in the pitch-black corners. After ascending a flight of stairs, she took a shortcut to her room.

Wyatt jogged around the corner, out of breath. "I've been looking all over for you. I need to put a tracking device in your ass."

"If you insert anything inside me, I'll shatter your skull."

He swaggered up, hands in his pockets. "Tell that to the man in your room."

Her eyebrows furrowed. "What's Niko doing in my private chamber? If you guys are playing a prank, I'm not up for it."

"It's not Niko."

"Is that so?"

"Niko's the one who let him in." Wyatt stretched out his arms before letting them fall to his sides like dead timber. "But since you put my hat on the damn statue, I'm not telling you anything else." With that, Wyatt whirled around and strutted away.

Blue had quickly learned that living in a houseful of men was like living with adolescent boys. They all had a relentless sense of humor and pranked each other to pass the time. Sometimes Blue and Gem were caught in the cross fire but rarely were they the center of the joke. Keystone men knew better than to target a woman with their juvenile sense of humor. Gem was sensitive and made them feel guilty.

Blue would just make them live to regret it.

"There better not be a bird in there," she muttered, reaching for the knob.

When Blue opened the door, she was startled to find a man kneeling before her fireplace, lighting the kindling. The lanterns in her room provided sufficient light, and it wasn't cold enough for a fire. Was Shepherd wearing a long wig, trying to pull a fast one on her?

No, the man was much taller.

His sleeves were loose and tattered, his clothes as brown as the mud on his boots. And his hair! It was as long as Niko's but messy and unwashed, adorned with a random braid here and there.

Blue tiptoed to the desk on her right and stealthily lifted her tomahawk.

"You can't sneak up on a Chitah," he said softly.

The rich timbre of his voice raised the hair on the back of her neck. After he set the screen in front of the fireplace, the man stood and looked over his shoulder at her, a sideways smile inching up his face.

Blue squeezed the handle of her axe, her heart pounding against her chest. It was *him*—the Chitah who'd helped them in West Virginia. The one who carried her naked and bleeding body back to the cave after the lion attack.

The man she'd kissed to repay a favor Raven owed him.

As he approached her with a purposeful stride, she suddenly began to regret that kiss.

The Chitah folded one arm over his middle and bowed. "Matteo Leone, at your service."

"I know who you are."

He straightened his back and locked his golden eyes on hers. Matteo was tall like most Chitahs, but few had his dark hair, and he made no effort to hide it with its long length. Even his beard was long and sparse, bound with a few small elastic bands.

"Forgive the formal introduction, female. I assumed that your memory of me might be hazy."

"There's nothing wrong with my memory, but I think there's something wrong with your head. What are you doing here? And I don't just mean in Cognito but in my bedroom. Did you change your mind about a cash payment for helping us? I was under the impression that you accepted a guide job at the children's sanctuary."

Matteo took a step forward and held her gaze. "When a man reaches a fork in the road, he must choose his path. It's an honor to help out those children, but I keep glancing at the other road, and I have to know if it's worth traveling."

"I don't understand."

He suddenly took her free hand and lifted it to his mouth before placing a lingering kiss on her knuckles. "Female, I'm here to court you."

Chapter 4

Early that morning, I received a text from my father. He asked me to stop by before going to see Ren, but I had no intention of taking him with me. Crush needed to stay uninvolved in dangerous affairs, even if the Shifters *were* his friends.

After putting on ripped jeans and a maroon T-shirt, I stood in front of the latticed window in my bedroom and gazed down at the vast estate behind the mansion. Hunter was running as fast as he could down a grassy hill, holding a spool of string in his hands. Shepherd held the kite over his head. Neither of them looked like they knew what they were doing, but they were having fun. The estate behind the mansion, cleared of most trees except a few here and there, resembled a rectangular carpet that rolled out before us. There were patches of wildflowers, especially near the hill that sloped down. The outer perimeter was surrounded by trees that went on as far as the eye could see. My gaze skated off in the distance toward the far tree line on the right near the pond, and I noticed a man circling a tent. I squinted, but it was too far to make out any details.

"What the hell?"

Panicked, I grabbed my purse and flashed down the hall to the second floor. "Someone's outside," I said, flying into Wyatt's office, out of breath.

Gem and Claude's apathetic faces greeted me from the black L-shaped sofa, where they were snacking on miniature donuts.

"Didn't you hear me?" I asked in disbelief. "There's a strange man lurking out back on our property. I couldn't see if there are any others, but he pitched a tent."

Wyatt slowly swiveled his computer chair and yawned. "That's Blue's new boyfriend."

My heartbeat slowed. "What?"

Blue peered over the beanbag chair in front of the TV and stared daggers at Wyatt. "What did I tell you about the jokes?"

Wyatt angled his chair to hide from her and gave me an exaggerated wink. "What I *meant* to say is that he's courting Blue against her will."

Claude dusted the powdered sugar off his hands. "That's Matteo. Do you remember the man who helped us deliver the young to the sanctuary? I think they called it Wonderland."

I jerked my head back. "That's him? He came all this way just for Blue?" Matteo the mountain man must have been desperate for female companionship to travel all the way up to Cognito. On the bright side, at least he wasn't here for me.

Gem practically swooned as her head fell against the back of the sofa. "I think it's *romantic*."

Blue stood. "There's a fine line between romance and stalking."

"Give him a chance," Gem urged. "He's a little dirty, but he's amiable and brave. Claude told me all about what he did."

Blue leaned against the vending machine and lifted her chin, daring anyone to challenge her. "I don't want him inside the house. If he wants to camp out on private property, Viktor can deal with him. I'm dead serious. The last thing I need is a lovestruck Chitah following me around."

"Courting is our way." Claude crossed one leg over his knee, wearing nothing but grey sweatpants and a lazy grin. "I don't know why Matteo would choose a Shifter when his kindred spirit could be out there, but don't dismiss the seriousness of his intentions. This is how we prove ourselves the most worthy of all males. If he's courting you, he'll do it in the most honorable way."

She folded her arms. "We'll see how much honor he has left when he has to bathe in the pond."

I hooked my purse strap over my shoulder and heaved a sigh. "Has anyone seen Christian?"

"Not since he left early last night," Claude replied.

Wyatt rolled his chair around. "Maybe he's cuddled up postcoital in the arms of a blond waitress, regretting his life choices."

"If anyone sees him in the next hour, tell him to meet me at Crush's house. If I'm not there, he can text me."

Before leaving the room, I casually strolled over to the surge protector and stepped on the switch. All the electronics on Wyatt's desk shut off.

"Hey!" Wyatt shouted as I left the room. "You're worse than the spooks!"

Following a lengthy detour, I pulled my truck into my father's driveway and parked behind his shiny red pickup. When I glanced at my passenger, I realized my father was going to murder me. After sleeping on it the night before, I decided that if he didn't want one of his Shifter buddies babysitting him, I would find a suitable replacement. So I'd stopped off at the local animal shelter and found him a dog.

Well, more like a beast.

Aside from a rabbit he'd once given me, Crush had never owned a pet. Now that I knew about all his biker buddies, I understood why. Shifters generally weren't fond of pets. It wasn't that they didn't like animals; they just didn't like the idea of owning an animal that, in their mind, should be living free. As if poodles and basset hounds could ever run wild. They needed a master.

And Crush needed a guard.

I had walked by every cage, trying to decide what type of dog he might like. The cute, fluffy ones were automatically off the list even though I knew Crush had a soft heart. He needed a fierce companion that could protect him. The pit bulls available were too hyper, the bulldog was too lazy, and the German shepherd had no teeth. I really hesitated on that bulldog. Not only was it my father's nickname, but he also had a tattoo of one. I finally settled on the dog that approached the cage door and looked ready for me to leash him up and take him home.

I glared at the pooch in the passenger seat, who sat taller than me. "You better make a good first impression."

Once out of the truck, I opened the passenger door and let the dog free. He was big and muscular, a beautiful shade of red with a black muzzle and ears. When I glanced over the paperwork at the shelter, I realized he weighed more than I did. The leash had to go, mostly because he kept chewing on it during the ride. Plus, I had my doubts it would be effective. If he decided to bolt, he'd wind up dragging me down the street. The dog shook his head before following me up the porch steps.

I rapped my knuckles on the door. "It's me—your spawn."

Crush answered while taking a bite from a hot dog. "Just in time for lunch," he said. Then his eyes flicked down and his smile vanished. "What the fuck is that?"

"Your new best friend. Let us in."

He narrowed his eyes at me and swallowed. "You got three seconds to tell me that's a Shifter friend."

I nudged him out of the way and went in, but the dog remained on the porch. "Happy birthday. This is your new best friend."

"It's not my birthday, and April Fools' Day is over."

The dog sat and cocked his head at the grumpy old man.

"What are you lookin' at?" Crush barked.

Easing back to the doorway, I leaned against the doorjamb. "He's a bullmastiff. I think the guy said it's a crossbreed, like me. A bulldog and a mastiff. He might have a little mutt mixed in, but he was the best-looking boy in the kennel."

"You need to take him back."

"He was scheduled to be put down in a week."

"Goddammit, Raven. Don't put that shit on me. I didn't ask for a dog. I got no room, no food, and no time. I work all day and like to watch my shows at night. He'll be barking."

"They said he's not a big barker, but he'll guard your property and make someone think twice about breaking in. Come on. Give him a test drive."

"He'll shit all over the lawn."

"Fertilizer."

A motorcycle engine throttled from the road as Christian steered into the driveway, his shades as dark as his clothes.

The dog shot down the steps and tore across the yard like a bolt of lightning. His rippling muscles were as impressive as his speed. Christian abruptly cut across the lawn to avoid him. The dog didn't slow down his chase, and the next thing I knew, Christian steered onto the road and sped off.

The dog trotted back as if he were on a victory lap, and when he made it up the steps, he wagged his tail at my father.

Crush stroked his goatee. "Smart dog," he muttered. "Come on in, and let's see how smart you really are."

We both sat at the table, and Crush set his half-eaten hot dog near the edge. "What am I going to do with a damn dog? I don't have the space."

"He was living in a cage, so this is an upgrade. You could even chain him in the yard when the weather's nice. If you don't keep him, I'm going to plan B, and you don't want to know what plan B is."

The dog sat next to the table and stared at Crush. The hot dog was a mere inch from his face, and his nose twitched. It was hard to tell if Crush was testing him or vice versa.

My father got that look on his face when he was about to give in to something he didn't want to do. "My buddies ain't gonna like it."

"Since when the hell do you care what anyone thinks? They're Shifters; you're not. They can't tell you how to live your life. Come on," I said, sugaring him up. "He's the bestest boy ever. Just look at that wrinkly old face. You two are practically twins."

"You're walkin' a thin line with that sass talk."

"Look, just keep him around long enough to see if you're compatible. Give it a few weeks."

"What if he tears up my house?"

A smile touched my lips. "Then I hope he starts with that recliner."

My father knocked the hot dog on the floor and watched the dog's reaction.

Drool leaked from one of his cheek flaps. He snorted and then looked back up at my father.

"If he's too much trouble, I'll figure something out," I promised. "The shelter won't take him back, and I'd rather see him go to a home. You live out here alone, and I think it's a good idea to get either a dog or a security system with cameras and an alarm."

Crush shot me a baleful look. "The dog stays. You're not putting cameras in my house so you can spy on me." Then he leaned toward the dog and softened his voice. "Go on. Eat it."

The dog bobbed his head but didn't make a move for the wiener.

"What are you trying to do?" I asked.

"Just testing to see if he knows who the alpha is around here. Alphas eat first. Betas only eat when the alpha gives them permission."

I snorted. "He's a dog, not a Shifter. I don't think that's how it works."

Crush reached down on the floor, swiped up the bread and meat, and then held it in front of the dog's muzzle. "Here."

With that, the dog gobbled up the tasty snack and then proceeded to lick Crush's hand, arm, and then his neck.

Crush rocked with laughter in that way I adored—a deep belly laugh that warmed me all over. Yeah, these two were going to get along just fine.

I slumped in my chair. "They gave me a squeaky toy shaped like a hamburger. It's in the truck if you want it."

Crush patted the dog's muscular body. "He doesn't need a damn rubber toy. What he needs is a good bone."

"So where am I meeting Ren?"

Crush glanced up at the clock in the kitchen. "We need to head out."

"*I* need to head out. *You* need to buy dog food before he starves to death."

"That wasn't the plan."

"Look, I know you want to be involved, but I need you to not be involved. Especially with any case I might be working. If you stick your nose in the middle of this, I won't be able to do my job. And another thing—Ren won't respect me if I walk in with my father holding my hand."

Crush let out a reluctant sigh and watched the dog, who was busy licking crumbs off the floor.

"He probably needs a good run in the yard," I suggested. "You two stay here and bond."

"*Sit*," Crush ordered. When the dog wagged his tail, my father shook his head. "We've got a lot of work to do. I can't have an animal this big that doesn't listen."

"I'm surprised he didn't knock over the table for your plate. He seems like a good dog. He just needs someone like you to teach him all the rules." I rose from my seat and pushed my chair in. "Christian and I are leaving. Where's the meeting?"

Crush stood. "He'll be at the Angry Hornet in a private room. Ren doesn't want his pack involved."

When I heard Christian's bike approaching, I shut the door so the dog wouldn't get out. "I don't remember a private room in that place."

Crush pursed his lips. "Every Breed bar has a private room. It's the one marked Utility Closet."

I looked down at the big beast of a dog. "Why do they call a Shifter bar that mostly serves wolves the Angry Hornet instead of something more... wolfy?"

My dad reached in the fridge and pulled out a cold hot dog and gave it a wiggle, which made the dog salivate. "When they first opened the place, there were hornet's nests everywhere—even in the bathrooms. They damn near got stung to death trying to clear it."

"Figures. Well, you two have fun bonding. I'm leaving my

truck here for now, so if you want to pick up dog food or whatever, the keys are inside."

"Maybe I'll give it the wash it deserves."

I strode out the door. "See ya, Crush."

With the engine rumbling, Christian kept watch on the door as I mounted the bike and wrapped my arms around his middle. "What the feck was that coming after me?"

"My dad's new best friend."

He throttled the engine. "For a minute there, I thought your da finally took a wife."

Chapter 5

THE ANGRY HORNET WASN'T FAR from my dad's trailer. They catered to bikers in the area—mostly Shifters. My father used to drink there in the early days, before his sobriety, and even though he didn't go there anymore, everyone knew Crush Graves. The bikers were a tight-knit community, and my father was a trusted human who worked on their bikes and other vehicles. Unfortunately, some of those guys would always remember him as a drunk. I wished I had never gotten wasted there that night. Now everyone probably thought like father, like daughter.

Once inside, we walked straight toward the bar and seating area. On the right was a sunken billiard room with red felt pool tables and mosaic lights. Nothing fancy, but it had its charm. Heeding my warning about Vampires, Christian kept his black sunglasses on. He obviously knew the drill, but sometimes he just didn't give a damn. We strolled toward the bathrooms, and then I lightly knocked on the door of the utility closet.

Ren opened the door and gave Christian a cursory glance. "Where's your old man?"

"Ren, this is my partner, Christian Poe. Christian, this is Ren." Christian took off his sunglasses.

I'd known Ren a long time, and it suddenly dawned on me that I didn't know his last name. Most of Crush's friends went by one name, and I had never called anyone a Mr. or Mrs. Anything.

Both men squared their shoulders and locked eyes like two

caged animals about to fight. After a few seconds, Christian lowered his gaze, a submissive gesture among Vampires.

Ren's black hair had grey strands that blended flawlessly. He had an old-school look, like James Dean or bikers from that era. Tattoos covered his arms, not that you could see them beneath his leather jacket. Like all alphas, he exuded power. It rippled off him. Ren wasn't a guy to mess with, but he was exactly the kind of man you wanted on your side.

Ren stepped back to let us in. Unlike most private rooms I'd seen, this one reeked of stale cigarette smoke and looked more like someone's living room. No contemporary wall lights, no wet bar, and no giant television. A round rattan coffee table with a wood top sat between two brown couches that had been collecting dust since 1976.

Ren shucked off his leather coat and flung it onto the left-hand sofa. "I've only got orange soda. I thought Crush was coming."

I sat on the opposite sofa and noticed the cluster of unopened bottles on the table, nary a beer in sight. "Everything going okay with you?" I asked, trying to be social before we dove into business.

He sat down, knees apart, fingers laced across his stomach. "Could be better. Could be worse."

Ren wasn't much of a talker.

He glanced up at Christian. "Sit down."

Christian tucked his sunglasses in the unbuttoned collar of his Henley. "When's the last time that upholstery has seen a steam cleaner?"

"Never. I don't do business looking up to anyone, so take a seat or take a hike."

After examining a white stain on the seat cushion, Christian shot me one of those "you're going to regret this" looks before sitting down.

Ren reached inside his pocket, retrieved a silver lighter, and snapped it open with two fingers. "You're my last resort."

"Well, that's a vote of confidence," Christian said, not hiding his contempt.

Ren's thumb rolled over the flint wheel, creating sparks. "A few

Packmasters recently got together at a long-overdue peace party, and after everyone left, we got to talking. Some of us have had a few unexplained deaths. Obviously Shifters don't live forever. Kids have accidents, and over the years, some people just drop dead for no apparent reason. It's not common, but it happens."

"If that's the case, what makes you think there's something fishy going on?"

"Well, it's not just the wolf packs. One guy heard about a few rogues who bit the dust without explanation. Another heard stories about other animal groups. One of the Packmasters in our group happens to be a Councilman, so he hired two bounty hunters to look into it. One guy said he didn't find anything, and the other's an old buddy of mine from Austin. Unless there's evidence, clues, or an assailant, there's nothing he can do for us. He suggested we talk to a Relic."

I watched Ren light up a smoke. "What did the Relic say?"

Ren took a long drag and then stretched his arm over the back of the sofa. "He works with some of the packs, so he already knew about a couple. He said we don't hear about half the deaths that really go on, and it's not out of the ordinary. He suggested we stop all the conspiracy theories before it leaks and starts a panic. I'm inclined to agree with him." After taking another puff and exhaling through his nose, he continued. "That could do more harm than good, especially if it turns out to be nothing. We're still keeping him in the loop, but it's not really a position I want to put him in if it means ruining his reputation. People won't trust him with their secrets anymore."

"Do you have a list of names I can look at?"

Putting the cigarette between his lips, Ren dragged his jacket toward him and retrieved an envelope from the inside pocket.

I reached across the table and took it.

"Don't let anyone see that," he warned with a shake of his finger. "We wrote down every single death we knew about in the past year, so maybe not all of them are connected. If the Relic's right, it could come back to bite me in the ass. It doesn't take much to start rumors, especially after all that bullshit that went down with the higher authority running cage fights."

"That's not what happened," I pointed out. "We busted some reps who work for them, but you can't pin it on the entire organization."

"All the same."

I glanced over the list of names and ages. "Were any of them in your pack?"

"One. Ruth died months ago, and the Relic said it was a defective heart. She didn't have a mate or kids, but it was still hard on the pack. Ruth was only two hundred. She mated into the pack, but her mate died during a scuffle we had a few years back with some Vampires. They hadn't been together but a few months. Damn shame."

"Was it a personal conflict with the Vampires? Do you think they might have come after her too?"

"Nothing like that. It was a fluke run-in, and things got out of hand." Ren flicked the ash from his cigarette into an ashtray. "Maybe it seems like I'm overreacting, but I don't feel right *not* looking into it."

"Did they all die in the same way?"

He shrugged. "No accidents. No injuries."

Christian clasped his hands together and sat forward. "You think it's something more insidious, don't you?"

Ren took another long drag and steadied his eyes on Christian. He blew out a cloud of smoke. "You tell me."

I noticed children on the list, and as tragic as that was, it made sense. Kids were more vulnerable since they weren't impervious to sickness or injuries. Adults could heal, so the idea of a mutation wiping them out was unsettling. Additional surnames were scribbled beside some of them—presumably their pack or other animal group. I turned to Christian and quietly said, "I think Blue needs to be in on this. If we have to talk to some of these people, they'll trust her more than they will us."

"Aye. But do you think it's worth the trouble? Viktor isn't a fan of mysteries."

"I'll make it worth his time," Ren said, stubbing out his cigarette. "A few of my boys pooled money for the bounty hunters, but this one's coming out of my pocket. Nobody knows we're talking. I've already exhausted my resources for the year, so if it turns out to be nothing, I guess I'm the fool. But these are crazy times."

"I'll talk to Viktor, but I can't guarantee anything." I tucked the paper back in the envelope. "If he accepts the job, I'll have to bring on another teammate or two. I know you don't like outsiders in your business, but we're Keystone. We work with partners."

Ren stood. "I want you to know I respect what you did, busting that ring and saving my kind. We hear about raids all the time, but we don't always get the details."

Rolling my eyes, I got up, and Christian followed my cue. "I'm sure Crush gave you more than enough details. He's not supposed to talk about my business, but I guess he can't help himself."

Ren chuckled. "He's a good man. I've known him since we served together."

I tapped the envelope against my palm and tipped my head to the side. I was curious about Ren and what made him tick. "Why would a Shifter serve in the military?"

"In times of combat, you do what's right. It's good for alphas and betas to have experience as either a bounty hunter or a soldier. That's the type of training you need to run a pack."

I snorted. "Yeah. I've seen how toddlers can get out of hand."

Ren lifted a bottle with two fingers and snapped off the lid. "How much have you learned about Shifters? We form groups for protection—not just from other Breeds but territorial disputes. People are land hungry. I've seen entire packs wiped out." After guzzling down half the bottle, Ren swaggered toward the door. "I'll call you after I talk to your boss. Crush gave me his number, but I wanted to talk to you first and make sure you were on board. Just so you know, if he wants to assign someone else to the case, I'll back out. I want you in charge or no one at all."

"If Viktor gives us the green light, set up a meeting with the

Relic. I want to pick his brain and see what he thinks about this whole thing."

"You'll have to be discreet."

"Didn't Crush tell you that was my middle name?"

He gave me a tight-lipped grin. "Mind if we chat in private?"

Christian inclined his head before leaving the room.

Ren looked me up and down but not in a lewd way. "You grew up, Raven. We haven't really had a chance to talk since you reappeared."

I'd shared a few words with Ren during a party at Crush's house, but he clearly had questions he didn't want to ask in front of his pack.

He tipped his head toward the door. "They're soundproof, so your friend can't hear us." Ren swaggered back to the sofa and took a seat. "Crush mentioned you're dating that Vamp. You and Crush have always been family, so what I'm going to say to you is what I'd say to anyone in my own pack." Ren coolly rotated the silver lighter between his fingers. "If the Irishman ever lays a finger on you, come see me. If you need to make him disappear, I'll take care of it. No questions asked."

Ren would have said that to me whether I was human or Breed. My father and his friends didn't show their love the way most people did. Actions always spoke louder than words.

"Thanks, Ren. I appreciate the offer, but I'm a girl who takes care of her own problems. For what it's worth, Christian's good to me. I used to hate Vamps. I still mostly do. But I trust him with my life. He also knows not to cross me. If you have any concerns about his involvement in this case, don't. He may be the biggest fanghole in Cognito, but he gets the job done."

"I won't lie—he makes me nervous. All that power they have. Wouldn't take much to crush your skull if things got heated between you two. Maybe you should settle down with another Mage—someone with equal power."

I gave him an oblique smile. "I have more power than you give me credit for."

"That I don't doubt."

Chapter 6

"I bought something for you," I said, handing Christian a wedge of watermelon.

He smiled up at me from his grassy spot on the hill overlooking Keystone estates. "You remembered."

I sat down beside him. "You told me about how much you love watermelon, but we never have any in the house. They're in season, so I bought a few. I was going to leave one on your bed as a surprise, but I didn't think you'd eat it."

He took a bite while staring at Matteo's campfire in the distance. "And exactly what do you think I might do with a large melon?"

"Toss it out the window?"

"'Twould be a shame if it struck you in the head," he mused before taking another juicy bite. "We'd have to bury you in a watermelon patch."

"My ghost would be a hideous sight. Like the headless horseman, only a watermelon for a head instead of a pumpkin."

He chortled. "I'd pay good money to see the look on Spooky's face." After finishing his melon, he stared at the rind. "Half the fun was choking on the black seeds."

"They're genetically modified now."

"Like you." Christian hurled the melon into the darkness.

I jerked my head back. "Are you possessed?"

He wiped his fingers on his pants. "Why do you ask?"

"I've never seen you litter a day in your life." I reached out and held my hand to his forehead. "No fever. Are you the real Christian Poe?"

He leaned back on his elbows. "Blue's suitor keeps himself busy. He'll have it tidied up before dawn. Have you noticed he's clearing out the property? Felled two dead trees just today. Gem ran out to stop him from cutting down the one she burned up. I guess that dead thing has a special place in her heart."

"I know how she feels." I mirrored his position, and we both gazed down at the distant campfire. "Does he really think pulling every weed is going to impress a woman like Blue? Would you do that for me? Clean acres and acres of—"

"Have you gone stark raving mad?"

I planted a kiss on his mouth, and his lips tasted sweet. "I'm with a Vampire. I *must* be mad."

He growled sexily and leaned in for another peck. "Climb astride me and I'll change your mind."

I slid my hand down his body and cupped his growing erection. He hissed at the contact and lost that cool facade. I loved watching him crumble beneath my touch.

He pinched my chin. "*Later*, Precious."

"Why not now?"

Christian eased to a sitting position, forcing me away. "We have company."

I heard the footsteps in the grass before I recognized Blue in the darkness.

When she reached us, she put her hands on her hips and stared at the orange glow across the open field. "I swear to the fates, I'm going to castrate him before he's done with this courtship business."

Christian twirled a leaf between his fingers. "Why not just throw all the trash into the field? That'll keep him busy."

Blue grinned. "Sounds like a man after your own heart."

I wiped the grass off my hands. "I say we give him a riding mower and a pair of shears."

Blue shook her head. "If this is how Chitahs court each other, count me out."

"Aye," Christian agreed. "If he can't bring you the head of your enemy, he's not worth having."

I gave Christian a long look. He was serious.

Blue captured a lightning bug in her hand. "Viktor has a new assignment for us. He's looking for you, Raven."

"I already know about it."

A faint glow appeared between her fingers. "I thought so. I guess I owe you."

"For what?"

"For putting my name in the hat."

I snorted and stood up. "I don't know what hat you're talking about. I may have grown up around Shifters, but conducting an investigation with them is another matter. I need someone with finesse in that department. You're not a wolf, but you know more about Shifters than I ever will." I glanced up at the dark sky. "I don't know if it's a case worth taking, but I owe Ren for looking after my dad all these years. He's done a lot of good things for us. He helped Crush get clean, and he made sure that I had someone looking out for me while my dad was in rehab. I don't remember much about it, but when my dad got home, Ren popped in every night to visit. I guess he didn't want Crush going through it alone. Anyhow, memories like that linger, and it wouldn't be right to turn him away."

Blue opened her hand and released the lightning bug. "You're more like us than you realize. When I met your loner ass, I wouldn't have pegged you for a girl who grew up around wolves."

"And I wouldn't have pegged you for a girl who went around kissing strange Chitahs."

She glanced back at Matteo's campsite. "Strange indeed."

I offered Christian my hand. "Coming?"

"I already spoke to Viktor about the job. I think I'll enjoy the fresh air for a while."

I retracted my hand. "You knew we had the assignment and didn't tell me?"

"Before you get your knickers in a twist, Viktor asked me to keep it private until he spoke with Blue. Thanks for the melon."

"Hope you enjoyed it," I said, heading back to the house. "You won't be getting the other two I'd planned on giving you tonight."

When we were out of Vampire earshot, Blue glanced back. "What made you want to get in a serious relationship in the first place? This job doesn't give us that luxury, and besides, you're always at each other's throats."

"We're Vampires. Of course we're at each other's throats. That's just our way. People who try too hard to please the other are just faking it. You have to do what feels natural."

"So you like sleeping with one eye open?"

"That's what keeps things interesting."

We reached the mansion and entered through the side door, which Blue had left unlocked. Blue didn't know how tender Christian was in private, how he would softly stroke my eyelashes and tell me about his world travels. Sometimes he just bored me to tears with facts about hippos while rubbing my feet, but those were the things I loved about him. Yet as close as we were, he was still a mystery. But I could see into the depths of his heart. Others didn't understand our complicated relationship, but outside opinions didn't matter. Christian gave me everything I needed: companionship, privacy, laughter, friendship, and one hell of a sex life.

Blue rounded the corner and gave me a quick glance. "What's that grin about?"

"I was just wondering how long that Chitah plans to camp on our property. He might win your heart after all."

"When pigs fly."

"He might be your soul mate."

She traced her finger along the wall. "I have no need for a mate. Keystone is my life."

Hunter suddenly flew down the stairs and past us, a long string flapping from his mouth.

Wyatt appeared at the landing, fists anchored on his hips. "That's it. I'm not going after him."

"What's with the string?" I asked, gripping the newel. "Did you convince him that he could fly like a kite?"

Wyatt jogged down the steps, drawing attention to his red socks. "He's got a wiggly tooth. I told Shep to wrap a string around it and tie the other end to a doorknob. When he started to slam the door, he chickened out. I think he feels guilty about causing the kid any pain, but that tooth has gotta go." He turned to walk with us. "When I was little, I knew a kid who choked on his own tooth."

Blue rolled her eyes. "Don't be ridiculous. Did you tell Shepherd that tall tale?"

"I'm not fibbing! It actually happened while he was riding horseback. I guess it freaked Hunter out, because he took the string off the knob and ran."

"You told that story while he was getting his tooth pulled? Good job," I said, smacking him on the arm. "Be sure to add that to your résumé. Hacks into computers and terrifies small children."

"Just give him an apple," Blue suggested, leading us down a hallway that passed the courtyard.

Wyatt shuddered. "He might swallow it. Then we'd have to fish it out for the tooth fairy."

Blue sighed. "The tooth fairy is a human fabrication."

"Uh-huh. Tell that to Shepherd. He's suddenly all gung ho about these weird-ass traditions. First it's a birthday, then it's the tooth fairy. Next thing you know, we'll be hiding Easter eggs."

"I always wanted to do that," I said, thinking back to my strange childhood. "My dad didn't like wasting food. In retrospect, he probably didn't know how to boil an egg."

Blue snorted. "In a house this big, we'd never find all the eggs. Not until we smelled them rotting."

Wyatt eased between us and put his arms over our shoulders. "Where are you ladies headed? Late-night pillow fight?"

I gripped his hand. "Pin the dagger on the donkey. Wanna be the donkey?"

He fell back and snapped his fingers. "Just remembered I've got fries in the oven. Maybe Shep can help you out with that one."

Wyatt hustled off. I was joking, but because of my kill record, I guessed he didn't put anything past me.

When we entered one of the libraries, Viktor was on his phone with his back to us. He spun a globe, chuckling softly.

"I also had a good time," he said intimately. "You are beautiful woman."

Blue slid her jaw to the side and folded her arms as we waited for him to wrap up his call.

When he noticed us, he held up a finger and then turned away. I couldn't hear what he said before ending the call.

Viktor smiled at us. "Apologies."

I summoned the urge to pry. "Was that Lenore? How did your date go?"

A blush touched his cheeks, and he stroked his silver beard, averting his eyes. "It went very well. Very well indeed. She has an impressive wine collection."

I raised my eyebrows. "You went back to her place?"

He cleared his throat. "I called you here to inform you that I've accepted Ren's offer on a conditional basis. He wants you in charge. I have no trouble with this as you have better relationships with his territory. Blue and Christian will provide any support you need."

"What were *your* conditions?" Blue inquired.

Viktor strolled over to an orange chair and leaned against the back, his hands clasped. "I have no desire to waste valuable time on theories. If you cannot find evidence there is something sinister going on, I will shut the case. Or is it close? Instead of flat fee, Ren is paying us by the day. He is aware this might be wild geese chasing each other."

I snorted and rocked on my heels. Sometimes it was funnier *not* to correct him when his English lost its way. It usually happened this time of night after a few drinks.

"That sounds reasonable," Blue said, jutting her hip as she leaned her shoulder against the doorjamb. "I hope he didn't give you any trouble."

"Nyet. Ren does not want his reputation ruined either, so we must exercise discretion. It is *very* important to be careful when you speak to these Shifters. We must not reveal our... intentions."

He scratched his jaw with an uncertain look and swung his gaze upward. "Packs are very suspicious of outsiders and protective of the dead. I do not want to create animosity in the territory. It is very unstable at the moment. I have spoken to Miss Parrish, and she came up with an idea."

I folded my arms. "You spoke to Lenore about our case? How's that keeping it private?"

"She is a trusted associate. This is not the first time I have consulted with a member of the higher authority on outside cases."

I released a long sigh, worried that we might be violating Ren's trust by involving someone from the higher authority. "And what did Miss Parrish suggest?"

"That we use the higher authority as a cover. It is the only way to protect the integrity of the case. You will pretend you are taking a census of all the packs and local Shifters—that way, if they talk to one another, they will not grow suspicious of our questions. You must call them in advance and schedule appointments. In light of the recent scandal with cage fights, we will say the higher authority wants to look at recent deaths and assist with conflict, accidents, or sick children. This is a show of goodwill, and the group leaders will acknowledge the gesture for what it looks like."

"So the higher authority isn't really going to help them," Blue said, not hiding the disappointment in her voice. "That's a rotten thing to do—extending an empty hand of friendship. What if they *have* had conflict issues or preventable deaths, and they look to the higher authority for help? Then what?"

"Miss Parrish has offered to work out the details, but we do not anticipate anyone will seek help. Shifters are proud people. You know this to be true. They do not trust outsiders. It is the rogues I am more concerned about, and there is not much we can do for them, even if we were helping. I have confidence that you two will come up with the right words."

"Do we start right away?" I asked.

"Da. I have instructed Ren to call you with more information. No one is working any large cases, so they are at your disposal if you need transportation or research. But this is only an investigation, so I do not want you armed. Blue, an axe on your hip will not be well received."

"I understand," she said, allaying his concerns.

He turned a sharp eye to me. "And you will do the same? No weapons?"

"Of course," I said, gritting my teeth. I didn't like going anywhere without my daggers. Even though I had Mage powers, a girl had to prepare for the unexpected.

Blue gestured to the glass of white wine on a table by the chair. "Let me get you some of that Gouda cheese you like so much to go with your wine."

"I-I am fine," he stammered. "Not necessary."

"Don't be ridiculous. You barely touched your plate tonight at the table. You have a lot on your mind these days, but now that you've settled all the details with this case, you can relax and let us take care of the rest. We won't let you down. It's not good to go to bed on an empty stomach." She turned on her heel. "I'll bring up some of those green olives while I'm down there. Maybe wheat crackers and sweet pickles," she added, turning the corner.

Viktor chuckled and lowered his gaze to the floor. "What would I do without my Blue?"

"Starve?" I noticed an old painting on the wall of wolves circling a campfire. Keystone's art was a collection of beautiful and haunting imagery, unlike any I'd ever seen in a museum. They celebrated the packs who had once inhabited these rooms.

"What is on your mind?"

I worried my lip. Viktor's newfound relationship with Lenore concerned me. She had a tumultuous past with Christian, and for that, I hated her. Yet we'd had some good interactions lately, and she seemed to be genuine. People change, so I had this strange love-hate relationship with her. Well, maybe *love* was too strong a word, but how that translated into her getting more involved with Viktor and Keystone affairs was fuzzy. "Do you think a personal relationship with a higher authority member is a good idea? If things go wrong, you could fracture our relationship with the entire organization. Christian and I gave serious thought to what would happen if the two of us split and couldn't live or work here anymore. Have you thought about the repercussions if things go south with Lenore?"

He licked his lips and reached for his wineglass. "Immortals do not seek long-term relationships. Miss Parrish is a Vampire—"

"But you're a wolf, and you *must* have that urge to settle down with a mate. It's practically in your DNA. If she doesn't have that same desire, maybe it complicates things. I don't want to meddle in your personal affairs. I love Keystone, so I guess part of me feels… protective of the one person that holds us all together. We don't know much about Lenore. Besides," I said, trying to kill the tension, "Lenore is a woman, and hell hath no fury like a woman scorned. That's why Christian's always looking over his shoulder."

He chuckled softly and sipped his wine.

I really didn't feel comfortable *at all* inserting myself in Viktor's love life, but sometimes passion blinds people from seeing the dangers. I'd never been the type who gave relationship advice, so that made the silence between us even more awkward.

"I'll keep you updated," I promised him, steering away from the topic of Lenore. "Thanks for taking the case. Ren's a close family friend, and I feel like it's the least I can do. I'll be careful. I don't want his reputation damaged any more than I want ours."

"Spasibo." Viktor muttered a few words in Russian before rubbing his eyes. "It is late. I still have much work to do."

"I'll leave you to it," I said, turning toward the door and making a hasty exit.

As I drew near a window in the back hall, I glanced out. The moon sprayed a dim light on the back property, and though I couldn't see all of it on ground level, there was no sign of Christian. When I went up to his room, he wasn't there either. A person could get easily lost in Keystone, and we often used our phones to call one another. But at this late hour, there were only a few places we gathered. I journeyed down to the second level and entered Wyatt's World, which sounded more like an amusement park but was nothing but a grey room filled with snacks, computers, beanbag chairs, and electricity. It was the only room in the house that looked like it didn't belong in a Gothic tragedy. Wyatt kept his desk and computer gear on the right side and let us have the rest of the room so we could watch TV or relax on the sofa.

"Has Christian been in here?"

Bopping his head to "Safety Dance," Wyatt made a few keystrokes on his keyboard before an image came up of the underground garage. "Have a look for yourself, buttercup. His bike's gone."

I stepped closer. "Since when do we have security cameras on the property?"

"Since the boss man wanted one in the garage."

Mental note: don't have sex in the garage with Christian.

"What's the purpose?"

He retrieved a set of keys from his pocket and hopped up to open the vending machine. "Viktor was out there talking to Lenore one night, and I guess he got to thinking how vulnerable they were all by themselves. If something happened in the garage, nobody in the house would hear it. So I set up a motion-activated camera that triggers an alarm on my computer. It's also handy when Viktor needs to know who's around and who's not for meetings and stuff." He reached inside the machine and grabbed a package of Nutter Butters. "With Hunter running all over the place, I think Viktor was afraid the kid might accidentally lock himself in there one night. I also had my buddies put in a garage door with a safety sensor." Wyatt closed the vending machine and locked it. "If he wants me to start childproofing outlets, I'm quitting. In my day, we called it survival of the fittest."

"Now I see why you never had kids."

He snorted and sat back down, tearing open the cookie wrapper. "The family name will die with Wyatt Blessing, and I'm okay with that." After tucking his light-brown hair back into his loose beanie, he gobbled up two cookies. "Kids are fun when they belong to other people. Most Gravewalkers I know hate their parents for cursing them with the gift of afterlife sight, so that's a therapy session I ain't got time for. My guess is everyone here feels the same about kids or else you wouldn't be here." He leaned back in his chair and tapped a cookie against his bottom lip. "Doesn't mean I don't like the act of making babies."

"Then you might want to wear a condom unless you want a hundred little Wyatts out there."

He frowned. "You need to run along, Dr. Ruth. I've got work to do."

As I turned, Kira glided into the room with a tray. A silver dome covered a dish, which I could clearly identify as french fries when I took in the unmistakable scent. She lowered her copper eyes, always finding small ways to make herself invisible. When I glanced back, I noticed Hunter hiding behind her skirt. He held his finger to his lips, and I mirrored his action, acknowledging that I'd keep his secret.

Halfway down the hallway, Shepherd appeared with a string dangling from his finger. His face flushed and dewy, he met up with me and caught his breath. "You seen Hunter?"

Switch must have gone to bed. Shepherd had that "I'm in over my head" look on his stony face, like a boxer who'd just walked into a ring with a guy twice his size.

"Maybe you shouldn't go around yanking his teeth out until they're ready."

Shepherd dropped the string onto the floor. "That was Spooky's idea."

"Since when do you listen to Wyatt? That's the same man who grows his own drugs."

Shepherd gave me a toothy grin. "Not anymore. I heard that Chitah dug them all up."

We both erupted with laughter. Shepherd abruptly stopped when Kira approached with an empty tray. She moved so swiftly that her wavy red hair danced behind her like a flickering candle.

As she passed us, Shepherd turned and spotted Hunter walking closely behind her. "Aha!"

Kira pivoted, and the tray slammed against the stone flooring. Her eyes were wide, her complexion as white as a ghost.

"Sorry, I didn't mean to—" Shepherd rubbed the back of his neck, his embarrassment obvious. "Hunter, get over here."

When she caught sight of the little boy emerging from behind her, she made two tight fists and blew out a long, slow breath. It wasn't a reaction of relief but one of control. Maybe she'd come close to flinging the tray at Shepherd's skull, killing him dead. The thought made me smile. Instead, she speared Shepherd with a hostile glare and collected the tray before heading off.

Shepherd took Hunter's hand. "What did I say about running off like that? You always need someone with you, little man. This place is big, and you'll get lost."

Hunter flashed his blue eyes up and held a defiant look.

Shepherd squatted in front of him. "I'm not gonna pull your tooth. Promise. Cross my heart and hope to die."

When Hunter wrapped his arms around his father's neck, Shepherd stood, his kid dangling. Hunter snickered as he kept his legs straight instead of wrapping them around Shepherd's waist.

"So that's how it's gonna be, huh? You'll break my neck."

We walked toward the stairwell, and Hunter finally let go. He didn't have on his light-up shoes, but his pink socks made him easy to spot.

"Do you know where Christian went?" I asked.

"Not my business." Shepherd took a cigarette from the pack before tucking it under his sleeve. After lighting it, he flicked the matchstick on the floor and walked over it. "You two fighting?"

"No," I said on a sigh. "He just likes taking off without telling me."

"Huh." After a quiet moment, Shepherd chuckled. "I thought for a minute Kira might shift. They sometimes do that when startled. She had that look."

"I guess she has more control than we give her credit for."

"I hope she's been letting her animal out. You've seen how Viktor gets when he puts off shifting. His wolf gets aggressive.

Wasn't her father a wolf? I don't need that kind of risk around my kid."

"Maybe she's a defect. I've heard about Shifters who can't shift."

Shepherd and I split ways, and I wandered to an arched window overlooking the courtyard. Gem floated in the swimming pool like a flower, her gown spread out and the blue-green colors shimmering.

"Christian, where are you?"

Chapter 7

My old blue pickup barreled down a dirt road, leaving a trail of dust as Creedence Clearwater Revival's "Fortunate Son" blared on the radio.

Blue held her hair back as the wind cut through the open windows. "Are you sure we shouldn't wait for Christian?"

I turned down the radio. "He knows we've got a case, but clearly he thought staying out all night was a better plan. I don't have time to figure out where he is since he left his phone in his room. I'll give him an update later, but it's probably better this way."

"That's for sure. The last thing a pack wants to see rolling up their driveway is a Vamp. Sorry. Vampire."

"The Vamp in me isn't offended." I laughed and shook my head. Breed were offended by the silliest things.

Both of us were dressed down. A T-shirt and jean shorts for me, and Blue had on a sleeveless turtleneck with brown cargo pants. Some of her scar showed on her left shoulder, but she didn't seem interested in covering it with a button-up shirt.

I removed my sunglasses when we reached a large house in the middle of the woods. Most packs had ample parking, so I found a spot by a sedan to the right of the house.

We received a lot of inquisitive stares from the kids out front who were swinging from a rope tied to a large oak tree.

Blue reached for my hand before I shut off the engine. "Don't let your guard down. Sticking our noses in pack business is a dangerous affair. People have disappeared for less."

"The Packmaster's expecting us." I killed the engine and gave her a long look.

"Shifters are an old Breed, and we're superstitious. Some of them practice the old ways, and the Councils have no authority."

"What are the old ways?"

"It's not just wolves that used to do this. People gravitate toward strong, fair leaders, and it's hard to get in those circles. Those at the bottom of the barrel either struggle alone or join anyone just to get protection. In the old days, they used to share some of the women. People were chained, and you really don't want to know all the rest. Councils put a stop to that, but sometimes you get these small clusters living outside the Council's reach." She ran her fingers through her long brown hair and then gripped the door handle. "Anyhow, just watch yourself. Don't insult the Packmaster or anyone's mate. Be careful what you say. We're not on neutral ground anymore. This is *their* territory, and they have every right to defend it if they feel threatened. We're outsiders, and tight-knit groups like these are suspicious."

"Why didn't you tell me all this before?"

She chuckled and got out. "I'd rather listen to your music than a barrage of questions."

Fair enough.

I didn't want to know every sordid detail. It might tarnish my view of those I cared about by learning the dark history of Shifters. I'd heard plenty about the brutality of pit fights and slavery but little on the dirty deeds some of them participated in. Did Breed children get a history lesson on this type of stuff? Might be something to ask Switch later.

I glanced up, and the treetops seemed to disappear in the sky. A flock of birds circled overhead, and the sweet smell of pine filled my nose.

"What's your business here?" A dark-haired man in overalls rose from his seat on the front porch and blocked the steps.

"We're here on behalf of the higher authority," I said, taking notice of the knife on his hip. "Your Packmaster is expecting us."

"You don't look like Regulators to me. Did they run out of red coats? Josiah's busy."

"He invited us."

The man smirked. "Were those his exact words?"

I refrained from plucking out his eye with his own knife. "Look, he said he was a busy guy. I get it. We just have a few questions."

The man narrowed his eyes. "What kind of questions?"

Blue stepped forward, immediately catching his admiration. "Just a routine errand. We're visiting all the Shifters in the territory, packs included, and have to complete some boring paperwork. We don't want to take up your time or interrupt your schedule. Since Josiah's a busy man, could we speak to the beta instead? If he can't see us, we'll just scratch your name off our list and be on our way." Blue leaned on the railing and tipped her head in a beguiling manner, her gaze softening as she reeled him in with a glance. "We get in *big* trouble if we go back with blank papers, so could you help us? Pretty please?"

The black-haired man gave a tight-lipped smile and actually blushed. "Well, I don't want to get anyone in trouble. Andy's out back, but don't get your hopes up. He's got certain opinions about the higher authority these days."

"You're a saint," she said, turning on her heel.

As we paced off toward the side of the house, he called out, "Hey, if you're single—"

"Thanks again!" She waved her hand while rolling her eyes at me.

"You need to teach me that trick."

"It's not hard," she said, twisting a leaf off a bush. "I've seen you in action. You're using your sexuality, but that's not the key."

"Then what is?"

"Men want to be noticed. So you notice them. And despite what they say, wolves just *love* a damsel in distress."

I snorted. "You could have just dropped your pen and bent over."

"Then I would have had to gut him like a fish when he made a move on me." She tossed the leaf into the grass.

Three kids zoomed by us as we neared the back of the house. The immediate surrounding area was clear of trees except two, and they each had target boards nailed to their trunks. An older woman emerged from a garden carrying a basket of tomatoes. In front of a shed, a man and woman hung sheets on a clothesline, one stretching them out while the other snapped a clothespin on the line. I searched around and noticed a slim guy smoking a cigarette on the porch steps. His skin was whiter than the sheets, so he probably spent all his time inside reading.

Yep. He looks like an Andy to me.

"Hi. You must be Andy. I'm Raven, and this is Blue. Josiah said we could stop by and ask a few questions for our census."

He shook his head. "You're not getting anything from me."

"Why not?"

With the cigarette wedged between two fingers, he pointed behind us. "Because *that's* Andy."

We both turned.

A man who looked to be seven feet tall threw a large knife. It twirled in the air and struck the target board dead center. Andy didn't have a shirt on, and a tribal tattoo covered his entire chest.

"Great," I said under my breath. "Don't they have any nerdy beta wolves? This is so stereotypical."

When I marched toward him, Blue jerked me back.

"Don't approach the beta. Let *him* approach *you*. We're here on business, and he might not want to cooperate. So look a little submissive."

I gave her a hard look. "That's not in my DNA."

"Just play the game," she said quietly as we neared the tree next to the one he was aiming at. "If the pack thinks their beta's in danger, they'll fight to kill."

I looked at Andy's rock-hard biceps. "Something tells me the beta can take care of himself."

Andy yanked the knife off the target board and ambled back

to his spot. He stopped midway, his back still to us. "Are you from the higher authority?"

"Yes," I replied.

"Josiah told me you were coming." Andy glanced over his shoulder, his dirty-blond hair unkempt and his beard like a Viking's.

"It's just a routine visit," I said coolly. "We're paying a visit to all the Shifter groups in the area who've lost someone in the past year. They want to see if there's some way they can help reduce unnecessary deaths. In case you need supplies or the Council needs assistance with settling pack disputes more efficiently."

With supernatural speed, he twisted around and threw the knife. I barely had time to draw in a breath as it sliced through the air, inches from my face. I reactively winced when I heard it whistle past. Once I realized my ear was still intact, fury boiled in me like lava rising to the mouth of a volcano.

Blue gripped my hand as if sensing it.

Andy swaggered toward us, his eyes centered on mine. "Wasp," he said, walking by to retrieve his knife some fifteen feet behind me.

I glanced down and saw the severed body of a yellowjacket by my shoe. This asshole wasn't trying to save me from a sting but wanted to throw around all that macho dominance bullshit.

Blue gripped my wrist tighter. "Keep your cool," she said under her breath.

People rarely pushed my buttons, but I was used to pushing back. I couldn't even draw a weapon or retaliate with a few creative insults about his intelligence.

I reached in my back pocket for a small notepad and pencil. "Josiah mentioned your pack recently suffered two losses. One of old age and the other a heart attack. Is that correct?"

When he strode back, he pointed the knife at me. "I'll give you one chance to rephrase your question, or this knife goes in your gullet."

Baffled, I flicked a glance at Blue. What the hell was wrong with the way I asked the question? I'd done so as thoughtfully and politely as possible.

She signaled me with a look that she'd take over. "I know how painful it is to suffer the loss of a packmate. There's nothing harder, and the pack is never the same."

He stopped a few feet ahead and turned to face us. "You don't strike me as a wolf."

"Falcon," she said, tucking her hands in her pockets. "My tribe divided us into smaller groups. When you live with someone for hundreds of years—love them and care for them—the loss changes you. It carves a hole in your heart that seems impossible to restore. The one who died of old age must have shaken everyone terribly."

Andy lowered his head. "Teresa was a mother to many. She was an old wolf," he said, a smile hovering on his lips. "Feisty. She used to say that the fates would have to drag her to the next life."

Technically, we weren't here to question him about the old woman. But Ren had given me the full list of names and made notes next to those who died from unsuspicious circumstances. Talking about her seemed to loosen him up.

"We had an old mother like that in our family," Blue said, steering her gaze up to the treetops. "She used to spy on the young hunters and shit on the ones who boasted too much."

Andy tossed his head back and laughed. "That sounds like our Teresa. They don't make them like that anymore."

"Truly," Blue replied. "And the other loss—we have in our notes she was only thirty. That's *so* young."

"I'm sorry for your loss," I added.

His eyes glistened as he studied the blade of his knife. "Alisa was to be mine. But the fates took her from me."

"We can't bring her back," I said, "but we can bring you justice if someone took her life. I know the Council lets the packs handle their own disputes, but that's why we're here. The higher authority wants to make some changes, so they're looking at a sampling of recent data to see where they can help. If this was murder—"

"No, it was nothing like that," he cut in. "She got sick one night after dinner." Andy placed a hand over his heart. "Said her chest was bothering her, and she wanted to lie down. I gave her some heartburn medicine and went downstairs to play cards. When I returned to the room, she was asleep. At least I think she was asleep." Andy turned his back to us and folded his arms.

Blue and I flanked him but kept a respectful distance.

"The next morning, she was still asleep. Alisa was always the first out of bed. She liked to have a cup of coffee before climbing back under the covers with me." His lips thinned as he stared at the dirt, his knife still clutched in one hand. "Her skin was so cold when I kissed her. I thought she—"

Andy hurled his knife across the yard, and the handle knocked against the shed, grabbing everyone's attention.

"The Relic said it was her heart." Andy heaved a mournful sigh.

With his weapon out of the picture, I felt easier asking the next question. "Did he do an autopsy? How did they know the cause of death?"

"Fuck you if you think I'd let anyone cut her into pieces." Andy stormed off without another word.

I put away my notepad. "Welp, that went well."

"It actually did." Blue gave the spectators a guarded look as if she expected them to jump us. "He told us a lot more than I thought he would given it was his mate. Had I known that, I would have asked to speak to someone else."

We strolled toward the house. "Maybe the Relic will have more information. We're supposed to meet him at Ruby's Diner in an hour."

"Good. I'm starving."

"There's something Andy didn't tell you," the lean man on the step said quietly.

I stopped near him. "And what's that?"

"They had a fight. Andy has a temper, and it stirred up some rumors when she suddenly died." The man stood and flicked his cigarette into the yard before opening the back door and going inside.

As soon as I stepped inside Ruby's Diner, I knew right away that I needed an Angus burger with extra cheese, and an apple pie. We had a long day ahead of us.

I approached a booth by the left-hand windows, exactly the spot where I'd asked the Relic to meet us. The man sitting there had his head over his plate.

"Hi, are you Graham?"

"In the flesh."

"Sorry we're late. I'm Raven, and this is Blue."

Graham Wiggins's rotund figure led me to believe he might be a stress eater. He sopped up his gravy with a yeast roll, leaving nothing to waste. To look at him, I'd never guess he was Breed. Just an average-looking guy who dressed like a middle school football coach who substituted as a history teacher. He looked like he was testing out a beard by the whiskers filling in his face.

Graham licked his fingers as we took a seat, and I was suddenly grateful that handshaking wasn't a Breed custom.

"The food here is spectacular. Spectacular! I'll have to come here again. I couldn't decide between the chicken-fried steak and the meatloaf."

Blue slid into the booth first.

Sitting beside her, I searched for Betty but didn't see her. "Not many people order the meatloaf, so I think you made the right choice."

After flagging a waitress, Blue and I ordered our food and waited for her to set our drinks on the table before talking business. It also gave Graham extra time to finish up his meal so he could work on the chocolate cake that just arrived.

I watched a group of teenagers smoking in the parking lot outside.

Graham finally wiped his mouth with a napkin and then eyeballed the cake. "Ren tells me you're looking into a few deaths.

Whenever Packmasters get together in large groups, nothing good ever comes of it. I'm sure your feathery friend can agree."

Blue leaned back and drummed her fingers on the table. "What's that supposed to mean?"

"Nobody wears falcon feathers except falcons. If you're not a falcon, you're bound to ruffle somebody's feathers wearing those earrings." Graham erupted with laughter, and it sounded like a hyena. It was silly enough that I caught myself smiling. He was probably a hit at dinner parties, the guy who had all the best stories and jokes.

"Where's your partner?" she asked.

"I don't have one."

"How the hell do you manage clients without backup? I've never met a Relic who didn't partner up with someone to share the workload."

Graham tore open a packet of sugar and poured it into his soda. "I only sleep two hours a night. It runs in the family and doesn't affect our mental state in the least. A slight genetic mutation. I suppose I could find a Relic who specializes in Relics, but what would be the point? Anyhow, less money for me to share."

I folded my arms across the table. "But it also means you can only be one place at a time. If you had a partner, you could have twice as many clients."

Graham chortled and set his phone on the table. "This is the twenty-first century. Clients can schedule a conference call on the phone for virtual face-to-face contact. Half the time they're just consulting me for advice." He twirled his phone to make a point. "Five years ago it wasn't as popular, but once they get used to the technology, they realize how convenient it is. Now I have more time to focus on the kids and occasional scuffles the adults get into."

Blue snorted. "Scuffle is one way to put it."

He picked up his fork. "Idiocy is another."

I sipped my soda, wishing it had a little tequila mixed in. "Do you think we're wasting our time?"

He ran the prongs on his fork across the top of his cake.

"Doesn't hurt to have a second opinion. But I examined some of the victims myself and didn't find anything suspicious. So from a medical standpoint, I don't see a connection. It really boils down to what you ladies uncover—if anything."

"We just visited the Boring pack."

Graham cackled. "Josiah should have chosen a different name, but wolves like to follow tradition with using the Packmaster's surname. I've heard worse, but I have to keep from laughing whenever I hear it. Wouldn't want word getting back to Josiah that I was making fun of his pack."

"I'd be more afraid of Andy," I said, leaning back as the waitress set our food on the table before leaving.

"Andy?" He waved his hand dismissively and stared at my food. "He's a pussycat compared to Josiah. Say, why did you order dessert first?"

"So if I die in the middle of my meal, I don't have any regrets about not eating pie."

"You are a smart woman. Smart indeed. So, tell me what you found out at the Boring residence."

"The beta's woman died young."

Graham's fork sank into his chocolate cake. "Alisa was the epitome of a healthy woman, but Shifters are prone to genetic defects like everyone else. It's a sad fact. Shifting usually heals most things but not conditions they're born with. Even with humans, a heart defect often doesn't show up until later. You see it strike down athletes all the time. Shifters can't get human diseases or cancers, but it doesn't mean they're impervious to aneurysms, heart attacks, and twisted bowels." He grimaced. "That's an ugly way to go. We should all be so lucky to go as peacefully as that woman did."

I scooped up the vanilla ice cream before digging into the pie. "How do you know exactly how she died? Andy said there wasn't an autopsy, so what makes you think it was her heart?"

Graham shook his head. "Shifters don't like autopsies. It's not common practice in general, but we do them from time to time with unexpected deaths. We Relics are wired to seek out knowledge. The more we learn, the more we can fuse to our DNA and pass it on. But we can't force people to do something they don't want to. Occasionally we'll get a pack that demands answers, especially if it's something that can be passed down to the children. Alisa didn't have any kids, so I guess they found it... excessive and unnecessary. As for how she died, her symptoms fell in line with a heart episode."

"What about a stroke?"

"Strokes aren't something I see with Shifters," he said, eating more cake. "They have a natural healing magic, and like I said before, it's usually something they're born with that goes undetected. In most cases, it has to do with the heart. Especially if it gets them that fast."

Blue sipped her milkshake and then played with the straw. "Did she have any marks on her body?"

Graham furrowed his brow before looking over his shoulder.

"Only humans come here," I said, reassuring him. "I think what Blue's driving at is someone in the pack suggested that Andy and Alisa got into a fight earlier that evening. If this turns out to be a case of domestic abuse, her name comes off our list."

Graham nodded slowly. "I see, I see." After another bite of cake, he wiped chocolate off his mouth. "I've known Andy a long time, and he's *definitely* got a temper. If there was any foul play, I didn't see signs of a struggle or marks on her neck. That's not to say he couldn't have put a pillow over her face. Perhaps *that's* why they were so adamant against an autopsy."

"What about the others? Ren gave me a list." I reached into my pocket.

Graham waved it away and lowered his voice. "You shouldn't carry that around with you. It's dangerous. *Slanderous.* I can't speak for all the names on their list, but there was nothing suspicious happening in the packs I work for. Natural causes. Alisa could be an exception."

"So you admit you could be wrong." Blue finished eating her oatmeal cookies and pushed the empty plate out of the way.

"About one," Graham admitted. "Maybe two. But if I can't

properly determine a cause of death, I might as well quit right now."

"What about the lady in Ren's pack?" I asked. "She was only two hundred. That's not even middle age. When you start comparing all the deaths, doesn't it look suspicious?"

Graham shrugged while licking icing off his fork. "I don't work for your friend's pack, so I only know what they told me: she died in her sleep. That's not what I chalk up to a suspicious death, and I've handled a lot of dead Shifters in my time. When they're found in an alleyway or inside a trunk—*that's* suspicious. My family's been working with Shifters for eight hundred years. Eight hundred! Generation after generation. I'm the last of the generation, and all my knowledge stays right up top until the day I die." He tapped his finger against his temple. "You see, I can't have children. So I know all about getting dealt a bad hand. It happens, and it's a terrible thing."

"I'm sorry to hear that," Blue said earnestly.

When the waitress arrived, she set down more plates and twirled away. Not as chatty as Betty, but we didn't have time for socializing.

Blue squirted mustard onto her chili dog in a zigzag pattern. "I know about unexpected deaths, but usually it happens with children. They can't shift to heal, and it's almost impossible to keep them from jumping out of trees or falling off a horse. It's rare to see people die in the prime of life—unless it was in battle or during a difficult pregnancy." She turned to look at me. "Pregnant women can't shift. Well, they can, but it's too dangerous for the unborn baby. Our animal will refuse to come out. It's the only time they sleep in peace."

When Graham leaned toward his soda a bit too quickly, the straw poked him in the nose. His cheeks bloomed red beneath the facial scruff, and he wiped his hands on a napkin instead of taking a drink. "You're basing it on your personal experiences. Do you know how many Shifter groups reside in Cognito? I'm not talking about the packs, but *all* animal groups. Not to mention all the rogues. The names Ren threw at me were scattered across the board. A few of them were my clients, but most weren't. I can't afford to jeopardize my career in this fruitless investigation of his. Do you think it would be easy for me to find new clients? The only time that happens with a good Shifter group is when their Relics drop them or die. If they thought I was keeping secrets or this stirs up unfounded gossip, I'll wind up working behind a gas station counter."

After biting into my juicy burger, I reached for an onion ring. Graham seemed levelheaded, and I needed an honest opinion. "Back to my earlier question: do you think we're wasting our time?"

He glanced at his watch. "As a Relic, my nature is to question everything. I only hope you're being careful. People talk, and what you're asking them will raise a few eyebrows."

"Our stories will match up," Blue confirmed, oblivious to the dab of chili sauce on her cheek. "What can you tell us about the cases you personally oversaw? How did they die?"

Graham scratched his scruffy jaw. "One was a boy of ten who drowned."

I dusted crumbs off my fingers. "Why the hell would he end up on our list?"

"I asked the same thing." Graham resumed eating his cake, not leaving a single crumb to waste. "I suppose the Packmaster thought it was suspicious since the kid was the best swimmer in the pack. His mother revealed that he wasn't feeling well earlier but still wanted to play. The boy had just eaten, and everyone knows you shouldn't swim after eating. It's not science-based, but people sometimes cramp up. I knew one lady who had food regurgitate into the esophagus, and she choked, which caused her to drown in a panic."

Just as he said that, Graham inhaled cake and went into a coughing fit. While he gulped down his soda and tried to regain his composure, I devoured my burger and wondered if I should have taken this case. Ren had assured me that none of the names were accidents or sickness, so why was a drowned kid on the list? There were only three kids he marked as a true accident, and none were by drowning.

Graham cleared his throat. "Another was a twenty-one-year-old male, motorcycle accident."

I got up from the table and stormed into the bathroom. After scrolling through my contact list, I called Ren.

"Got anything?" he asked.

"A growing bout of indigestion. Am I wasting my time? Tell me now, Ren."

"What happened?"

"A drowning? A motorcycle accident? One of them looks like domestic violence. You convinced me the deaths were suspicious, like they dropped dead out of thin air. You said there weren't any accidents."

"Dig deeper, Raven. You're better than that." Ren hung up.

As tempting as it was to quit the case, I knew Ren wouldn't risk his reputation if he didn't think something was fishy. It probably wouldn't amount to anything, but maybe all he needed was someone to tell him that.

I sighed and stared at my reflection. My ruby necklace was tucked beneath my shirt so it wouldn't draw attention from the packs. They wouldn't expect someone from the higher authority to show up wearing fancy jewelry. I clutched it and stared at myself. "From killer to private investigator. Don't fuck this up."

When I returned to my seat, some of my onion rings were missing. "Sorry, I had to freshen up."

"We heard," Blue quipped.

"All right," I said, getting back to business. "So we have a drowned boy, a motorcycle accident—what else?"

Graham stared at his empty plate. "This past winter, a man in his fifties passed away. Another one of my clients was a twelve-year-old girl." Graham raised his head and met eyes with me. "Be very careful. These people are grieving, and you're going to be poking at a fresh wound. Don't put any wild ideas in their heads. Shifters are paranoid—more than other Breeds. They always think someone's conspiring against them. People die every day, and not always from trauma. Some just have faulty genes. I've looked at the names, and I just don't see any plausible connection. If there is, I want to be the first to know about it. That means I overlooked something I shouldn't have. If only they'd let me perform autopsies… I'd be able to confirm with absolute certainty, and there wouldn't be all this tiptoeing around."

After finishing my burger, I pushed my onion rings toward Graham, who had been eyeing them like a hawk. "We have another stop today with a group of bears."

"They call themselves a sleuth," Blue interjected.

I nodded, not really knowing all the proper terminology. "Are the Franklins one of yours?"

Graham shook his head. "Nope. But watch yourself around bears. They can be quite temperamental."

I gave the Relic a murderous grin that made him freeze. "So can I."

Chapter 8

The Franklin residence took us far out of the city. I loved driving my truck around—the windows down, wind in my hair, classic rock on the radio. It still carried the same smell as when I was a kid and brought back memories of Crush taking me to get a snow cone on a hot summer day.

When I turned onto the dirt road, Blue pivoted in her seat and looked out the back window.

Alarmed, I slowed down. "What's up?"

"I thought I saw something." She faced forward and took off her sunglasses. "My falcon is itching to scope out the area."

"Why don't you do that? I can handle this."

"That's not what I'm here for." She rolled up her window and sat back with a hard jerk. "Surveillance is instinctual—I can't see a damn thing in human form."

"You probably just saw one of their lookouts running around."

"I know. You're right." She pulled at the collar of her turtleneck. Her feather earrings were probably a strategic move to make Shifters feel more comfortable talking to her even if they weren't the same animal. I was the interloper, so I paid close attention to Blue, hoping to glean some of that knowledge. The only way to excel at my job was to learn everything about the Breeds. What to say, what not to say, the best way to get information. Shifters were still a mystery to me, and learning that each animal type had their own customs and hang-ups made me dizzy.

When we reached a tiny cabin, I parked in front, noticing there weren't any vehicles or people. "I must have taken a wrong turn."

"No, this is it."

I reached in my back pocket and pulled out the paper. "It says here that there are thirty-three people in this group. There's no way in hell they all fit inside that matchbox cabin. Where are the cars? It looks abandoned."

Blue set her sunglasses on the dash. "Some bears live underground or in modified caves. I've heard they have a really nice setup, but they don't like strangers seeing where exactly they live."

"So they build these tiny shacks to deal with outsiders?"

"Exactly."

I admired the tiger lilies surrounding the cabin. When we got out, a breeze rustled the leaves in the tall trees surrounding us. Aside from that, it was eerily quiet.

"They know we're here," she said, cocking her head when a bird screeched.

I swatted a mosquito buzzing around my thigh. "I picked the wrong day to wear shorts."

We approached the little shanty and knocked. When no one answered, I stepped off the rickety porch and rounded the building. I passed a pile of bones, flies buzzing all around them.

When I reached the back, cold dread washed over me.

A brown bear paced toward us, a chain locked around its neck. I backed up, almost stumbling and falling on my ass. The beast let out a weak roar before sitting on its haunches.

"That's a female," Blue said quietly as she eased up beside me.

"How can you tell?"

"Intuition. She's weak. I don't like the looks of this."

"Why is she chained up?"

Blue scanned the woods around us. "When the lower-class groups have trouble getting fresh blood for mating, they sometimes trade women. If the women give them trouble, they break them."

I clenched my fist. "Should we free her?"

Blue shook her head. "That's not what we're here for."

My gaze darted back to the bear. "We can't just leave her like that."

"She would probably maul you to death. I can fly to safety, but you—"

"I can flash."

Blue pivoted toward me and folded her arms. "Then what? We'll lose our chance of getting information, and on top of that, we'll have bears hunting us down. This goes on more than you think. Freeing her won't stop them from doing it again, and they'll just find some other woman to replace her."

"So you can just… walk away?"

She glanced over her shoulder at the bear. "Let's get what we came here for. The leader isn't the one meeting us, is he?"

"No. Some guy named Ferro. Father of one of the victims on our list. He died eleven months ago. Age twenty-one."

We both turned at the sound of footsteps approaching from the left. Breaching a thicket of trees, a rugged-looking man approached us. His hair was black and shorn close to his head, his eyes dark and mysterious, and his chest hair covered him like a thin vest.

"Which one of you is Raven?" he asked, coming to an eventual stop.

I squared my shoulders, putting on an air of authority. "That would be me."

"I'm Ferro. Frank said you wanted to talk about my son. We don't have to report deaths to you. We're out of territory limits."

"I know. That's not why we're here." I waved my hand at a mosquito whirring in front of my face. "The higher authority is looking to see what they can do for Shifters in the area. They want to make amends after that fiasco with the fighting rings."

"I heard about that," he said flatly, as if the idea of cage fights didn't bother him.

"They're looking at recent deaths in the past year—anything that falls out of the norm of old age."

His brows furrowed. "Why?"

"In case there's something they can do to help."

Blue stepped forward. "That might mean making Relics available to everyone and not just those who can afford them. Or ensuring packs have basic medical supplies. Possibly offering advice on territorial disputes, but that's not one I can promise anything on. They want to look over the data first and then decide where to extend their resources. I'm sure your leader does the best he can, but we both know how some groups are favored over others."

Ferro's mouth twisted, and his eyebrows arched in a manner that suggested he agreed with her statement.

"I'm sorry to hear about your son," I began. "Twenty-one is just a baby."

Ferro rubbed the side of his nose, and I wondered if he might break down crying. But he didn't. He held it together as best a grieving father could.

Losing a kid at any age must be tough, so I tried to be as sensitive as possible. "What can you tell us about him?"

Ferro heaved a sigh. "Rain was my firstborn. Strong like me but kind like his mother. He had the right temperament."

"For what?" I asked, uncertain of the implied meaning.

"Rain was an alpha bear. He could have led this group or started his own."

"Can I ask about his death? I know it's hard, but it might help."

"Bike accident five miles up the road." He glanced toward the front of the cabin.

"But you don't believe that," Blue suggested. "Parents have a sixth sense. What's yours telling you?"

Ferro folded his arms, his dark eyebrows drawing together. "Rain's been riding a bike since he could walk. If it wasn't a dirt bike around the property, it was on the back of my ride. Well, the front. He always wanted to steer," Ferro said with a wistful smile. "It was perfect riding weather that day. They found him in the middle of the road."

I let the scenario play out in my head of what could have happened. I'd grown up around bikers and heard all the accident stories, so I knew what some of the most obvious dangers were. "Maybe he made a quick stop because of an animal or car."

"No skid marks. His tires were fine. No head-on impact to the bike. If he was swerving, he would have gone off the road. But he was dead center, still wearing his helmet. He was scraped up, and Frank said he died of internal injuries."

"But then why didn't he shift?" Blue said under her breath, talking to herself. Then she snapped her attention up. "Did he have any suspicious wounds or puncture marks that didn't look like they were from the accident?"

Ferro slowly shook his head. "Frank said he didn't find any. I would have looked, but I couldn't."

The pain on Ferro's face was as palpable as the bulging vein on his forehead. I pitied the guy and suddenly found myself relating his pain to what my father must have gone through years ago.

Yet I had to ask the obvious, given Rain's age. "Was he drinking?"

Ferro's lip curled. "Rain didn't drink in the daytime. He didn't drink much at all, but he knew better than to drink and drive."

Blue lowered her voice and drew closer to him. "Do you think Frank felt threatened by your son?"

"I don't know. My boy was young with ideas of his own about how to run a sleuth. I heard a few of his friends cut ties when they found out he was seeing a wolf."

I jerked my head back. "Was it serious?"

Ferro shook his head, dismissing the notion. "Young boys need to sow their wild oats. I don't know who he fucked or what their names were—I just heard about the wolf thing a few weeks before he died. Rain was talking about leaving."

I swatted another mosquito that was feasting on my thigh. "Do you think maybe her pack found out and chased your son on the road, causing the accident? Maybe she had a jealous mate."

Ferro's dark eyes locked on mine. "I thought I put this to rest, but you're putting ideas in my head. Everyone in this territory knew Rain. Everyone. He rode that bike all over the place. Hell, he even did wheelies at speeds that scared the fuck out of *me*. Rain got along with wolves, lions, eagles—you name it. It wasn't in his nature to be deceptive and take a mated woman. If you want to know if my Packmaster or some overprotective father came after him, I don't know." Ferro rubbed his face. "I don't know."

I pulled out a fake business card from my back pocket. It had a temporary email and number we'd set up for this case. "If you think of anything else, call me. It goes to voicemail, but just leave a message and we can talk or meet somewhere."

Ferro took my card between his index and middle finger, giving it a cursory glance before sliding it in his back pocket. "Anything else?"

"No, that's all we—"

"Actually, I have one question," Blue said, tapping her chin. "Does Frank have any sons?"

"Yeah."

"Alphas?"

Ferro huffed out a laugh. "No. That's why he keeps going through women like underwear. None of them can produce a son, let alone an alpha."

Blue didn't look back at the chained bear, who was growling, but kept her eyes steady on Ferro. "Who's in line of succession?"

"No one." Ferro turned away and disappeared into the woods.

I turned to Blue. "What was that about?"

"We have to explore all angles to rule everything out. Frank might have felt threatened by a young alpha male. Most groups follow an order. When a leader gets too old, they choose a successor—usually their son—and step down. But sometimes you get a challenger who wants to overthrow the leader. It doesn't sound like Rain was that kind of alpha, so maybe Frank was afraid that some of his best people would follow Rain if he started his own sleuth."

I glanced at the bear. "Why would he want to take anyone from *this* family?"

"Likable or not, it would have been impossible for him to form a reputable sleuth because of his ties to this family. So he might have just settled for some of the men in this group. I'm sure they're not all bad. Sometimes people get stuck for lack of options."

"I don't see why he couldn't have started with a clean slate."

"Let's just say that groups like these sometimes have interbreeding going on. They share their women with the leader.

Shifters looking to join a new group don't want to mix themselves up with an alpha who came from *this*," she said, gesturing toward the bear. "They usually don't care about things like inbreeding."

"It sounds like we're going to have fifty different cases on our hands. Jealous mates, jealous leaders—what Pandora's box did I just open? This wasn't in the brochure."

She poked my arm. "That's what you get when you pick your own cases. Viktor has a vetting process for a reason. If we can't solve a case, we look bad. *He* looks bad. Makes it harder for us to get the good-paying jobs. I think he felt a little obligated because Ren is like your family, but you should be careful with favors. People take advantage, and it doesn't always work out."

I scanned the property and noticed an axe lodged in a tree stump. I put my foot on the wood to steady it and pulled the axe free.

"And what do you plan to do with that?" Blue asked, her eyes dancing with amusement.

"Break the chain."

She strutted up and tossed the axe onto the ground. "Don't be ridiculous. The only thing you'll break with that is your pride. That bear wouldn't even let you get close to her with a weapon in your hand. This isn't what we're here for."

"Maybe not, but this is *exactly* what I signed up for. We got what we needed from Ferro, so now it's time to take care of business."

She put her hands on her hips. "So you're willing to start a war on an impulse?"

I met her steely gaze. "It's only impulsive if you haven't thought it through. I know exactly what's at stake, and freeing her is worth a few pissed-off bears."

A smile touched her lips. "I knew I liked you for a reason. But Viktor won't approve."

"Look, I know you follow his orders to the letter, but we're not a military unit. You and I both know that Viktor doesn't care what goes down on these jobs so long as we clean up our mess and don't jeopardize the case."

She toed up some dirt with her boot. "If word gets out we're stirring up trouble on Shifter territory, we won't get very far with the case."

"What rumors are these assholes going to spread? That two women single-handedly shamed them? That they were chaining up Shifters in order to break them? If some of the elite groups in the area get wind of what's going on out here, these guys will have bigger problems on their hands than the bear that got away."

Blue stroked her bottom lip, and I sensed she wasn't trying to talk me out of this. She was trying to get *me* to talk *her* into it.

I studied the bear, who was lying on her belly. "Why doesn't she shift? The cuff around her neck would fall off."

"Because her life is threatened. When our animal senses our life is in danger, they'll take over. That's what these guys want. You have to break the animal, or they'll never be submissive. As long as she's in those chains, she'll protect her human side because the human is weak. I've heard of Shifters staying in animal form for years—some even decades." Blue took a deep breath and relaxed her shoulders. "Once I release her, she goes her way, and we go ours. If she wants to lie there, then we let her. Got it? Unless you want to help me lift a three-hundred-pound bear into the back of your pickup."

"No, thanks."

Blue twisted her long brown hair and wound it up in a bun, using an elastic band to secure it. Her lush lips and doe-eyed look were a stark contrast to her strong bone structure and thick eyebrows. She had qualities that made a person look at her for longer than normal, and I supposed that was why she often wore a hood.

She unzipped a pocket in her cargo pants and retrieved a small tool. "I'll pick the lock around her collar."

I chuckled. "You have everything in those pockets, don't you?"

"Everything a woman needs. Except for weapons."

"Should I call Viktor and tell him you've finally lost your mind?"

Blue propped her foot on the tree stump and surveyed the

scene. "Animals can usually sense other Shifters. She'll know right away I'm not above her in the food chain, so that might keep her from mauling me to death."

"And if she swipes those big-ass, razor-sharp claws at your face?"

Blue shot me an impish grin. "I'll fly away and leave you two alone."

"Thanks."

Blue didn't bat an eyelash as she approached the massive creature, her pace steady, her back straight, her eyes downcast. When the bear unleashed a deafening roar, the hair on the back of my neck stood on end. I briefly eyed the fallen hatchet just in case we had to do the unthinkable. As Blue neared the animal, she held out her hands—palms down—and spoke softly. I was out of earshot and couldn't hear what she was saying, but it was more about her tone and not the words.

After a few short huffs, the animal lay back down in a pile of dead leaves.

Where did this woman get the balls? I'm not saying I wouldn't have done it myself, but Blue was recently mauled by a lion. Her scars were as fresh as the memories that must haunt her at night. And yet there she was, facing a beast that could finish what the last one hadn't. Maybe she had a death wish.

I sharpened my light and paced forward, ready to distract the animal if it got agitated. Blue inched closer and then gingerly reached for the thick metal collar around its neck. I watched nervously as she dug through the matted fur and turned the collar, searching for the lock. She was dangerously close to the bear's jaws. One snap and it was all over.

"Stay where you are," Blue said calmly. "Don't make her think it's a trap. Isn't that right, girl? Yeah. We're gonna get this ugly thing off you."

I waited for a painful minute while Blue used her lock-picking tool. The bear grunted a few times, shifting its weight and growing restless.

"Almost done," Blue said as if she were tying the laces of an impatient child. "And then you'll be free."

How did this woman wind up here? Was she duped? Had she been traded off? At what point does a Shifter lose free will? How can someone let their family decide their fate?

Even though I'd grown up around Shifters, it was clear I would never fully understand them.

"Hurry up," I sang.

"One more second."

"Oh, I don't think so," a voice boomed.

I hadn't sensed them coming, but as soon as I turned, I felt a weak lick of energy radiating from two men who looked ready to slit our throats.

I was about to pelt them with rocks when I remembered the axe. I hustled back to where Blue had left it and scooped it off the ground. "Frank invited us."

One guy stepped in front, tattoos covering his pale, hairless chest. Unlike Ferro, who had a robust physique, this guy's ribs were protruding from his chest above his concave stomach. Maybe they fought for their meals, and he always came up last. His buddy had more meat on his bones but was just as pasty. I would have never pegged them for bears.

More like weasels.

Skeleton Man pointed his knife at Blue. "Get off our female."

Our? Just hearing that word made me want to trim his toenails with my axe.

The bear stood, chains falling away. Blue sprang to her feet and backed up, her eyes trained on the bear and not the two men.

Skeleton Man retracted his arm. The moment the knife left his grip, I dropped the axe and flashed after the blade, knocking it off its trajectory. I skidded to a stop just short of the bear and slowly backed up. Maybe flashing around an unchained animal wasn't the best idea.

After a brief look around, the bear loped out of sight.

I shook the blood off my knuckles and aimed a hot glare at the men. "Go crawl back under the rock you came from. We're here on official business. If you want the higher authority up your ass, that's up to you. Just keep in mind that I'm a Mage." Static flickered at my fingertips.

"Since when does the higher authority give a shit what we do out here?" he spat out.

The woods came alive when at least ten more men emerged from hiding spots behind the brush.

I looked over my shoulder at Blue, deciding this wouldn't end well. "Take off. I'll meet you at home."

She glowered. "I'm not leaving you here alone. We'll fight together."

"You're unarmed. You can escape. I have no choice," I said, noticing the men had spaced apart so that I'd never make it back to my truck.

"Have you got enough fang to take down fourteen men? Because it'll take a hell of a lot of Mage light to drop a bear. I'll fly if you promise to run."

I gave her a regretful smile. "I can't leave my truck. My father gave me that truck, and I'll bet they're stealing the tires as we speak."

Blue sighed. "Go for the dagger. I'll get the axe."

"We require compensation," Skeleton Man called out. "Tit for tat."

One of the men slid his gaze down Blue's body. "Yeah… tit."

Once I spotted the knife, I flashed to it. One man made a wild lunge, but I spun around and sliced his arm.

Blue ran past me toward the axe, the ground thundering beneath her feet. She skidded to a stop when Skeleton Man reached it first.

He approached her with a menacing stride. "Are you a bird? Because I sure have a taste for fried chicken."

I gasped when he lifted the axe in a sharp movement and brought it down.

One minute, Blue was in the line of fire. The next, a tall figure appeared in front of her and stopped the axe midair. He gripped Skeleton Man's wrist, standing like a pillar between Blue and certain death. The stranger's boots were as dirty as the ground beneath him, his long hair unkempt. When he turned his head to look at the other men, I saw his full profile.

Oh shit.

It was Matteo. *What the hell is he doing here?*

The men backed up when they saw that Matteo had gone primal. Chitahs weren't Shifters, but they had something animalistic living inside them that was ruthless when it took over. Ruthless enough to take on fourteen bears? By the looks on the men's faces, they didn't want to take that bet.

I joined Blue's side, uncertain how this would end.

Matteo bared his teeth, all four incisors in view. The venom inside was only poisonous to a Mage, but they could probably do serious damage. Skeleton Man stood frozen, his wrist still caught in Matteo's clutches, his hand turning purple. When Matteo inhaled deeply and audibly, the man whimpered and let go of the axe.

Blue wasted no time collecting it. "What kind of depraved men chain up women? Go back to your cave now unless you want us to call our boss."

"Don't get any bright ideas," I added, using my most authoritative voice. "If we don't report back in an hour, they'll send in Regulators to find us."

That was enough for most of the men to retreat, but three lingered behind. "Let him go," one guy demanded.

Ignoring him, I glared at Skeleton Man. "You better tell your goons to back off. Have you ever seen a Chitah rip out a man's throat with his teeth?"

A low growl rumbled in Matteo's chest. He slapped his hand behind the Shifter's neck and yanked him so they were nose to nose. And Matteo had to bend down to meet his gaze.

The scrawny Shifter trembled, his eyes saucer wide as he looked at Blue. "I wasn't gonna hurt you. I just wanted to—"

"I wouldn't finish that sentence if I were you," Blue said as she circled behind him and put her mouth close to his ear. "He can smell a lie, and you know it." She finally sidestepped and nodded at Matteo. "Let him go."

Matteo drew closer to the man's neck.

"I *said* let… him… go," Blue commanded through clenched teeth.

Matteo roared, and it didn't even sound like a man. It was chilling enough to silence the forest. He flung the Shifter backward, and the man struck a tree like a rag doll.

"Don't come around here again," his buddy snarled, helping Skeleton Man to his feet. "Next time we won't roll out the welcome mat."

His feeble threat deserved a laugh, but frankly, I didn't care. Once they were out of sight, I heaved a sigh. "That could have gotten ugly real fast." I twirled the knife, only slightly disappointed that I wouldn't get to use it. "I hope the bear's long gone by now."

Blue signaled for my attention with a graceful wave of her hand. "Raven, put the knife down. Slowly."

Matteo was glaring over his shoulder at me. At the knife. Then back at me. His savage eyes drilled into mine, the tension as taut as a spring on a mousetrap.

"I thought most Chitahs respect women?" I said quietly. "He's a decent guy."

Blue gave him a guarded look. "Yes, but he thinks you're threatening his female."

"*His* female?" I snorted. "Should I book a caterer? When's the big day?" I let the blade fall to the ground.

Matteo drew in a deep breath and, when satisfied with my emotional scent, scanned the woods.

Blue erased the distance between us and blew out a breath. "Thank the fates he didn't kill anyone. Claude's hard enough to control, but I don't know anything about Matteo or his intentions. Go on without me. I'll take care of this idiot before he sniffs out their cave and starts a war."

"Are you sure? We could always tie him up in the back of my truck."

"Or tether him to the bumper," she muttered.

"You need to have a talk with him," I said, irritated by the whole affair. "He can't follow us around when we're working a delicate case, and he sure as hell can't interfere. If Viktor found out, he'd pull us off this assignment so fast."

"Gotcha."

"I'll keep my phone on. If you change your mind and need a lift, just call. It's a long walk home."

She smiled. "But a short flight. He's the only one who's on his own. I just need him to unflip that switch so I can hit him over the head with a rock."

"Careful. That's how cavemen fell in love," I said, heading back to my vehicle. I stopped halfway and turned. "If you plan to fly home, do you want me to take anything? Like your boots?"

"No need. Usually I leave my clothes in a place where I can retrieve them. But if I lose them, no big deal. My axe is all that matters, and that's at home."

On my walk back, I mulled over how close we'd come to fighting those morons. Blue would have probably flown off, assuming she survived the axe, and I would have taken my chances. Sure, we could have left the woman, but that wasn't in my DNA. And reporting the incident wouldn't have made a difference. The sleuth would have hidden her by the time anyone could investigate, and the higher authority would demand to know why we were impersonating them. We had to be more careful, and Matteo needed to find another obsession.

Once inside my truck, I beeped the horn twice to signal I was leaving just in case she changed her mind at the last minute. As I drove away, I watched my rearview mirror, but Blue never appeared.

Chapter 9

BLUE WIPED THE SWEAT FROM her brow, still rattled by how close they'd come to a bloodbath. She would have never taken the risk with a high-class Shifter group, but then again, reputable families didn't chain women.

The birds resumed their chatter in the treetops, and dappled light covered the ground like broken shards of glass.

"Are you going to stay like that all day?" she asked Matteo, unsure about the best way to snap him out of it. Claude had flipped his switch enough times that Blue knew how to talk him down, but it was personal for every Chitah. Claude once described it as riding in the passenger seat of a speeding car, and Blue could relate but only to an extent. She shared physical form with her spirit animal, but Chitahs didn't. What came out when they flipped their switch was themselves in their purest state, stripped of all reasoning and logic, acting only on emotions and instinct.

Mainly they had to feel secure again, so she spoke matter-of-factly, knowing he would pick up her emotional scent and realize the threat was gone. "I can't talk to you like this, so I'm leaving."

When she reached the front of the cabin, he called out, "*Wait.*"

Blue turned on her heel, relieved to see that his eyes had returned to their golden hue and his fangs had retracted. She pulled the elastic band from her hair.

Matteo canted his head, watching her like a hawk. She knew that look. He was trying to figure her out, study her habits.

"I'm not going to ask what you're doing here," she began,

deciding not to point out the obvious. "Did you run Chitah speed the whole way?"

With the grace of a panther, he drew closer, his gaze mysterious. "That's not easy to do in a city with humans. A female gave me a ride."

"I find that hard to believe. You look like a hobo."

He gave her a sideways smile. "She called me charming."

Blue swiftly branched away so she could roll her eyes. "You shouldn't be here."

Matteo caught up, his long legs taking short steps to match her stride. "That male almost killed you."

"Is that so? I could have shifted."

"Balderdash. He was too close. You wouldn't have had time."

She gave him a piercing look. "And how do you know what I *can* and *can't* do? Or maybe you think because I couldn't escape the lion that I'm weak."

"I never said that."

"You implied it. Skulking in the shadows and following me all over the city proves you think I need a bodyguard. Maybe that's the kind of flattery Chitah women need in their lives, but I won't tolerate it. This is a secretive job, and if my boss found out you were following us, he'd have your memory scrubbed. What you did helping us with those kids won't matter. You have no right to meddle in our business."

"For that I apologize. I have no desire to… *meddle* in your affairs."

"No. You just want to make me your bride and fill me with babies."

Matteo came to a hard stop.

Blue faced him and studied his downward glance. A shadow crossed his features, one so black that she could almost feel its presence as if it were a living thing. "Look, I don't want to get deep with you. I also don't want to tiptoe around your feelings. You shouldn't be here. I'm not the one. I'm just a girl you rescued one night when no one else could carry me."

He lifted his gaze. "If you choose me, I'll always carry you."

"I don't want to be carried. And I don't want a man who thinks I *need* to be carried."

Incensed, she marched up the road. How the hell was she going to shake this guy off her tail? Chitahs and Shifters had one thing in common: they were persistent. Shifters she understood, but how could she turn off a Chitah?

Matteo caught up again. "Tell me about your kin."

"Next question."

"How can I woo you if I don't know what you desire in a family? Did your name come from your eyes?"

"Don't be ridiculous."

"I just assumed…"

Blue stopped in her tracks and shot him an icy glare. "You assumed what?"

He lightly shrugged. "It's uncommon to see a Native with blue eyes."

"It's also uncommon to see a Chitah with dark hair. What's your point? Do you think I'm a product of a mixed mating? Or maybe you're suggesting something more sinister." She turned away, thankful she didn't have her tomahawk.

His hand gripped her arm. "Wait. I have no wish to insult you, female. I want to know you. I want to learn all there is about you." He released his hold, and his gaze softened. "Tell me something."

She pondered a minute before giving in. What could it hurt? "My name is one I gave to myself, and that's a story you don't get to know about. Yes, my eyes are blue. All my people have blue eyes."

"Is it because you're a falcon?"

"No. It's just a trait within my tribe. I'd never seen people with brown or green eyes until I left my childhood home."

He tipped his head to the side. "You were isolated as a child. That's unusual in these times. What did you think when you first saw brown eyes?"

She thought back. "I thought they were beautiful. They were rich and came in many shades, like the earth. Some light, some yellowish, some as dark as a bear's. The blue eye color in my tribe didn't have as much range—just the same dull shade."

"Not dull," he said, brushing his knuckles against her cheek. "Like two sapphires under the sun. And what do you think of my brown eyes? Do you find them desirable?"

She slapped his cheek and then held out her palm to him. "Mosquito." After resuming her hike, she thought about Claude and all his stories. She knew just enough about Chitahs that she might be able to scare this guy off by becoming the antithesis of what he desired in a woman.

He jogged up beside her. "I'm grateful for your kindness. Many would have let the insect feast on my blood, but you have a thoughtful spirit," he said, his voice laced with humor.

She stopped again and wrinkled her nose. "You smell like a feral hog."

"Does it please you?" He tossed back his head and laughed. "Don't worry, female. I'll wash in your creek upon our return."

Oh, this guy is a riot.

"Viktor's only tolerating your presence because of the favor you did for us. Don't count on it lasting."

"Then I better work harder to win your affection."

"You seem to have a habit of accepting jobs with little payment."

His gaze fell to her lips. "The last payment received was the greatest of my life. I thought the kiss would satiate my broken heart, but all it did was make me hunger for you."

"Those are sweet words you should save for a woman who has a heart to give. Did you really think I'd just ride off into the sunset with you? Live in a cabin in the woods?"

He leaned in, his eyes predatory and his mouth wanton. She remembered the taste of his lips. "I know your heart yearns for the wild. I see it in your eyes."

"You'll tire of this."

"Men tire climbing mountains that reach the heavens. Some journeys are worth the uncertainty of success."

"Exactly how old are you? You look fairly young, but I get the feeling you could be my grandfather."

"I'm a young six hundred. In my time, we didn't ask a person's age. Do you think wisdom comes with youth?"

She patted his chest. "Apparently it doesn't come with age. You're chasing a mouse that can't be caught."

Before he could reply, Blue released her human form and let her animal take over. Clothes fell away from her body as she morphed into a winged creature. Matteo's mouth fell open as she soared upward to the one place she truly belonged.

The world was much quieter from above. She didn't have any clouds to ride, but the earth unfolded beneath her like a patchwork quilt. Land was divided between territories, farmland, and the wild. Small rivers and creeks carved through them, and the urge to hunt grew strong as her falcon scanned the open fields below. Late afternoon to early evening was the best time to catch wild rabbits, and even though it was too early for hunting, Blue decided to let her falcon take the helm. Through her animal's eyes, she became a passenger on a spectacular flight.

Far from Matteo and his honeyed words. Far from obligations. Far from remembrances.

Chapter 10

Before going home, I drove by Crush's trailer. I was curious how he was getting on with his new companion. Crush's red truck was out front, but I didn't see any sign of the dog in the yard. Had he gotten rid of him? I sped off before Crush heard my motor humming and came running out with his shotgun.

After gassing up my truck and driving it through the car wash, I went home. The sun had gone down by the time I got there. Judging by the lingering smell of pot roast and the empty dining room, I'd missed dinner. The burger had filled me up anyhow, so I ascended the wide staircase in search of Blue. The wall lanterns guided my way through the stone hallways. In the daytime, Keystone was a castle. But at night it was a place that could make children afraid of monsters.

Maybe I'd bitten off more than I could chew. Hunting murderers was more my speed, but detective work had too many moving parts. Hopefully those bears hadn't gone back for Blue. She'd left her phone in my truck, so I had no way of getting in touch with her.

I poked my head inside Wyatt's office. "Have you seen Blue?"

Wyatt—who was stretched over his desk, plugging something in—jumped. "You scared the ghost out of me! Don't creep up on people like that."

I leaned against the doorjamb, arms folded. "What's got you so wired up?"

He scratched the back of his neck, his eyes darting around. "I put on a kids' movie for Hunter earlier, and I'm creeped out by it."

"Which one?"

"*The NeverEnding Story*. Have you seen it?"

"I don't think so."

Wyatt took off his beanie, revealing a tangle of messy brown locks. Sometimes it was easy to forget he was born in the 1800s because of his charismatic, youthful appearance. The patchy whiskers on his face, unruly hair, and casual clothes made him look like a guy who quit college to backpack through Europe. He tossed the hat on his desk and plopped down in his leather chair. "It's about a kid who reads a book."

"Sounds terrifying. I think the most I've ever seen you read is the ingredients on a Doritos bag."

He stared at a basket of french fries on his desk, hand inside his shirt as he scratched his belly. "The characters in the book are living their life, oblivious that they're just part of a story. The kid reading the book holds all the power to save their world."

"And?"

He rubbed his arms. "What if *we're* just characters in a book? What if someone is reading about us, and we only exist on a page?"

I chuckled softly. "Seriously? I have an unsolvable case, Blue has a stalker living on the property, Hunter's on the run from everyone trying to yank his tooth out, you see dead people all the time, and your worst fear is that you might not be real?"

He circled his finger over the trackpad on his laptop, deactivating the screen saver. "Actually, my worst fear is butterflies, but we'll pack that up and save it for another day."

"How many of those mushrooms have you had tonight?"

He gave me an indignant look. "That has nothing to do with it."

"Eat your fries. If you see Blue, tell her I'm back and to call me." I handed Wyatt her phone to charge.

Wyatt suddenly turned his head and stared into the empty room. His olive-green eyes locked on something, and he said, "If there's anyone out there reading this, don't kill me off. I've got a whole life ahead of me. I promise to be more entertaining."

Hearing heavy boots tromping against the floor in the hallway, I turned to see who was coming. I guessed Shepherd since not even Claude walked that loudly.

Shepherd puffed on his cigarette from the doorway. "If you don't give me some work to do, I'm going to put your ass in that vending machine with a thousand-dollar price tag."

Wyatt scoffed as he grabbed a cluster of fries. "The joke's on you. I'm worth at *least* ten."

"I could have used some backup today," I remarked.

Shepherd squared his shoulders. "You run into trouble?"

"Just fourteen or so bears itching for a fight."

He chuckled darkly. "What clusterfuck did you get yourself into?"

"We took care of it."

He flicked ashes on the floor. "I sure as hell hope so. You don't fuck around with a family of bears. They're vindictive little bastards. Packs and dens have a little more order and leadership, but some of those bears are wild animals. You need weapons?"

"Viktor doesn't want us armed. We won't be able to question anyone if we're packing. They won't trust us."

Shepherd dropped his cigarette inside Wyatt's soda can. "One of *those* cases, huh?"

Wyatt gestured to my legs. "Looks like what you really need is mosquito repellent."

Shepherd ambled toward the sofa. "Nah. Then it might keep her boyfriend away."

"Have you seen Blue?" I asked.

Shepherd blew a breath of smoke toward the ceiling. "She's around."

That was a relief.

"I'll see you two knuckleheads later." I stepped into the hall, my leg itching like crazy. What I needed was a stiff drink. My last assignment had reawakened old nightmares I'd just as soon forget. But I wanted to stay as clean as I could for this case. One fuckup would not only get back to my father but possibly damage his reputation.

Switch rounded a corner, his circle beard a little thicker as it often was late at night. The man grew hair at the speed of a werewolf.

"What are you up to, Switcharoo?"

"Shep and I just finished a few games of pool." He gloated, eyes shining as he leaned against the wall. "I kicked his ass. Three times. What are you up to?"

"Trouble," I said, strolling toward him.

"Sounds about right." He stripped off his shirt and fell into step beside me. "I'm about to let my wolf go out for a run. Nice night, lots of land, and a few rabbits to chase."

"Did you hear about our visitor?"

"The dickhead with the tent?"

I smiled. "You should chase *him* around for a while. He's trying to court Blue. I don't know what he thinks he'll accomplish by camping out in the woods outside our house."

"Nietzsche said: There is always some madness in love. But there is also always some reason in madness."

"How did you get to be so smart?"

"I read a lot of books."

"I don't remember that in my high school classes."

Switch swung the shirt around. "News flash—you don't need school to expand your knowledge. Most Shifters don't go to human schools—not unless they want to. All you need is a good teacher and a lot of books. Look around, Raven. You're surrounded by books. You have libraries in this place, and I bet there are more in some of these closed-off rooms."

"I'm too busy hunting killers to catch up on philosophy."

"Well, if you ever need a teacher…"

"I know a thing or two about a thing or two." I approached the stairs that led up to my floor, and Switch lingered by the ones that went down. "I bought Crush a dog today."

Switch frowned and rested his arm on the stone railing. "Why would you do that?"

"Because he needs a companion and protector. Don't judge. It's not like I bought him a Shifter."

Switch draped his T-shirt over his broad shoulder. "A pet isn't a good look for him."

"As Crush would say: I'm all out of fucks to give. He works his ass off every day, then he goes home and sits in his chair all night. Alone. I got a dog that would protect him, but I also wanted to give him something he could love. Something that could love him back."

"So you got him a dog out of guilt."

I gripped the railing and sighed. "He probably gave it away by now. He knows how the packs feel about pets—especially dogs. Despite everything that happened after I left home and disappeared, he stayed clean. He didn't have to. Crush isn't the type to settle down, so maybe I just want to see him happy."

Switch rested his arm on the other balustrade. "He *is* happy. You're back in his life. Maybe you can't see him all the time, but that's part of growing up and leaving the pack. Or in your case, home. You can't feel guilty because he chose to live alone. Some people enjoy the life that others pity them for."

I sat down on the step and removed my boots. "I know he likes his routine, but you know Crush. He's always been a big teddy bear."

Switch belted out a laugh. "More like a grizzly."

"I don't mean to everyone else, but to me." I stood with my boots in hand. "I love him. I just want someone else to love him too, even if it *is* a mangy old dog." After a quiet beat, I settled my eyes on the large owl and clock tattooed on his left arm. My father told me that ink has a personal meaning for everyone, and sometimes a painful one, so I didn't go around asking people about it. As far back as I could remember, Switch had that tattoo. Maybe he liked the idea of something wise on his arm. Teaching seemed to be in his blood.

He gave me a pensive look, as if he wanted to tell me things. "I need to find Hunter. I told Shepherd I'd round him up for bed."

I raised my eyebrows. "You guys just let him wander around by himself?"

"Hell no. Gem took him exploring. God knows where the hell they are, so I'm gonna let my wolf sniff them out. Gem's a sweet girl, but she's a little awkward around kids. He might have snuck away from her."

I didn't bring up Gem's business. She'd been robbed of a childhood and had lived as a slave. In many ways, she was childlike herself. I noticed how uncomfortable she became when Hunter was upset. I'd seen her that way once with an infant. Through no fault of her own, she lacked the skills to know how to comfort a child and make them feel safe. Their distress made her panic, and her attempts were ineffectual.

"I'll see you around," I said, marching up the steps.

"Raven?"

I paused and looked down at him.

Switch didn't look up. "Nothing. Never mind." He shifted, his brown wolf giving me a sideways glance before racing down the stairs.

A few months ago, I might have thought that look was all about his feelings for me. But I no longer got the love vibes from Switch. That look was something else entirely.

Switch had a secret.

When a woman holds a secret, it's either deeply personal or juicy. When a man holds a secret, it's nothing but trouble.

Christian rarely entered my room uninvited, so I didn't bother going there. His Honda and Ducati were both in the garage, so unless he'd gone for a long walk, he was probably in his room or having a drink downstairs.

I knocked and then pushed open his bedroom door. Viktor had assigned us rustic living quarters, but I'd dressed mine up with sumptuous bedding, a painting, rugs, and flower arrangements. Christian hadn't done a damn thing to his room since day one.

A fire crackled in the hearth on the far wall, only a basic chair in front of it. I peered around the left-hand entryway into the bathroom but didn't find him there either. Tempted by the candy dish, I padded over to the bed, set my boots on the floor, and plopped down. His crystal dish was the only real décor in his room, if you could even call it that. Christian liked the old-fashioned stuff my daddy used to buy: butterscotch, ribbon candy, various hard candies, and sometimes lemon drops. Tonight it was green peppermints. After twisting off the wrapper, I popped the delicious sweet into my mouth and set the wrapper on the bedside table.

"There's a waste receptacle by the bed, you know."

I noticed his shadow in the doorway. "I wasn't sure when you were coming back, so I wanted you to know I'd been here."

The door closed behind him. "I always know when you've been in my bed, Precious." He strode to the table and tossed the wrapper into the trash.

"How?"

Christian bent over and put his mouth to my ear. "I can smell your blood."

That sent tingles where it shouldn't have.

"Since when are you a fan of the brassiere?" he asked, lifting my shirt over my head.

"I can't interview grieving families with my tits out."

"'Tis a shame. They're fine tits."

"I tried to find you this morning before we left. Where did you go?"

He tossed the shirt on the floor. "Shifters aren't fond of Vampires on their land."

"You could have stayed in the truck."

"To what purpose? I'll go with you tomorrow on the rogue cases. How's that? Now tell me about your day at the office."

I lay back and locked my fingers behind my head. "Two completely different deaths. One woman died in bed. Her boyfriend and the Relic said it was her heart. The second death was a young guy who fell off his motorcycle."

He unzipped my jean shorts and slid them off. "Hardly sounds suspicious."

"They found the bike in the middle of the road. No skid marks, no front-end damage to the bike, nothing to indicate it was hit by another vehicle." I yawned and crawled all the way onto the bed, my head just below the pillow.

Christian rounded the bed to the left side and sat against the headboard. "Motorbikes are death machines."

The wood snapped in the hearth and split in two, sending a shower of sparks up the flue.

I turned on my side and propped my head in my hand. "He was wearing a helmet."

Christian frowned. "That's peculiar. A Shifter would heal his wounds unless he was knocked out. Any other injuries?"

"The usual scrapes you would get, but his father didn't mention anything out of the ordinary. Their alpha suggested internal injuries. I guess it's possible he could have passed out from the pain."

"Aye, but eventually he would have woken up and shifted. Even a broken neck isn't enough to kill a Shifter. If something knocked him unconscious, he was out long enough to die. No blood?"

"Nothing obvious."

Christian stroked his beard, his eyes fixed on the wall ahead. "I don't see how they could be connected even if they were foul play."

"I guess the Packmasters thought it was enough to look into. They've seen it all, so maybe something just doesn't feel right in their gut. I said I'd look into it, but I didn't promise to solve it." I rested my hand on his inner thigh and gave it a light squeeze. "I'm glad you're coming with us tomorrow for the rogues. We only have one pack—you can sit in the truck for that one."

"I'll not squeeze into that infernal contraption between two women."

My hand slid upward, and I cupped him. "Sounds like every man's fantasy."

Christian's onyx eyes drank me in as I massaged him. "You're my fantasy. You and you alone." His breath hitched when I unzipped his pants.

"Don't you like people watching us?"

He chuckled. "Aye, but not someone I know. That would be like my sister watching."

"Too bad you don't have a window in here."

"Why? So you can jump out of it?"

I scooted closer and freed his cock. "So you could take me in front of that Chitah," I said, stroking his hard shaft. "I bet he'd like to watch."

Christian tensed all over. Teasing was one of his favorite pastimes. It was a game between us to see who had the most willpower. There were nights both of us wound up going to bed completely unsatisfied because of our competitive nature. That made every single encounter between us even more explosive.

I circled my tongue around the blunt head.

"Careful, now. That tickles."

"Show it to me."

Knowing what I was referring to, Christian crossed his arms and threw off his shirt faster than I could track. I wanted my eyes on that big, beautiful raven tattoo while I took him into my mouth.

Christian stroked my hair. *"Jaysus,"* he breathed.

I loved all the smooth and rough edges of Christian Poe. From his sharp tongue to his soft look. From his hard muscles to his pliant lips.

I fell into a slow rhythm, just the way he liked. When his eyes hooded and shoulders tensed, I drew back and let him see my fangs. Christian's dark eyes went wild, his fangs punching out in response.

I stroked him from base to tip. "Do you want it?"

Without answering, he reached back and gripped the top of the headboard. The wood creaked from the pressure of his tight grasp, and his muscles were solid.

So much power.

So much control.

When my sharp fangs grazed the tip, he hissed. Vampires never got winded, but Christian's chest rose and fell at a rapid pace as he gazed down at me like a feral creature—an image that would have terrified most with his deadly fangs and bottomless black eyes. I moved down the shaft to that lovely patch of skin where his leg joined to his hip. My fangs throbbed, hungry for his blood. Eager to please him, eager to please myself, I got on my knees and yanked his pants down to his ankles.

Christian groaned.

I sensed his anticipation as I softly kissed his skin, searching for just the right spot—the one he had shown me. My other hand stroked him fast and furious.

The headboard snapped.

Fear kept him from touching me. The fear of breaking my bones or crushing my skull in a moment of passion. There was only one way to level the playing field.

I drove my fangs deep down until blood filled my mouth.

Christian's sharp groan hung in the air as I drank deep and continued stroking him. I braced myself for him to flip me onto my back and fuck me hard. That was how we played this game.

But he didn't. He stretched out and let me take control.

He was *actually* going to let me drink until he climaxed.

God, yes. His blood united us, and I could *feel* his lust. It only heightened my desire, and with each swallow and each stroke, I could feel him getting closer and closer, the biting pulse of arousal at his fingertips.

I also felt a swell of Vampire power rising within me.

After licking the wound closed, I sat up, crawled onto his lap, and watched him snap my panties away as I reached to put him inside me.

His eyes were that of a depraved man as I rode him. Hard and fast. As if my life depended on it.

Christian gripped the back of my neck and pulled me down. The moment his fangs pierced my neck, it felt as if my eardrums were vibrating. His blood was coursing through me—ancient blood. The blood of his maker and every Vampire before him. Everything went still as he slid down on his back and I draped myself over him.

Christian drank greedily, his arms encircling me. The moment his tongue swiped over the wound to seal it, I yelled out, the sound filling the room and probably the hallway.

I sat up and studied his lips. Not a single drop of blood in sight, but it clearly intoxicated him judging by the way his lustful gaze settled on my bra. He made no attempt to remove it or tear it to shreds even though I knew he wanted to see my nipples, to taste them. To prick them with his fangs just enough to tease. But instead, he memorized their outline against the white cotton.

"You're a fecking goddess," he said, his hands on my thighs.

"Do I have to move the heavens to make you come?"

"Ladies first."

And there we were, back in the game of who could hold out the longest. Once blood entered the picture, neither of us lasted long. We didn't do it all the time, but it intensified everything.

I pinched his nipples until he bared his fangs at me. "The next costume ball we go to, we're dressing as a llama."

He gave me a quizzical stare.

With my palms on his shoulders, I leaned in and slowed my rhythm. "That way you can fuck me from behind in the middle of the room with everyone watching."

"Won't people wonder what the back end is doing bumping up against the front end?"

I kissed his mouth. "Stop overthinking it."

His breath came in rapid pants against my lips as he chortled. When he saw my stunned reaction, his chest rocked with laughter, tears streaming from the corners of his eyes.

I sat up and gave him a baleful look.

"*Jaysus*, I can't help it, lass. Don't be cross with me."

"I thought you liked the dirty talk?"

He wiped his eyes with his palms. "Your dirty talk just took a left turn at the intersection of Stark and Raving Mad."

I playfully ran my finger down his chest. "Says the man who once told me I tasted like the Dead Sea." Falling out of the mood, I caught my breath and relaxed. "Sorry. I guess I'm distracted."

"I can see that." With Vampire strength, Christian lifted me up and laid me down beside him, still erect but no sign of disappointment on his face. No feelings hurt or desire to finish what we'd fallen out of. Christian didn't believe in forcing desire, and if he knew how to read blood as well as he claimed, he probably sensed my distraction mingling with the passion. If my head wasn't all the way in the game, he wasn't in a hurry to play.

And that was what was so great about our relationship. No forced expectations. No hurt feelings. No petty arguments. Maybe it was the blood connection, but everything between us felt natural and easy.

I watched him pull up his pants and then kick off his shoes. Christian was a man of mystery. Most people would have gotten undressed, but he wasn't one for lying around naked all the time. Not unless I was his blanket.

Which was a shame. Christian had a remarkable body I loved to admire.

He adjusted my pillow before lying on his side, head propped in his hand. "What's on your mind? You're anxious."

"Maybe we should just lie here for a while and bask in our failures."

He circled his finger around my navel. "I'm as satisfied as a man can be. Now tell me what vexes you."

I crossed my ankles. "Blue and I did something today I'm concerned about. We went to see a sleuth and wound up releasing a chained woman. Well, she was in bear form."

"And you were caught," he said, twisting his mouth to one side.

"They weren't too happy about it. Tensions flared, but nobody died."

"Well, thank the heavenly angels for that. I wouldn't envy the task of picking your carcass out of a bear's teeth."

I slapped his chest. "Who said I'd be the one to die?"

He arched an eyebrow. "How many bears?"

I stared up at the ceiling. "Just fourteen."

He let out a single, sharp laugh. "*Just* fourteen, she says. And now you're worried they're coming after you. Is that it?"

"You know how fragile the male ego is. Normally I wouldn't

worry, but I'm going to be in Shifter territory for a while, and it's possible I might run into them again. I'm not sure I'd even recognize all their faces. Everything happened so fast." I turned on my side to face him.

"Worry not, lass. I'll not let anyone harm you."

My finger traced the raven's wing that spread from his arm to his chest. "You would die for me?"

"That's what heroes say, and I'm no hero."

"Then what *are* you saying?"

He lifted my chin with the crook of his finger. "I'll slay for you. Any man or woman who tries to end your life will answer to me."

Those weren't empty words. Christian had killed hundreds for Lenore.

"I'm not asking you to kill for me. I'm not asking you to do anything but… rub my feet," I said on a stretch.

A crooked smile appeared. Christian kissed the tip of my nose before sitting up. "It looks like I'm not the only one who got my fangs into you," he said, running a finger over a swollen mosquito bite.

"Apparently your blood wasn't strong enough to heal the itch. What kind of Vampire are you?"

He pressed his thumbs into the arch of my foot and stroked all the way to the ball. "The kind who can make a woman orgasm from a mere stroke of his hand."

I rolled onto my back so he could get a better angle. "Some days I wonder if I'm cut out for a job like this."

"You pull your weight."

I looked up at the ceiling where shadows danced. "That's not what I mean. I'm not used to going to a job unarmed. If I didn't work for Keystone, I would have taken on those bears. Every last motherfucker. Even if it killed me. We couldn't even do that. Viktor's expecting an investigation, not a body count. I'm going to screw this job up someday. Big time."

"I'll not lie," he said, massaging my toes. "Going clean isn't easy. I struggled with it for years when I worked as a guard not to kill the person I was guarding or their numpty companions."

"What kept you from it?"

He rested my foot on his shoulder and rubbed my calf. "I suppose a desire to do something good in this godforsaken world. It's an honor to guard another man's life."

"So you thought every life saved would make up for one you took?"

He kissed my ankle, his beard tickling my leg. Christian kept his eyes on mine even though I was half naked and open to him. "You're fighting against instinct when you have rules to abide by. Once you master self-control, you'll make the right choices in every situation. Even if it's one that breaks the rules."

"So I should have taken on the bears?"

He laughed darkly. "I didn't say that." Christian rested my leg next to him and slid over me, his nose touching mine. "You have to weigh all the risks and choose your moments wisely. Sometimes that means taking a rain check. An immortal learns patience, and the earlier you master that trait, the better it will serve you. These are things I can teach you."

I kissed the corners of his mouth. "What else can you teach me, Poe?"

"Fetch me a candle, and I'll show you."

Chapter 11

BECAUSE WE HAD A LONG list of names, Blue and I decided we'd cover more ground by splitting up over the next few days. The booked appointments and locations made it difficult to question more than a few people a day, so that would shave our time in half. I handled the rogues, and since Blue had more experience with animal groups, she managed those. After our recent fiasco, we both agreed not to go alone, so we took our respective partners.

I wasn't sure who wound up with the shorter end of the stick. Blue and Niko had a serious confrontation with a family of tigers who thought the higher authority was trying to confiscate their land. Yesterday Christian and I met with a bodyguard who lost his brother. The conversation was going well until I asked if his brother had any enemies. He got fidgety, Christian tried to charm him, and all hell broke loose when he shot us with a semiautomatic pistol and fled. As much as I wanted to chase his ass down and return the kindness, I let him go. Sunlight healed my wound, and Christian's bullets popped out a few minutes later on their own. He was more peeved about the holes in his shirt than he was about getting shot.

Christian glared at me as we entered the club.

I smiled. "I don't know why you're still upset. Most of your clothes have holes in them."

"Aye, but that one was new and expensive."

"Shouldn't have worn it on the job," I said, pulling the door open.

The evening crowd was dancing as if it were their last night on Earth. The tables were full, and thirsty patrons encircled the oval-shaped bar.

"You'd think she would have picked a more discreet place to talk about the death of a loved one," I said quietly.

I loved that I didn't have to yell over the music with Christian. But that also meant not muttering smart-ass remarks under my breath, which I had a tendency of doing.

A flirty Mage flashed up and blocked my path. "Can I buy you a drink?"

Christian shoved him across the room. "No."

I nudged him as we kept walking. "That's one reason I hate flaring in a Breed bar. I understand why we have to do it, but then I have to deal with all these light-horny bozos who just want to bind with me. No, thanks."

Christian's hand rested on my lower back. When we reached the bar, I scanned the patrons, searching for our fourth and final appointment.

"How will you know if she's here?" Christian asked.

"She said she'll be in a red leather jacket at the bar." I found myself standing on tiptoe and leaning over to look at everyone's attire.

Then I spotted a pretty brunette with bright-red lips that matched her jacket. As I signaled to Christian that I'd found her, a redhead grabbed his ass and didn't let go. I nonchalantly wrapped my fingers around her wrist and gave her a sharp electric jolt before moving on. Christian must have heard the gasp, because his head turned, but I tugged him forward.

"Are you Harper Nichols?" I asked the woman.

She slowly turned on the stool, her black skirt riding above her knees. Harper wasn't young, but she wasn't old either. In human years, she looked to be in her forties. "You're from—"

"Aye," Christian said, cutting her off so she didn't announce to everyone in the bar that we worked for the higher authority. Nothing would clear out a room faster. "Did you reserve a private room?"

"No need," she said, rising off her stool. "Follow me."

When we reached the far end of the club, Harper chose a corner booth and took the bench against the wall. I didn't like having my back to people, but I reluctantly sat in the chair across from her, Christian to my right.

Harper set her white wine on the table and took off her jacket. "I know you asked to meet privately, but I don't know you. A girl has to protect herself. Would you like to order a drink first?"

My mouth watered at the idea of tequila sliding down my throat. "No, we're good."

"Fetch me a pint, lass!" Christian barked at a waitress.

I glared.

He rested his arms on the table. "I'm not the one driving."

After the waitress swooped in with a glass for my thirsty partner, I began the interview. "You know the reason we're speaking. I think I explained everything on the phone. It wasn't easy to find your number."

She lifted her wineglass. "I'm not that accessible these days."

"We're just looking into recent deaths to see if there's anything the Shifter community needs. That includes you, even though you're not part of a group," I assured her.

Her eyes rolled as she set down the glass. "You sound like a man on a first date."

Christian cocked his head to the side. "And how's that?"

She arched an eyebrow. "Lots of sweet talk and empty promises. You look like the kind of man who knows what I'm talking about."

"I'll have you know that I never make promises I can't deliver on."

"Someone isn't getting enough pussy." She lifted her wine to her lips. "So much pent-up frustration."

Though his tone remained placid, he lightly tapped his fingernail against his glass. "What you know about my sex life would fill a thimble."

After a sip of wine, Harper leaned in. "I sell sex toys for a living. If there's one thing I'm familiar with, dear, it's that desperate look in your eyes. Besides, I'm a wolf. I can practically smell an unsatisfied man."

I stifled a laugh.

"What was that?" he asked me.

"Nothing. I just had a tickle in my throat."

I loved seeing Christian get flustered. We never finished our sexual encounter the other night—just heavy petting followed by my falling asleep in his arms.

Harper spoke, her voice textured and sultry. "It's not an insult; it's merely an observation. Maybe you have trouble keeping it up. Completely normal. Or maybe your busy schedule doesn't allow for much playtime." A smile touched her lips as she circled her finger around the rim of her glass. "Maybe you need someone to crawl underneath the table and suck you off." Her eyes narrowed slightly, studying his reaction. "You need excitement, don't you? Risk. Danger."

Christian put his hands in his lap. "Now that'll be enough. We'll be the ones asking the questions."

I glanced up at him. My God, was he actually blushing? I wondered if he was also as hard as a diamond down there, but I kept my hands to myself.

Harper chuckled quietly. "Sorry. I'm good at my job because I know how to read people and figure out what they need. Sometimes *they* don't even know."

"What toys do you sell?" I asked, genuinely curious if that was something Christian might like.

"All kinds. Some I guarantee you've never heard of. Some I'd rather not talk about in present company."

Apparently, Harper was dealing in illegal items. I pondered as to what they might be. Mage-infused cuffs? Sensor-infused vibrators? Penis-shaped impalement wood?

She reached inside her jacket and slid a business card toward Christian. "Anytime you feel like spicing things up, give me a call. I've got something for everyone."

He lifted the card between two fingers. "I know just where to put it."

"What can you tell us about your mate?" I began, easing into the subject.

Harper gave a mournful sigh. Grief flickered in her green eyes like embers in a fire. "Bono was my life mate. They say every wolf has one. Not everyone is lucky enough to find their other half, but I found mine. And I'm not just saying that because I loved him. I felt it."

I furrowed my brow. "What do you mean?"

"It's not something talked about, but when a Shifter finds their true life mate, they can sometimes sense when they're in danger. It's more than love—it's a connection. And I felt that connection sever the day he died." She took a slow sip of wine, her eyes glittering. "He was younger than me. His parents liked the band U2, and that's how he got his name."

Harper was at least a hundred. Probably two. But I didn't dare ask. Even if Bono was forty, that was a pretty significant age gap.

"Did it cause problems with his family?" I asked, feeling out every angle.

"Bono left his pack at seventeen. He had a difficult relationship with his father, and they quit talking." She reached for her coat and pulled out a silver cigarette case. "Do you mind?"

I shook my head.

Harper lit up a slim cigarette, took a drag, and then stared at the lipstick on the filter. "I met Bono while running across a street on a rainy day. It was the perfect meet-cute."

I frowned. "A meet what?"

"A meet-cute is what they call it in the movies when a couple meets in a charming or funny way. I lost a shoe in the road and huddled beneath one of those awnings. Bono dashed toward me, collected the shoe, and asked if I could be his Cinderella." Harper smiled and tapped the cigarette ash into a marble ashtray. "He was always corny when it came to romance. He courted me the old-fashioned way. Maybe because I was older, he wanted to show me what I'd been missing my whole life. I was a bit dubious about the whole thing, but it didn't take long for me to fall head over heels. Bono was six three, charismatic, and had a smile that got him in trouble with women. He looked like a young Heath Ledger. Do you know who that is? Bono always made me watch those old movies." She took another puff from her cigarette. "Anyway, we didn't have an official mating ceremony. Those are optional and more customary with packs. Going to the Council is just a formality, so we exchanged our own vows and made it exclusive."

"How long were you together?" I asked.

Harper kept staring at her cigarette. "Six short years. Bono couldn't start his own pack, and nobody wanted us in theirs, so we had to fend for ourselves."

Christian set down his glass and wiped foam from his lip. "Why couldn't you join a pack? A handsome couple, looking for a place to start a family."

Harper stubbed out the cigarette. "We couldn't have children." She gave me a deliberate look. "I was born without ovaries."

Christian tipped his head to the side. "Is that possible?"

I kicked him underneath the table. "I didn't think packs would turn away childless couples. Shouldn't kids be a choice and not a requirement?"

Harper indulged in more wine. "Sometimes I think they make things up just to keep the family tight. But I get it. Shifters are all about procreation to keep the Breed alive. People fall in love. People who are different animals and different Breeds. But you don't usually see those couples in a pack, do you? Packmasters don't want that kind of influence under their roof."

"Now let me get this straight." Christian cut in, his fingers steepled and a confounded look on his face. "You don't have ovaries, or you don't have eggs?"

Her lips thinned. "Ovaries."

"And what about your other lady parts? Do you have a uterus?"

I regarded him for a moment. "Do I know you?"

Harper adjusted the silver watch on her wrist. "I don't know how to spell it out for you that wouldn't involve a whiteboard. Honey, I was born with a penis."

Christian stroked a hand over his beard. "Jaysus, Mary, and Joseph. You don't say? And your beau didn't mind?"

Harper chortled and shook her head at me. I had suspected her secret based on a few physical clues, but I wasn't certain until she confirmed it. Christian seemed less embarrassed about his faux pas than he was curious.

She leaned back and dusted a rogue ash off her black dress. "Bono knew from the beginning. You can't hide a shoe size."

Christian gave her a crooked smile. "I've known a few women in my time with large hooves."

Attempting to shut Christian up, I asked, "Do people know about you, or do you keep that private?"

Harper pinched the stem of her wineglass. "Admittedly, most can't tell. I was born a girl in a male body, and as I got older, people started calling me a girl. I didn't grow up in a pack. My mother wanted to shield me from all the hate, but to be honest, I never felt any until I mated Bono."

"Why's that?"

"I took a virile male out of the mating pool. We wanted kids but obviously couldn't have them. I went through extensive surgery, but that doesn't fix the problem." She waved her hand around as she spoke. "Some packs didn't want us because of the controversy. Others were afraid it might upset the single women. *Heaven forbid.* I suppose we could have tried other cities, but frankly, I was tired of the rejection. We didn't need that negativity in our relationship. *I* didn't grow up in a pack, and I turned out fine. Bono grew up in a pack, so that was all he knew. We had a long talk, and I convinced him we could make it on our own. Bono suggested getting a kid off the black market, but I was against it."

"Is that so?" Christian asked, not hiding his skepticism.

She narrowed her eyes at him. "I'm not just saying that because of you. Bono could have children, so it didn't make sense to acquire someone else's child. But he also didn't want to have sex with another woman. It would complicate things. We talked to a Relic, but in vitro fertilization wasn't his specialty. Aside from that, it's impossible to find a Shifter who's willing to carry someone's baby and give it away. It's not in our nature. That meant finding a woman who wasn't in a pack and had no desire to join one. A secret like that would ruin her. Anyhow, we never got that far. Bono died." Harper's lip quivered as she stared at the last drops in her wineglass. "It would have been nice to have a piece of him left behind."

"I'm sorry." I lowered my eyes for a moment to offer sympathy before delving into the details we really needed to know. "How did he die?"

"Watching TV. He was alive one minute, and the next…" She shook her head. "I'd gone into the kitchen to get ice cream and then found him slumped over. I thought maybe he'd nodded off or was playing a prank, but his eyes— When you see a dead person's eyes, you just know. They don't always close."

I furrowed my brow. "He was just watching TV?"

Harper nodded slowly. "No hanky-panky. Nothing that would have spiked his heart rate. Bono was fit. It's not like he sat around all day on the couch. He was a jogger, but I think he ran because of his sweet tooth."

"How long were you out of the room?" Christian asked before sipping his beer.

"I wasn't. We had an open floor plan, so there wasn't a wall between the kitchen and living room. I just turned my back for a minute. No one could have sneaked in and done something without my knowing. And besides, there would have been a struggle. I just couldn't believe it. The Relic said it happens sometimes—babies born with defects that go undetected. It just seems like that would have shown up on a regular checkup when he used to see a Relic as a kid. I asked the Council for an investigation, but they turned me away. They wanted to cremate him, but I—I probably shouldn't tell you this."

"Go on," I said. "We're not here to arrest anyone."

Harper pinched the stem of her wineglass. "I stole his body. The higher authority prefers cremation so humans won't get ahold of the body, but packs are allowed to bury the dead on their land. I don't see any difference in giving me those same rights. Bono didn't want to be cremated."

Christian straightened his back. "So you put him in the trunk of your car?"

She gave him a look of derision. "I'm not telling you where he is, and if you charm me, I'll make you regret it for the rest of your unnatural life. Burials aren't against the law."

I picked at my black nail polish. Ren was right. This didn't feel normal at all. Maybe I didn't know enough about Shifters, but people dropping dead while couch surfing? This story was similar to some of the others we'd heard. A few deaths we ruled out entirely. They were suspicious, but we had no evidence to prove the deceased was murdered by their partner or, in one case, a disgruntled landlord. That still left a decent number of unexplainable deaths. One minute they were fine, and the next, gone.

"Had he been feeling sick?" I asked, wondering if Bono might have exhibited the same symptoms as a few others.

Harper shrugged. "Just heartburn. Nothing a little ice cream couldn't cure. He didn't look sick. He didn't look like a man who was about to die. I just don't get it. Is the higher authority going to open an investigation on his death? Is that why you're here?"

The heartburn could simply have been a precursor to a heart attack. What exactly could I promise her? "I don't know," I said truthfully. "We're just looking into things to see where help is needed, but I don't know what can be done in this case. If you need anything, you have my number. I'll see what I can do."

Harper put on her jacket and flipped her wavy hair out from beneath the collar. "You two make a handsome couple."

Startled, I blinked at her. "We're partners."

As if sensing my surprise, she stood and gave me a cunning smile. "A girl can always tell. He's handsome in a brooding, serial killer kind of way. A fanghole, but some women like a challenge. I'd keep an eye on him if I were you." She steered her gaze to Christian. "And if you want my help achieving the ultimate satisfaction in bed, give me a call." Harper rounded our chairs and placed her hands on Christian's shoulders, leaning in close. "Don't worry. You're not my type."

After she left, Christian quietly resumed drinking his beer.

"What do you think?" I asked.

He wiped his mouth. "I don't need any sexual assistance in bed. You hear? If that lunatic thinks I require special toys, she can saunter on and shove that little cigarette case where the sun doesn't shine."

"I meant about her mate. Do you think…" I mouthed the word *virus*.

"Your guess is as good as mine. Maybe you shouldn't have committed to a case you can't solve. We're not a charity."

When I got up to sit across from him, I sat on Harper's cigarette case. "She left this," I said, opening it up.

"Throw it in the bin. It's a vile habit for a woman, to be sure."

I read the inscription etched inside the lid: ALL MY LOVE, BONO.

"Order me some onion rings. I'll be right back." Before leaving, I leaned down and whispered in Christian's ear, "Aren't you a little bit curious about a few kinky sex toys?"

After kissing his neck, I weaved through the crowd toward the front door. She couldn't have gotten far, and maybe I could ask her some personal questions that she wouldn't answer around a Vampire. Especially one with a mouth like Christian's.

Jogging through the parking lot, I called out, "Harper!" I scanned the area, hoping she hadn't driven off. As I distanced myself from the club, I could still hear the music thumping. Pockets of laughter and chatter erupted from the front of the building. A white car drove past me, but it wasn't Harper in the driver's seat.

"Harper?" I tried again, tucking the cigarette case inside my back pocket.

Something hard thumped against the back of my head, and a soda bottle fell to my feet. I staggered forward, pain briefly radiating throughout my skull as I turned around. Four men moved on me in a flash, and I didn't have time to sharpen my light, let alone flee.

Two seized my arms, and a third backhanded me across the face. Certainly not the hardest I'd ever been hit, but I was annoyed as hell that I didn't know why. When he shook back his stringy hair, I recognized the scrawny physique and concave cheeks.

"Skeleton Man," I murmured. These guys were from the sleuth we'd run into earlier.

Damn bears.

"What the fuck did you just call me?" he growled, backing up and raking his gaze over me.

I kicked like a soccer player aiming for the goal, striking his chin so hard that his teeth clicked together.

My hands were bent behind my back, so I couldn't blast the two men holding me. Instead, I leaned over and sank my fangs into one guy's shoulder.

"*Owww*...Fuck! She bit me!"

When he let go, I swung my free arm and punched the guy to my left. Then I bent forward and gripped his arm, blasting him with energy while simultaneously kicking the man behind me in the stomach.

Skeleton Man suddenly shifted, and if he was the smallest guy in the group, I'd never be able to tell by the size of his grizzly. The bear craned his neck and roared, slobber dripping from its massive jaws. I stumbled back, putting as much distance as I could between us before bumping into a sedan.

When the two other men morphed, I flashed to the end of the parking lot, which ran into a brick wall. I whirled around, facing three bears who were coming for me. I jumped on top of a Mercedes, ran down the trunk, and hopped onto a taller vehicle. One of the bears stood up on its hind legs and rocked the SUV.

Surrounded by angry and potentially hungry predators, I pulled out my phone in a panic.

"I just ordered a second pint. Can this wait? Your onion rings just arrived," Christian said.

A bear swiped at my feet, and I jumped. "I need your help."

"Is that so? Could have sworn this was all about phone sex. Don't be thinking that woman was right. I don't need help in the bedroom."

"Dammit, Christian. I'm surrounded."

"You can't handle a few juicers? You're getting rusty."

"They're not juicers." I looked around but couldn't see a safe way off the vehicle without getting mauled. God forbid if I slipped and wound up a meal.

"I'm disappointed in you, Raven. Didn't we teach you better than that? All those hours in the training room, and you're asking me for help? *Jaysus*, lass. What could possibly be so important that you'd actually pick up the phone to ring me for help?"

"Bears. Fucking bears! Now get your ass out here."

I hung up and felt like a dancing fool on top of that large SUV. It wasn't easy to take down a big animal with Mage energy, not without a struggle. Two additional bears only added to the likelihood that I would wind up somebody's dinner.

And I was nobody's snack.

My eyes widened at the massive claws on Skeleton Man's bear as he clawed my leg and tore through my pants and flesh. He and the others circled the vehicle, watching my every move to prevent me from jumping down. They knew that all I needed was some flat land to flash to safety.

Christian coolly strode up, hands in his pockets. "Well, that's a dandy predicament you've gotten yourself into." He pulled a piece of candy from his pocket and casually unwrapped it as I dodged another attack. "Did you know that a bear's fangs are three inches long? But it's their claws that do the most damage." He looked over my attackers. "I don't know—they look rather hungry to me. Bears eat up to ninety pounds of food per day. How much do you weigh?"

Once again, destiny screws me over.

Christian chuckled darkly. "Will Goldilocks escape to live another day, or will she perish in the jaws of three hungry bears?" He popped the candy into his mouth. "Tune in next week for the exciting conclusion."

"I'm not asking you to save me, you fanghole. Just make it a fair fight."

"Since when is life fair?" He tucked the wrapper into his pocket.

One of the bears rocked the vehicle so abruptly that I almost tumbled into the clutches of another.

Christian wanted to see me grow as a warrior, but he was also being a dick. Admittedly, I probably would have done the same thing to him.

I pointed at the darker bear. "That one clawed my leg. He's still got my blood on his paw."

A black look crossed Christian's face, and he stalked toward the animal. The bear must have weighed half a ton, but Christian grabbed his neck and threw him into the front end of a BMW as if he weighed nothing. The animal bellowed in pain as it slumped to the ground and shifted into a man.

My hero, I wanted to say in jest but jumped into his arms instead. When our eyes locked, sexual heat bounced between us like static electricity.

He smelled amazing. Like onion rings and expensive cologne.

What Harper didn't know was that the only thing Christian and I needed to spice up our sex life was a battle. While toys sounded kinky, nothing titillated me more than the smoldering look in Christian's eyes after he watched me fight. He winked and twirled me away as if we were dancing. While the two remaining bears circled the SUV to see what was going on, I kicked the naked man in the head until he fell unconscious.

"I'm gonna have a talk with Viktor about this 'no weapons' rule."

Christian pushed up his sleeves as he faced the bears. "Where's your creativity?"

I flashed around the parking lot, peering into cars until I found what I was looking for. After smashing the back window, I pulled out a sheath. "*Hello*, darling."

Christian punched one of the bears before looking back at me.

I sliced the air with the katana. "How's this for creative, Mr. Poe?"

He nonchalantly struck the bear again when it lunged at him a second time. "You should have torn the bumper off a car."

"Are you serious? They don't put real bumpers on cars anymore. Besides, what would I do with a bumper? Thump his twelve-inch-thick skull with it?"

"I was thinking more along the lines of impaling him in the arse." He kicked the second bear when it grabbed a mouthful of his pant leg and ripped it off at the thigh. Christian stared down at his bare leg. "You insipid excuse for a fur coat. I'll give you a good thrashing."

"What is it with you sticking things up people's asses tonight?" I swiped my sword at one of the bears, lopping off his ear. "Thinking about what you want me to do to you later?"

"Over my rotting corpse," he growled, tearing the roof rail off an SUV and stalking toward the bear.

Yeah, this night was about to get interesting. But not half as interesting as the hot sex we'd be having once we got home.

If we even made it that far.

Chapter 12

Earlier that same day.

BLUE PARKED HER MUSTANG IN front of a jaw-dropping white mansion that looked like something out of Beverly Hills. The iron gates by the road should have tipped her off, but this was beyond anything she'd ever seen. Most Shifters who lived in the country liked the rustic look—it blended in with the woods around them. But some families were loaded, and they liked to flaunt their wealth by constructing modern homes that rivaled anything out of an architectural magazine for billionaires.

"Keep your guard up, amigo. I don't like the looks of this."

Niko unbuckled his seat belt. "Is that not what you said about our last stop?"

"I didn't like the looks of that either. I still don't. Where the hell were all the women? I only saw three in that whole pack. But I sure saw a lot of kids. Mostly girls."

"Yes," Niko murmured. "I noticed deception in their light, but that could have been for any reason, including having strangers in their home."

Blue scoffed. "A run-down warehouse is hardly a home."

"What is it about *this* house you don't trust?"

"This isn't a house—it's a compound." She flung open the door and got out.

This assignment hadn't opened her eyes to the crap going on with some Shifters—it just reminded her of it. The vast majority of animal groups were decent, but there were far too many who weren't. Wolves weren't any worse than lions or horses or cougars. She'd seen her fair share of immoral behavior even in a herd of deer.

The sun glinted off the electric-blue paint on her Mustang. Wyatt said she should have purchased a classic, but Blue liked the power in her newer engine. She didn't drive it much—a falcon has little need for a car. But if she was going to own a vehicle, why not drive something with a little kick?

Her attention wandered around. Instead of gravel, a paved driveway led up to the house. Concrete covered the entire front except for a circular patch of grass and topiary in the center. Most people would have put a fountain there, but she liked their design better. The driveway branched to the left and disappeared, likely to an underground garage. She cast her gaze to the three-story mansion. The levels weren't stacked neatly on top of each other but were set backward, creating ample patio space. She thought she heard splashing water—probably one of those fancy infinity pools.

Niko rounded the car and joined her side. "Everyone's inside. That's unusual."

"Not really. They've probably got a bowling alley and movie theater inside this place. You should see how many windows there are."

He clasped his hands behind his back. "Perhaps you shouldn't judge a man until you've been inside his home. Forgive my bluntness, but your opinions of people are highly subjective."

Blue couldn't deny it. It wasn't easy for her to trust people, especially those with power.

"Well, let's get this show on the road," she said, offering Niko her arm.

Blue was used to guiding her partner around in unfamiliar places. He was quite adept at learning the layout of a club, restaurant, and even the sidewalks outside their regular haunts. But while Niko could see energy and avoid colliding with people, animals, or even plant life, inanimate objects rarely gave off energy. Not unless they'd been recently touched or were made of certain stones. Sometimes he could simply follow someone's energy trail, but it wouldn't always point out stairs, chairs, or other obstacles.

"Three steps," she said as they approached the front door.

He followed her movement, and when they reached the top, she let go, signaling there was nothing more to guide him through.

Blue looked for a door knocker or doorbell but only saw a speaker box. She pushed the button and waited patiently.

"State your business," a woman said.

"Blue and Niko to see Sambah Freeman."

They waited another moment before the massive door opened. An older woman with a colorful wrap on her head that matched her ankle-length blue dress greeted them with a long look before stepping aside. "Come this way. He's expecting you."

When Blue noticed the lady was barefoot, she reached down to unlace her boots. Then she tapped Niko's leg to signal he needed to take off his shoes.

The marble floors gleamed, pulling in light from all the windows. They passed a group of children gathered on a massive brown shag rug. Two older women were styling the children's hair while keeping an eye on the others who played.

Niko followed her energy trail without touching her. Sometimes it drew attention when she led him around, so he was always cognizant about how much assistance he took from her in front of watchful eyes.

She glanced up at the lofty ceilings. The art was resplendent, including a gorgeous painting of lions walking through a golden field toward a ruby sunset. The other pieces were images of Africa, elephants, and a few abstracts. There were also masks, woven blankets, spears. She couldn't take her eyes off each one as they approached the curved staircase.

"Beautiful stairs," she said, gripping the metal railing. "I like the way they curve upward." That was her discreet way of warning Niko. There was no danger of him falling since glass siding ran all the way up.

Once they reached the top floor, the woman led them through a large gym filled with expensive equipment. Two men lifting weights didn't give them a second glance, but she had a feeling they were Sambah's bodyguards. When they reached the windows, two glass doors automatically opened.

Blue lifted her toes when she stepped onto the hot concrete. Lucky Niko. He could adjust his internal body temperature and make his feet a few degrees cooler to counter the burn. They veered right toward a swimming pool that went around the corner of the house.

"He will see you when he is ready," the woman said before taking her leave.

The splashing grew louder as a man appeared from around the corner and swam toward them. The smell of chlorine hung in the air as he made long arm strokes, his head only surfacing when he took a breath from the side. Once the man neared the edge of the pool, he disappeared beneath the water. A few seconds later, he emerged and ascended the wide pool steps.

The water glistened on his dark skin, and admiring his body was unavoidable. Her eyes strayed down to his white Speedos, which looked painted on. She could probably wash laundry on his sculpted abs.

He lifted a towel off a nearby chair and dried his face. "You are early, are you not?"

Blue shifted her weight to her other foot. "We agreed on a later time, but our last stop went pretty quick."

The man wrapped the towel around his waist and approached. "I am Sambah Freeman," he said, bowing. "You must be Blue and Niko. Come, let us sit in the shade."

Sambah led them to a patio set on the opposite side of the pool. A blue-and-white rug blanketed the hard concrete, and a white umbrella shaded the glass table, blue sofa, and wicker chairs. Sambah gestured for them to take the sofa, and he sat in the chair to their left.

Blue had barely gotten her butt in the seat before a man appeared with drinks. He set the frosty glasses on the table, each with a lemon wedge and sugar on the rim.

"Thank you, Joba." Then Sambah said something to him in a language that Blue didn't understand, and Joba went back inside.

Blue licked her dry lips, resisting the urge to drink.

Sambah stared at Niko. "I wonder how it is that a blind man works for the higher authority. They are so particular. You must be very special."

Niko inclined his head. "No one is more special than another. May I?" He reached toward the glasses. "Lemonade sounds refreshing."

"And how do you know what I'm offering?" Sambah asked.

Niko ran his hand along the table until he found the lower edge of a glass. "I heard the ice clinking when he set them down. I can smell the freshly squeezed lemons, and I haven't had anything to drink since this morning."

Sambah rocked with laughter. "I see which one of you is driving the horse." He steered his eyes to Blue as he reached for his own glass. "You must be parched."

"Was that your servant?" She kept her hands on her lap.

After a long sip, Sambah set his glass on the table. "That was my brother. We serve each other in this house. Unlike most prides, we have no rank."

"But you are their leader."

Sambah hooked his arms over the back of the chair. "Formalities. It is the women who run this house. I am merely the instrument of their bidding. Not everyone likes taking on all the responsibilities." He flicked his fingers toward her glass. "Joba is *not* a servant. But consider this: if you refuse to take what's offered by a paid servant, you devalue their position. Sitting there, refusing their service, does not honor them any more than taking their offerings dishonors them."

Blue gulped down half her drink and grimaced at the sour bite of the lemon. There wasn't enough sugar in there. "And what would you know about being a servant?"

"Nothing. But I was a slave for three hundred years, so I know that accepting or refusing food means nothing. Look every man in the eye—acknowledge their existence. People use money and power as a way to elevate themselves above others," he said, tapping his glass. "When you truly see a man for *who* he is and not *what* he is, only then you can change the world."

"How can one person change the world?"

"Change germinates within you, and that is where the world begins."

"And where does it end?" Niko asked.

"In me. In her. In Joba. In the children downstairs and the lions chasing each other on the lawn. In your daughters and sons. Be the example that compels others to change."

Blue placed the chilly glass against her neck, the icy condensation dribbling down her chest.

"Where are my manners?" Sambah rose to his feet and held out his hand. "Let me take your jacket. The rooftop soaks up the sun."

Blue lowered the glass and shook her head. She had thrown on a flannel button-up over her tank top, expecting to be indoors most of the day. Shifters usually kept it chilly inside their homes.

"Come now," he said, crooking his fingers. "Do not drag my reputation as a hospitable host through the mud."

"You can sit, Mr. Freeman. I'd rather keep my clothes on if you don't mind."

A smile touched his lips. He inclined his head and returned to his seat. "If there's one thing I've learned in my life, it's to never argue with a woman."

There was no hint of a breeze. Blue set her glass on the table and felt her chest beginning to sweat. "This is never an easy conversation to have, but we're here to inquire about your son's death. Do you have any questions from what I conveyed on the phone?"

"That the higher authority wishes to stick their noses in our business to find out what else they can control?"

"That's not what I said."

"That's what I heard. I never hear what is said: I hear what is unsaid. In all the years since the higher authority came to be, they have never done anything for Shifters outside of giving us land to keep us quiet."

"Land is a generous asset. Other Breeds would kill for it."

Sambah shook his head. "We have numbers, and that makes them afraid. The land offerings were made to conciliate Shifters, but since the recent cage fights, people no longer know what to believe. Their representatives were involved in wicked affairs, and it undermines the trust we had in them. So I am taking a wild guess that they are searching for our weaknesses. Why else would they look into deaths?"

Sambah made a good point—too good.

I need to make him trust me, she thought.

She crossed her legs. "In case you're having issues with other prides that the Council won't resolve. In case someone doesn't have access to a qualified Relic."

"Perhaps," he muttered, looking off toward the setting sun.

"I know it's not easy talking about the loss of a child," Blue said, softening her tone. "What can you tell us about his death?"

"Less than what I can tell you about his life. I have twelve sons and seven daughters, but King was my youngest. The others were given American names at the request of my mate, but King was very special. He was born to do great things, and that is why I gave him an auspicious name."

"Was he to inherit your fortune?" Niko asked.

"I would have given the world to King. So smart. So full of joy and honor. All my children are different, and I am grateful I can give them all this. They don't know what it's like to belong to someone—to be property. And it's my intention that they never do. They've heard the stories from their elders, but as we old ones begin dying, so will our history."

"You're a first-generation slave?" Blue asked. "I'm so sorry for what you went through."

Shifters could live for hundreds or even over a thousand years, but it wasn't as common as one might think. Due to fights, battles, and even accidents, many never saw past middle age. The more invincible a person felt, the more reckless they behaved.

"First we were sold to humans. But when the immortals discovered some of us were Shifters, we were sold to the highest bidder. Now imagine a world where you're free and you must see your previous master walking the streets. None of these men were held accountable."

"If immortals were held accountable for their sins, there wouldn't be enough jail cells."

Sambah paused for a moment in thought. "My tribe was slaughtered and stolen from our home. They killed the old ones and gathered up everyone else—mostly men and young women. Many children were either killed or left behind to die of starvation. We were shackled around the wrists and neck, so we couldn't shift to fight back. I won't describe the graphic nightmare aboard the ships. Some fled when their shackles were changed or temporarily removed, but few of them survived. Where is a lion to go in a strange country? They were hunted and killed, so we had to escape in human form in order to survive. So many tribes lived isolated from the world. I had never met a Vampire or a Mage until I came here. Our elders told stories of Chitahs—pale men with golden eyes and skin that would change patterns like that of a cat. But we never saw one. Not until I came here."

Blue thought about all the people she'd seen in the house. "Is everyone in your home from Africa?"

"They're all of African descent. Maybe that's not how most Shifters invite members into their family, but we have formed a brotherhood from common experience. We have a duty to preserve our culture and keep our stories alive in our children. What can they learn from a lion who lived a privileged life in England? One who could only shift in the privacy of a large estate to protect themselves? They don't know what it's like to hunt in the open plains, following the thundering hoofbeats of gazelle with the hot sun on their backs. We could go anywhere—the land was ours. Now we are restricted to territories. My family shifts in the courtyard. So many roads. So many cars. So many camera phones."

Blue sympathized with him. "I guess you have problems I haven't endured."

He flicked a glance at her feather earrings. "Owl?"

She snorted. "They're nosy little bastards. I'm a falcon."

"It must be nice to be free in the heavens."

"It is," she admitted, turning her head toward a rogue breeze. "I guess I take my freedom for granted. Is that what happened to King? Did he wander off the territory?"

Sambah lifted his glass and licked the sugar off the rim. Somewhere nearby, Blue heard drums and singing.

"Apologies," Niko said. "Did we disturb a ceremony?"

Sambah gazed off to the west. "No. There's a small tribe within our family who sings to the setting sun. There are many customs here, and we honor them all."

Joba returned with a colorful round tray. On it, a supremely large plate filled with many different foods. Blue arched her eyebrows, surprised by the feast.

Joba chuckled and used a piece of flatbread to scoop up what looked like a mixture of cooked cabbage and onions. Then he took a bite. "Don't let good food go to waste."

When he left, Blue reached for a folded-up piece of bread and used it to grab food on the tray. She wasn't exactly sure what they were eating, but it smelled good.

"Here," she said, placing it in Niko's hand. "Eat up."

Niko held it to his nose before taking a bite.

It was rude to decline food offered in a Shifter home. Mainly because it was considered a show of trust by both parties. Leaders could poison enemies under the guise of hospitality, something Shifters once did. Sambah was testing them, and that was why she shoved food into Niko's hands before he had the chance to decline.

She looked at the doughy bread lining the plate. "This is all vegetables?"

Sambah chuckled. "We lions have a bad reputation. Many of us prefer to eat meat only in animal form. This is *bayenetu*. Many options."

Blue tried some. "It's delicious."

"So are enchiladas and candy bars. We eat all of those too. But if you come into my home as a guest, we will serve you our food." He flicked his gaze to the tall trees. "You asked me how King died. It wasn't from a territorial dispute. Gossip and speculation surrounded his death, but the truth is he fell down the stairs."

"Fell?" Blue asked, unable to mask the surprise in her voice.

Sambah shook his head. "Great men die in battle. I cannot understand it myself. It happened after midnight, and I don't know what he was doing up that late. It's not unusual for our lions to stir in the late hours, but we keep the house quiet for the children. There has to be a schedule."

"Maybe he wanted a midnight snack, and it was dark," Niko suggested.

"The kitchen is closed after our last meal," Sambah informed him. "And I installed a glass railing to keep the children from falling. They light up at night. Our worst nightmare is a home that is not safe for children. Young ones are so precious and fragile. But King was a man. He struck his head, and that is why he didn't shift."

Blue swallowed her bite. "Do you think someone pushed him?"

"I don't know what to believe. I teach my children well. I have taught them to shift before they are injured. If you pushed me from a falling window, I would shift before my feet hit the ground. Our animals are less frail. I will never know. They found him on the stairs in the morning, and I cannot imagine how long he must have lain there. I have the power to force him to shift—I could have saved him if he'd still been alive. Even if I couldn't, I could have held him in my arms. But that was not the will of the fates."

A black feeling enveloped Blue, one she tried to suppress.

Niko touched her arm. He must have noticed her light change.

Having lost her appetite, Blue lifted her glass and cleansed her palate. "Was he himself that day? Did anything about his mood or behavior seem off? Maybe he wasn't feeling well, and that's why he lost his balance." She avoided allusion to the possibility of a virus.

"I should remember all those last moments," Sambah admitted, "but I don't. They are gone from me. I remember him as we gathered for breakfast the previous morning. He was giving my brother an ulcer. We often joked that King could talk a ghost out of his grave." Sambah reached for the plate. "My son was an insistent man. He got his way many times because I couldn't win a debate with him."

Niko chuckled, and that pleased Sambah.

"I could tell many stories," he continued. "The living are memory keepers of the dead. It honors their spirit to remember them, but more importantly, those stories inspire younger generations. I'm afraid I have no conspiracy to report to the higher authority if that's what they're looking for. No murder under my roof. No cover-up. Just a tragic accident."

Blue stood. "I'm sorry if we wasted your time."

"Not at all." After eating what was in his hand, he rose to his feet and rounded the table to escort them inside. "It is not often we get visitors from the outside—especially falcons. If you don't mind my saying so, most of your kind avoid us."

Blue gave him a sideways glance. "Maybe it's because some of you consider us dinner."

"That was many centuries ago. Food is plentiful now." He stopped and turned to face her. "I promise not to eat you if you visit again." Then he directed his gaze to Niko. "May I steal a minute alone with your partner?"

Blue patted Niko's shoulder. "The door is about seven steps ahead and it automatically opens. I'll be right in."

Niko bowed. "Thank you for inviting us into your home, Mr. Freeman. It was a pleasure being your guest."

When he left, Sambah folded his arms. "I have many questions about your friend."

"Why didn't you ask him?"

"Because it is not he who intrigues me."

Blue tucked her hands in her pants pockets as the wind blew her shirt collar to the side. "I'm not available."

Sambah tossed back his head and laughed. "I am not a collector of mistresses. There is only one woman who has my heart."

Confused, she frowned. "Then what is it?"

"Where are your people? Where is your tribe? Why do you walk alone?"

"I'm not alone. I have Niko."

"But he is not one of us."

"No, but I chose my family. Not everyone is born to live in a big house and knit all day."

He squinted and looked deep into her eyes. "You're not foolish enough to believe the women in my house are subservient, are you? We are evolved from the way our ancestors ran a home."

"Not everyone is as progressive as you are."

He gave a short nod as if she had answered a question. That annoyed Blue—it irritated her when people felt entitled to her privacy.

"This is not a ruse, is it?" he asked, making her suddenly nervous. "Over the years, I've amassed a fortune. I know some envious immortals who would like nothing more than to disband my pride so they can make themselves rich."

"I promise that's not what this is about. I would *never* be a part of something like that."

Sambah turned toward the setting sun, which Blue could see in the reflection of the tall windows. "In my homeland, there wasn't always peace. We battled for land among other Shifters. Sometimes lions, other times hyenas or leopards. All warriors carried scars they chose not to heal. Scarification was practiced among human tribes, but with Shifters, those marks held a different meaning. They weren't just symbols of courage but also of beauty. We call those marks fingerprints of the gods. We are not born warriors—we are chosen."

Blue realized her shirt had moved away from her shoulder, revealing some of the nasty scar that ran beneath her tank top. There was no point in buttoning up.

"If your people cast you out because of your scars, they were foolish. It is a bad omen to turn away those touched by greatness," he continued.

"That's not what happened. I left them a long time before."

"You carry pain inside you. It makes me wonder if anyone has told you how beautiful you are—how beautiful your scars must be. They're a remembrance of pain, but if I were a single man, I would undress you and admire them."

Blue snorted. "Well, I'm glad you're mated. And anyone who undresses me without permission gets his hands cut off. Don't worry, Mr. Freeman. The pain I carry is old and has nothing to do with the marks on my body."

He suddenly turned and put his arm around her, leading her to the doors. "Good. Then I would very much like to introduce you to one of my brothers. He doesn't live in my house anymore, but he has no issue with interbreeding. Though a goose once gave him grief."

"Until you cooked her?"

Sambah laughed. "There is a sense of humor in there after all."

Chapter 13

"What did he talk to you about?" Niko asked from the passenger seat.

"He wanted to set me up with his brother."

The car was too dark to see if Niko was grinning, but she could feel it.

Niko shifted in his seat. "And what did you say?"

She steered onto another road. "I'd rather clip my wings than mate with a lion."

"Bad blood?"

"Sambah's a decent man—I can't disagree with that. More than some of the families we've visited, especially the last one. Not everyone follows the old customs about feeding visitors, and he gave us a tour of his home. But it doesn't erase the history between different animal races. It wasn't uncommon to skin the hides of your enemies, and some probably still do it even though it's a primitive custom. But there were a few who *ate* their enemies—roasted them on a spit. Lions were one, and I've also heard stories about leopards. It's one thing if your *animal* consumes another, because we don't have much control over what our animals do, but when you eat another Shifter while you're in human form, it's practically cannibalism."

"Even if the victim is in animal form?"

"Doesn't matter," she said, tightening her grip on the wheel.

Niko took out one of the peppermints she kept in the armrest. "Perhaps it's time you let go of that stereotype. People change, and more importantly, newer generations phase out the old."

"I know. Like I said, I've got nothing against him. Nice guy, nice home, nice family. But I still wouldn't mate a lion. Their ancestors might have eaten one of mine, and that would anger the spirits."

"Wyatt says most of the spirits go somewhere after death, and only a few linger."

"You're talking about the same man who thinks Ding Dongs should have their own national holiday."

Blue swerved when something darted in front of her headlights. The car went careening off the road and took a few hard bumps before she slammed on the brakes.

Niko unbuckled his seat belt. "My eyes were closed. What happened?"

"You tell me." Blue looked out the back window but couldn't see anything, so she pulled onto the road and put the car in park. "I thought I saw a man. Do you think I hit him? Viktor will kill me if I ran over some poor human."

Niko opened his door. "Maybe we should check it out."

"I'm one step ahead of you, amigo." Blue already had her door open, one foot out. The headlamps of her car lit up a thin veil of fog, but without the aid of streetlights, she couldn't see the road behind them.

"There's a body," Niko said. "Still alive."

"Thank the fates."

Blue hustled across the asphalt until she reached a dark shape on the ground. She knelt and rolled the man over and was searching for a pulse when he suddenly seized her wrist.

She pulled back, but he didn't let go. "Were you hit, sir? I can take you to a hospital."

"You're the one who's going to need a doctor." The man rose to his feet, taking her with him. The red taillights on her car didn't illuminate his features, but she could see he was tall.

"Blue, there's one more in the woods," Niko said coolly.

It was then she realized that this was a trap. Niko climbed onto the roof of her car, scanning the area. He could see what others couldn't in the cloak of darkness.

"I thought falcons were smarter than you," the man said, jerking her wrist. "Walking around unarmed, especially in wolf territory?"

Wolf. They weren't in wolf territory. Wyatt had given her the specs of all the places she planned to visit, and outside of the Freeman pride was a whole bunch of unused land owned by the higher authority.

She squinted, trying to make out his face. "Do I know you?"

"You stupid cunt." He grabbed a fistful of her hair and shoved her toward the vehicle. "Tell your blind friend to get back in the car."

Blind. Yep. This guy knew them. And as many cases as they'd worked together, there was no telling what the hell this was about. Every blue moon, they ran into a thug they'd busted or roughed up, and all these jerks wanted was revenge.

Something moved within the tree line. Blue expected to see this guy's buddy, but instead, a wolf trotted up to the car, sniffed, and barked. Not a ferocious bark she'd heard from Viktor on the attack, but one to call attention.

"They're alone," Niko said. "What do you want to do?"

"Give us what we came for," the man gripping her hair snarled.

She stopped short and gave him a steely glare over her shoulder. "An ass kicking?"

Blue struck him in the chest with her elbow, then twisted around and punched him until her knuckles throbbed. Bloodied his nose, knocked out a tooth, and then she went for the windpipe. Despite her best efforts, he didn't drop to the ground but swung his arms as he gasped to breathe. Hand-to-hand combat wasn't her style. She could throw a mean punch, but this guy must have been twice her weight.

Niko jumped off the car and hustled toward the wolf. With outstretched hands and webs of light dancing at his fingertips, he addressed the animal. "Leave us, and I won't kill you."

Blue's adversary simultaneously hacked out a cough and a laugh. "You blind motherfucker. You couldn't kill an elephant. Get him!"

The second the wolf lunged. Niko ran a step and somersaulted over him, his fighting techniques pure magic.

Blue looked down when the man punched her in the leg. No, that was no punch. It took a second to feel the knife piercing bone, and she lost her balance, dropping to her knees.

In that moment, Blue had what could only be called an out-of-body experience. She punched him in the groin with immense power and did it repeatedly until he crumpled to the ground, gasping as he clutched his testicles. Then she yanked the knife from her leg and crawled over him, her pain no longer existent. As she raised the knife, something tickled her memory, filling her with so much rage that she drove it straight through his heart.

Again and again.

"Blue, stop." Niko grasped her hands, forcing the knife out.

Blue mechanically rose to face him. By the car, the wolf lay motionless. "Are you okay?"

He reached out until his hand found her temple. "I should ask you the same."

She limped toward the car. "What the hell do they think we have?"

Niko touched the trunk lid and bent down low. "I didn't sense it before. Open the trunk."

Unfortunately, she didn't have a model with the button on the trunk lid itself, so Blue dragged her leg behind her as she reached inside the car and activated the trunk release.

"Blue, quick!"

Her leg dull with pain, she hobbled to the rear. The trunk light Shepherd had installed revealed a child curled up in a fetal position. She couldn't have been more than ten or eleven.

"*Fates*," Blue whispered. "How long has she been in there?"

"Her light is weak. Does she look familiar to you?"

Blue reached in and swept back the girl's long brown hair. "Yeah. The Donner pack."

"You mean the one from this afternoon?"

Blue thought about how suspicious the men had behaved and how few women she'd seen. That in itself wasn't unusual, but it was all the children that raised red flags—mostly girls. This one had been sitting inside the garage when they arrived. She had a hopeful look in her eyes when she saw Blue, but sometimes that was simple curiosity from packs cut off from the outside world.

"She's been in there for *hours*," Blue said, a sinking feeling coming over her as she pulled the girl out. She set her on the ground and patted her cheek. "Wake up, honey. Can you hear me?"

"I'll get water." Niko disappeared from sight.

The girl's eyelids fluttered before she looked up at Blue. "Please don't send me back," she rasped. "*Please.*"

"Okay. Don't you worry about all that."

Niko reappeared and held out a bottle.

"Here, you take her," Blue said.

While Niko cradled the girl, Blue slowly poured water into the girl's mouth. A few swallows went down before she passed out.

"She's burning up," Niko said. "She'll die if we don't find help."

"We can't take her to a hospital—she's a Shifter."

They had a hard-and-fast rule about bringing strangers home for medical care. Blue reached in her pocket and dialed Graham, the only Relic she personally knew. When it went to voicemail, she pulled herself up. "We have no choice but to take her home. Turn on that cooling thing you do and see if you can bring down her temperature."

Once they were safely inside the vehicle, Blue hit the gas and left the bodies behind. She didn't have time to call cleaners in, but if these guys were expected back, their packmates would come for them sooner or later.

"You're injured," Niko said. "I can heal you."

"Don't be ridiculous. You can't do two things at once. Focus on her. She's just a kid."

"I can't heal her," he said remorsefully. "My gift heals wounds, but I can't fix something like this, especially not a child."

"Just keep her cool. Shepherd will know what to do."

The air conditioner combined with Niko's Thermal ability sent goose bumps up Blue's arms. She couldn't stop her hands from shaking, but it wasn't from the cold. She sped down every shortcut she knew, trying to get home as quickly as possible.

What were you thinking, kid? Blue wondered why a child would have done something so foolish. She might have chalked it up as an accident, but the girl would have had to get inside the car, pop the trunk, and then quietly lock herself in.

Please don't send me back. Those haunting words echoed in Blue's head.

She dialed Shepherd. "Set up the medical room. ... I'll tell you when we get there."

Thank the fates I bought a fast car. The engine roared as she glanced at the girl's lifeless body, sand slipping through the hourglass with each passing second. Niko would notice if her light extinguished, but Blue wasn't going to let that happen. Not on her watch.

When they arrived, the front gate was already open. She sped up the private driveway and screeched to a halt in front of the door. Blue hopped out.

"Is it Niko?" Shepherd approached the vehicle.

She limped around the car to open Niko's door. "Help us."

Shepherd's eyes widened. "Who's that?"

"A little girl who's going to die if you don't get moving."

Blue snapped her attention to the footfalls rushing toward them. Matteo emerged from the darkness at Chitah speed, his nostrils flaring as he undoubtedly picked up their emotional scent.

"You're like a stray cat we can't get rid of," she muttered.

Shepherd took the girl from Niko's arms and carried her inside.

When Blue went to follow, Matteo gripped her arm. "Female, you're bleeding."

"I don't have time for this." She freed her arm from his grasp and gave him a sharp look. "You can't come inside. That's the rule, Chitah."

"You need help," he insisted, trapping her against the car.

Blue touched his arm, realizing he was close to flipping his switch. "It doesn't hurt. I'll be fine."

He dipped his chin. "Balderdash. Not only can I scent your pain, but I can also scent your lies."

"*My* life isn't what matters here," she said rapid-fire. "Your tongue isn't going to fix my wound. That little girl needs me. Let me go unless you want to be responsible for her death."

Concern bled from his expression, but he finally capitulated and backed off.

Blue brushed by him, hoping it wasn't too late. She couldn't have a child's death on her hands.

Once inside, she slammed the door and dizzily followed the commotion coming from the middle of the house. Halfway to the stairs, she collapsed.

"Blue!" Viktor appeared over her like an angel. "Why do you not shift?"

"I need to see the girl." Blue sat up but had to lean on her hand to steady herself. "I have to make sure she's okay."

Guilt set in. Why hadn't she noticed someone in the trunk of her car? How long had that girl suffered in the heat? Even though it was late afternoon and she had parked the car in the shade, it was too hot for a kid that age to lie in the trunk that long. Blue thought about sitting on that rooftop, sipping lemonade and eating while that little girl was probably beating on the trunk lid to get out.

"You *must* shift," he insisted. "So much blood."

"Not enough to kill me, Viktor. Help me up—I need to see if she's going to make it. I have to be there. I have to see."

Viktor lifted her into his strong embrace. She wrapped her arms around his shoulders, nuzzled close to his stubbly neck, and caught a faint whiff of cologne. He swiftly moved down the hall, whispering Russian words she didn't understand. Was he admonishing her? Praying for her? Reciting the grocery list?

None of it mattered. She was home.

Chapter 14

"How's your arm?" Christian asked, a twinkle in his eyes.

I glanced at the dried blood where a bear clawed me and then finished pouring his whiskey. "My arm's fine, but I still have phantom pain in my leg."

"You get used to it."

I set the glass down and sat in the bench seat opposite him. We had the dining room to ourselves, and it was nice to have a moment of peace after our scuffle with the bears. Blue and Niko hadn't made it back yet, so we were waiting to see if they had anything exciting to report.

Candlelight flickered on his handsome features as he lifted the crystal glass. "Thirsty?"

"Depends on what you're offering, Mr. Poe. I've had my fill of the red stuff tonight."

"'Tis a shame." After sipping his drink, he gave me a hot look. "Are you sure you don't want to take a short walk upstairs and rub your knockers on my knob?"

"Not when you put it like that." I sat back and stared at his glass. "Blue and Niko should be back soon. We need to figure out what we've got—if anything."

"My money's on the apocalyptic virus." He swirled his drink before gulping it down.

I sighed, glancing at a lantern by the entryway. "I can't rule it out."

A piercing chirp sounded from somewhere in the house. I

looked over my shoulder. "That sounds like a fire alarm. Do we have a fire alarm?"

Christian guzzled his drink and stood. "Get your arse up. Someone's hurt."

"How do you know?"

"Wyatt sounds the alarm to get everyone in the medical room."

I jogged behind Christian down the hall until we reached the foyer. The moment the door swung open, Shepherd bolted through the dim room with someone in his arms. I barely saw anything but a blur.

"Was that Blue?" I asked Niko, who walked in next.

"It's a child."

"Where's Blue?"

The team appeared from all directions and rushed to the medical room, Niko in the lead. Claude and I entered the room while everyone else watched on.

"She's burning up," Shepherd said, feeling her forehead and neck. "Claude, get the IV pole. Niko, keep her cool. I need bags of ice!"

Christian vanished from sight.

I neared the table but kept out of the way. Her yellow Mickey Mouse shirt was dripping with sweat. "What can I do to help?"

"Look in the cabinet to the left of the sink and get me the red vial. Everything's color coded. Niko, what's her Breed?"

"Shifter."

I rummaged through Shepherd's weirdly organized cabinet until I spotted three red bottles. "Which one?"

"Any. They're in the same drug family. I need it for when we cool her down. She's gonna start shivering, and that'll raise her body temperature again unless I do something about it." He set up an IV bag and started putting in a line. "Shit. I've never treated a kid before. What the fuck did you do?"

Niko kept his hands on her neck and forehead. "We found her in the trunk of the car."

"Jesus fuck," Shepherd breathed.

Viktor came in with Blue in his arms. "She's bleeding."

"Tell her to shift," Shepherd said, adjusting the IV drip. "I can't give up the table."

"Maybe you should have two," Gem suggested, peering in.

There wasn't much to Shepherd's makeshift medical room. Just a metal table and a long cabinet with a sink in the corner by the door.

"Set her in the chair for now." Shepherd touched the girl and furrowed his brow. "She's not thinking clearly, her head hurts, and she's scared. But not of us. Something else I can't read."

The girl lurched to her side and vomited on Shepherd's pants.

"I can read *that*," Wyatt remarked from his spot in the corner. "She doesn't like your style."

"Button it up or I'll make sure you never have children."

"Don't want them."

Viktor and I hovered over Blue, my hands pressing against the wound on her leg to stanch the bleeding.

She craned her neck to see the kid. "Is she going to be all right? I didn't know she was in there, Viktor. I swear it. Her pack showed up and ran us off the road. They thought we stole her."

"Why did you not give her back?"

"I promised her I wouldn't."

Viktor removed his shirt and used it to tie around her leg. "If she dies, her pack can legally seek retribution. You understand this."

Blue nodded weakly. "If they want a life, I'll give them mine."

I wiped my bloody hands on my shirt and swung my gaze to Viktor. "They can't just kill one of us as payback. This wasn't her fault. You heard what they said—the girl hid in the trunk."

"It is the way of the pack." He finished tying the tourniquet. "This will keep you for a while. But you must shift before you pass out, and we cannot wake you."

"Not until she's okay." Blue's normal olive complexion was now a sickly grey, her cargo pants soaked in blood.

"You are indispensable," he said, leaning in close. "We will do what we can to help the child, but you must not go too far over the edge."

Christian returned with several bags of ice. He and Claude arranged them under the girl's armpits, along her torso, and everywhere that Shepherd instructed.

"What the immortal hell happened to your pants?" Wyatt asked, looking at Christian's missing pant leg. "If that's the new fashion, don't sign me up."

"Get him out of here!" Shepherd boomed, startling me enough to look back at the door.

Hunter had wandered into the room and was staring at the blood on the floor.

Claude rushed over, scooped up the little boy, and carried him out.

The next thing I knew, Shepherd and Christian were bickering.

"I'll not do it," Christian snapped.

"She might die. One little drop in the bag won't hurt."

Christian shook his head. "It doesn't work like that."

Blue tipped forward. "Don't you *dare* give that baby your blood!"

Shepherd listened to the girl's heart with a stethoscope. "I'm just saying it might help speed things along. What if she's got brain damage?"

Wyatt snorted. "Then you two will have a lot in common."

Shepherd lunged, but Christian held him back.

"Get your aloof fucking Gravewalker ass out of here," he growled, pointing his finger at Wyatt. "She's a kid. Out of my medical room. Out!"

Wyatt threw his hands up. "Maybe she wants to go to the other side. Ever thought of that? When it's your time to go, it's your time to go. Sometimes holding on to the living world is worse than death. But go ahead. Play God," he said, leaving the room.

Shepherd scowled. "Next time he wants me to save his ass, I'm going to throw him onto the ferryman's boat myself."

"What's in the IV?" I asked.

Shepherd rolled up a stool and attended to the girl. "Just some water and electrolytes. She's dehydrated, but the first thing we need to do is get her temperature down. Then we can see the damage done."

He wiped the sweaty hair away from the girl's beet-red face and then rested his hand on her forehead. His touch seemed to slow down her panting, and I guessed he was using his Sensor gifts to make her comfortable. When she started shivering, Shepherd reached across the table, and I handed him the red vial.

After administering an injection, he switched off the overhead lights so only the dimmers beneath the cabinets were on. I wondered why at first, but new places and medical rooms could be scary for kids—especially with everyone watching. We waited for several long minutes in the darkened room.

Finally, the girl stirred. "I gotta pee."

Everyone breathed a sigh of relief.

"She's gonna be just fine," Shepherd announced.

Gem rushed in. "I woke Kira. She doesn't know what's happening, but I put a blanket and pillow on the floor for the girl. I think you should put her in there tonight. Kira can watch her, and she'll be close to the kitchen, bathroom, and medical room."

Shepherd lifted her into his arms. "Get the pole and stay close behind me. I don't want you yanking her line out."

Once they left the room, Blue grimaced as she stood up and then lost her balance. Viktor put his arm around her middle so she could put her weight on him.

"Take me outside," she said.

"Nyet. Your falcon will be weak and vulnerable."

I trailed behind them in case Blue needed something.

"My animal can't sleep inside," Blue pointed out, blood dripping onto the floor. "Just bring out some raw chicken. I'll be fine. She's small, so the blood loss won't be as severe. I just need her to sleep."

I slowed when they reached the front door. As it opened, Blue's clothes fell away, and her falcon flew into the night. Viktor was left holding her flannel shirt, and he stood there for a moment before heading to the kitchen.

Niko reached the stairs. "I think we should reconvene tomorrow to discuss our findings. Blue needs time to heal."

"Sounds good. Maybe I should call the Relic and see if he'd be willing to meet with us again."

"As you wish."

I watched him slowly ascend the stairs. "Later, alligator."

"After a while, crocodile."

I smiled. Sometimes it felt like I'd been with Keystone for a million years. I sat down on the steps and stared at the pile of clothes by the front door.

Christian sat next to me. "Never a dull moment."

We watched Claude walk by with a bucket and mop. When he disappeared from sight, I asked, "Why didn't you give that girl your blood?"

"Why didn't you?"

"My blood isn't pure. You could have healed her."

"That's not how it works."

"You once ran through fire to save a little human girl. You can't give up one drop of blood?"

"You were going to burn alive. That girl was already halfway to the other side, and who knows what I might have brought back." He rested his forearms on his knees. "If you think it's a mark on my character, then so be it. Vampire blood is sacred, and it's powerful. It's not a magic pill that fixes everything. If people begin to think of Vampires as cattle, they'll treat us that way. My maker told stories about Vampires who were staked and held against their will, used for healing by humans and other Breeds. Decades and centuries of lying in a tomb, only to have it opened when someone needed blood."

"She could have died."

"Aye, and it would have been an easy death. We should all be so lucky. I don't like seeing the wee ones suffer, but something else you should consider is that not everyone takes kindly to those who have consumed blood. Her pack might turn her away, thinking a Vampire now has influence over her. Shifters think it taints their purity, and maybe it does. We don't know what might happen if that child grows up with one drop of Vampire blood inside her. That's one reason we don't share it with everyone."

"But you'd give it to one of us."

"You're not a minor. I'd be forcing a dark magic inside her that she didn't ask for. There was a good chance she suffered brain damage, and I'm afraid some things blood can't cure. What if all I could do was save her from death, but she lived out the rest of her days as a vegetable? Besides, I know the sound of a dying heart, and hers was thumping against my eardrums like a battle song."

I nudged him. "You should have told Blue. She was bleeding to death, waiting to see how it turned out."

"Everyone likes a good suspense." Christian stood and rested his hand on the newel. "Do you think she would have taken my word for it? Don't be daft. That woman doesn't trust me as far as she can throw me." He glanced up at the tall ceilings. "What a ridiculous saying. Trust can't be measured by distance."

I propped my elbows on the step behind me and stretched out my legs. "You looked sexy tonight fighting those bears, Mr. Poe. I like seeing what you can do with your hands."

Christian gave me a hot look that made my heart quicken. His black eyes shimmered as they skimmed over my bloodstained shirt. "Are you tempting me, Miss Black?"

"It doesn't take much." I sat up and looked at my bloody hands. "This is the most convoluted case. I thought I'd ask a few questions, get a few answers, but now we're fighting bears and stealing children. We could end up pissing off more people than we help. But I can't quit." I yawned, exhausted from the flashing I'd done earlier. "It's too bad we can't see into the future." When I looked up, Christian held a guarded look.

He clasped his hands behind his back and frowned. "I don't know if that's entirely true."

"Thinking of getting a tarot reading?"

Christian retrieved a peppermint from his pocket and paced the floor. "Have you ever heard of a Gemini?"

I got up. "I've heard the name, but I'm still learning about the Breeds I know. Why?"

He folded one arm across his middle and pinched his beard. "I know of a Gemini. Not a friend, but more of a friend of a friend. They're a rare Breed."

"What's your point?"

He lifted his gaze. "They have an uncanny knack for predicting things. No one knows exactly how much they can see or sense, but people pay them good money for advice."

I snorted. "Advice? Like the Dear Abby of immortals? Give me a break."

"I don't know if he'll even see you, and if he does, I don't know how much he'll tell you. They can be rather infuriating, only giving away just enough details to influence the future. Or not influence. I've never quite figured that one out."

"And you believe them?"

"*Jaysus wept.* Your friend just flew out the door, and you fought bears with lightning bolts coming from your fingertips. I never took you for a skeptic."

I shrugged. "It just seems like if there was a Breed who could see into the future, they wouldn't be so rare. Couldn't they see their own extinction?"

"They were hunted. It's a wonder any of us are here, and that's why we keep our gifts to ourselves. Maybe it's a bad idea," he said decisively, marching up the stairs.

Curious, I followed. "Wait a second, if he can help us, why not? I'm up for trying a mystical fortune-teller. Does he use a crystal ball?"

When Christian hit the landing, he turned. "And *that's* why I'm not so sure it's a good idea. You can't make this one angry."

"I make everyone angry."

"Aye, but a Gemini won't be amused by your insolence. There's something dark inside them, and if you anger them, they'll hunt you until the end of time. The beast is sated only by blood. I've heard about them in stories; they're not to be trifled with even if they've mastered the art of switching off their emotions. They have few friends because no one wants to get that close to a Gemini. If you break their trust, it might cost you your life."

"I've got a lot of people hunting my ass down. What would make him any different?"

Christian's gaze darkened. "They'll kill everyone that stands in their way. Gemini are the things of nightmares—they're the Big Bad Wolf in our world. You know how Claude gets when he flips his switch? Imagine that for centuries until they see you dead. They're very old, to be sure, and every bit as strong as a Vampire. I've heard they're perceptive to emotions, like a Sensor."

I gripped the railing. "Are they the origin Breed? Do they also shift into an animal?"

"I don't know, Raven. They guard their secrets."

"But you think your friend might help us?"

"He's not my friend. But if you're looking for advice on whether or not to pursue this case, he'd be the one to ask."

"Then we have to do it. Call him up and arrange a meeting. I'll pay."

"I'll speak with him," he said, turning on his heel.

I caught up and tugged Christian's shirt. "*I'll* speak to him. This is my case."

Christian chuckled softly. "You'll have us killed with your sharp tongue."

"If it's that dangerous, I promise to behave."

"You're incapable of keeping that promise."

"That's not true. You have more of a temper than I do."

"It's not your temper I'm worried about. It's your tongue."

I wrapped my arms around his waist from behind and held him still. "The same tongue that's going to be all over your cock tonight?"

He stiffened. "Don't make promises you can't keep."

I slid my hand over the front of his pants and felt him hardening beneath my touch. "This time I promise to satisfy you completely."

He peered at me over his shoulder. "Why do I get the feeling this comes with strings attached?"

I withdrew my hand but kept my arms around his waist as he turned to face me. "Introduce me to the Gemini. I need to know if this case is worth pursuing or if I'm going to wind up destroying my career over it."

He cupped my head in his hands. "I'll move time for you, Precious. All you need do is ask."

Chapter 15

I TOOK ANOTHER BITE OF MY jelly donut and set it on the flattened paper bag next to me. One thing I liked about my old truck was the long bench seat. Lots of room to set things on, fit extra people, or even snuggle with Christian.

"I like watching you eat," Christian remarked. "It's like watching jackals on a kill."

"I deserve a pound of sugar. I burned a lot of calories last night."

"I have that effect on women."

"I was talking about the bears. Hand me my coffee?"

I didn't need to explain that I was joking. He knew. Last night, Christian and I had tried positions that were new to me. Because I'd had some of his blood to heal, he didn't have to treat me like a fragile piece of glass. I sipped coffee from my thermos, thinking about the way his tongue had explored my body. The weight of his gaze, the heat of him, his rough hands all over me. I felt flushed all over just thinking about when I'd whispered his name and he slowed everything down. We stared into each other's eyes for a long time, and I'd never felt more connected to anyone.

Christian lowered the visor and adjusted his dark sunglasses. "Did you notice Wyatt acting peculiar at the breakfast table?"

"If he was acting normal, I'd worry. Where is this place anyhow?"

"Keep going straight. We're almost there."

I handed Christian my thermos and reached for the donut.

"Why didn't he invite us to his house? It's a little early for going to a club."

"This is where most people like to conduct their affairs. You don't invite strangers into your home."

"A club isn't exactly private."

"I reserved a private room."

I took a giant bite. "Swell."

"You shouldn't talk with your mouth full."

I winked at him. "You didn't complain last night."

Christian pointed to a parking lot, and I steered into an empty space. When I offered him a nibble of my donut, he captured my wrist and devoured the glazed pastry, licking my fingers in the process. The amorous way he looked at me sent shivers down my spine.

"Isn't that trench coat a little warm?"

He got out of the truck and followed me to the front. "Now that's a peculiar thing to say to a Vampire."

"You stick out like a sore thumb wearing a coat on a hot summer day."

"Do you think these numpties care? I like all the pockets. More room for candy."

I opened the main door. "You're a twisted man."

Once inside, Christian led the way. Clubs were generally quieter in the morning, the music low but the crowd not always smaller. People showed up for morning drinks or breakfast. Others were conducting business. Some just seemed to live there. Immortals without jobs must lead a boring existence.

We reached the back hallway where the soundproof rooms were.

Christian stopped by door number ten. "I'll be here if you need me."

"Wait, you're not coming in?"

"I just arranged the meeting, but this is *your* case."

"You're my partner."

"Aye, but like you said, I've got a temper."

Annoyed, a folded my arms. "Why didn't you tell me this earlier?"

"I wanted a peaceful drive." He tapped his finger on my nose. "It's better if he focuses on one person. My presence might distract him. I don't know how their magic works, but I don't want to muddy it up." Christian pushed a button by the door.

Christian always liked to be in the middle of things, and I couldn't imagine why he'd want to leave me alone with a Gemini. Was he afraid this guy would see something he shouldn't about Christian's past or future?

The door opened, and a somewhat tall man with a slender build greeted me with a smile. I wasn't quite sure what to look at: his mesmerizing eyes or the terrifying dragon tattoo on his neck.

Touching the ends of his brown shoulder-length hair, he regarded Christian with familiarity. "As a favor to Justus, I've agreed to meet with your companion. But I require payment."

Christian reached inside his coat and pulled out a wad of money. It was bound but not in an envelope. "It's all there. We would greatly appreciate our money's worth. Raven will speak with you about the details."

The man slowly turned his gaze toward me. He had hazel eyes, but when I looked closer, they shifted in the light to a deep orange. I couldn't be certain if it was a Breed trait or simply that beautiful shade I'd seen in magazines.

He inclined his head. "I'm Remi. Come inside, Raven."

I anxiously moved past him, my hand resting over the small handle of a push dagger on my belt. Viktor didn't want us going into Shifter territory armed, but I wasn't making the same mistake twice about going into a club without my knives.

Remi whispered something to Christian before finally closing the door. "What do you drink?"

I watched him approach a long black counter and fill a glass. "I'm not thirsty."

"But you are." His hand brushed over the row of bottles until he settled on the tequila.

"I'm driving," I said firmly.

"Do sit."

The room was dark blue and the furniture black leather. Even the accent lights were blue. One couch faced a giant television screen on the right-hand wall, a table filled with snacks below it. I strolled to a circle of leather chairs and sat in one.

Remi set our drinks on the glass table and eased into the chair across from me. "It's seltzer water. You should accept a drink when offered, especially when doing business."

"Why? I'm not thirsty."

"You are, but that's beside the point." He crossed his legs and sipped his green drink. Remi's gaze was intense—more so than even Claude's. "When you refuse a drink, it reveals you're either nervous or don't trust the person. Breed are very particular about rituals. One might assume you're keeping secrets, and you'll find it difficult to gain the trust of the party you're doing business with. Always play the game even if you're not thirsty. No one says you have to drink the alcohol." He set down his glass and rested his arms on the armrests. "On the other hand, if you refuse a drink from a man hitting on you, and he buys you one anyway, throw the drink in his face."

I sputtered with laughter. "Why would I do that?"

"Because you didn't want it, and he didn't respect your refusal."

I crossed my legs, keeping my cool and heeding Christian's warning about my tone. "I'll make a note of that."

"You're a fast learner, aren't you?"

"So I've been told. I'll just be honest—I don't know anything about Geminis and what you guys can do. Christian said you see into the future and give people advice."

"People pay me for advice, yes. I have the gift of intuition."

"Are you always right?"

"I am. But there's a caveat." Remi laced his fingers together. "Fate isn't linear. In most cases, people think they always have a choice. But it's the things we cannot predict that truly change fate."

"Like what? I could get up and walk out of here."

"But you won't. You want to hear what I have to say. Sometimes choice is an illusion."

I reached for my seltzer. Remi felt old, and there was something profoundly detached about him that gave me the creeps. He seemed like a sensible, polite guy, but I'd never met anyone so emotionally distant. The vacant look in his eyes and even the unnatural way he moved made it easy to imagine what sitting with a god would feel like—absolutely terrifying.

The top buttons on his black silk shirt were undone, as if he wanted the world to see his tattoo.

I set down my glass. "So if my choice doesn't ever change, what does?"

"That's an interesting question. Accidents happen. Serendipity. Is that how you wound up with this organization?"

"That's how I wound up in this world. My entire life is one big accident. So… do you read palms? I have questions about a case I'm working."

"Just to be clear, I can't elaborate on my abilities, but we were once trusted advisers to kings. I can understand the outcome of a situation."

I scratched an itch on my head. "Have you ever played the lottery?"

"Money should be earned."

So much for a sense of humor. "Someone gave me a list of names and thinks there might be a connection between their deaths. Most of them are unexplained, they're all Shifters, and we even have some kids. Can you tell me how they died?" I reached in my jeans pocket to pull out the paper.

Remi waved the paper away. "No need. It doesn't work that way, Raven. I can't reveal details."

"And why not?" I asked, trying to quell my anger.

"Too much knowledge can alter the outcome. I already see the path, but if I give you too much, it'll change. And I'm not certain which new path will open up."

"Doesn't speaking to you change things?"

"The future I sense is without the influence of my reading. That's why I'm careful about details that could affect the outcome. I don't see everything, Raven. There is too much to know, and choices are constantly altering the landscape. But I know enough. I know that you are thinking about quitting, and that's why we're here."

I leaned forward and looked at my drink. He didn't seem to know when to stop staring, and it was unnerving.

"Crossbreeds aren't accepted," he said, shifting topics, "but there are more out there than you think. Some have both gifts, some have neither. And some keep very special secrets. You seem caught between two worlds."

I slowly looked up, my body tense. "Did Christian tell you about me?"

"No, Raven. I see you. And you walk between light and dark. Your past is haunting you."

I shot up to pour myself a glass of tequila. "I didn't come here to lie on your therapy couch." I knocked back the drink and felt my irritation dissipate. "What do you need to know about my case that will help? I've got all these new distractions. This job has opened up a lot of closets, and skeletons are falling all over the place." I returned to my seat and met his gaze. "Am I on a wild-goose chase? Should I quit and take something else?"

"You can always drop the case. That's not what you want to know."

"Are the deaths connected?"

Remi leaned forward and mirrored my position. "It's quite a conundrum. These distractions you mentioned—what would be the outcome had you given up right away? You can't walk a path without making footprints. And yet you seem more concerned about what's happening behind you than ahead. Does that make sense?"

"It kind of does actually. I live with someone who talks like you. But you see, bears and wolves are chasing me down the path. Literally. We're inadvertently pissing off a few people, and I just don't know if it's worth it. Obviously the woman and girl were worth it, but isn't there anything you can tell me? Something that'll speed things along? I don't want to keep working on this if it leads nowhere and ruins our reputation. Is the path a dead end?"

Remi's hair slid forward, but he kept those stony eyes on mine. "I have conflicting feelings about your future. There's so much darkness in your past that it threatens to put out your light. I don't mean your Mage light, but the humanity that still dwells within you."

"Immortals think humanity is a weakness."

"Emotions are a weakness. Humanity is something else entirely. It's what keeps us from becoming monsters."

"Maybe it's too late for some of us."

He flicked a glance at the door and sat back. "Your love will be tested."

The hair on the back of my neck stood up. "I didn't ask about my love life."

"No. You asked about a job. One that doesn't end your life or end the world. You want an easy answer so you have a reason to quit. Perhaps I wanted to give you your money's worth of advice—something of value."

I stood. "I know I'm not supposed to piss you off, but if that's all you're going to tell me, you're nothing but a grifter. At least have the decency to give Christian a refund." I headed out. While he'd made some valid points, none of it helped me solve this case.

"An outsider will give you the information you seek, but it won't be me," he said. "It's a worthy endeavor, and you've already changed the path of many lives without even knowing. The truth is right in front of you. All you have to do is open your eyes."

I turned on my heel and stared at the man, who sipped on his green drink. I wanted to ask what he meant about my love being tested. Did I want to know? Would it change anything? Would I fall out of love with Christian or find myself plotting his funeral?

Remi snapped his fingers to snag my attention. "Put what I said about Christian out of your mind. Long ago, men wanted to know the time of their death. You can't imagine the negative impact that knowledge had, and it subsequently changed their fate. If you know the details about your death, how will you ever enjoy your life? You'd live in fear, become reckless, lose your passion. Your chosen fate would change because of that knowledge. That's why I can't give you all the answers, but I give enough. And it's the truth, Raven. Someday you'll appreciate the value of a man's advice even if it isn't what you seek. Even if it's not enough. What may seem trivial will set you on the right course if you so choose."

Chapter 16

After I met with the Gemini, Christian lifted his motorcycle from the back of my truck and took off to buy medical supplies for Shepherd. I had a meeting with Graham I'd arranged earlier that morning, and he wasn't comfortable speaking to anyone but Blue and me. He'd expressed his concern about meeting too often in public during the day, so we brainstormed and came up with a private location—my father's trailer. My dad would be at work, and I had a spare key.

When I pulled into the driveway, I spotted Blue lounging in one of the Adirondack chairs by the firepit. A gust of wind blew her hair to one side, her feather earrings dancing in the breeze. I parked beside her blue Mustang and got out.

"How long have you been here?" I asked, slamming the door.

"Not long. Your dad has a nice place. No cars go by."

"This street doesn't go anywhere," I pointed out as I approached. I didn't usually see her in T-shirts, but today she had on a white one with brown pants. "Nothing but a few more trailer homes. He doesn't own all the land behind him, but it's undeveloped, so it's pretty quiet out here. No traffic noise." I sat on the flat arm of the chair across from her. "This is where I spent most of my childhood."

"You were lucky. I pity the children who grow up in the city. They don't know peace and quiet, the sound of wind in the trees and—"

"Neighbors firing off shotguns," I said with a laugh. "It's not totally quiet out here. How are you feeling? How's your leg?"

She stretched it out and then knocked her heel against the ground. "Perfecto. I just feel so damn guilty."

"About the girl?"

She leaned forward. "I can't believe I didn't notice. Even Niko didn't sense her. She's a kid, so her energy is weak. But that's no excuse. We were so preoccupied talking about the case that we didn't notice someone in the car. Had I parked that car directly in the sun, she wouldn't have made it. And if we had stayed just a few minutes longer…"

"But she's fine. Viktor gave Kira time off to take care of her, and Shepherd's checking in on her every hour. Christian mentioned that she ate something this morning, so that's a good sign." My chair started to tip, so I got up. "I've got a key. Let's go inside."

"We should wait for the Relic. He might get spooked if he pulls in and doesn't see us here."

"He's a big boy. Did you bring your file?"

When she stood up, she revealed she'd been sitting on it. Both of us were feeding Wyatt information—every detail we uncovered about the victims. A few had given us pictures even though being photographed was discouraged among immortals. I collected her file and put it with mine.

"Are you sure your father won't mind we're in his home?"

"He won't even know."

I hiked up the porch steps and knocked on the door. When I didn't hear any barking, I unlocked the door and peered in. No sign of the dog. Maybe he took it to work. Then again, maybe he took it to the pound. I tossed the files onto the kitchen table when I heard a car pulling up. Blue jogged down the steps to meet Graham. Except for his belt, which was too tight around the waist, he dressed nicely. He took a comb out of his back pocket and combed back his short, wavy hair.

When I noticed sweat stains on his blue button-up, I grabbed a few cold soda bottles from the fridge and set them on the table.

"I keep saying I need to move farther north to get away from this heat," he said, entering the trailer. "But how far north do I have to move? Alaska?" Graham pulled out a vinyl chair and sat, the metal legs creaking.

Blue took the chair next to his. "I've heard that cities with a higher Breed population have more extreme weather than other places. It's never consistent but always warmer or colder than everywhere else."

I set the bottle opener on the table. "Would you rather have water?"

He dabbed his forehead with a paper napkin. "Do you have any cold chicken? That would hit the spot."

My brows arched, and I turned back to the fridge. Who the hell walks into someone's house and asks for chicken? I had to laugh. Probably my father, and if anyone had cold chicken in the fridge…

I peeled off foil from a plate and set it on the table. Crush was not only a connoisseur of frozen dinners, but he also liked to buy large quantities of meat at the local barbecue pit. "Want some?" I asked Blue. "I can get you a plate."

She shook her head while popping the lid off her soda bottle.

I sat on her right, across from Graham. We opened up our respective folders and began laying out the papers.

Graham chewed the meat off his chicken leg. "Tell me everything you found. All the details, and don't leave anything out."

"We don't have anything concrete," Blue began. "But several people mentioned the victims not feeling good." She glanced at me. "Did you get any more of those?"

I fished out a few papers I'd clipped together. "These guys. Most of the others were away from home or alone, so no one really knows anything other than they died." I held up one paper. "I'm not sure about this guy. He was a lone wolf—no mate or partner. I had a hard time getting details about his death. Ren put him on the list because he dropped dead in the middle of a bar."

Blue looked around. "Do you have a pen?"

I rummaged through my dad's junk drawer in the kitchen

and tossed her a ballpoint. She scribbled question marks on a few papers and set them aside.

Graham pulled a few of those toward him and reviewed the info. "You can't connect every single death. You have to factor in how and where they died. This lady died from a snakebite."

I looked at the file. "Her boyfriend didn't mention that."

"Of course he didn't. She had a lot of money, and he didn't. I know the Relic who saw her. She had all the symptoms and a swollen leg, but the boyfriend wouldn't allow him to treat her."

"Why did he call a Relic?"

"He didn't. A concerned neighbor called. I don't think the boyfriend had anything to do with the accident, but I suspect he didn't mind nature taking its course." Graham cleaned off the meat from the bone in one bite and set it on the plate. "Do you have any statements from a Relic who examined them? Any clues left at the scene for these?" he asked, looking at the papers with question marks on them.

Blue shook her head. "Not those."

He wadded up the papers and tossed them into the kitchen. "Then they have to go."

I shrugged. "Fair enough. But what about the guy who fell off his motorcycle?"

He held a chicken wing close to his face and inspected it. "If I had a nickel for every Shifter who died in a car accident. Some of them think they're immortal and can heal from any injury. But they can't heal if they're impaled or unconscious or bleed out. Most of them are young, arrogant boys. What's next on the list?"

I created a separate stack. "These are all your clients."

"I questioned most of them," Blue said, tapping her finger against her orange soda. "The twelve-year-old girl collapsed. Do you have any medical history on her? Kids just don't drop dead."

"That one had anxiety issues since she was little. Medication didn't help, so I suspect she had an underlying medical condition. Even something as simple as sleep apnea can wreak havoc on the body, and it's not easy to catch. Parents don't want to put their kids through a battery of tests."

I played with a paper clip. "That's not true. I once had a rash, and my dad took me to five doctors until they decided it was an allergic reaction to a detergent he was using."

Graham chuckled. "You're a Mage, right? Your early experience is with humans. We're talking about Shifters."

I glanced at Blue. "Who found her?"

Blue's shoulders sagged. "Her mother found her in the kitchen with a glass of milk spilled all over the floor. She hadn't been feeling well. We've got a lot of similar stories about chest pain and headaches. If this *is* a virus, it hits them fast."

Graham wiped his barbecue-stained fingers on a paper napkin. "A virus by design is contagious. It jumps from one host to the next, either through airborne droplets, saliva, or blood. We would see more cases."

I gulped my drink and sat back. Graham had a point. "Maybe it just affects people with a certain blood type or something. Nobody studies Breed genetics or DNA, do they?"

He tore meat off the second wing. "That's a loaded question."

"I'm not talking about you, but are there secret labs somewhere? You're a Relic. You'd know about that kind of thing."

He lifted his gaze to meet mine. "Would I? Do you think we have some national alliance with secret meetings?" Graham erupted with laughter. "It's a competitive field. We all have inherent knowledge passed down from our ancestors that suits us for specific areas of work. Some specialize in Chitah disorders. Others are skilled therapists and counselors who work through harmony issues within a group or help with mental problems. No two Relics possess the same knowledge, so there's no way for me to know who specializes in what. For the right money, I would imagine that some go rogue and work in secret labs. I've heard stories, but I don't know if those are just rumors."

"What's your skill?" Blue asked.

"I mostly have wolf clients but not all. Most human medicine is ineffective on Breed. It's weak and, in some cases, doesn't work at all. I'm basically your average medicine man. Nothing exciting about that." Graham sipped his drink and grimaced. "I'm a milkshake guy myself."

"Sorry. No milkshakes in this house," I informed him. "What about Ensure? I could throw that in the freezer."

He frowned. "What's Ensure?"

I chuckled. "A human drink with vitamins and protein. Never mind."

"Why would you have human drinks in your house?"

"This isn't my house. It belongs to… a friend."

Graham blanched and looked over his shoulder at the hallway behind him. "Are we alone?"

"Want me to give you the tour?" I offered. "I don't want to jeopardize your reputation or career for helping us. I promised you a private location, and this is it."

He shook his head, looking at the papers with a chicken wing still in his hand. "This is scandalous research. Scandalous! If you can't find a connection and any of these Shifters find out what you're researching, they could file formal complaints."

Blue and I shared a look. Formal complaints were the least of our worries after a night battling bears and wolves, then rescuing a child.

"Some of the packs bury the bodies on their land," I said. "What if we dig up a few and run some tests? You might find something in their blood."

Graham choked on his chicken. "You must have a death wish. They're not going to let you dig up the dead. Do you have anything on the rest? Anything new that was overlooked? If not, you should drop it."

I shook my head. "I'm not dropping this. I've made a decision, and I think this is worth pursuing."

Blue folded her arms on the table. "It could ruin us, Raven. Some of these look really fishy to me, but he's right. If anyone gets wind of why we're really asking questions, and they think for a second it might have something to do with a virus, that's going to set off a panic."

"One you can't undo," Graham added. "The higher authority

lost a lot of credibility after that recent scandal. Even if the reps made a public statement that the virus gossip was a misunderstanding, no one would believe it. You could inadvertently start a war. That might dissolve the only law organization we've got, and nobody wants that. Nobody!"

I spread out the papers. A young woman found dead in her sleep, an older woman dead in a chair, a young boy who drowned, several young men who had all collapsed. And as much as I wanted to rule out the bear on the motorcycle, I couldn't. I got up and unwadded the papers Graham had discarded on the kitchen floor so my father wouldn't find them. "What about the Donner pack?" I asked Blue. "The one you saw yesterday afternoon."

I felt a sharp stab of guilt when I remembered that they were the ones she had a run-in with.

Blue held a look I couldn't discern. "The victim was a young man—eighteen, I think. They said he collapsed while repairing a broken window. They're saying it was dehydration or a heatstroke, but I wouldn't rule out foul play. They were in a rush to get us out of there. Something fishy was going on in that pack. Not many women, but a whole bunch of little girls."

Graham heaved a sigh. "Some people shouldn't be allowed to breed."

I stared at the papers. It was so random. None of them had anything in common except that they were Shifters. Different ages, genders, animal types, and even causes of death. The only thing we could trace to some of them was that they died unexplainably. "Could it be a genetic mutation instead of a virus?"

Graham sucked the sauce off his thumb. "What do you mean?"

"What if some Shifters are born with a mutation that kicks in at random times, like an autoimmune disorder? Except instead of making them sick, it just kills them."

"I don't think that would go over well in the Shifter community either. Unless we can prove it, we can't even suggest it."

Blue rubbed her temples. "If it's true, they have a right to know. Someone will have to organize a task force to research it.

They'll have no choice but to dig up the bodies since it's something that would affect the entire population."

Graham shrugged. "Sure. Tell everyone that their pack might have a genetic mutation and see how many of them start killing or kicking out relatives who might carry the gene. You need to think about it this way—if we can't cure it, we can't suggest it. It's better if they just accept the deaths as part of nature. We don't have specialized hospitals for Breed. We don't have organized research teams who come up with cures for defects. We accept them. Otherwise you'd see more of these interbred children getting attention—the ones born with both gifts canceled out. Maybe in a few hundred years but not now. It's possible they were born with a genetic flaw. That's something I can't rule out as a science man. But if so, there's nothing we can do but protect the stability of the community."

I folded my arms on the table and put my head down. The human side of me wanted to do all the things we would do in the human world. But that wasn't my world anymore. Everything had an impact. The stability of the Breed world was as thin as a sheet of ice over a lake. One wrong decision would cause fractures far and wide. The ramifications for spreading rumors or slander were substantial, and because it would affect our organization, I had to tread carefully.

Yet Remi's words resonated, and I felt compelled to see this through. Even if we could never publicly disclose our findings, I needed to know where this road was taking us. Maybe nowhere, but maybe we could save a few people along the way from bad situations.

"Do you have any potato salad?" Graham inquired politely.

I needed to end this meeting before he cleaned out Crush's fridge. I lifted my head. "Can we schedule another meeting with you when we have more information?"

"Absolutely. I want to help in any way I can, but I just don't see anything suspicious." He continued reading a few more papers while finishing his chicken. "You spoke to the Freeman pride?"

I tucked my fist against my cheek. "Blue did."

Graham set down his chicken. "What did they say?"

Blue guzzled her drink and then sighed. "Sambah lost a son. What do you think they said? He's upset. They found him on the stairs."

"You spoke to Sambah?" Graham cleaned his hands with a napkin. "That's a powerful pride, and King was next in line. At least that's what I heard."

"You know them?" I stood, dumped the chicken bones into the trash, and put the empty plate in the sink.

"I'm not their Relic," he explained. "I tried to apply once, but they turned me down. They have a lot of money and power. I hope you didn't upset him. Did he seem upset? I hope you're not mentioning my name to any of these people."

Blue scooted her chair back. "We've been careful about what we tell them. We don't want anyone getting suspicious about our visits."

Graham heaved a sigh. "Good. The last thing you want to do is make enemies with the Freeman pride. I've heard stories about them."

I leaned against the sink. "What stories?"

"Someone murdered one of their lions. Or was it a lioness? I can't remember." Graham loosened his belt a notch, causing me to look away. "It was a bar fight, I think. The Council rarely gets involved in family disputes. Sambah didn't go to the killer's pack. He sent his men to hunt down the two people involved in the killing and bring them back. Nobody knows what happened to them."

"If the killing wasn't provoked, it's within his rights," Blue said, scooting back her chair. "An eye for an eye. The leader can ask for any compensation he desires."

Graham wiped his forehead. "Did you know that lions eat their enemies?"

Striding to the door, I announced, "You better go. Blue and I have more work to do, and I'm sure we're keeping you."

He rose from his seat. "Thanks for the snack. That should tide me over until lunch."

Blue couldn't stifle her short laugh.

Graham pushed in his chair. "It's genetic. I have a slow metabolism and a big appetite."

I gripped the doorknob. "I'm not judging. I'm exactly the opposite."

He moved around the table and looked me over. "If you need an appetite stimulant, let me know. I have something for that, and it seems to work on all Breeds. Vampires are my biggest customer. Some of the old ones have gone so long without eating that food makes them queasy. Can you imagine?"

"If food makes them sick, why would they want to eat?"

He cleared his throat. "Everyone does business in restaurants and clubs these days. Food is a social activity, and they're trying to gain people's trust. Anyhow, let me know if you need a little boost." He took a package of gum from his front pocket. "Gum?"

"No, but thanks. I'm not a big gum chewer."

Blue raised her hand. "I'll take one, amigo."

He tossed her a stick before shoving one into his mouth. "Call me if you come up with anything. I work with some of these packs. I need to know what's going on just as much as you do. Have you given any updates to Ren or the other Packmasters?"

I opened the door. "No, I'm leaving him out of it for now. It's better that way. He's a good guy, but he's tight with a lot of packs. They talk, and I don't want this becoming a topic of discussion while we're still in the middle of it."

"Good idea. Well, *sayonara*, ladies."

After clearing the table, I returned to my seat and listened to Graham's car speeding away.

"Raven, we should think about dropping this. We've got nothing. You didn't promise Ren you'd solve it—only that you'd look into it."

I tapped my finger on the table. "I spoke with a Gemini this morning."

Her blue eyes widened. "You *what*? Did Viktor authorize that?"

"Hell no. Christian knows him through a friend."

"I've heard about those guys. Nobody wants anything to do

with them. Consulting them for advice, yes. But friends? Lovers? No way."

"He seemed pretty affable. Real detached though. I can't explain it."

She blotted an orange stain on her shirt with a napkin. "What did he say?"

"I think he knew more than he was telling me, but he led me to believe I shouldn't quit. He said an outsider will give us information, but he didn't say if it would help the case or bury it. Maybe saving a few lives in the process is what we're meant to do. We freed a woman and—"

"Almost killed a little girl," she finished. "I didn't steal her from the pack."

"I didn't say you did. But you had a bad feeling about them. Maybe you inadvertently saved her from a dangerous situation. I'm sure Viktor will speak with the local Council to see what's going on with the Donners."

My heart ricocheted in my chest when a vehicle pulled up the driveway. Had someone been spying on us?

"Oh shit. I hope those bears didn't follow me." I got up and peered out the small window before releasing a breath. "It's just Crush. What the hell's he doing home?"

A ferocious bark sounded along with toenails skittering up the wooden steps.

Blue sprang to her feet. "He has a dog?"

"I gave it to him. Don't say anything, okay? He knows how it looks with other Shifters, but he needs a guard."

Crush flung open the door and peered in.

I jutted my hip. "Hi, Daddy."

"Don't you *hi Daddy* me. What the fuck are you doing here in the middle of the day?"

The dog tore inside and bumped the table as it charged me. I sharpened my light to blast it in case it went for my jugular, but instead, it slobbered all over my face and almost knocked me down.

"Get down!" Crush clapped his hands, and the dog obeyed.

Then the bullmastiff sniffed Blue, who didn't look all that comfortable around him. From what I understood, animals could sense Shifters, but I didn't know what they thought of them.

"It's fine," Crush said on a chuckle. "His tail's wagging."

She eased alongside the wall. "I better go pick up Niko. We have a stop on the west side of town, and it's going to take a while to get there. I'll talk with you later. Nice seeing you, Mr. Graves. Sorry for the intrusion."

I gathered up the dirty napkins from the table. "See ya."

Right on time, Christian's motorcycle rolled into the driveway.

Crush peered out the window. "Grand fucking Central. What the hell's going on around here?"

"I just needed to borrow your house for an hour. What are you doing home?"

He walked into the kitchen, his blue coveralls stained in oil and sweat. "I forgot something." Crush ran the sink water, dunked his head under the faucet, and audibly sighed with relief.

Christian quietly entered. "I see I arrived just in time for the shower scene."

The dog turned and bared his teeth. Christian lowered his head and stared daggers at the animal.

I rushed around the table and stood between them. "Don't hurt the dog. He doesn't know better. Crush, you need to lock him up."

Crush kept bathing his head under the faucet. "You want me to lock up my guard dog? Then he won't be guarding."

When I heard him chuckling, I searched for a leash. The dog didn't even have a collar on. "Fine. We'll just be on our way. See ya."

"Hold on." Crush shut off the water and dried his head with a dish towel. He whistled sharply, and the dog gave one last snarl at Christian before trotting into the kitchen.

I leaned my back against Christian and gave Crush an apologetic look. "I didn't mean to break in."

"You should have told me." He opened the fridge and bent

over. "You know I don't care. I just don't like people sneaking around behind my back."

"So you decided to keep the dog?"

"Yeah."

"What did you name him?"

"I was thinking about Pickles."

Christian barked out a laugh. "Now that's a grand name for a beast like that."

I frowned. "Pickles?"

Crush finally stood, a giant dill pickle in his hand. The dog gobbled it up before he could offer it to him.

"Don't feed him those. They're probably loaded in sodium."

Christian wrapped his arms around me. "Sounds like a match made in heaven."

My father shut the fridge door and gave me a stern look—the same one I used to get when I came home late as a teen. "Where the hell's my chicken?"

"Oh shit. Was that your lunch? Is that what you came home for?"

He sighed. "Never mind. I'll grab something on the way back. Where's my hug, baby girl? Or are you too good to hug your old man around the Vamp?"

I broke out of Christian's arms and gave my father a hug. He wrapped me in his strong arms, water dripping off his head and the smell of oil and sweat filling my nose. The dog began growling again.

"Don't let your dog eat my boyfriend," I said quietly.

"I'll have you know I can snap this animal's neck in less than two seconds," Christian remarked.

"Keep it up, peckerhead, and I'll give him wooden teeth," Crush snarled.

I backed away. "All right, break it up."

He twisted his mouth and returned to the fridge. I gathered our papers from the table and tucked them in a single file folder.

Crush rattled plastic. When I looked, he was tossing cheese slices at the dog, who practically inhaled them.

Christian shook his head. "*Jaysus wept.* You're going to back up that mutt's colon until he shites all over the place."

Crush tossed the dog another piece. "I ran out of fucks to give."

The red bullmastiff gobbled up another slice of cheese and walked back to keep an eye on Christian. He had a dark face with droopy jowls, but he was solid muscle.

"Oh, for feck's sake!" Christian suddenly covered his nose and flew out the front door.

Confused, I went to go after him when I caught a whiff of what had driven him out. "Jesus, Crush. You need to start feeding him dog food. Do you really want all that gas in your house?"

Crush straightened his back. "*I* get gas. So what?"

"If you light up a cigar, you're likely to blow this place up."

He gave a rolling belly laugh, and it made me laugh right along with him.

"I'm serious. Stop giving him all that cheese."

"Fine, fine." He threw the dog the last slice and pitched the wrapper into the trash. "I was using food to train him."

"I think the pet store sells special treats for that."

"And I bet they charge an arm and a leg for it."

"I'll pay for all the expenses," I said, patting the dog. "If you make him fat and lazy, he'll be useless."

Crush tied his goatee up with a small rubber band. "True. I liked the way he chased after your Vampire. What's in the file?"

"Work stuff."

"The same work stuff you won't involve me in but you're using my house for?"

"Have you talked to Ren?"

Crush scratched his ear. "Two nights ago. Why?"

"Did he say anything?"

"No. He's keeping things tight-lipped now that you're working on it."

"Good. I want you to do the same. I don't think we've got anything," I said, lying through my teeth. "So if they're sitting around swapping stories, they're better off putting an end to all that gossip. You know how your friends run wild with ideas."

"Give me a hug before you leave."

My father never held back on his affection for me, and I loved the hell out of him for it. Every hug made up for all those years lost, and I wasn't sure if he was doing it for him or me.

"I believe in you," he said, squeezing me tight. "You'll figure it out."

"Daddy?"

"Yeah?"

"Don't name that dog Pickles. What if I named you after your favorite food?"

"Hungry Man is a respectable name."

We both laughed, and for a brief moment, I forgot all about lions and tigers and bears.

Chapter 17

I STARED AT MY DINNER PLATE, my stomach turning.
Wyatt took off his hat and dropped it in his lap. "What the immortal hell is this?"

Gem spooned a helping onto Claude's plate. "It's my world-famous bacon macaroni salad."

Shepherd lifted his plate to his nose and sniffed the mystery meal.

Viktor turned away from his liquor table and held up a bottle. "Who wants wine?"

Everyone but Gem simultaneously raised their hand.

"None for me," I said.

Wyatt poked at the pasta salad with his fork. "What are the green things?"

Gem wiped her hands on her long apron, her fingernail polish every color of the rainbow. "That's spinach."

"And the orange things?"

"Jelly beans."

Niko snickered. "Apologies. I need wine to prepare my palate."

I lifted my glass. "I think I'll have that wine after all."

While Viktor filled our glasses, we quietly poked at our food. All except Shepherd, who shoveled it in.

Hunter fished out the candy, wiped each one with a napkin, and made a neat little pile next to his plate. Claude scooped out his and gave them to Hunter, who looked like he just won the candy lottery.

Shepherd buttered bread and set it on Hunter's plate. "Eat some of that."

When Hunter shook his head defiantly, Shepherd glowered. "You can't keep skipping meals. I know you're hungry."

Wyatt spread his macaroni salad between two pieces of French bread. "Maybe you need to yank that tooth out."

"Keep it up, Spooky, and I'll extract your teeth with pliers the next time you get high on those mushrooms."

"It'll fall out when it's ready," Niko assured him.

Shepherd grumbled something inaudible before gulping down his wine.

"It's my fault," Blue confessed. "All that blood on the floor probably scared him. No wonder he doesn't have an appetite."

Shepherd laced his fingers together. "I know he needs to learn about what we do and what happens when we get hurt, but maybe he's too young."

"Nonsense." Viktor set down his glass. "If the boy lives here, he must see the dangers. It is the only way he will respect this organization. It is not an ideal situation, but we cannot shield him from the world. If he doesn't learn the consequences, he will not make good judgment."

"Decisions," Gem said quietly.

"Da. He is part of our family now, and there is no guarantee that he won't overhear things he shouldn't. We must teach him the importance of secrets. He must also know that there is always a chance one of us may not come home."

Shepherd finished his drink. "I gotcha, but he's also a Sensor. He didn't have his gloves on."

Viktor nodded. "Understood."

Claude set another jelly bean on Hunter's plate. "Maybe we can move this morbid conversation to another night. You're frightening him."

"Where's the girl?" I asked, glancing at the empty booths on the other end of the room.

"Kira is looking after her." Viktor studied a macaroni noodle on the end of his fork. "That is why we have this wonderful dinner Gem has prepared for us."

Wyatt snickered.

"The girl would not allow Switch to watch her, so Kira cannot return to her duties," Viktor continued, deciding to risk a bite of the pasta. "I have given Kira time off for next few days. She will stay with the girl day and night until we have resolved that situation. Until then, we are on our own again."

"I'll cook," Claude volunteered.

"Dishes," Blue chimed in.

Wyatt set down his half-eaten sandwich. "I'm *not* doing laundry."

Viktor lifted his glass. "Then you light candles. Shepherd will wash clothes."

Wyatt's shoulders sagged. "Wait, I'll do laundry."

"Too late," Shepherd said with a chuckle.

Wyatt held up his sandwich. "It's not fair. Candles are a full-time job. And then I get wax all over my shirts."

Shepherd lifted his wineglass. "Cry me a river."

"I'll help with the candles," Niko offered.

Wyatt glowered. "You can't even see the wick."

"Exactly."

"Nobody asked you, buddy," Wyatt muttered as he picked up his sandwich. "Says you."

Shepherd looked at Hunter and pointed his fork at Wyatt, who was talking to himself again. "*That's* why you don't do drugs."

Gem chewed while studying her plate. "I think I should have used the green jelly beans."

"The girl can't stay here," Christian said, twisting the stem of his wineglass. "What's your plan?"

Viktor buttered a heel of bread. "We have no choice but to return the child and hope the pack does not seek compensation. We have no reason to keep her from her family, and they will come for her if we do not send her back."

Blue leaned into view. "Something's not right with that pack."

"We have no evidence. She is not ours to keep. Shepherd, how is her health?"

Shepherd set down his glass. "Better. She won't talk to me, but she's up and about."

"Then it is settled. The girl goes home tomorrow."

"No!" a voice cried.

We all turned toward the doorway. The young girl had on a nightgown that was too big for her—probably one of Kira's. Her eyes darted between the group of adults before she ran behind Blue and clung to her.

"Please don't let them take me back," she whimpered.

Niko shifted to face her. "How old are you, little one?"

"Twelve."

She sure as hell didn't look twelve, and everyone else was thinking the same thing. Maybe she just looked young for her age, but she also didn't look well-fed. Her arms were thinner than they should have been and her cheeks concave.

Blue coaxed the girl to stand between her and Niko. "What's your name?"

"Marelle."

"Are you hungry? Do you want some pasta?"

She stared at Blue's plate. "I'm not eating that."

Wyatt chortled. "Smart kid."

Gem elbowed him, and he shut up.

"Are you feeling better?" Blue asked.

"Uh-huh."

"We're glad to hear that. You had us really scared."

She guiltily looked around the table before lowering her head. "Sorry."

"Why did you get in my car?"

Marelle shrugged.

"You can't stay here. We have to take you home."

"Please don't."

Claude's nose twitched, and a black look crossed his face before he sat back. Gem caught it, and she gripped his arm.

Blue swept the girl's hair away from her face. "It's not up to me. You need to ask Viktor."

She peered at Viktor and shook her head.

I reached out my hand. "Come stand next to me. My name's Raven."

Blue nodded, and the girl quickly walked around Christian and stood on my right side.

"I bet you've never seen anyone with eyes like mine," I said, trying to distract her.

She looked at me, and her expression shifted. "Oh cool. Are those real?"

"Yep. No contacts. Pretty neat, huh?"

"Uh-huh."

"Is there a reason you don't want to go home? I bet your mom misses you."

"I don't have a mom."

I rubbed her back consolingly. "I'm sorry, Marelle. I lost my mom too."

"You did?"

I nodded. "My dad took care of me, and he's a really good guy. I bet yours misses you."

She looked down at her feet, one of them sweeping against the floor. "I don't know who my dad is."

Viktor shifted to face her. "How do you not know your parents in a pack?"

Marelle shrugged.

"Who takes care of you?" I asked.

"I take care of myself."

Viktor sighed. "I am sorry for your parents. But your Packmaster is your protector, and we must return you to him." He reached for her hand.

Marelle recoiled and clung to me. She was trembling, and just then, Claude's chair flipped over.

"Son of a ghost," Wyatt exclaimed. "Someone get him out of here."

I couldn't turn my head with her arms around my neck, but I knew that Claude had flipped his switch.

"We can't take her back," Niko said, not inviting any argument.

Viktor's face told it all—he was in absolute agreement. Chitahs could pick up emotional scents, and when Claude flipped his switch at the girl's fearful reaction, it was clear something sinister was going on in that pack. And Niko must have seen something in her light.

I gave the girl a gentle hug. "It's okay."

Viktor sat back. "You will stay here until we find a solution. This is a safe place. It is not your home, but if you are in danger, I will protect you." He scratched his silver beard, a pensive look on his face. "I will call your Packmaster and threaten to expose him if he comes after us."

The girl eased her hold, and when I looked at Gem, she had tears welling in her eyes.

Gem shot to her feet. "Do you want to sleep in my room tonight? I have lots of pretty rocks and fairy lights all over the place."

Marelle shook her head. "No, I like Kira's room. It's small, and I feel safe in there."

"Then what are you doing out here?" I asked.

She gave me a sheepish look. "Kira fell asleep, and I wanted to see if you had any snacks."

Wyatt snorted. "Kid, we got snacks. Tell me what you like, and I'll get it for you." He glanced over his shoulder. "I wasn't talking to you."

Marelle stood behind me. "Do you have any cookies?"

Wyatt twirled his hat between two fingers and then draped it over his shoulder. "Do you like chocolate or peanut butter?"

"Um…"

"I'll bring you both. I'm all finished with *dinner*," he said, making air quotes.

Blue dropped her napkin on her plate. "I'll take her back to Kira's room. Marelle, you have to stay in there. You can't wander around without one of us."

"I'm sorry. I like your earrings," she said as they left the room.

Viktor steepled his fingers. "How many children were in that pack?"

I shrugged. "Blue mentioned there were a lot of girls but only a couple of women."

"Are you thinking what I'm thinking?" Shepherd asked, the tip of his steak knife twisting against the tabletop.

Hunter grabbed his jelly beans and raced out of the room.

With that, Shepherd scooted his chair away from the table. "I'll be back. This kid's gotta eat."

"Maybe some soup," I suggested.

Gem hopped up. "I can make soup!"

Shepherd gave her a skeptical look.

Gem took off her apron and folded it over the chair. "From a *can*, Mr. Grumpy. I was just experimenting tonight."

"If it's all the same to you, I'd rather eat meat."

"Alas, there wasn't an animal carcass available in the fridge. Maybe next time I can serve you a whole hog on a spit."

"Those are pretty good," Wyatt remarked. "I had some in Hawaii a million moons ago."

I turned my attention to Viktor. "I'm staying on this case. I think it's worth our time."

Wyatt stood up. "Well, it sounds to me like you don't know anything."

Christian pointed a knife at him. "Did anyone ask your opinion?"

Wyatt put his hat on. "I wasn't talking to her. I should have known a spook-free house was too good to be true. Usually one or two wander in, but they always leave with one of you when I ignore them. This one won't keep his mouth shut." Wyatt made a talking motion with his hand, aimed behind him. "I'm not for hire. You're going to have to find yourself another Gravewalker to settle your affairs, buddy boy." Wyatt pushed in his chair. "Singing doesn't bother me. That's what earphones are for."

I used to think Wyatt was divorced from reality, but now I was beginning to see the reason behind his recreational drug habit.

Back when I'd first arrived at Keystone, there were apparently a lot of specters in the mansion. After they cleared out, Wyatt seemed calmer—maybe because he was getting more sleep. Whoever was haunting him was probably one of the bears we'd taken out or maybe the wolves who ran Niko and Blue off the road. In any case, they were Wyatt's problem now.

"What'll happen to that girl's pack?" I asked. "Are you going to do anything?"

Viktor's grey eyes narrowed. "I was not certain what we were dealing with until just now. I know these animals. I have seen many like them in my time. They keep just enough women to breed children but not so many as would rise up against them. Men like these find each other and form packs with evil intentions."

I wondered how many jails cells were available. "Are you going to turn them over to the Council?"

He lifted his glass and swirled the wine. "Nyet. Wyatt, get as much information on these packmates as you can. I am certain that all have violated the law or were kicked out of other packs for nefarious reasons. Gather evidence to prove a conspiracy. I cannot take action unless I know this is what it looks like."

"I'm on it," he said, strutting out of the room. "Let me get those cookies first."

Gem gripped the back of her chair. "What can I do?"

"Work with Wyatt. Some of these Shifters may be old and in one of your historical books."

"And me?" Shepherd asked.

Viktor stood. "Polish your weapons."

After taking Marelle back to Kira's room, Blue changed into her red dress and walked to the back of the mansion. She didn't feel like flying tonight—too much was on her mind. She breathed in the night air, the most wonderful scent in the world. After a short walk, she reached the part of the grass that sloped down and gave her the best view on a moonlit night. The mansion was a dark shadow looming behind her, the blue circular clock window in Claude's room visible because he had all his candles lit. When she found a nice spot at the crest of the hill, she took a seat in the grass, her knees drawn up and her eyes on the stars.

Matteo appeared out of nowhere and sat to her left. "That dress is becoming on you."

"How did you know I was out here?"

"Your scent calls to me."

She snorted. "And what do I smell like?"

"Everyone has a different scent to a Chitah. Yours is like a spice. Cinnamon or something close to that." He took a deep breath and slowly exhaled, which Blue found a little creepy. Claude had never mentioned her personal scent, but maybe that was because it would be inappropriate.

"Are you cold, female? I have a coat in my tent."

"Did you wash it in the pond?"

Matteo chuckled. "You forget I'm a man of the wild. The woods are my home. Are they not yours?"

"They were."

He flicked his gaze down. "How is your leg?"

"Like new."

"I've always envied Shifters for their gift of healing. Chitahs heal—just slower."

"I work with a Chitah. He's pretty tough."

"Should I worry if he's put his tongue on your wounds?"

She smiled. "Claude has put his tongue on almost everyone. You Chitahs are strange."

"It's a gift that comes in handy when healing superficial scrapes. Mothers can heal their young so they don't grow up with scars."

Blue looked away.

"My apologies."

"Shifters admire scars. Just not so much on women," she muttered.

A lightning bug flashed in front of her.

When Matteo didn't say anything in return, Blue stole a glance at him. He had a strong profile. His nose had a slight bump, and his convex forehead gave him an intense stare. But those lips—she couldn't help but remember how soft they were, even with that ridiculous excuse for a beard. Matteo looked like a nomad—a warrior without a home. "When is the last time someone cut your hair?"

He gave her an amused look. "Is it not to your liking?"

"I think how a man grooms himself says a lot about him. You look like you lost interest decades ago."

"Perhaps I did. When you live alone, there's no need for grooming."

"It makes me think you don't have a high opinion of yourself."

"That doesn't change my opinion of *you*."

She admired the universe above. "Maybe it says more about where you are in your life. What was that look you gave me?"

"What look?"

"When I came home bleeding. I know that look. Want to tell me about it?"

He wrung his hands. "I lost my kindred spirit."

Blue understood that most Chitahs who lost a kindred spirit to death never recovered from the traumatic loss. Even the rejected ones suffered, just not nearly as much. A kindred spirit was their perfect match—the one they were born to love.

"I'm sorry" was all she could say.

"I gave up everything, and I still failed her."

"How?"

Matteo cleared his throat. "I was once a bounty hunter, and I made a lot of enemies. Sarah changed everything. How we met isn't a romantic story. She was the daughter of one of the men I hunted. She proved his innocence, and it changed how I felt about my job. She made a new man out of me and talked me into building that cabin. Then she gave me a daughter, and my life was complete. I thought we'd be safe in the woods."

Blue knew where this story was going. "But someone found you."

"Yes. And I wasn't there. I'd gone to negotiate a trade—we were low on meat, and I needed more traps. When I returned…"

Matteo's voice cracked, and he shielded his face. It seemed like a decade passed before he put his hands down and finished. "I should have been there to protect them. I can't even remember what I said to her before I left. I can't remember if I kissed her or told her that she was my world. And our baby—"

Matteo's upper and lower fangs punched out, giving him the appearance of a wild cat.

Blue didn't dare move. If a Chitah flipped their switch, they could be unpredictable. She didn't know this guy well enough to guarantee her safety.

His nose twitched, and he covered his mouth. "Forgive me. I didn't mean to frighten you."

"I'm sorry for your loss, and I know those words are so weak. There's nothing a person can say to lessen the pain. Sometimes just hearing condolences makes it worse, like poking at a wound."

His fangs retracted. "Share your past with me." Matteo placed his hand on her knee. "Please. You would honor me, and something tells me it's why you aren't with your people anymore. What brought you to this band of misfits?"

She gave a mirthless chuckle. "Fate, I guess."

"Does your family not miss you?"

"I have no family."

He lightly squeezed her knee and withdrew his hand. "Was it that bad?"

"Worse." Blue sometimes imagined her pain as a lake beneath a thin sheet of ice. She had spent years freezing the surface, working on protecting those waters with a solid layer that nothing could penetrate. But ever since finding that girl, hairline cracks had begun to form, and some of that water was leaking to the surface.

"It's easier to talk to a stranger," he said. "I've never told my story to anyone, and even though I didn't reveal every gruesome detail, I feel comforted in a strange way. Think of it this way: if you choose me as your mate, you'll have confided your deepest secrets and shown me your trust. If you reject me, you'll never see me again, and you won't be reminded that someone knows your secrets."

The temptation beckoned her. Blue had given Niko a few small details, but not nearly all of it. Even Viktor didn't know the full story.

She found herself unable to sit, so she rose to her feet. Could she tell this memory without unraveling? "I once had a family. There was a land dispute between my tribe and another. Isn't that what most wars are all about? Land." Blue turned her back to Matteo and faced the expansive grounds that rolled downward to a valley. "The enemy tribe owned land that our ancestors were buried on. My father couldn't acquire the rights back, and the leader wouldn't sell it to him. So they made a treaty. My father would give up his most precious possession in exchange for them agreeing not to build on that land, to only use it for hunting."

"And you were that possession."

Blue turned toward him. "Yes. My tribe believed in arranged marriages, and mine was supposed to unite two enemy tribes. I took pride in my role. I had a decent mate, but he wasn't a tender man. He provided for me and our two sons, and that was enough."

Matteo stayed seated, his arms draped over his knees, caught in her spell.

"I had good boys though. They loved their mother and made me laugh. They showered me with all the affection that he didn't, and that made up for everything. My sons were my world." Blue's lower lip trembled, and she steered her eyes to the ground. "One day, my chief gave someone permission to build on that land. They had broken the treaty after twenty years. My father's tribe issued a threat, and I don't know all the details of what was discussed or not discussed." She clenched her fists. "They should have worked it out. It didn't have to be that way."

Memories sliced through her like hot knives, and she turned to face the darkness. In the distance, a dying fire by Matteo's campsite seemed to thaw those frozen memories.

Blue swallowed hard, trying to keep that ice beneath her feet as cold as possible. "Once a year, all the warriors gathered for a special tribal ceremony. My mate and older son went, and I stayed home with Chen. We called him Chen for short—his father gave him a ridiculously long name." Blue tried to smile, but the good memories never stayed for long. "I woke up to screaming and war cries. Chen was only thirteen, but I'll never forget seeing him face that door with a spear in his hand. My boy was replaced by a man in those moments. He was protecting his mother." She heard another crack in the ice. "When the door flew open, the first man inside got a spear in the chest. Right through the heart. But the second and third and fourth man who barged in couldn't be stopped. I took one down with my axe, but the others had taken Chen, forced him on his knees, and..."

Tears streamed down Blue's face as she stared at that distant fire. "Those men held me down so I could watch my son die. Then they left me. I didn't have the strength to get up and fight, because my whole world had just ended." Blue couldn't bring herself to give Matteo the details of how they had sliced Chen's throat. How Chen had gasped for air, clutching his neck until he collapsed in a heap. *Her child. Her boy. Her cherished one.*

She felt Matteo's hands rest on her shoulders as he stood behind her.

Gathering her courage, she continued. "When my mate and the others returned, they found everyone dead. Everyone except me. My father had given orders to keep me alive. He didn't care about his grandsons because they shared my mate's blood—the blood of his enemy."

"What was your mate's name?"

Blue whirled around. "He doesn't deserve his name to ever be spoken on this earth again," she said through clenched teeth.

Matteo's nose twitched, and he took a step back.

Blue felt the emotions culminating within her like a cyclone, and that pain turned to fury. "They blamed me. They said *I* had cursed them. But *they* were the ones who broke the treaty! My father assumed by planting me in that tribe that I would make sure that the treaty was upheld. Those weak and worthless men were to blame."

"They cast you out, didn't they?"

Blue shook her head, her eyes sliding down to a brown rabbit nibbling on a patch of grass. "My mate was pressured into taking action—pressured by the tribal council. But he did it without hesitation. They had a ceremony the next day, calling to the gods for strength. They planned to go to war with my father's tribe, but a sacrifice was in order. All of their women and children were dead." She lifted her head and held Matteo's gaze. "They tied down my eldest—the baby I nursed and sang to. The son I had so many dreams for. The young man who was handsome and strong and had caught the eye of several prominent women. Even in his last moments, he looked at me and told me to run. Afraid for my life, he wanted me to flee. He tried to talk me into it the night before, because he felt safe within the tribe. He shared their blood, but I didn't."

Matteo released a breath but was unable to say anything.

Blue folded her arms, bracing herself. "Nayati went with such bravery. He braced himself as his father stood over him with the knife. He cursed his father. He called to the spirits of his ancestors to curse everyone in the tribe. Then my mate knelt down, shook his head, and stabbed my son in the chest."

When the memory took hold, Blue couldn't keep it together. She grimaced from the pain, the memories so raw and vivid that she relived all those last moments. All the what-ifs and regrets. Why hadn't she told her son that she loved him? Could she have bargained for his life? All she had done was scream *no, no, no.*

Matteo's arms were around her, but they didn't ease her sorrow. No one had ever comforted her through this pain because it was a tragedy she bore alone. "I'm so sorry, female. Pain like ours should never be endured."

When Blue remembered the men releasing their hold, how she had rushed to her son and draped herself over him, her knees buckled, and she crashed through the ice. She remembered so vividly placing her hand on his chest and watching his breath grow more and more shallow. She couldn't even speak in that moment. Bleary-eyed, she had managed to sit up and cradle his face in her hands. Nayati stared up at the sky, his eyes fixed. She remembered the singing around her, celebrating that her firstborn was dead. She remembered the feel of his cheeks in her hands and how chubby they once had been as a child. Blue had held her son until his heart finally stopped, something she felt against her fingertips. His spirit had already departed, but she couldn't bring herself to let go until he was truly gone.

Now on her knees, Blue fisted the grass, tears spilling down her nose. "I took that knife out of his chest and put it in my mate's back. Then I found an axe and killed eleven warriors before they could hold me down. I wanted to die fighting. I didn't care anymore." She sat back on her heels and wiped her runny nose. "Nothing mattered. My heart and soul both died, and I had nothing to lose. My life was inconsequential."

Matteo knelt in front of her. "How did you escape?"

"The chief wanted me to live. He wanted me to suffer for my entire life as they would. And I have. I want to remember my sons, but all I can see is the look in their eyes when they died. Be thankful you were at least spared that. My father and my mate stole good memories and replaced them with pain and regret." She took a calming breath, felt that ice solidifying beneath her feet again. "We argued, you know. Our last night together, and we fought. Nayati was willing to go to battle to avenge his brother's death. Battle against his own grandfather. He loved his little brother, and it crushed him when he saw the body. He wanted revenge. I was scared. I didn't want to lose another son, so I told him he couldn't go to battle with the others. You never think the last conversation you have with someone is going to be the last, and I live with that."

"I understand that pain more than you know. What happened to your mate?"

"I suppose he's still alive somewhere. They went to war with my father's pack, and I walked away. My father betrayed me. My mate betrayed me. I spent years grieving, and when all that rage and sorrow went away, I felt nothing. I *had* nothing. My life was nothing... until I met Viktor. He needed a scout, and I was the best." Blue quickly wiped her face, stood up, and stalked off.

Why the hell did I tell him all that? she thought. *I've spent years hiding my past, and now I spill my feelings all over the place in front of a virtual stranger? What is wrong with me?*

She finally stopped near an old tree, Matteo's footsteps just behind her. "Nobody tells you that losing a child is like being an amputee. You can live without your arm, but you're never whole again. I lost both my arms. Sometimes I forget about them, and then I feel guilty for forgetting."

"I know that feeling. I wept every day for my family. One day I realized they hadn't crossed my mind, and I wept from the guilt of forgetting. The guilt of enjoying a day without them."

"How did you get used to not having them in this world?"

Matteo furrowed his brow. "I haven't. Sometimes it comforts me to know that they're still alive, just in a different time. I'm caught in the present, and they're still in the past. But maybe we exist simultaneously."

"Men are so much better compartmentalizing their pain." Blue rested her back against the tree trunk. "I can't figure out what it was all for. Why did I bring those beautiful boys into this world, only to watch them die? What was the purpose? That's why I don't believe in love, Matteo. Not the way you romanticize it. My own father betrayed me. My mate loved his pride more than his own child. And my love wasn't enough to save my sons."

He reached up and gripped the bough above his head. "It must have been hard to leave everything you knew. Not just the loss of your children but your entire community."

"I might look young, but I'm an eighty-five-year-old Shifter. I've had a lot of time to adjust."

"You're just a toddler," he said with a lazy smile.

Blue dried her eyes on her sleeve, grateful for the shift in topic. "And how old are you?"

"Six hundred. I don't know the exact years, but that's about right."

She strolled past him. "Old man."

"Dignified."

"Maybe you should find someone your own age."

He chuckled softly. "Are you ashamed to be seen with me?"

"Ashamed to be seen with a man who never bathes and wears a mop on his head? Never."

"If I cut my hair, I cut my chances of wooing you."

"That's superstition."

"Say what you will, but my people believe it."

"You must have courted a lot of women judging by the length of your mane."

Matteo suddenly twisted her into his arms. "I haven't stopped thinking about our kiss. Day and night. No matter what I do, where I go, all I can taste are your sweet lips."

When he leaned down, Blue panicked and stepped back.

Matteo still clutched her hands. "Give me a chance. I'll love our children no matter what Breed they are—even if they're human."

"I don't want a family."

"But if you mated again, what *would* you want? I can give you so much love."

Blue shook her head. "I don't care about love. I would just want a man with integrity—someone who's wise and always does the right thing. Someone who would never betray me. A noble man who lifts himself up in this world without stepping on others or becoming a victim of greed. A man who doesn't run from his problems."

Matteo's grip loosened until their hands parted. "I can be those things. I can try."

"Your wounds are still fresh, and somehow you think I can erase all that. You're where I was decades ago, and you have a long way to go before you figure out your purpose. Some people aren't meant to have all the happiness in the world. Maybe the best we can do is give it to others. You have a noble job guiding children to that safe haven, and maybe that'll heal your wounds."

Matteo clasped his hands together. "And the girl you saved, does that lessen your pain?"

Blue didn't have an answer for that.

"Which one gives you more peace: the lives you save or the lives you take?" he asked.

"I don't know. That's my honest answer. I'm glad the girl's with us, even though it's temporary. Her pack shared the children."

Matteo's upper fangs descended. "They *what*?"

"Don't flip your switch on me. This is the stuff I deal with every day, and maybe it *does* give me a little pleasure to take out criminals who might otherwise get away with it."

"That pack can't be allowed to exist."

"It's not up to me. We can't keep the girl. I know we've got a big mansion, but this isn't a place for kids. I don't know what'll happen."

"Someone has to save the children. Do you want me to take the children to West Virginia?"

Though tempted, Blue shook her head. "They don't belong there. That's a place for Potentials. A young wolf needs a family."

"What happens to girls like her?"

Blue paced. "They go to an orphanage. She'd never survive that place. They take care of them, but a Shifter needs a special kind of nurturing. I don't know. I guess we'll see what happens. Look, I have to go. If you know what's best, you'll go home. Buy some clothes, trim up those split ends. Maybe you'll find yourself a girl, or maybe you won't. But don't give up on guiding those kids. Your job is invaluable."

Blue unlaced the front of her gown and let it drop to her ankles. Matteo was the first one who had seen her scars, and he might be the last man who saw them. Part of her was curious what a man's reaction would be. She wished she could ignore the hideous gashes, but they were a huge part of her now, and there was no avoiding how this would continually impact her life in ways she couldn't predict.

His jaw slackened, and though he turned his head as if to look away, his eyes softened as he gazed upon her body. She felt him admiring her breasts, her shapely hips, and her long legs. The initial look of surprise immediately vaporized, replaced with a look she was familiar with—desire.

She stepped out of her gown. "Why is it people are so shocked by nudity?"

"You took me off guard."

Blue grinned. "Looks like I've found a way to shut you up."

Matteo bowed. "Feel free to shut me up anytime, my lady."

With that, Blue raised her arms and flew away.

Chapter 18

BLUE AND I HAD TEMPORARILY put our case on hold. After a few more days of questioning Shifters, Viktor wanted everyone to drop what they were doing to perform a special rescue mission taking down a Shifter pack. We didn't have nor seek approval by the Shifter Council or higher authority; Viktor had taken it upon himself to collect as much evidence against these devils and rescue the children. We mostly avoided talking about it because of the grim nature, and we didn't want Claude flipping his switch every five minutes. When Viktor finally called us to go, we didn't have a meeting. We understood what was expected of us.

"I still don't understand why you wouldn't report them first," Gem said from the back of the van. "We have so much evidence."

Christian and I exchanged looks by the rear door before looking at Viktor, who was driving. Everyone else had taken a spot in the back—all but Claude, who was trailing behind us in a rented van. We needed something to transport the kids.

Viktor flicked a glance at us in the rearview mirror. "Men like this are crafty. If we reported them first, they might somehow find out and move the children elsewhere. These packs trade children."

"Are you sure they're *all* involved?" Gem pressed. "I don't want to kill anyone who's innocent."

"Trust me, they're all involved," Blue said, arms folded. "I had a long talk with Marelle this morning, and she told me everything. It's all of them. They use the three women for breeding, and the packs trade those children to keep the mothers separated from them. She heard them mention other states, so it seems like they don't want them living in the same area."

Gem looked down at her black shoes. "Oh, that's horrible."

Blue tied her hair into a bun. "The women were once kids in their pack. These guys like it that way because they don't have to worry about them blowing the whistle. It's the only life they've known, and most of them are probably too scared. Who knows? Maybe they're just brainwashed and think it's how everyone lives."

I gripped the bench when we hit a hard bump. "Besides that, do you think jail is a fair punishment? And what if someone lets them out?"

Shepherd returned a knife to the holster on his chest. "Last chance if anyone wants a firearm. I'm not gonna have time to load it when we get there."

Niko gripped the pommels of his katanas. "I'm good."

Wyatt looked down at his all-black outfit. "I need one."

"Horseshit. You've got five, and you probably won't use a damn thing. I'm all out of holsters unless you want to shove it up your ass."

Wyatt tugged on his black knit hat. "I was under the impression that my commando days were over, General Patton."

Viktor snapped his fingers. "I need everyone on this mission. There are twenty-five of them."

"Twenty-three," Blue said. "We took out two, remember?"

"Spasibo. Twenty-three."

"Maybe we should start having a meeting before a raid," I suggested. "Just to get all the questions out of the way."

Christian barked out a laugh. "We would never be able to leave, and Spooky would find a way to weasel out of it."

Wyatt glowered. "Rollergirl and I aren't meant for this kind of Rambo stuff."

Gem straightened her back. "Speak for yourself."

Wyatt crossed his feet at the ankles. "I tag along when you need a professional to hack computers and gather evidence. I did that already. My job is done. But here I am, sitting in a van with guns strapped to my crotch. You know I can't kill anyone. That's the worst thing a Gravewalker can do." He swung his gaze to the space next to him. "Nobody asked the freshy. Go find a light to jump in."

I checked the push daggers on my belt, inside my leather coat, and strapped to my hip. I also had a stake inside a fitted loop in my jacket. Shifters couldn't heal if impaled—another reason Shepherd brought guns. Sometimes bullets went through, but sometimes they didn't.

The van stopped, and Viktor turned off the engine.

It was quiet enough you could hear a pin drop. Was it possible to sneak up on a wolf pack?

As if reading my mind, Viktor twisted around in his seat. "A pack won't flee on their territory, especially if they have something more than land to protect. Remember what I said earlier: no one leaves the building except the children. I want each of you working with your partner."

"Swell," Shepherd grumbled.

I met eyes with Christian. Something about going into a fight filled me with arousal, and I could see the same amorous look in his eyes.

"Remember what we are here for," Viktor stressed.

Shepherd stood. When he neared the back door, he looked between Christian and me. "Whenever you two are finished eye fucking…"

Christian winked and popped open the rear door. "After you."

Claude waited outside, also dressed in black. His golden locks were tucked inside a black knit hat. Wyatt stuck out more than the rest of us since Have a Nice Afterlife was printed on the front of his shirt.

Gem leaped out of the van, her chunky boots crunching on the concrete. There was an air of confidence about her I hadn't seen before on one of these missions.

I noticed my surroundings—concrete roads, dilapidated buildings, and a stop sign bent in half. "I thought we were going to their house?"

"We're here." Blue jumped out of the van next. "This pack lives in the city."

"I thought packs liked woods and shit."

"Not every pack is approved for Shifter land, so they buy up large apartment buildings or abandoned warehouses. Wyatt couldn't find the blueprints on this place; that's why we didn't have a meeting. There's not much to discuss. Here we are."

Wyatt stepped out and twisted his ankle. He leaned down, gripping his leg. "It's not that I couldn't find it. The blueprints weren't in the public records. Someone deleted them. Ow..."

Viktor joined us. "Cowards erase their existence so they are off radar."

Christian peered around the van. "You're not concerned they'll see us?"

"Nyet. Shepherd scouted the building yesterday."

Shepherd folded his muscular arms. "They only have a few windows in the back, and they're up high. It's a two-story warehouse. They welded shut all the doors. The only way in and out is through a garage door."

"That's how Niko and I went in," Blue explained. "We parked just inside, and I guess that's when the girl snuck into the trunk. There's a staircase that goes to the upper level and a walkway that takes you through the building. It's an open plan, like a running track. You can see the entire first floor over the railing. We didn't get the full tour, so I don't know where they keep the kids or if they have a bazooka. We're all going in blind."

"Who volunteers to guard the front door so no one escapes?" Shepherd asked.

"I will." Niko squared his shoulders.

Shepherd shook his head. "No offense, but if someone slips by, you'll stumble all over the city trying to chase after them."

Niko pulled one of his swords halfway up, revealing the shimmering blade. "Perhaps I should make it clear: *no one* will get by me." He pushed the sword back in place.

Viktor gripped Gem's shoulder. "I need you to get us inside like we talked about."

Gem's fingertips sparked, and she seemed to stand a foot taller. "I won't let you down."

Viktor addressed everyone in the group. "I do not want one child hurt. Not a single one. Do whatever you must—I give you permission to send those devils straight to hell, but protect the children first. We must get them out."

Blue took a deep breath, and we all stole a moment to ready ourselves. This wasn't a delicate operation with a lot of moving parts. We didn't have to collect sensitive data or capture someone alive. This was a rescue mission, and the only ones leaving alive were the children.

Shepherd drew his gun. "Let's roll."

We marched up the street like vigilantes. The building was located in a desolate industrial area. No streetlamps, no traffic, and no witnesses. The weeds had taken over the sidewalks and random potholes.

"No movement on the roof," Christian confirmed. "No cameras that I can see."

Gem's purple hair bobbed up and down like ribbons as she jogged to the front of the line. Blue light dripped from her fingertips like broken spiderwebs dancing in the breeze. When we reached an oversized garage door, everyone stood aside and let Gem do her thing.

She smiled blithely and widened her stance. "Watch this."

Gem cupped her hands in front of her until they began to shake. As a Wielder, her energy balls were typically blue. But this time, a powerful orange light illuminated her hands.

Blue took a giant step back. "Maybe we should pick the lock instead."

Gem's hair stood on end, charged with static electricity. Remembering how her energy could reduce an immortal to nothing more than charred remains, I put more distance between us.

"Worry not," Christian said. "The wee lass has improved her aim."

Gem's hands were spaced apart, and between them formed a blinding orange ball. Once the light was as big as a softball, she gripped it in one hand and swung her arm like a pitcher. I drew in a sharp breath.

The metal door exploded. I shielded my face with one arm as hot sparks shot out and quickly dissipated before hitting the ground.

"*Holy Toledo*," Wyatt said. "That's a perfect hole."

Shepherd held up his gun and marched forward. "Save that line for your next date."

When Shepherd disappeared inside, we heard rapid gunfire. Everyone rushed in at once and immediately split up in different directions.

I jumped over a body by the door and jogged up a set of metal stairs, a dagger in hand. As I rounded a corner, I ran into a Shifter. It was tempting to toss him over, but he'd only become someone else's problem. I sliced his neck and delivered a powerful electric shock to his chest, knocking him unconscious. He would bleed out before waking in time to shift.

The walkway on the second floor looped all the way around, but you could easily shortcut across the bridge. Below, I saw people scrambling and heard screams. Without overhead lights, it was difficult to make everything out. I noticed a playground, a seating area, and a kitchenette. Focusing on the second level, I busted open the first door on the right.

A man shot up from a chair. "What the fuck?"

Christian barged past me, scooped a young girl off the bed, and put her in my arms. "I'll be right with you."

When the door closed, I heard nothing but bloodcurdling screams.

I set the girl down, who looked to be around six. I still had a dagger in my hand and no idea what to do with her. She screamed and covered her ears when gunshots went off.

Panicked, I scanned the building. On the other side, Shepherd kicked down a door, Wyatt behind him with two kids in tow. A wolf lunged at Shepherd, who brandished a large knife.

I cupped my hands around my mouth. "Wyatt!"

Then I took the girl's hand. "Come on, sweetie. Don't be scared. We're the good guys."

She jogged alongside me in a daze, tears streaming down her face. When I reached the walkway that crossed over, I ran to the center to meet Wyatt. "Take her."

I turned back and spotted a man running toward a door in the back. I flashed down the walkway and came up behind him. "Where do you think you're going?"

When he turned, I latched onto his neck. My fangs punched out and pierced his main artery as I delivered an electric shock. He pounded his fists against my back, but I gripped him like a boa constrictor killing its prey until I crippled him with weakness.

His blood was so vile that I almost threw up. When he collapsed in a heap, I staked him.

"I'll finish this one," Christian said, blood staining his lips and beard.

"You didn't drink that guy's blood, did you?"

"Viktor asked me to collect evidence should anyone question us. I've tasted his sins, and now this one gets my special attention." Christian dropped down on his knees, slowly unbuttoning the man's shirt. He was too weak to shift and barely conscious. But his soulless eyes went saucer wide when Christian yanked out the stake and trailed it down his belly. "Have you ever been disemboweled?"

I spat out as much blood as I could before heading toward another door. Claude's roar filled the open room, as did the sporadic gunshots and terrified screams of children. I flung the door open, and two children cowered in the corner—a boy and a girl.

"Come with me," I said, trying not to imagine what I must have looked like with blood on my mouth and a knife in my hand. "Hurry up!"

Eyes brimming with terror, the two children clutched each other and reluctantly moved toward me.

"I'm not gonna hurt you." I gently touched the boy's head. "I promise. Okay? It's a little scary out there, but we're here to save you from these bad guys."

The girl nodded.

I bumped into Christian outside the door. "Jesus. I nearly stabbed you."

He winked. "Wouldn't be the first time."

"I need to get these kids to Wyatt, but I don't know where he is."

"Worry not, lass. I can hear the little gobshite now." Christian scooped up a child in each arm as if they weighed nothing. "Back in a jiffy."

I sprinted to the far end of the building. When I glanced down at the lower level, I could have sworn I saw Matteo. Viktor's wolf viciously attacked a much larger wolf, and the savage noises were enough to curdle blood. I looked up, and to my horror, a toddler was peering down at the chaos. The railing was only made up of three bars, and she easily fit through them as she leaned over the bottom one.

I flashed down the walkway and slowed at the curve. My heart wound up in my throat when she teetered too far from the edge. With lightning speed, I raced toward her, dove to the floor, and clutched her in my arms before rolling onto my back. She wailed and wriggled with all her might.

When I crawled to my feet with the child in my arms, I scanned the building. There wasn't time to comfort her—only to save her. Just ahead, Blue emerged from a room, blood dripping from her axe and a look of murder on her face I'd never seen before.

"Can you take the baby?" I asked, the toddler kicking her feet. "Give her to Wyatt."

Blue shook her head.

"Blue, I can't. I'm charged up with energy, and I'm afraid I'll shock her by accident. Please."

Blue scooped up the little girl and propped her against her hip as if she'd done it a thousand times. With the axe in her other hand, she turned around and strutted away.

I spotted Christian below, slamming a wolf against a wall. We couldn't leave one child behind, so I looped back to the rooms I'd passed. One was a bedroom, and though the light switch didn't work, my Vampire eyes allowed me to verify it was empty. The second door revealed a stairwell. Ascending the steps, I put away my small dagger and took the larger one from its sheath. Once at the top, I pushed the long metal bar on the door and stepped outside.

A gust of wind whipped my hair around. The rooftop was an ideal spot to hide. Dark shadows, ventilation pipes, but likely no fire escape. I'd never seen them on old factory buildings. I branched away from the door. Without lights, it was difficult to see long distances.

And this was a big fucking rooftop.

I treaded carefully since there wasn't a parapet to prevent me from stepping off the edge. I walked around, using my Mage ability to detect energy. Someone was definitely up here.

"You might as well come out and fight instead of cowering like a chicken," I said, taunting him. "Are you sure you're even a wolf?"

Two eyes gleamed at me from the shadows. A black wolf emerged, powerful and larger than most I'd seen. Viktor had cautioned me that wolves were clever enough to kill a Mage by chewing off their hands before going for the jugular. Usually it took more than one, but this guy was big.

I waved my dagger so he could see the weapon. Was the man conscious in there, or was I only dealing with the beast?

A growl rumbled in his chest before he lunged. I flashed around him and swiped the blade, but he turned and snapped at my wrist. When I recoiled, he went for my other hand. I windmilled my arms and quickly flashed away before he jumped at my throat.

The wolf didn't stop. Unlike a human, who would assess the situation and develop a new strategy, he kept up the attack until I was on the defense. I sliced his back, but his fur was too thick and dark for me to see any blood.

Pipes became obstacles as I tried not to stumble over them in the dark. I gripped a tall pipe like a stripper on a pole and swung around, kicking him in the head. When I let go and landed, his fangs locked onto my left arm. Panic set in when he thrashed his head and tugged the leather, tearing it to shreds. I brought down my dagger, but he spotted it and dashed off.

I wound up cutting my own arm.

"Dammit!" As I stalked toward him, I noticed Christian perched like a vulture on the raised doorway. "Get your ass down here if you want a piece of this."

"Oh, I'll get a piece of that later, Precious." He gave me a crooked smile, his trench coat splayed behind him, his knees drawn up and arms folded over them.

Damn if I didn't want to impress him. It wasn't just my lover watching me—it was a professional who had spent hours in the training room with me.

I sensed a dim energy from the other side of the roof. After sheathing my large blade, I gripped the two push daggers secured to my belt. The blades protruded between my fingers, the handles fitting snugly in my closed fists.

Toenails scraped against the asphalt as the beast sprinted toward me. I braced myself, and seconds before he leaped into the air, I fell onto my back. As he sailed over me, I drove my daggers into his sides, and the force of motion ripped the blades down his flank.

He yelped, and for a split second, I felt pity.

But then I remembered what these men had done, why we were here. When I flipped over, I stared at a naked man on the ground. He was a giant. By the time I sprang to my feet, he'd shifted back to a wolf. I flashed toward him, dropped to my knees, and drove the daggers through his skull.

The beast made one final lunge, but death came swiftly. He smothered me with his weight, groaned, and then his thundering heart finally came to a stop.

A slow applause sounded. "Well done, Raven. The daggers were a nice touch."

I shoved the animal off and sat up. "You can't shift with daggers in your skull—not unless you want brain damage."

Christian extended his arm and helped me up. "That was the smart way to go about it. Torturing a man like that is a pleasure, but you have to know when you're at a disadvantage."

"Disadvantage? I had the upper hand."

"He was twice your size. I saw you stumbling about in the dark. One misstep, and you would have tumbled off the roof."

I frowned at my torn jacket. "Heights don't bother me—I wouldn't have fallen. But he wasn't shifting to heal the little stuff, and look at him. He's a moose. He probably could have shifted a dozen times before getting weak. That's why I had to finish him off quick."

"And tell me why you didn't sizzle him up with your battery juice?"

"I'm already tired from flashing. It would have weakened me more."

"Good girl. If I could give you a pointer—next time, go for the eyes. It's far easier to gouge out an animal's eyes than a man's."

"You're disgusting."

"Aye. But this isn't a competition where the winner gets a trophy. It's a game of survival." He folded his arms. "Your technique is improving."

"I just wish I hadn't sipped on that guy's blood downstairs. I feel sick to my stomach."

"We should go back down."

I jerked my daggers out of the wolf. "Thanks for letting me fight alone."

"You're thanking me for not interfering? Is this the same Raven who called me to help her with bears?"

I wiped the blood on the wolf's coat before sheathing the daggers. "That was different, and you know it."

"And that's why I took a front-row seat. 'Tis a shame I didn't have any popcorn."

I put my arm around his waist as we walked. "You haven't had popcorn in decades. What if you choked on a kernel?"

"Don't you know CPR?"

"I think you mean the Heimlich maneuver. Don't worry, I would serve popcorn at your funeral."

When we reached the door, he opened it for me. "The only thing I want served at my funeral is revenge. Invite all my enemies and slaughter them."

"Right before 'Amazing Grace,' I'll douse the church with kerosene. How's that?"

I jogged down the hot stairwell until I reached the door. After pressing my ear against it and listening, I cracked it open and peered through.

Christian yanked me away. "Anyone ever told you not to put your eyeball up to a crack?"

"No, but something tells me you've heard that a lot."

"It's all clear," he said, jerking open the door.

We both rushed out and split apart, keeping the same stride as we ran toward the crossover. Down below, bodies littered the floor. Each room I passed, I glanced inside the open doorway and looked under furniture to make sure it was clear.

Wyatt jogged toward me, his face sweaty and hat missing.

"I checked the rooms," I said. "All empty."

He leaned on the railing to catch his breath. "There's one more."

"How do you know?"

He jerked his thumb at nothing behind him. "The freshy said there's someone on the roof."

"I was just up there. The guy's dead."

"Well, you missed the kid." He fanned his shirt away from his chest. "All the others are loaded up in the vans. Tell Shep I'll be right down."

After he took off, I met with Christian, who had just crossed over the bridge.

"I didn't hear any wee ones up there," he remarked, brows furrowed.

"It's a big roof. Lots of hiding spots. Maybe you were distracted, or maybe Wyatt's finally lost his marbles."

We headed toward steps that descended to the first floor. Blue was covered in blood spatters as she searched through a toy pile.

In the center of the room, Viktor's wolf rose up on its hind legs and savagely attacked another wolf. The vicious snarls and snaps along with three dead wolves made me want to get the hell out of their way.

I reached Blue. "What are you looking for?"

She finally stood with a toy in her hand. "One of the kids wanted her dolly. I hope this is it, because we can't stay much longer."

"I'll take care of the bodies and make sure we didn't miss any children," Christian said, stalking off.

I fell into step beside her as we headed back to the garage. "What do you need help with?"

"Getting everyone together, I guess. Once Viktor takes care of that last wolf, Shepherd's going to set the place on fire to burn up evidence that we were here."

"That's a little dramatic."

"It's the only way to erase fingerprints in the Breed world. Sensory fingerprints, blood—you get the picture. Claude's tracking down the women."

"Are we taking them home?"

"Not the adults." When Blue reached a well-lit area, she stopped and noticed the blood on her arms. "Viktor wants to give them money so they don't wind up on the streets. Apparently, none of the kids belong to them. Anyhow, two of them took off, and the other one is sitting outside."

"Maybe Christian should scrub their memories of us, just in case."

She bent down and wiped her arms on her pants, trying in vain to get the blood off. "That's a good plan. Someone might get the bright idea to blackmail us or report the incident to the higher authority."

I kicked a bullet shell. "Technically, we didn't do anything wrong. Those men were hurting the kids."

"Yeah, but nobody hired us. That's not how Viktor operates. He's trying to protect us from an investigation, and there's no way we could justify this bloodbath. Operations like ours aren't supposed to go rogue."

I handed her my leather coat. "Put this on. I'll check outside the building. Maybe the women are just hiding."

The kids were inside the vans parked by the garage, some

crying and others firing off questions. Gem approached the back of one van and put on a light display, which quickly distracted them.

I veered left and walked down what was once flat concrete. Some of it had broken and shifted. Time had ravaged the property, weeds and vines erasing what man had once created. I peered behind a sheet of metal and then looked inside a patch of weeds as tall as me, scuttling backward when something slithered around my feet.

A piercing cry set me into motion, and I jogged around to the side. My eyes widened at the sight of Wyatt hanging halfway off the roof, both hands clutching the hand of a young girl no more than ten. She was slipping through his fingers. I bolted toward them a split second before she fell. I caught her, but not with grace. Our bodies collided, and then we fell in a heap. A few seconds later, a sickening thud hit the ground behind me.

"You okay?" I rubbed my shoulder and sat up.

The girl lifted her arm, her elbow bleeding and covered in grit. Judging by the knot on her temple and my throbbing lip, we must have smacked our heads together during the catch. I twisted around and gasped when I saw Wyatt.

"Niko!" I shouted. "Someone help!"

The first person on the scene was Shepherd. When he caught sight of Wyatt, he holstered his gun and dropped to his knees. "What happened?"

"He fell off the roof."

Shepherd glanced up. "*Jesus fuck.*" He rolled Wyatt onto his back. "Open your eyes! You in there?"

"I didn't see it happen," I explained. "He was hanging upside down, so I don't know how he landed."

Shepherd felt for a pulse. "He's still alive. I can't sense anything but the pain he felt hitting the ground." After assessing his neck, Shepherd reached inside his back pocket and pulled out a handkerchief.

"Do you want me to get your bag out of the van?"

He pressed the cloth to the gash on Wyatt's head. "Niko!"

he shouted over his shoulder. "Get your ass over here!" Then he glanced at the girl. "How about the kid?"

"My arm hurts," she whimpered.

"It might be broken," I whispered to Shepherd.

He reached over and touched her knee. His palm glowed red, and the girl sighed with relief. While he couldn't heal her, he could temporarily remove her pain.

Niko navigated the uneven ground as quickly as he could. He must have read everyone's light, because he went to the girl first. "Give me your arm, little one. Don't be afraid."

The girl quit clutching her elbow, and Niko gingerly held it.

"Can you do that on a kid?" I asked.

"I'll have to use less power. As long as she has Breed blood, I can heal fractures."

A light pulsed, and a loud snap of electricity sounded. The girl recoiled but then immediately bent her arm and stared at it in amazement. A gentle touch later, the gash on her head was healed.

"Wake up, Spooky." Shepherd lifted Wyatt's eyelids. "I can't see a damn thing in the dark."

I held my palms close to Wyatt's face, pushing light into my hands until tiny blue webs danced at my fingertips. It wasn't much, but maybe it was enough. "Does this help at all?"

He leaned in close. "His pupils aren't fully dilated, so that's a good sign. I think."

"You *think*?"

"I'm not a damned doctor. I patch people up."

"You also put holes in them."

Niko crawled above Wyatt's head and held it in his hands. A dubious look crossed his expression. "So much damage. I can heal him, but it doesn't mean he'll awaken."

Viktor jogged over while trying to put on his sweater. "What happened?"

Shepherd sat back. "Humpy Dumpty took a spill off the damn roof. That's what happened."

Niko sighed. "It's your call, Viktor. If he doesn't wake up on his own, I can't promise he'll wake up at all. And if I heal him and he's comatose…"

Yeah, we'd all been down that road already with Niko.

Viktor wiped his hand down his mouth, a nebula of emotions clouding his expression. "Is there nothing you can give to wake him? Like in movies."

Shepherd glanced up. "You mean smelling salts? I don't like carrying ammonia around with me. Chitahs can smell it." He looked down at Wyatt and frowned. "Should I punch him? That might wake him up."

"You'll do more damage," Niko warned him.

"Spooky, wake your ass up!" Shepherd slapped his cheek a few times. "You in there?"

Suddenly Wyatt's HAVE A NICE AFTERLIFE T-shirt wasn't so funny.

Shepherd kept holding the handkerchief against Wyatt's head to stanch the bleeding. "You gotta wake up, man. Don't do this to me."

I could see Viktor pressing on a tough decision. I couldn't get the sound out of my head of Wyatt hitting the asphalt. Staring at his lifeless body, I charged my light and cupped his crotch.

Wyatt gasped, and his eyes went wide.

Next best thing to CPR paddles.

Niko wasted no time before cradling Wyatt's head. Concentrated light culminated at his fingertips. When it flashed, I shut my eyes from the blinding flare and heard the crack of a whip. Watching Niko heal never got old. After repairing Wyatt's head, Niko went for his chest. This time, Wyatt cursed under his breath.

We all breathed a collective sigh.

Wyatt cupped his crotch. "Why do my balls hurt?" When he scooted to a sitting position, the bloody rag fell onto his lap.

Shepherd squeezed Wyatt's shoulder. "What's your name?"

"Wyatt Blessing."

"Do you know who I am?"

"A dickhead." He looked down at the bloody handkerchief in his lap. "Did you save me with your snot rag?"

Shepherd stood. "Yeah, he'll be fine."

Viktor eased up next to Shepherd. "My wolf searched the building. Christian is removing the last of the bodies. Burn it down."

I jumped to my feet. "What are you going to light?"

Viktor took the girl's hand. "That is Shepherd's job."

"I brought gasoline canisters in the second van, but it looks like they've got a gas line." Shepherd took a box of matches out of his pocket and rattled them, a sinister smile on his face. "Let's get this party started."

Chapter 19

As soon as we got home, I showered and changed into my sweatpants. Though I'd promised myself I wouldn't drink on this assignment, the dark blood drove me to it. Prior to leaving the burning warehouse, I'd vomited as much of it out as I could, but it had already seeped its way inside me, slithering through my veins like a venomous snake.

"Slide over." Christian set an empty glass on the booth table and stole the spot next to me.

While he poured himself a drink, I stared through the open archway into the gathering room. Despite the late hour, some of the children were awake and talking. Blue was brushing one girl's hair, and Gem was reading an old Russian fable to the little ones. None complained that she didn't translate it to English. She was an animated storyteller, capturing their imaginations. Given the circumstances, Viktor thought it best to keep the men out of the room so the kids felt safe. He chose an isolated hall with only one way in and out, and Kira and Switch were busy setting up their rooms.

"How's Wyatt?" I asked sleepily.

Christian traced his finger around the rim of his glass. "Knocked out from what Shepherd said. That's one lucky bastard."

"No kidding. He almost landed straight on his head; it's a wonder he didn't snap his neck."

"A broken neck isn't a sure thing."

"I'm not going to ask how you know that. Wyatt must have spooked the girl. She took a step backward, and off they went."

Christian chuckled darkly. "He has that effect on women."

After finishing my tequila, I folded my arms on the table and put my head down. I heard someone sit on the bench across from us.

"It is good to hear the sound of children in this house," Viktor remarked. "It has been many years since these rooms were full."

Christian gently stroked my back, and it felt so damn good. "How long do you wager we'll keep them?"

"We cannot risk them escaping or running about the house and finding weapons. Kira and Gem will watch them at all times, and that is an immense task."

Christian shifted in his seat. "Drop them off at the orphanage."

"Nyet. We have fifteen little ones who require special care. Shepherd will give each a health checkup in the morning, but only with Kira by his side. Just thinking about what they have been through—" He slammed his fist against the table, and I jerked up, my head pounding. When he noticed the silence in the adjacent room, he waved his hand at them with an apologetic look. "Any progress on your assignment?"

I rubbed my eyes. "I don't have enough facts. Maybe these deaths weren't connected after all. Who knows? Maybe all we were supposed to do was rescue those kids." I swung my gaze toward the gathering room. "And you know what? That's good enough for me."

"Says *the Shadow*," Christian quipped.

I steered my attention to my Vampire. "What did you do to that guy when you closed the door?"

Christian slowly arched an eyebrow.

"That's what I thought. It feels good to put the bad guys behind bars, but in this case, nothing beats the death penalty. If I never figure out the mystery behind my case, at least we saved those kids. I just hope we can find them a decent home."

"Aye."

A little boy appeared at the table and stared up at Christian. He had ruddy cheeks and wide brown eyes. "Are you a real Vampire?"

I chuckled softly.

Christian—arms folded on the table—dipped his chin. "I am."

"Can I see your fangs?"

Christian flashed them before I could object.

The boy scampered back into the gathering room. "I told you so!"

Christian lifted his glass. "The wee ones aren't afraid of us like they used to be. There was a time when the sight of my fangs would make people shrink back in terror."

"You sound disappointed," I said.

"Little ones should be scared of monsters. They shouldn't ignore those primal instincts."

Viktor stroked his silver beard and cast a somber gaze into the adjacent room. "They have seen monsters—real ones."

Switch swaggered in. His messy brown hair fell to his grey shirt, which looked like it had shrunk two sizes in the wash. "Everything's set up. A few of them will have to share beds. I can sit at the end of the hall and make sure nobody wanders."

"That might frighten them to see a strange man outside their door," Viktor said, rising to his feet.

Switch furrowed his brow. "What if I shift? My wolf won't harm children, and I think they'll be okay with that. I'll make sure he knows to keep them in the hall."

Viktor rubbed his bloodshot eyes. "That is acceptable. But everyone is exhausted, and you won't have a backup."

I raised my hand. "If he needs a break, I'll take over."

Christian gave me a loaded glance. "I didn't think you were feeling well."

Dancing around that topic, I said, "I'm not, but that doesn't mean I can't stay awake. It's not like my core energy is depleted."

Viktor clapped his hands. "Come, little ones! It is time to sleep."

Gem closed her book and woke some of the children. Blue lifted a toddler on one hip and a young girl on the other. Most of the kids had their eyes closed and were doing the zombie walk as they followed Gem through the dining room.

Viktor gestured for Christian to join him. "I need your help moving large furniture from upstairs. I would like each child to have their own bed for as long as they are here. I cannot do this alone."

Christian eased out of his seat and sighed. "Perhaps you should go to bed and let me handle all the hard labor. I need something to keep my hands busy."

"Place them in the empty rooms. Kira will put fresh linens on them tomorrow morning."

When Christian passed by Switch, the two men locked eyes. While they were finally getting along better, I had a feeling that Christian still didn't trust that Switch wouldn't change his mind about me, and I suppose Switch might have felt the same about Christian.

I scooted out of the booth to head upstairs. "Is your wolf up for this, or are we going to find him sleeping on the job?"

Switch fell into step beside me. "My wolf and I have a symbiotic relationship. As long as he does what I say, he gets to come out whenever he wants. Well, almost whenever."

"What do *you* get out of it?"

He gripped the stone railing as we ascended the stairs. "Nice dreams. That Chitah out there is messing with my schedule though. I don't like him on the property."

"Neither does Blue, but Viktor's taking a hard pass on getting in the middle of it."

"I can see his attraction to her. Blue's a badass."

We reached the second floor and strolled around to the other ascending staircase.

"You okay?" he asked.

"Tired."

"I know I can't ask why, but I'm pretty good at putting together puzzles. You got fifteen pieces downstairs."

"Yeah, we just need to find them a home."

"What's their animal?"

"I don't really know. I'm guessing they're wolves."

Switch flipped his hair back when we reached the top of the

stairs. "Not many packs have that kind of room or the money. I wish I could help, but you'll have to split them up."

I wasn't certain if that was a good idea, but I didn't mention it to Switch. The kids might be related, and in any case, they'd grown up together. It didn't seem right breaking them up.

"We'll see," I finally said. Pausing at a hallway entrance, I gave him a skeptical look. "Are you following me?"

"I figure your boyfriend needs help hauling that shit down."

My lips twitched. Christian hated being referred to as a boyfriend, but he wasn't exactly my husband or mate. "I think he can manage. He's got superstrength, you know."

"Maybe so, but if he doesn't know how to pivot, he's going to bust up those beds trying to get them through the doorways."

I tightened the drawstring on my grey sweatpants. "Be nice to him. We've had a long night, and—"

"I got it." Switch unexpectedly wrapped his arms around me. "I'm glad you're okay. I worry about you sometimes."

Tired, I leaned into him and accepted the hug. It felt nice to have a friend who cared about me.

"Christian's going to a sex club," he whispered in my ear.

Taken aback, I let go and gave him a quizzical stare. "What?"

"He also goes somewhere else, but I don't know where," Switch added, his voice barely above a whisper.

Knowing Christian was upstairs, I did the same. "Are you following him?"

"You can't follow a Vampire. I was in the city one night and spotted him. Decided to see where he was going."

I let those facts resonate for a minute. "Was it the White Owl?"

His heavy brows furrowed. "How did you know?"

"It's not what you think. Stop following him. I mean it."

I ventured upstairs, leaving Switch behind. He was probably anticipating a big fight, but I knew exactly what this was about.

Following the sound of wood scraping against a wall, I headed down a dark hallway and stopped by a door. "Christian, I need to ask you something."

Holding a large bed frame over his head, he gave me an exasperated look. "Can it wait? I'm a wee bit occupied."

I folded my arms.

"For feck's sake." He set the bed down and glided to the door. "I don't care for that look you're giving me."

"You mind telling me why you're hanging around the White Owl? I closed that case, remember?"

"How—" He slanted his eyes to the side, probably trying to recall where he'd made a mistake.

"It doesn't matter how I found out. Honesty, remember?"

"Someone spiked your drink that night, and I'll not forgive a deliberate act that put your safety in danger."

I leaned against the doorjamb. "So why aren't you trying to find out who buried me? Isn't that more important than someone who slipped Sensor magic into my bottle when I wasn't looking?"

He reached up and gripped the doorframe. "One thing at a time."

"And what did you plan on doing once you found this person?"

"Having a wee bit of fun. Is that a crime?"

I hooked my fingers in his pants and gave them a tug. "I know your version of romance is a head on a platter, but let it go. If you want to find someone, find the person who buried me. Do I have your word you'll drop it?"

"You can have much more than that if you keep tugging on me."

I stood on my tiptoes and gave him a chaste kiss. "I'll hold you to it."

"I wouldn't expect otherwise."

"Switch is on his way up to help."

Christian snorted. "And what does the Shifter think he can help with that I haven't got under control?"

I poked him in the belly button before striding off. "How to pivot."

When I reached a window that opened onto the roof, I climbed out and found a nice spot that overlooked the property. I couldn't see anything except Matteo's campfire, but the stars were courting me with their lustrous glow. Reclining on my back, I admired the view.

A white owl swooped over me, and I almost had a heart attack. When I sat up and twisted around, I saw Houdini was standing behind a chimney stack.

"You wouldn't happen to have a pair of pants up here, would you?" he asked, folding his arms over the brick.

I stood and gave him a baleful look. "What are you doing here?"

"One of these days, Butterfly, you'll be happy to see me."

"Maybe I don't care to see that much of you."

He remained behind the chimney stack, clearly naked but hidden from the chest down. His white hair soaked in the starlight and the rising moon. Houdini didn't have in his black ear studs since jewelry never transferred with a Shifter. Some Shifters could probably use liquid fire to make the holes permanent, but I didn't see any large holes on his ears, and I also didn't presume that Houdini spent much time in animal form. He seemed more in touch with his Vampire side than anything.

"It's so hard to find you alone these days," he said absently. "I came by to warn you."

I widened my stance. "Is that a threat?"

"Poe has been skulking about my club, and I don't like it. He's tried to get in twice, and I have reason to believe he charmed two of my workers. If you're conspiring against me, you won't succeed. I'll see to that."

"Like you saw to my burial?"

His eyes narrowed slightly. "Do you really believe I'd do that?"

"I wouldn't put anything past you, Chaos. The last thing I remember is leaving your club. Next thing I know, I'm clawing at the lid of a coffin. Have you ever been buried? It's the worst nightmare you can imagine. Convince me you didn't do it, because you once tried selling me on the black market."

Houdini leaned away from the chimney stack. "Casting you into the unknown is one thing, but killing you is another. I have a special affection for you, Raven. You're my youngling, and I desire to see what you're capable of in this world. If you think I would waste my time burying such potential, then you don't know me at all."

I turned away and approached the edge of the roof. If it wasn't him, then who? This mystery would forever plague my thoughts. It was likely one of the Vamps I'd attempted to kill in my past life, before Keystone. But it was the not knowing that I couldn't live with.

"You don't have to worry about Christian," I said calmly, still feeling sick from the dark blood. "He won't be coming around anymore." I turned on my heel to face my maker. "But he wants to know who spiked my drink that night. If he finds out the truth, he'll come after you, and I won't be able to stop him."

"Then the game is afoot."

"This isn't a game."

Houdini flashed a smile. "Everything is a game. Why would you caution me if you didn't feel something for me? Loyalty perhaps? It's in your blood, Raven. As much as you want to hate me, I'm your maker. I gave you my blood, and your instinct will always be to protect me. The real question is: Who would you choose in a death match? Your lover or your maker? What a conundrum." His expression relaxed. "Come on, Raven. Not everything has to be black or white. Live in the grey."

"The world is your puppet—you've made that abundantly clear. You don't care about anything or anyone, so why should anyone care about you?"

Houdini rounded the chimney stack and unabashedly strode toward me. Even in darkness, his hazel eyes were mesmerizing, and though not muscular, his body conformed to an ideal masculine shape. An inch away, he gazed down at me, his regal but ancient features sending a chill down my spine. "Your team is basking in the praise after exposing that fighting ring. I would imagine you were paid a hefty sum."

"We deserved it."

Houdini leaned in tight with an impassive look. "Who do you think gave you the blueprints to the auction house?"

My blood ran cold.

"If your team had bothered to look up my username, they might have noticed that the numbers spelled out *chaos*. If I didn't care about anything or anyone, I would merely be a spectator in this world. I would offer nothing. Not my blood, not my company, and certainly not my blueprints. Be careful with those assumptions, Butterfly."

Houdini spread his arms and melted away into a beautiful white owl. With a few flaps of his wings, he soared over my head and into the black night.

Chapter 20

I DIDN'T SEE CHRISTIAN THAT EVENING. He stayed busy moving furniture downstairs, and I was busy lying in bed, mulling over what Houdini had said. Thankfully, Switch didn't need any help guarding the kids. The blood I'd consumed hadn't left my body, and I still felt sick. Why it didn't bother Christian was beyond me, but I suspect he never took nearly as much as I did. Around noon, I headed down to the gym in my black shorts and a sleeveless shirt. Niko practiced swordplay while I hit the weights.

When my muscles couldn't take anymore, I grabbed a leftover sausage biscuit from the kitchen and followed the sound of squeals and laughter to the courtyard. It was a beautiful day, nothing but blue skies and sunshine. The kids were playing games, sitting in the green grass, and climbing trees.

I found Wyatt lying on a chaise by the hot tub, his chair reclined horizontal, green sunglasses shading his eyes. I strolled down the shady veranda and sat in the chair beside him.

He rolled to his side to face me, his grey shirt twisting up. "Is that for me?"

I glanced down at my half-eaten biscuit and handed it over. "You feeling okay?"

He didn't eat with his usual vigor. Crumbs showered the concrete as he chewed like a sloth. "My head hurts. Niko says everything's healed, and it's just my synapses misfiring or something."

"I get that sometimes. It goes away. Need some aspirin?"

Wyatt finished his biscuit and slowly wiped his hand on his jeans. "Shep gave me a strong painkiller."

"Ah. That explains it." I drew up one leg and propped my foot on the edge of the chair.

"Believe me, I wanted my own herbs, but some caveman Chitah dug them all up. Now I have to replant everything." He sighed dramatically. "Do you know how long the tiny tots are staying here?"

I swung my gaze to a little boy playing by a winged statue. "I guess until Viktor finds a place for them."

"They better not let them out of their sight. I've got a lot of sensitive equipment upstairs that I don't want nosy little fingers touching."

Hunter suddenly burst through the door, his shoes lighting up with each step. He looked at the gathering of kids with uncertainty, and I watched as he walked the opposite way down the veranda, his gloved hand tracing alongside the wall. Had he ever played with other children? A red-haired girl about his age wandered up to the other side of the wall and faced him. She spoke for a minute, but he didn't say anything back. Then she reached out to touch his face.

No, not his face. His scar.

After another moment, she turned and pointed somewhere. Next thing I knew, Hunter climbed the wall and followed behind her. When they reached a row of purple flowers, they went chasing after a butterfly.

"They seem okay," Wyatt said. "A few scrapes and bruises. Shepherd checked them this morning before I woke up. Three of the older girls were malnourished, and one boy had an infected cut on his foot. Too bad they're not old enough to shift. Then again, I don't think I could handle fifteen wolves crapping all over the place."

I twirled a lock of hair around my finger. "You did good, Spooky. You saved that girl's life."

"You're a good catch."

"Apparently, not that good. You almost died."

He snorted. "I would have crushed you."

I waved a pesky gnat away from my face, thinking about how we weren't so immortal. Some of us bounced back better than others. Wyatt could have easily died had Niko not been there. I wasn't entirely sure that Christian would have given up his blood. Most Breeds didn't want it—they feared its power. I was only half Vampire, so I wasn't sure that drinking *my* blood would have made a difference to anyone but a Vampire.

Kira floated out the door with an armload of blankets. Without her kerchief, her red hair lit up in the sun. She found a shady spot by some trees and spread out the blankets. A minute later, Switch rolled out a food cart and helped her set up a picnic.

"Viktor wanted to lock them in their rooms," Wyatt murmured. "But Blue said that kids need fresh air and sunshine. She's right. You lock up kids, and they start getting into trouble. Especially boys."

"I don't think you have much to worry about with this group. They had to grow up fast, and that changes you." I heaved a sigh and crossed my legs. "Makes me wish I could go back in time and kill those men more slowly."

Wyatt rolled onto his back and ran his fingers through his messy brown hair. The patchy whiskers on his youthful face made him look like a college kid looking for work in a coffee shop. "I saw some of Christian and Blue's handiwork. That's a therapy session I ain't got time for."

Something Houdini had said was still on my mind. I shifted toward Wyatt. "You know the last case we worked on—the fighting ring?"

"Yup."

"Who sent you the blueprints to the auction house?"

"Man, did I get those at the eleventh hour." He turned his head, my warped reflection in his sunglasses staring back at me. "Some anonymous user. Ghosted before I could ask what he or she wanted in return."

"Is that normal?"

"If it were one of my contacts, maybe. Sometimes we do each other favors. But on that site, you don't get something for nothing.

Everything has a price. Maybe they somehow knew what was going on and had a personal vendetta against the people involved. Why?"

"I was just thinking about it."

"Well, if you find out who it was, I wanna know. People aren't helpful out of the goodness of their heart. Creeps me out."

My thoughts drifted back to the conversation the night before. Why the hell would Houdini have helped us? It didn't seem in character. Maybe he'd done it to redirect focus away from his business. I found myself keeping so many secrets lately to protect him. If Wyatt or anyone else knew he had provided the blueprints, they might go after him. Worse, they might think that we're conspiring and I'm feeding him information about Keystone. Maybe his plan was to sabotage me. Or maybe he wanted to test my loyalty to Viktor since telling the truth might get me fired.

Damn his games.

I spotted Blue perched in a tree. Like me, she was comfortable with heights, but I suppose that had to do with her being a falcon. "I guess my case is closed."

Wyatt draped his arms over the armrests as if he were tanning on a Hawaiian beach. "What's the trouble?"

"I'm running in circles trying to find a missing piece, and maybe there isn't one. Now I'll just have to tell Ren we've got nothing."

"I wouldn't be so sure about that."

The little boy who'd approached Christian last night jogged down the veranda with a girl at his side. They skidded to a stop at the foot of Wyatt's chair, and the boy asked, "Why do you have Lost Soul written on your hands?"

Wyatt drummed his fingers on the chair. "None of your beeswax."

"Are you sure you didn't mean *lost sock*?" The two giggled.

Wyatt sat up and lazily waved them off. "Scram!"

I watched them race each other down the long walkway, laughing the entire way before scaling the wall and flopping onto the grassy side. It gave me hope that they might be okay. At least they knew how to read.

I turned my attention back to Wyatt. "What were you going to say?"

"About what?"

"The case."

He scratched his scruffy jaw. "Oh that. About a week ago, someone tracked in a freshy."

"Yeah, sorry about that. We ran into a few uncooperative Shifters we had to put in their place."

"See, that's what I thought. So I ignored him. The minute you start paying attention to the dead, they stick to you like glue. They want *favors*," he said, using his fingers to make air quotes. Wyatt sat up and adjusted his chair to an upright position. "If they don't get what they want, they turn into little demons. That's why most Gravewalkers look like they're running on two hours of sleep. Things were peaceful for a while, and now the new guy decides to keep me up all night singing."

"Wish I could help, but it's not my problem."

Wyatt slid his glasses down his nose so I could see his bloodshot eyes. "He keeps asking me to give a message to his father. What am I, the Pony Express?"

"Does he want you to do it for free, or does he have some way of paying you?"

"See, that's where it gets weird. He says if I do him this favor, he'll help us. Normally I don't trust freshies, but I'm desperate. Even after my near-death experience last night, he kept me up. All night. I lost him earlier in the east wing and came out here, hoping to avoid him long enough to get a nap. When they attach themselves to a house, they don't like leaving. I'm sleeping out here if that's what it takes."

"How exactly can he help us?" It didn't seem logical. "Can they see something we can't?"

"They can go wherever they want and eavesdrop on anyone. But most freshies have short attention spans. They spend more time focusing on their life, trying to hold on to the memories before they get all mixed up. Seriously, if ghosties could be spies, we'd have a real business. But most of the older ones have the memory of a goldfish. And the new ones have a whole catalog of issues I don't subscribe to."

"What exactly does he know?"

Wyatt shrugged. "It's up to you if you want to find out."

I stood and put my hands on my hips. "Then I think we need to have a séance later on. Have you seen Christian?"

"He took off."

"Did he say where?"

"Maybe for a Brazilian wax." Wyatt pushed his sunglasses back up. "I'm not his babysitter."

"Keep your calendar free. Meeting in your office tonight."

Chapter 21

After parking my blue pickup in Crush's driveway, I finished listening to the tail end of "Bad Company" before cutting off the engine. My father was on a ladder propped against the metal garage, a hammer in one hand and a spray can in the other.

I got out and squinted up at him. "What the hell are you doing?"

His hellhound sat nearby, head cocked to the side as he watched his master.

Crush sprayed the can, and a flurry of obscenities came pouring out of his mouth as he beat on a brown clump of mud with a hammer.

"Go on, you bastards! Not on my garage!"

As I drew closer, I realized he was pounding his hammer on a giant wasp nest while simultaneously spraying all the pissed-off wasps who were flying out to see who was demolishing their home.

"Crush! Get down from there before you fall!"

The ladder teetered, and I rushed to steady it. Part of the nest fell a few feet in front of me, and I wanted to bolt when the hornets flew out and angrily swirled around us. I waited until Crush hustled down the ladder, but not before one stung me on the arm.

"Fuck!" he growled. "I'm gonna get the gasoline."

"Don't you dare." I gripped his shirt. "You'll set the whole garage on fire. Just leave it here. They'll go away. Come inside before they figure out what's going on," I said, spotting a red welt on his head. "How the hell did you live past thirty?"

The dog barked at the nest, ready to defend Crush at his own peril.

Crush clapped his hands, and his companion trotted toward the trailer and bounded up the porch steps. Once inside, Crush disappeared into the bathroom and then returned with a Band-Aid box. He ran the faucet in the kitchen, wiping a few stings. "You want a drink?"

"No, I'm good," I said, sighing while I sat down.

He set a box of baking soda and a bowl of water on the table. "My mama taught me this," he said, mixing them together into a paste.

"You don't talk about Grandma much."

"I guess there's not much to talk about. They were old, even when I was young. They died before you were born, so I didn't think you wanted me boring you with all my stories."

"Bore me sometime. The only thing you ever told me was how your dad showed you how to fix cars, and your mom made you finish everything on your plate."

"That shit was no joke." He applied the paste to his hand and put a bandage over it. "She was the worst cook in the history of the world. You haven't suffered unless you had that woman's version of stew. She worked in a factory making clothes or something. That was before companies started making everything overseas. I guess she never had time to learn how to cook."

I stood up to put the paste on his stings. "That explains a lot about your eating habits."

"I left home, and then the military cooked my meals. Never had time to learn all that, but I'm a microwave champion."

After applying the white mixture to his forehead, I dried the area around it and applied a Band-Aid.

"Dammit, Cookie. Your arm. Can you heal that?"

I reached for a strip of sunshine beaming through the window, but the painful bump didn't go away. "I don't think healing works on venom. It's fine. It'll look better than yours by tomorrow."

When I sat back down, he took my arm and spread paste on

the red spot. "I remember when you were about eight, you got stung by a bee at school. Remember that?"

"How could I forget? You showed up and flipped the principal's desk over."

He pressed the bandage on. "They didn't tell me what happened. Just something about you being in the nurse's office and how I needed to come and take you to the doctor. He was sitting on his ass, finishing a phone call. My baby girl comes first. For all I knew, you could have had a severed leg."

I chortled. The places a parent's mind goes when their child is hurt.

Crush gently rubbed his rough hand over my bandage and gave me a tender smile, flashing his silver tooth.

I patted his hand. "Hope you don't mind me using your house. I got permission this time."

"It's fine as long as you ask. I don't like you snooping around."

"Afraid I'll find your cigar stash?"

He sat back. "I don't smoke those things."

"Bullshit."

He did that thing where he stroked his mustache and goatee in a sad attempt to conceal his smile.

I glanced into the kitchen and noticed an empty bowl on the floor next to a water dish. "So how are things working out with you two? He seems to listen."

As if sensing we were talking about him, the bullmastiff sat next to Crush and gave me a happy smile as Crush scratched his floppy ears.

"I hate to say it, but I think he's working out just fine," Crush admitted with a look of pride on his face. "Keeps me company, and I take him to work. Looks out for the property when we're busy. Don't ya, boy?"

"Hope he's not scaring off the customers."

"Nah. He seems to know who the bad guys are. Dogs know. Maybe that's why he keeps running after your man."

"Then maybe you should keep him away from me."

"You're sugar and spice."

I crossed my legs and thought about the cold-blooded murders we'd committed the night before. "I'm the bad guy."

"Maybe so, but you're bad for the right reasons. That cancels shit out. Isn't that right, boy?" Crush gave the dog another good rub on the head before resting his arms on the table.

"Please don't tell me you named him Pickles."

His lips twitched. "He didn't respond to that name anyhow." Crush laced his fingers together. "Meet Harley."

"As in Davidson?" I reached out and rubbed his jowls—Harley's, not my father's. "That's a good name for a good dog."

"I guess he heard me using it a lot around the garage and thought I was talking to him. Makes sense that a dog should choose his own name."

A bike rumbled in the driveway.

Crush stood. "I guess that's my cue to get lost. Come on, Harley. Let's go for a walk."

"Don't you need a leash?"

Crush opened the door and winked. "Where's the fun in that?"

The only traffic that went by was the neighbors, so he basically had the road to himself. I had a feeling he was enjoying showing off his big bad dog.

I walked onto the porch as Ren dismounted his bike. Ren had a leather vest over his white tee. He reached the steps and rested his arm on the wooden rail. "That is one big-ass dog."

Harley clumsily trotted down the steps, and when he reached the bottom, he sniffed Ren. His tail wagged like crazy.

Ren gave him a short grin and looked back up at Crush. "I still don't like it."

"I don't give two shits what you like or don't like. It's none of your damn business what I do. He keeps me company, and he's a good guard dog." Crush lumbered down the steps until he was at the bottom. "I'm thinkin' about getting a sidecar."

Ren tucked his aviators into his shirt collar. "Don't be one of those assholes who puts goggles on his dog. I'll ban you from my property."

"Fine." Crush swaggered off, change jingling in his pockets.

"See who'll keep your bikes running as good as I do. And you can forget about that custom paint job."

Ren ascended the steps. "Your old man's an asshole."

"Didn't he once save your life?"

Ren struck his chest with a closed fist. "Respect."

"Thanks for coming. Do you want a drink?" I asked, heading inside.

"Whatever's cold."

I reached in the fridge for a can of ginger ale and set it on the table. Then I seated myself across from him so I could face the door. Ren cracked open the can, took a long gulp, and I listened to the sound of fizzy bubbles filling the sunny kitchen.

"How's the case?" He rested the cold can against his tan neck.

"A wild-goose chase. If there's a connection, we haven't found it. We crossed a few off because they didn't fit the criteria of suspicious death. We questioned everyone, and tonight we're going to go over the details again and see if we missed anything. But I got a strange offer, and I want to get your thoughts on it before I go down that rabbit hole."

He let out a small burp and set the can down. "What kind of offer? I thought we weren't involving any outsiders?"

"Well, this one involved himself. Apparently a freshy followed us home during one of our outings."

"A what?"

I scooted my chair in. "That's just another name for the recently departed. I work with a Gravewalker who has a lot of nicknames for them. Anyhow, he wants to help us in exchange for helping him. I'm not going to lie: I'm entertaining the idea. Might as well hear what he has to say."

Ren's brow furrowed. "You shouldn't strike deals with the dead."

"That's what I heard. But it's our last lead. If I can't find a connection, I'll have no choice but to drop the case. If it's a virus, you'll just have to wait for more Shifters to die. Maybe Graham can take a blood sample and find an infectious disease expert."

Ren tapped his finger against the can. "If it *is* a virus, we need to find out why it's only killing some and not all."

"Maybe the ghost has something to say. If he does, do you want me to pursue it? This is your dime."

After a long sigh, Ren nodded. "If it seems legit, and you got something to go on, I'll pay. It's costing me, but fuck it."

I gathered up the Band-Aid wrappers and tossed them into the nearby trash. One of them floated to the floor, and I squatted to pick it up. "Can I ask you something if you promise to keep it between us?"

He took another swig. "You know my word is my bond."

"This can't get out, even to your Packmaster buddies." I returned to my chair.

Ren folded his arms and leveled his dark eyes at me. "Ask."

"Last night, Keystone took out a pack."

Ren's face got stony.

"Before you say anything, this wasn't a normal pack. Only three women, I think, and a lot of kids. Mostly girls." I waited to see if anything would click, but he kept staring. "Young girls. These were insidious men, and one of those little girls almost died trying to escape them."

Something shifted in his look, and it gave me goose bumps. "Predators?"

I nodded. "If we had turned them in, who knows if they would have gotten the justice they deserved? Shit happens. People in high places pull strings, and money talks. I don't know who those guys were, but one wolf I took out was big. I've never seen a wolf that big before."

Ren eased back. "Sounds like a pureblood."

"Pureblood?"

"Most Shifters have bred with other animal types. Even if you've been living in a pack for generations, somewhere up the line, someone mated a cougar or panther or whatever. But purebloods were once considered royalty. Every animal type had one, and they never crossbred. It kept their blood pure—their power pure. Not all the wolves are big, but it's a trait only associated with them. Doesn't matter anyhow. You took him out?"

"We took them *all* out. But we can't turn these kids over to the higher authority, or they'll find out what we did. Nobody hired us to do that specific job, and they'll think we've gone rogue. Viktor's afraid they'll break up Keystone. Aside from that, they'll find out what we were doing there in the first place, and that leads back to you. I'm doing everything I can to not only protect our reputation but yours. That's why we're not involving the higher authority."

"Yeah, I can see how that would be a problem."

"These kids are probably related, but we don't know for sure. They grew up together, so we don't want to split them up. They deserve a better home than an orphanage."

He combed back his dark hair with his fingers. "Are you asking me? Is that why you're telling me all this?"

"I guess so."

"How many?"

"Fifteen."

His shook his head. "I can't do it. That's… that's a big number. You gotta understand how complicated it is. It's not only about space and having enough rooms—a Packmaster needs to make sure there's enough money secured in his pack to feed and clothe his packmates. Most are making ends meet with just enough to sock away. When a new packmate joins, he or she brings in money. But kids can't work, so they reverse the income. Since they don't have parents, I'd need to find enough watchdogs. *Fifteen?* Holy shit. I don't know anyone who could take on that many kids at once. You can't split them up?"

I shook my head. "Viktor wants them together."

"A pack would call attention to themselves with that many new additions, and if you spread them out among different packs, people are gonna start asking where they came from."

I propped my elbows on the table and rubbed the outer corners of my eyes. "We sure as hell can't keep them. Viktor wants them in a pack environment with family. I just thought maybe you had the space."

"Not for that many. I barely got room for my own packmates the way they keep having babies and bouncing between jobs. I told them the heat house is there for a reason. Give a woman some privacy. But they catch one whiff of their mate in heat, and it's all over. Next thing you know, boom. I got another mouth to feed."

"Do you have any suggestions?"

His eyes slanted down. After a thoughtful pause, he said, "Can't say I do. There might be packs in another state, but you'll be taking chances. Nobody's going to accept that many kids without question, and besides, you don't want to pick some random pack you don't know. You could be putting them in an even worse situation, and they'll be too far away for you to monitor."

I heaved a sigh and got up. After pushing my chair in, I glanced at the Band-Aid on my arm where the pain was pulsing beneath. "I know you and Crush like to give each other hell, but ease up on the dog situation. He refuses to accept help from anyone, and I worry about him being out here alone. Especially with all the enemies I make. A dog is a security system, and he needs a companion. I'm not here as much as I'd like to be."

Ren stood up and stretched out his arms. "Can't complain about his mood lately. He's struttin' around like a peacock. I don't think I've seen him this happy since you came back. Besides, it'll give him exercise." After finishing his soda, Ren lit up a smoke and moseyed toward the door. "If I were you, I'd keep an eye on him when he goes for those long walks."

"Why's that?"

Ren put on his aviators and cracked a smile. "I'd bet my left nut he took that dog up the road to shit in Lou Johnson's yard. Those two haven't been on speaking terms since Lou knocked over his mailbox. See ya."

As I held my spot in the doorway, I noticed Crush ambling back. Harley was trotting alongside him, tail wagging and looking about three pounds lighter.

Chapter 22

"Who is Aaron again?" I asked.

Blue spread out papers on the floor and then handed me one. "Age nineteen. Wolf. Planned to leave his pack but died three days before. They found him lying in a field."

Blue leaned against the sofa, one elbow on the cushion and her head propped in her hand. We'd been discussing the case for the past two hours, using the floor in Wyatt's office since it had the best light. Wyatt was at his desk, bopping his head and typing away on his computer while the singer shouted "Stroke me, stroke me" through the speakers. He had all the bright lamps off on his side of the room, but his cylinder desk lamps were set on a purple hue.

"Is your friend here yet?" she asked him.

Wyatt swiveled his chair around. "Nope. Maybe it's my lucky day and he slipped out the front door and into oblivion."

Blue yawned and pointed her toes as she stretched. "Those kids wore me out today."

I leaned against the connecting sofa. "I bet."

"Switch slept all afternoon so he could guard them tonight. Are you his backup?"

"I guess so, but he didn't need me last night."

She swept her long hair to the side and drew up one knee. "That's gonna wear him down. He can't sleep a few hours, teach Hunter in the day, and then guard the kids all night. He'll have to suspend his teaching duties, and that means Shepherd will have to put aside work and look after Hunter."

Claude strutted in and tossed something at Wyatt. "That's all there was."

Wyatt held up the bag. "What the immortal hell is this? Organic kale chips?"

"Is something wrong with your machine?"

"I'm out of chips, and I don't get my next order until Tuesday."

Claude plopped down to my right and hooked his long arms over the back of the black sofa. "Take it or leave it. At least she's buying snacks."

Wyatt flung the chips into his wastebasket. "Whoever showed her the organic section of the website is going on my hit list."

I sniffed and turned my head toward Claude. "What's that smell?"

He smiled lazily, a smile that had certainly seduced many a woman. "Organic mint bodywash. You like?"

"You smell like a Christmas tree. All you need is a star on your head."

Blue chuckled. "He's got the shiny gold shorts to match."

"You slay me." He leaned forward and gestured to the paper pile. "Any progress?"

I reached back and kneaded my shoulders. "The night is young."

His hands rested on my shoulders. "May I?"

Blue smiled knowingly. "He's got magic fingers. Say yes."

I glared up at him. "Okay, but no funny business."

Claude wasn't just an excellent hairstylist—his hands were also made for working out muscle knots. Once he started, all the tension melted away. I lowered my head, closed my eyes, and didn't protest when his thumbs made circles around my shoulder blades.

"Careful, Raven. I've heard that's how he gets women in bed," Blue quipped.

The purr rumbling in Claude's throat quickly died. "Pleasing a woman is in my blood, but I have too much respect for the females in this house to seduce anyone."

This conversation was heading south, so I leaned away. "Okay, that's enough fingerplay." I glared at Wyatt. "Can't you put out an all-points bulletin? If he doesn't poof his way in here, I'm shutting this case for good. It's probably not a good idea to accept help from someone we killed. It feels like a trap."

Wyatt used his heels to walk his chair toward us. "Patience, buttercup. They can sense electricity, so the office is easy to find. Trust me on that one." He flung his beanie onto the sofa and ran his fingers through his wavy hair. Wyatt looked more like himself again. Not so tired and sickly—his cheeks had color, and his eyes weren't bloodshot. He glanced over his shoulder. "Speak of the devil."

I straightened up, trying in vain to sense an energy change in the room. We followed Wyatt's gaze as he looked up to his right.

Wyatt signaled me. "Well, tell him what's up."

"Maybe you should do it. I don't like talking to thin air."

"It's not like he can't hear you. Anyhow, this is *your* case." Wyatt crossed his leg over his knee and fiddled with his loose sock.

Instead of staring up, I looked at the files on the floor. "Wyatt says you want us to relay a message in exchange for information. We agree to those terms, but we need to have the information up front. You can trust we'll uphold our end of the bargain."

Wyatt glared at the empty space beside him. "Because I want you gone, and if we don't make good, I have to stare at your ugly face every night." He shook his head. "I've never had any complaints from the numerous ladies that—"

Blue snapped her fingers. "Hey! *Focus.*"

Wyatt's stubborn mouth stopped moving. For a second at least. "Specterpath," he mumbled. "It's a crazy lost soul that doesn't know what the hell he's talking about, that's what it is."

Claude reached out and shook Wyatt's chair. "*Silence.*"

"We've got all these deaths that we think might be connected," I said, gesturing to the papers. "Lots of young people. It happened all of a sudden, similar symptoms reported in some. That's why we're questioning all these Shifters; we're trying to figure out if there's something more devious going on. It could be natural causes and accidents, but nobody lived to tell the tale. If there's something you know about one of these people who might have been in your pack or den or whatever, that's what we need."

Wyatt straightened his legs and crossed them at the ankle. "He says that *he* lived to tell the tale." Wyatt glanced up. "Technically, you didn't live."

Blue surged forward. "He's one of the victims? Which one?"

Wyatt took on a mocking tone. "He says his name is King Freeman, son of Sambah Freeman." Then Wyatt smirked. "That's what you sound like."

"King?" I uttered, completely dumbstruck. "Your father said you were found on the stairs. Did you fall?"

"No," Wyatt replied.

Christian waltzed in. "And what do we have here?"

"*Shhh*," we all said at once.

Christian threw his hands up and stayed on the other side of the room, leaning against the desk with his arms folded.

"He was sick," Wyatt continued. "Says he was going downstairs for… a glass of *what*?" Wyatt shuddered. "A glass of boiled roots. He was having some chest pain, and it wasn't going away like before."

"So he was chronically sick?" I asked.

Wyatt paused a minute as he listened to King. "Occasionally he got heartburn. Says he was under a lot of stress about whether to start his own pride or take over for his father."

"Start his own pride," Blue repeated. "Sambah didn't mention King was an alpha, but maybe I should have asked by the way he spoke about him. Usually the firstborn is the alpha of the family."

"That's why he has so many siblings. *Insert laughter here*," Wyatt said, making air quotes. "I'm not apologizing. You kept me up all night when I was at death's door."

Christian snorted and lowered his head.

"Twelve sons and seven daughters," Blue added, telling me something I hadn't known. "Shifters live a long time, but usually at some point, they stop making babies. They like to sit back and enjoy the fruits of their labors. Sounds like Sambah was trying for a successor. No wonder he chose the name King. That's too bad."

"He says he was going down the stairs," Wyatt continued. "He suddenly got a terrible pain in his head that blinded him. He fell. When he hit the landing, he was still alive, but he couldn't call for help. The pain got worse, and then he couldn't breathe. After that, everything went black."

Blue cupped her hands over her mouth, appearing deep in thought as she stared at her feet. "Alphas are stronger. It doesn't make sense."

"Has anyone else in his family died under similar circumstances?" I asked. "Or of unknown causes?"

Wyatt shook his head. "Some people just have a bum ticker."

"I'm not sure that was a heart attack," I said. "It sounds more like a stroke. Did he have any other pain before it happened?"

Wyatt cocked his head to the side as he listened, and then he replied, "Just the chest pain, only it was different than before. Sharper and more intense."

"Sounds like a pulmonary embolism," Christian remarked. "But I can't say those happen at the same time as a clot in the brain. What are the odds?"

I shoved a short stack of papers aside that we had ruled out. I thought back to every interview. Some who were among the last to see the deceased alive made remarks about them not feeling well. "Chest pain, heartburn…," I muttered.

"Even Andy mentioned it," Blue said. "Remember that guy?"

"You mean the beta who threw a knife at me? Yeah, I remember."

I noticed Christian ease away from the desk.

Blue glanced down at the floor. "He said she was having chest discomfort and went to bed. That fits the pattern."

I fished his paper out of the stack. "Damn. I thought maybe his snitch of a packmate was right about him killing her. He seemed like the aggressive type."

"Could be some gene mutation." Blue sat cross-legged and lined up a few papers. "But they don't belong to the same animal species."

"Then we have to consider it might be contagious." I turned a paper clip between my fingers. "If that's the case, not everyone's getting infected—or at least, not everyone's dying from it. Maybe they're just carriers. But what do these people have in common? It can't be the same blood type, or we'd have a bigger list."

"How would *you* know?" Wyatt asked, staring at the empty space beside him. "I thought you only hung around your own kind."

Blue looked up. "What did he say?"

Wyatt rolled his chair back a little. "That there are a lot of alphas in your pile."

I stared at the papers, remembering Ren had mentioned a few alpha wolves. "Who does he recognize?"

Wyatt kept rolling backward. "He knows the young motorcycle guy—Rain. Met him in an Italian diner. And—slow down, you're talking too fast. They don't need to hear your life story." Wyatt changed direction and scooted toward us, still staring up at nothing.

I twisted my hair back. "Ferro mentioned his son was an alpha, so that's not a surprise. We're just not sure about his death. He fell off his motorcycle."

Wyatt spun his chair in a circle. "He says that boy wouldn't fall off that bike if you turned it upside down. And he also heard about the little alpha who drowned."

I perked up. "The boy was an alpha?"

"Alphas always know another alpha. Even children." Blue suddenly lurched forward and opened a file where we'd put a few photographs that were offered to us. Then she held one up. "She's a redhead. And so is the teenage girl. Do you think—?"

"Do I think what?" I asked. "The men could be alphas? That's possible. We didn't exactly ask everyone, and they probably didn't think it was relevant to mention. But what about the rest?"

"Redheads have a higher probability of producing alphas. Nobody knows why, but maybe it's something in their DNA. Something that makes them just as vulnerable to a virus as the alphas."

I tossed the paper clip onto the floor. "We need to make some calls."

Blue sat back and stroked her feather earring. "We have to play it cool. If we ask that kind of question, it'll raise a red flag."

"Everyone's got a phone these days," I said, mulling over an idea. "Why not ask them to send us a photo? People are discouraged from collecting pictures, but we know they probably have at least one."

Claude lifted his legs onto the couch and twisted so he was lying on his side, head propped in his hand. He was so tall that one leg hung over the armrest, the other bent at the knee. "I enjoy watching you females at work. It's better than a detective novel."

"Photos are a good idea," Blue said, ignoring him. "How do we verify if the males are alphas?"

"Compensation," Christian offered.

We all gave him the same "what planet do you live on?" look.

Striding toward us, he put his hands in his pockets. "If you're working on behalf of the higher authority, who has Shifters' best interests in mind, ask them if the victim is an alpha. They'll answer, to be sure. Alarm will set in, so that's when you give them assurance that the higher authority will offer compensation for the loss of an alpha for the obvious reasons."

I collected the loose paper clips. "We can't lie to these people. Not unless you want to make a ton of enemies."

"'Tis not a lie if you pay. Lenore and Viktor are quite chummy these days, and I'm certain he can twist her arm. Heaven knows she probably has an obscene amount of money to waste. Use her name if you're pressed, and we'll make it work."

A smile touched my lips. "I like the way you think, Mr. Poe."

He bowed.

Blue gathered up the papers. "Wyatt, give me your phone."

He frowned. "Not even a thanks?"

"Your friend did all the work."

He rolled all the way back to his desk. "See if I dial the dead for you again."

Chapter 23

As tempting as it was to call everyone right away, we had to take into consideration the late hour. I spoke to a few rogue Shifters, and Blue dialed three or four packs before putting off the rest until morning. The ones we offered compensation to bought the lie. It sounded like a move the higher authority would make to save face. Ren seemed a little skeptical about sending me a picture of his former packmate, but he still gave me what I needed.

Wyatt set up a temporary email address for those who didn't have photos saved on their phones. Blue and I camped out in his office all day, eagerly waiting for callbacks and emails. It was important that we were thorough, made no assumptions, and heard from everyone.

"Delivery girl!" Gem sang, skating into the room with white paper sacks in her hands. She did a twirl in front of my beanbag chair and handed one bag to me before skating over to the sofa and giving Blue the other.

"What about the drinks?" I asked.

She pulled her long duster to the side before plopping down on the sofa. "Niko's on his way up with the drinks. Since you're hard at work, we thought you might want everything while it's hot."

Blue unwrapped her bacon burger. "Thanks. Where's yours?"

"Alas, they didn't have the salad I wanted, so I'm making one later."

Blue held out her fries. "You can have these. I think two burgers will do it for me."

"Don't mind if I do." She happily accepted the large container.

Blue finished chewing a mouthful of burger. "Are you sure Viktor doesn't mind us eating in here?"

"He's got his hands full with all the kids," she said, her cheeks flushed. Some of the black liner around her violet eyes had smudged in the corners. "Shep and Wyatt are busy unloading food from the van. I think they're going to sit in the dining room, because Claude was looking for extra chairs earlier."

I pinched off a piece of cheese and ate it. "I bet Kira's having a heart attack over the junk food."

We all quietly snickered. Junk food made the stress melt away. The fries were deliciously salty, and the burger had the right amount of cheese and secret sauce. All I needed was a vanilla shake.

"Coyote Burger is the bomb," Blue said, staring at her half-eaten burger. "It's too bad they don't have more locations."

Niko walked in with a handsome grin on his face. "Who's thirsty?"

I raised my hand and then felt instantly stupid. "Everyone."

Niko approached with the cardboard carrier that held four drinks. I peered at the transparent lids and claimed the vanilla shake.

He approached the couch and sat between Gem and Blue.

"Thanks, amigo." Blue's cheeks hollowed as she sucked down the chocolate.

"Strawberry for me," Gem said. "Unless you want it."

Niko set the tray beside him. "I'm not picky. Whatever's left is fine."

Gem set her drink on the floor. "This is fun. We never get to eat dinner in here together."

Niko finished sipping his drink. "How are your calls coming along?"

"Almost done," Blue said, wiping sauce off her cheek. "Just a few people we can't get ahold of. We're also waiting on photographs. I think there are two left who haven't sent us anything."

I set down my burger and wiped my fingers on a napkin. "I think they're afraid of getting in trouble. King's ghost confirmed a few, so we didn't have to call those people. I still haven't been able to reach Harper."

Blue licked her thumb. "Harper was the woman you and Christian met at the bar?"

I nodded. "I guess she's busy with work. Either that or she's done talking about her dead mate. We're probably picking at old wounds."

While digging into my fries, I watched Wyatt saunter into the room with his drink and a fast-food bag. He sat down at his desk, switched on the computer, and opened up his desk drawer.

"So disgusting," Gem said as he cracked open a can of cheese dip.

"Another email," Wyatt announced.

I flew up from my seat and stared over his shoulder. "From who?"

"Some guy named Andy." Wyatt opened up the attachment and wolf whistled when a beautiful redhead smiled back at him. It looked like a private picture of Alisa, taken on the bed with her head resting on a pillow and a loving smile on her face.

"Well?" Blue asked.

I sighed and returned to my beanbag chair. "Yep."

Blue checked off her name from a list. "We're almost done."

Wyatt tore his bag into a flat square, poured two large fries in a pile, and then drizzled the cheese dip over them. If it weren't for his Gravewalker DNA, he would have needed a quadruple bypass. "Viktor's in a foul mood today," he said, stating what we'd already noticed. "Anyone know what's up?"

Blue coughed and reached for her drink. "He was supposed to go on a date with Miss Parrish tonight. But now he's preoccupied with finding those kids a permanent home."

Wyatt used a fork to shovel in some of the fries. "What about the packs you've visited?"

"Some are decent," she said. "But none were up to snuff. Nobody had a house big enough to accommodate that many kids, and a few of the Packmasters were too strict. Unless they're new, packs don't keep adding and adding. They establish a number of packmates, and when someone leaves, they fill the opening."

Wyatt spun his chair around, cheese on his chin. "Viktor was on the phone with Finn when we came in just now."

I furrowed my brow. "I thought Viktor wasn't involving anyone."

"Finn works for the higher authority," Wyatt explained.

"Why wouldn't he just go to Lenore?"

Blue finished sipping her drink. "Finnegan's a Shifter. I only met him once. He's young but smart. At the end of the day, Shifters trust each other more, and that's probably why Viktor called him."

"Is he a representative or a Regulator?" I asked.

"Neither. I think he's positioning himself for a seat, but those don't come into play very often. You have to know someone or pay your dues. He has a lot of access to files. Don't worry—we can trust him. He's related to some HALO members, so he knows all about secrecy. You're still pretty new, so you don't know everyone yet. I bet Viktor was asking if he knew anyone who could take the kids."

Niko removed a green throw pillow from behind his back and tossed it aside. "This home was built for children, but it's no longer a place for them. Though, I admit, I enjoy the sound of laughter in the courtyard. It reminds me how carefree life can be."

Blue wadded up her wrapper. "Life isn't carefree. The minute you let your guard down, everything's taken from you. Just remember why we're all here. And I doubt you could convince any of those abused kids that life is carefree."

"Yes," he agreed. "But it's an idyllic world we endeavor for. That's why we're all here—so one day our kind can enjoy the same life that many humans have."

"Humans have their own set of problems," I pointed out. "Granted, they're not battling Vampires or rogue Shifters who want to slaughter their families, but it's not always an easy life. I don't think we can ever create a perfect world, but maybe we deserve more perfect moments."

Gem raised her cup. "To perfect moments."

We all silently toasted.

Viktor walked in, dark circles under his hooded eyes. "This room smells like a dirty hamper."

Gem pointed at the floor beside him. "Wyatt took off his boots. I don't think he's cleaned those since the eighteenth century."

I reached in my bag for extra fries. "Any luck placing the kids?"

Blue cleared up the napkins and bags. "Come sit down." She fluffed an orange pillow just as he took a seat to her left. "Did you eat? I have an extra burger."

"I cannot eat. I have too much on my mind."

Holding my drink, I stretched my legs out and sighed. "We might have to split them apart."

Viktor rubbed his bleary eyes. "I spoke to a trusted friend who has access to information on local packs. He will keep our secret because exposing us would be exposing himself for accessing files he should not. I cannot place them with just anyone who has room—they must be good men. No troubles, no criminal backgrounds, enough room. But he was not able to find a pack that fits the criteria." Viktor rested his elbow on the couch arm and covered his eyes. "We have a moral obligation to these children."

"We'll come up with something," Blue promised him. "Sometimes when you think about a problem too much, you can't see the answer. Maybe if you just get some rest, the answer will come to you."

"She's right," Niko agreed. "We all want what's best for the children, and we'll find a solution. Your light is stressed. You don't want your wolf coming out at the wrong time."

Viktor folded his arms and muttered something.

"In *English*," Gem said softly.

"You are right," he said. "I am no good unless I sleep. Perhaps Matteo can take them back to the sanctuary."

"It's not the right place for them, Viktor. You know it." Blue handed him her drink. "That place is for Potentials, and they don't belong. They need parental figures. Shifter kids won't do well without proper guidance. The guardians there won't be able to help them through their first change or teach them how to control their animal. They'll never be fit to live in a pack if they didn't grow up in one. It'll be harder for them to be chosen by good Packmasters."

"You are right, my dear. I am just talking out loud. We are running out of options." He stretched his arms across the back of the couch and yawned. "You two are busy in here today."

Slumped in the beanbag, I stared up at the ceiling. "We think we've made a connection. We're still waiting on a few callbacks. I don't know what it means, but if everyone's an alpha or a redhead who can make an alpha, then we need to figure out the mystery before everyone else does."

"Perhaps you should consult the Relic," he suggested. "It is always best to take advice from a professional. He might have a better understanding. May the fates help us if it is bio warfare. Why does that not sound right?" Viktor repeated the phrase, testing it on his tongue.

"Biological warfare is correct." Gem noisily slurped her strawberry shake all the way to the bottom. "It could also be the beginning of a mutation."

Wyatt belched. "What's that supposed to mean? We're all mutations."

"Yes, but nobody knows if one Breed began another. Or did we all form separately? And we're not the only Breeds there have ever been. I've read ancient books that talk about species I've never seen nor heard of. The extinct ones."

Wyatt wiped his fingers on his shirt. "So you think natural selection is taking out Shifters? Seems a little drastic."

She tossed a pillow at him. "I never said I was a scientist. But think about it—the weather is always more intense where there's more Breed. We know it's true even though no one has ever done scientific studies on it. Remember that year a whole bunch of Shifters were relocated to that small town in California, and they had that drought and all the fires? So maybe that same type of energy is affecting our DNA. Not many cities have as many immortals as Cognito. What if we're actually harming ourselves by living in close proximity?"

Wyatt tossed the pillow back. "If that's true, then we're all screwed. Might as well start reserving our slots at the cemetery."

Viktor stood. "Let's not be dramatic." He crossed the room and paused in the doorway. "Speak to the Relic and see what he has to say. I have more calls to make in the morning. *Spokoynoy nochi*."

"Good night," Gem said in return.

When he left, I stole Viktor's spot. "Let me see the list."

Blue reached for the notebook next to Niko and handed it to me. We wrote down all the names, excluding those we ruled out as unrelated.

I set down the notebook. "I think we've got enough. We're only missing two."

"Yes, but what if those are the outliers?" she asked.

"Then we scrap the idea. But this is over our head. We need to call Graham and see what's going on. If he thinks it's contagious, he'll have ideas about how we should handle it or who we should turn it over to. There has to be someone who specializes in this stuff."

Gem curled up with her head on a purple pillow. "Don't forget, it could also be a genetic shift. Maybe it's not contagious. Or maybe they have a shared defect." She yawned noisily. "I couldn't find anything in my books that looks remotely similar. I wish I could help."

Blue rubbed her arms as if a draft had blown through, and I could only imagine her fears. What if her own blood was diseased and it was only a matter of time? Alphas supposedly had the most powerful blood and magic. If they all perished, and there was no one left to lead Shifter groups, it would be chaos. They might wind up wiping each other out before the virus did.

Blue rose to her feet. "You're right. We have enough evidence to connect the deaths. We might never hear from the remaining two. Let's call the Relic and see what we've got."

Chapter 24

WE CALLED GRAHAM, BUT HE couldn't meet us on such short notice. We made an appointment for Friday evening, and that gave us an extra two days to follow up on the final names on our list. I spent the next day in the rock-climbing room downstairs, trying to scale the walls without a safety harness. After falling twice, I hooked up and took my time until I reached the top. Climbing helped me focus and learn patience. I had a habit of wanting to rush things.

Sweaty and thirsty, I made my way to the kitchen.

"We need to buy a water dispenser for the gym," I said as I passed Shepherd, who was sipping a drink in one of the booths.

"Take a bottle down with you next time," he fired back.

Smart-ass.

I walked into the kitchen, grabbed a chilled bottle from the fridge, and returned to the dining room. Instead of joining him, I flipped a dining chair around at the head of the table and sat facing him. "Is Hunter with the other kids?"

"Switch is teaching them all at once so he can keep Hunter on his lesson plans."

I raised my eyebrows. "I thought they weren't comfortable around the men."

"They saw him teaching Hunter and got curious—wanted to learn what Hunter was learning. Switch has a way with kids. I guess I don't have that knack. They run screaming."

I chuckled softly. "Maybe you should shower. Or cover up all your tattoos."

"Maybe I should smile more."

I screwed the lid back onto my bottle. "No, don't do that. When you smile, you look like the guy in the action movie who just landed a chopper and is about to blow away fifty terrorists."

Shepherd lifted his cigarette. "And that's a bad thing?"

I perked my ears, listening for the kids. "Where are they?"

"Far end of the property in the woods. Some of them were getting brave and running down the halls, opening doors—they were all over the place. Kira went along, and they're doing some nature shit out there."

We both shut up when the front door slammed in the distance. There was a low murmur of conversation.

When Lenore floated in, I froze. Her beautiful blond hair was braided and wrapped around her head like a crown. My hair was wild and midnight black. She walked like royalty, her shoulders squared and grace in her step. I sat slumped with my legs apart. While her peach-colored dress was open down the front and held together by a few spaghetti strings, the matching crocheted jacket gave the illusion of modesty. There was nothing modest about my attire, and my shirt had sweat stains. Sometimes I didn't understand how Christian could be attracted to polar opposites.

She had a peculiar look in her eyes when she noticed me. "Raven, what a delight to see you again."

Shepherd jumped to his feet, bowed, and made a fast exit. I should have done the same, but my legs were sore, and I decided to let Viktor make the call. The dining room was a common area, not a private room.

He gestured toward me. "You know Raven." He flicked a glance down to my skimpy shorts.

I shrugged. "Sorry. I wasn't expecting company. You normally take your guests into the private rooms."

Lenore swung her gaze up to the unlit chandelier. "I find closed rooms so drab and stuffy. This room has just the right amount of light."

"I insisted on the library, but Miss Parrish is very persuasive."

Viktor looked nervous. A perceptive Vampire could pick up a

racing heartbeat or pupil fluctuations. He didn't ever behave this way around Lenore, so I knew it had to do with all the children. That was probably where Shepherd had run off to—to make sure they stayed far away from the house until Lenore left.

"I bet you raced down the stairs again," I said, providing an explanation for the beads of sweat on his brow. "You should let one of us answer when Wyatt buzzes someone in. I don't mind."

He nodded and gave me an appreciative look.

Lenore moved to the chair on my right and waited until Viktor pulled it out for her. Funny—she had given me every reason to believe that she wasn't a woman who relied on men for anything.

When Viktor moved to sit across from her, I stood. "I'll leave you two alone."

"Do let her stay," Lenore said sweetly. "After everything you told me about Raven rescuing those Shifters and shutting down the cage fights, nothing would please me more."

Viktor gestured for me to sit, so I flipped the chair around and sat. I wasn't feeling particularly social, but I had to be on my best behavior around Viktor.

Lenore folded her hands, her nail color matching her dress precisely. "I hope you're giving Raven the vacation she deserves."

Viktor chuckled. "Raven is not one to sit idly."

"He speaks highly of you," Lenore informed me. "Viktor sings praises of all his people, but I think he has favorites."

"Don't be ridiculous." Viktor gave me a diplomatic look. "All of my people are talented in different ways. What kind of leader would I be if I favored one over the other?"

But Lenore's cryptic grin led me to believe that maybe Viktor boasted about me in private after all. He always pulled Christian in on more jobs than anyone else. He spent private time with Gem with her translations, so I always felt out of the loop. I'd always imagined myself as a thorn in his side—a necessary evil he needed to keep around for the good of the team but a ticking time bomb he would eventually want to dispose of. He definitely didn't play favorites, but knowing he bragged about me in private conversations was strangely reassuring.

"What brings you here this time of day so unexpectedly?" Viktor asked, not mincing words. I could tell he was annoyed with her unannounced visit this time, perhaps having second thoughts about encouraging personal drop-ins.

She tilted her head slightly as if searching for the right words. "Several packs are under the impression that I will be providing them with monetary compensation for the loss of an alpha. Do you know where they could have come up with such an outlandish idea?"

Viktor began to shake his head but then searched my eyes.

I gave him a guilty look. Viktor didn't always want to know every tiny detail about our cases while under investigation, but maybe we should have run this one by him first. I steadied my gaze on Lenore, careful not to suggest that Viktor wasn't in the know. "I needed a cover. To be honest, it was Christian's idea. He thought with you being new, it would be a good way to make an impression with the local Shifters. It's not easy to win people over, but money talks. We should have given you a heads-up, but I didn't think anyone would be calling you this soon."

It hadn't even been twenty-four hours since Blue and I had made those calls. Fucking hell, these guys were quick to check us out and make sure we weren't lying to them.

Viktor glanced at his vodka bottle across the room, but he probably knew getting a drink would only invite her to stay longer. "I will, of course, be handling all the payments. We would never impose in such a way."

Lenore slid her gaze from Viktor back to me and finally said, "Now that I know someone's not pulling a fast one on me, it's no trouble at all. I'm the one who volunteered the idea of using the higher authority as a cover. In fact, I think it's a splendid idea. Not only can we make amends with the locals, but it's also an opportunity for me to make personal connections." She looked across the table at Viktor and canted her head to one side. "I do think it would be best to include me on your plans the next time so I'm not taken by surprise. When three messages mentioned your people by name, I knew you could solve the mystery."

"Apologies," he said. "It was a very late night."

Viktor was clever not to lie to Lenore. Would she be able to see it as easily as a Chitah could smell it? He could have told her that we planned to call, and that might have smoothed things over, but he danced around the apology like a professional ballerina. Or were men called ballerinos?

"So this was *Christian's* idea." Lenore was impossible to read, but she remained amiable, leading me to believe she wasn't as opposed to the idea as I'd thought. "It'll win over some of the powerful Packmasters in the region to know that the higher authority has their best interests at heart. I'll have to make financial arrangements, but I need you to confirm each person who called. I'm assuming this is an exclusive list? Do tell me more."

"I'm afraid we cannot divulge explicit details of all our cases," Viktor said, leaning back. "It would bore someone of your high intelligence. We work so many jobs. Many are small and keep us busy. Very, very busy." He glanced at his watch.

"Of course." Lenore rose from the table. "I know enough. Since I don't want to take up your valuable time, would you mind if I stole Raven for an hour or two? I know you have plenty of work to do, but I'm judging by her appearance that she has a little free time this afternoon. Did you tell her I was your primary contact for the last assignment?"

My eyebrows popped up. "Is that why Christian was guarding you?" Now it made sense. If Lenore had helped, that would have inadvertently made her a target, especially since some of her peers were involved in the fights. "I thought maybe you'd made a bunch of enemies."

She laughed melodically. "I do enjoy your sense of humor."

I shivered, having a weird sense of déjà vu.

"Perhaps you should shower and put on something decent," Lenore suggested.

I caught Viktor's look, and he knew how precious every second was. They needed to keep the kids away from the house and quiet. Viktor was smitten with Lenore but not enough to trust her with his livelihood. That was telling.

I stood and pushed in the chair. "Since it's your invitation, you'll have to take me as I am. If I go upstairs to shower, I'll wind up taking a nap. That's my routine, and I've been working out all day. Just give me a couple of seconds to wash my armpits in the kitchen sink."

The sheer look of horror on her face made every bit of my uncouth behavior worth it.

Lenore owned a white Rolls-Royce. She also had a black car, but this one definitely fit her style. The back doors opened the opposite way, and I'd never seen anything so classy.

"It's a 1948," she said, running her hand across the interior wood paneling like one of those game show models. "Mint condition. I had to restore the leather bench, but isn't it a dream?"

I pointed at a cabinet door in the center. "Is that where you keep the booze?"

Her black eyes sparkled as she studied me. "How did you know?"

"I've seen a lot of old movies, I guess."

My dad would have loved this old car even though he would have called it a prissy waste of money. Deep down, he admired vehicles kept in their original condition.

"Have a drink with me," she insisted, opening the cabinet and placing two glasses on a tray that lowered from the back of the front seat. "Is bourbon all right?"

"It's fine."

She handed me one and clinked her glass against mine. "To unexpected friendships."

I wouldn't have gone that far, but I kept quiet and gulped down my drink. Christian was right about keeping enemies close. Though, truth be told, I wasn't sure if Lenore was friend or foe. I hated the bitch, but that was when she was after Christian. Now that she had her sights on Viktor, I didn't feel threatened by her. She helped sell my necklace at auction and lent me money. That didn't mean I trusted her either, but I was in her debt for that damn loan. It was wiser to have a good rapport with someone I owed a favor to, so I had to play it smart.

When I set my empty glass down, her eyes settled on my necklace. "Do you wear that all the time, even when you're sweaty?"

I gave her a sly grin. "Especially when I'm sweaty."

"Dear, oh dear. You should take better care of precious things."

"The chain is unbreakable."

"But your neck is not."

I stiffened at that remark.

Lenore chuckled softly. "I'm only saying if that necklace were to ever get hung up on something, what would happen to your neck?"

"It's long enough that I can slip it off if that were to happen, but thanks for thinking of ways to avoid my decapitation. That's not always the first thing that comes to mind when I'm admiring someone's necklace."

She savored her drink. "One has to be practical. You can't always keep something you love close if it might be the death of you."

I set down my empty glass and glanced out the window. "Where are we going?"

"It's a surprise."

As the car turned, grassy fields came into view. A tree here and there, sometimes a bench. Eventually we came to a stop.

"Oh goody. We're here." Lenore waited for the driver to open her door.

I shoved my door open and climbed out. Small waves lapped against the shore, and though the water was blue, there was a murky smell to it.

Lenore hooked her arm in mine and led me toward the shore. "I prefer the ocean and salty air on my tongue, but this will have to do."

"Isn't this a little blinding for you?"

The sun shimmered on the water like a million mirrors.

"Nonsense. I'm an old Vampire. When you're my age, you simply build up a tolerance for the intolerable."

The driver waited by the car as we walked down a gentle slope of grass until we reached the muddy banks. Lenore left her high heels in the grass, lifted the hem of her dress with one hand, and walked close enough for the waves to splash over her feet.

I stayed closer to dry land, not wanting stinky lake mud to cake all over my black sneakers. Strong wind plastered my hair to one side, but damn, it felt good.

"Viktor didn't know about your little financial arrangement, did he?" she asked.

"He's the boss. He knows everything."

Lenore smiled at me. "You're a better liar than he is. Why do you think I prefer meeting people face-to-face instead of using these confounded telephones? I can pick up tiny fluctuations in their breathing and heart rate, but to be honest, most people who lie give the same exact signals."

I stepped onto a flat rock and faced her. "Does it really matter? We work cases nonstop, and Viktor's too busy to know every detail. He trusts us."

A few tendrils freed themselves from the braided work of art on Lenore's head. "Maybe I find it curious that he protects his people… even from me. What does a woman have to do to gain that man's trust?"

"Seduce him?" I said facetiously.

"Is that what you do?"

I stepped off the rock and strolled away. "I don't use my sexuality to get what I want."

"Yes you do. We all do. Their weakness is our power." She matched my stride, her toes filthy with mud and tiny pebbles stuck to them.

"Maybe that's true for some men, but that's not how it works with Viktor. I earned his trust by doing the job."

"Perhaps I've been going about this the wrong way. I thought he wanted a woman of equal power, but maybe he's old-fashioned and desires a little dominance."

"I'm not interested in your love life, and to be honest, I think there are other men who are more your speed. I know he comes across as polished, but Viktor's a down-to-earth kind of guy. His version of fun is having a drink and telling boring stories about his boyhood. He likes sweater vests, hates electricity, tells bad jokes, and loves to jog."

"And exactly what kind of man do you think is my match?"

"Some rich asshole who throws big parties and travels the world in a private jet."

"A dime a dozen."

"Viktor's a workaholic."

"I'm realizing that. So, woman to woman, how can I impress Viktor and show him my true intentions? You know him better than most, and I don't know the others in the group well enough to solicit their opinion."

"You've got a good start with the vintage wine. Liquor him up and turn on the charm. Isn't that what you're doing?"

Lenore stopped me. "Why do I get the impression you don't approve of this match? I can't say I approved of yours, but one has to move on. Perhaps you have feelings for Viktor you're bottling up."

I erupted with laughter and turned back the way we came. Just the idea that I could be attracted to a man who wore silk pajama pants and a robe to bed was too much.

"You shouldn't allow Christian to shape your opinions," she said in the way a friend might when giving advice. "He doesn't want me to find happiness because of our history. But you and I have no history."

"Christian doesn't tell me what to feel."

"I'm relieved. I know how much you admire Viktor, and a man like him deserves happiness. If Christian secretly plans to sabotage our coupling, I hope that you'll have enough common sense to stop him. It would be a selfish cause, and it might destroy Viktor. He's more fragile than you think. And you should consider how one person's influence could affect your future. Always think for yourself. Contrary to what some believe, it's not a betrayal of love to have opposing beliefs or opinions."

"I'm not trying to keep you two apart. I just think it's an odd match. I like Viktor, and I don't want to see him get hurt. Don't get your hopes up for anything long-term. Keystone means a lot to him, and I don't know how well a serious relationship would work out."

"I've wondered the same about you and Christian. A woman like yourself would be better matched with a man in power."

The hair on the back of my neck stood up, and I had that weird feeling in the pit of my stomach again. This didn't feel right. I shouldn't be out here talking to Lenore about Viktor. I didn't want to influence his personal life—that could drastically backfire on me. What if Lenore told Viktor that I tried talking her out of their relationship? *Fuck.* Was she doing this to hold something over me?

"I should get back," I said, climbing the hill.

"Can I trust you won't drive a wedge between Viktor and me? You have to put aside your personal feelings and let people make their own choices. Viktor's a catch. There aren't many other men in this city I'm better matched with in terms of power and money."

"What about love?"

"Love is irrelevant. It's the other qualities you share with a partner that matter more. Trust, loyalty, affection, and companionship. I'm sure if you think about it, those are the things you value most with Christian."

"Actually, I'm fond of the hot sex."

Lenore stopped. "You're beginning to sound like him. Viktor sees a lot of potential in you, as do I. Just be careful. Bad influences rub off on people like mud."

I swiveled around, my gaze settling on her dirty feet. "I'll see myself home. I've got a few errands to run, and I like walking. Thanks for the scenic ride."

"Raven, it behooves me to pay those Shifters, especially after the egregious mistakes the higher authority made over the past few months. I'm a classy lady, and I'll stay true to my word. But don't pull a stunt like that again without consulting me first. You can't play with a person's money and reputation that way."

"You got it."

She strolled to the back of the car and rested her arm on the open door. "It was a pleasant surprise running into you, Raven. I have a feeling we'll be seeing a lot more of each other."

Perish the thought.

Chapter 25

AFTER MY CONVERSATION WITH LENORE, I walked to a nearby bar and sat down to think. I didn't have my purse or wallet, so it was just like the old days. Only now I wasn't hopping from table to table, suckering men out of a meal. In retrospect, my desperation must have been an undesirable perfume. Immortals must prefer the scent of aloofness, because one after another kept approaching my table or sending me drinks. I didn't accept their advances. I just sipped on my complimentary water and pondered our case.

If we could confirm this was a virus, who would we report it to? There were multiple Shifter Councils for each territory, and the higher authority was set up similarly except in different cities. We didn't have a Breed CDC or health department. We could set off a widespread panic. Even if it didn't wipe out all Shifters, taking out the alphas would do irreparable damage to the structured world surrounding them. Alphas ran packs. Period. Without them, Shifters would murder each other for that position in a constant battle for power. Some of the animal groups would break apart, and the Council only sold large plots of land to reputable alphas who formed a family unit. Would the Council revoke land from the dissolved groups? Would a war be imminent in a battle for land? What responsibility did Keystone have in all this? I wondered if Viktor would decide that nothing good would come out of revealing something we didn't have the science to stop.

When I felt time slipping away, I left the bar and strolled down the busy street. A man was playing a Pink Floyd song on a guitar, the setting sun encasing him in golden light. I passed a fortune-teller shop that, come to find out, was mostly run by Sensors. Deciding to take a shortcut, I jumped on the back of a moving truck to hitch a ride home. The idiot behind me was recording me on his cell phone, and I wished we didn't have all this technology. It made it difficult for me to flash. If something like that was caught on video, we had insiders who could shut down accounts and make videos disappear, but we still had to be careful about using our powers in public.

After a while, the truck put on its left-hand blinker, and I stepped off. Close to home, I flashed part of the way and walked the rest. Wyatt buzzed me through the gate, and as I strutted up the driveway, I noticed Christian standing on the upper balcony. He remained as still as a statue, his hands gripping the stone railing, his gaze fixed on my every move.

When I walked in, Gem flashed toward the east wing, presumably heading to her secret study. On the upper landing of the staircase, a little red-haired girl tossed a blue rubber ball. It bounced on three steps before it hit the edge and changed its trajectory. Hunter, who was at the bottom, dove after it like a baseball player. Both were in pajamas, although the girl wore an old-fashioned gown that someone must have found in one of the storage rooms.

She giggled at Hunter's feeble attempts, and it dawned on me that the same fate that had befallen our victims could affect her too. Maybe the best thing for Shifters to do was isolate.

"Raven." Niko greeted me as he entered the room from the hall ahead. "One of the children is missing. It's bedtime, and she ran off while they were brushing their teeth."

Hunter looked at me pleadingly, one finger over his lips. He knew Niko was blind, but Niko wasn't so blind that he wouldn't notice that girl's energy at the top of the stairs once he turned around.

Did I really want to encourage Hunter to be deceptive? I'd probably regret it in the long run, so I said, "It's time for you kids to say good night. You can play in the morning. The sooner you go to sleep, the sooner you can wake up to play."

The little girl jogged down the steps, gave Hunter a big hug, and dashed past Niko and down the hall.

Niko had on his oversized drop-crotch pants he often wore to sleep, so it looked like everyone was winding down for the night.

"Would you like to join me in the kitchen for hot tea?" he asked.

"I need to see where we are with the case. If I get hungry, I'll buy something from Wyatt's vending machine with my retirement money." I directed my attention to the boy. "Hunter, do you want us to walk you to bed? Where's your dad?"

Niko swept his hair away from his face. "Shepherd's guarding the hall while Switch and I search for the girl. Hunter, I think your father is a very sleepy old man. Can you help him to bed?"

Hunter slapped his hand over his mouth, covering his smile.

Shepherd strutted into the room, a five-o'clock shadow dusting his face. For some reason, he was wearing a green shirt and camouflage pants.

"What's with the getup?" I asked since that wasn't his usual style.

He stopped at the foot of the stairs and stretched his muscular arms. "The kids wanted to play war. Guess who was the enemy?"

I snorted. "Did they beat you up?"

"Fuck Wyatt and all his water balloons. Sorry, kid," he said, shifting his focus to Hunter. "I'm trying not to say those words."

"My dad said those words all my life," I said, hands on my hips. "I turned out fine."

He gave me a deliberate look before kneeling in front of Hunter.

I inched closer to Niko and lowered my voice. "What was that about?"

Niko canted his head toward me. "Some of the kids started repeating Shepherd's vocabulary, and it upset Viktor. You missed a colorful dinner conversation."

"I'll bet."

"He doesn't worry about Hunter since Hunter doesn't talk. But try convincing fifteen children."

Shepherd held Hunter's wrist. "Why are you covering your mouth?"

Hunter shrugged.

"Did someone hit you? Let me see."

When he pulled Hunter's hand away, everything looked normal. No bruising, no scrapes. Those were typical injuries you saw when kids got together.

"You had me worried, little man." Shepherd poked Hunter in the belly, and Hunter giggled and smiled wide.

When he did, I barked out a laugh. "Looks like someone lost a tooth."

Shepherd lightly held his chin and looked at it. "When did that happen?"

Hunter shrugged.

"Did he swallow it?" I asked.

Shepherd heaved a sigh. "Oh shit."

"You think the tooth fairy makes toilet-bowl pickups?" I laughed as I ascended the stairs. "G'night."

When I glanced back, Shepherd gave Hunter a hug and said quietly, "I love you."

That was probably the first time I'd ever heard him say it, and it made my heart melt a little.

"Hunter will make Shepherd a better man," Niko said, catching up with me.

"I thought you were going to make tea."

"Maybe later." When we reached the second floor, he said, "Hunter has softened him in a good way."

"Yeah. Kids have a way of changing people. My dad was always a good father, but when he became my sole guardian, he tried to do better. I can't say he always made the right choices, but Shepherd reminds me of him."

"I think having the children here has been good for Hunter. His light is brighter when he's around them."

"Kids need to be around other kids."

"It will be hard for him when they leave."

We climbed up another set of stairs to the third floor. "Maybe Switch can invite him to hang out with his old pack. He used to teach a lot of kids, and I bet they miss him. It might be good for Hunter to get out and make new friends, especially since we can't invite anyone over for a playdate."

"A play what?"

"Just a human phrase for getting the kids together. Who knows? Maybe Switch and Shepherd will get along better. Everyone's nice to Switch, but he still feels like an outsider here since he's staff and not part of the team. There's not much we can do about the reality, but it wouldn't hurt for us to hang out once in a while outside the house."

"I think that's an excellent idea. Hunter has a lot to learn outside of books, and I would imagine there are valuable lessons Shepherd must teach him about being a Sensor. He wears protective gloves in public, but he doesn't interact with people when we're out. Taking him on these... playdates would foster that unique education."

"Maybe I can take him to see my dad sometime. Crush is great with kids, and now he's got a dog. I bet Hunter would get a kick out of that mutt."

"Perhaps your father can look at Shepherd's car. I noticed a sound coming from the engine the last time we went out."

"Tell him to take it to Graves Auto Repair. My dad doesn't just work on bikes. My truck is older than dirt, but it purrs like a kitten."

"It sounds more like a lion to me."

I laughed and eyed the door to the balcony. "Since your room is on the second floor, can you let Blue and Wyatt know I'm back? I'm guessing there isn't any news, or you would have mentioned it. If they need me, they can knock on my door. I'm more exhausted than I thought and need to lie down."

He bowed. "As you wish."

"Old man," I muttered, musing over his joke about Shepherd. "That's the pot calling the kettle black. How old are you again?" I opened the door.

Niko casually walked away. "I better hurry back before my knees give out on me. My arthritis has been acting up," he said from a distance.

When I walked onto the interior balcony, Christian greeted me with a smoldering look.

"Niko's quite the comedian," he remarked.

I breezed by him to the other door. "He's not as funny as the man who's standing outside like a dad waiting for his daughter to come home from her date."

He shadow walked past me, snaking his way down the dark hall until he stopped by a candle in the distance. With his shoulder against the wall, he stood there, waiting for me to catch up.

"And what are you looking at, Mr. Poe?"

"Just admiring your gams."

"That word is so last century."

He turned on his heel to walk alongside me. "What can I say? I'm an old-fashioned man."

"What were you doing out there?"

"Wyatt's playing that infernal music again."

"Air Supply?"

"Aye. Probably pining over an old lover."

I walked into my bedroom and grabbed the matches on the dresser. "I guess Blue's keeping an eye on the mailbox then." I lit the lanterns, including a few candles in the fireplace. The light emphasized every crevice and crack in the stone walls. I sat on the scarlet bedspread, kicked off my sneakers, and lay down, staring up at the painting above the headboard. The bleak, grey landscape reminded me of what Houdini had said: live in the grey. The red trees suddenly looked like blots of violence.

Christian sat facing me, his back against the headboard. "You were gone for a while. Where have you been?"

I clasped my hands behind my head. "Can we not be that couple? I have to learn to trust you, and you have to trust me. I know you were gone today, and I don't know where. You promised me you wouldn't go to the White Owl, and I believe you. So that's why I'm not asking."

"On my word, I haven't been. I won't go there again."

I took off his shoe and then his sock. "I didn't ask, Mr. Stinky Feet."

"I beg your pardon? My feet are as pristine as the nuns of Vatican City."

I propped his foot on my chest and began rubbing the sole. Christian didn't have smelly feet, and even if he did, I wouldn't care. I just loved pushing his buttons.

"Mmm. I like that, Precious. You have the hands of a saint and the mouth of a sinner." He glanced at the floor. "I won't ask where you've been, but that's a curious amount of mud on the bottom of your shoes considering it hasn't rained recently."

"Shut up and rub my feet."

My legs parted when he rested my foot on his stomach, and I caught his gaze wandering up to my tight black shorts. It didn't take long before I felt something hard growing beneath my leg. Ignoring the passion stirring between us, I continued rubbing his foot until he fell in my thrall. Christian closed his eyes and stopped my massage.

"Lenore popped in this afternoon."

"Do you mind? I'm in the middle of a fantasy, and you bring up that woman." He opened his eyes when I didn't say anything. "All right. What did she say?"

"Some of those Shifters wanted their money and didn't waste time calling her. We should have told Viktor sooner. I thought you were going to talk to him."

"I haven't seen him since returning. Perhaps the children sent him to an early grave."

"Anyhow, Lenore seemed okay with it. She's going to pay everyone who goes through our approval process."

"Of course she's all right with it. It's good PR. Despite her balking, Lenore considers public relations to be one of the most important things in life. I have no doubt if there was a Breed newspaper, she'd arrange a feature on the front page about her contribution."

Christian's erection lost its enthusiasm.

"It made us look bad in front of Viktor. I'm not sure if he would have agreed to it even if she did, but we can't do something like that again. It was a great idea and got people to trust us, but we did it ass-backward. Something like that could backfire on us, and even you warned me not to make enemies with Lenore."

He gave me a pointed look. "Did she speak to you?"

"They both asked me to stay in the dining room. That's how Viktor found out. He lied for us."

Christian's head thumped against the headboard, and he cursed under his breath. "I meant to speak with him today, but I didn't think those shitebags would be calling so fast to collect. Was he cross?"

"I don't know. It could have made him look bad in front of a higher authority member, like he didn't know what the hell we were doing behind his back. I'm not sure with them dating if that makes it better or worse. We need to watch our step."

Christian continued rubbing my foot. "I'll speak to him later and smooth things over. 'Twas my idea, so I'll accept the blame." He patted my foot and sighed. "Do you want to get that, or shall I?"

"Get what?"

A knock sounded at the door.

I pinched his little toe. "I hate it when you do that."

When the door unexpectedly opened, I rolled to my side.

Blue paused at the threshold. "Sorry to bother you. I just got a message from the Boring pack. I think it was that scrawny guy who suggested that Andy killed his mate."

I sat up. "What did he say?"

"He says Alisa was secretly pregnant. He overheard the Packmaster talking about it before her death. The snitch thinks it was someone else's baby, and that's why Andy killed her."

"But she fits all the criteria."

Blue leaned against the doorjamb. "Yeah, it's just sad. The pregnancy is worth mentioning to the Relic. We might have to consider that one a question mark."

"Thanks for the cheery news," Christian said, tossing one of my socks to the floor.

Blue chuckled under her breath. "I'll let you two get back to whatever it is that you're doing."

When the door closed, I crawled next to Christian and nestled against his warm chest.

He stroked my hair before giving my shoulder a light squeeze. "If it's a virus, there's something else to consider."

"And what's that?"

"Viktor might perish."

I shook my head. "He's not an alpha."

"Aye. But who is to say what comes next? You can't control a microscopic enemy. First it's the alphas, but does it stop there?"

Chapter 26

ON FRIDAY NIGHT WE LEFT early to meet with Graham. Blue and I were eager to present our findings now that we'd found a link between the deaths.

"I hope he knows a specialist." Blue gripped the window crank and rolled up her window. "I bet there are secret labs that study this kind of thing."

"And I bet there are secret labs that cook it," I suggested.

"Why the hell did you take this case? I don't want this responsibility. If this is a virus and people find out we were involved, they'll blame us. They'll either say we didn't do anything soon enough or that we were the ones who started it. That's how this always goes." She wound up her long hair and tied it in a messy knot. "I guess Harper is the only one left on my list. Has she called?"

I glanced at the backup phone Wyatt had given me. "Not yet."

"Do you remember anything about your conversation with her that would suggest Bono was an alpha?"

I turned the steering wheel at a light and tried to recall every detail. "I think she said something about how he couldn't start his own pack, and nobody wanted him in theirs, but she might have been implying that he *wasn't* an alpha."

Blue pointed toward a brightly lit corner. "This is it. I'll look for him while you park."

It was Friday night in the human district. Neon lights drew people to the pizza shops, theater, arcades, diners, and bars. A group crossed in front of my truck, one woman stopping to adjust her bra straps.

"It could be a while," I grumped. "Looks like all the parking spaces are taken up. I'm going to have to circle around and see if there's anything open."

"Try valet somewhere."

"Fuck that. I'm not giving a stranger the keys to my truck."

"Shall I kidnap him so we can go somewhere else?"

"Please do."

Blue got out and looked toward the hot dog stand. "I see him. Do you want me to fill him in or wait for you?"

I honked my horn at a drunken idiot who decided the front end of my truck was something he could lean on while chatting with his friend. "Go ahead and start. I don't want to reschedule if he's got other appointments. I'll see if I can find a tiny car like Wyatt's and park on top of it."

"Good luck." Blue laughed and shut the door.

I coasted down the street and turned right at the hot dog stand. There were designated parking spots on the street, but most people took the train to this side of town due to the lack of parking. The few open garages were valet parking only.

A group of twentysomething girls lingered by a Porsche to take selfies. Relieved that I'd finally found a parking spot, I waited patiently despite all the honking cars behind me. The girls did their sexiest poses, all decked out in their cutest skirts and heels. It felt like an alternate reality. I could have easily been one of them had I not met Houdini. They were so blissfully unaware of all the secrets in the world living right beneath their noses. When they finally walked around the Porsche to cross the street, I got pissed off it wasn't their car and blared my horn. One girl shot me the middle finger.

I circled the block and kept going farther until I was ready to park in a tow zone. "We should have taken the subway," I sang, regretting we hadn't researched the location. While I'd grown up in Cognito, I hadn't been everywhere. I knew about this area of the city, but it wasn't my scene. It was too crowded and geared toward social groups. By the time I found a spot, I'd turned in so many circles that I didn't know where the hell I was anymore.

My thin jacket had a lot of pockets. It was actually Wyatt's—the first thing I grabbed from the coat closet. One of the phones vibrated against my chest. I should have let it go to voicemail, but we were waiting for just one more call. I dove between two buildings to escape the loud music pouring out of one of the taverns.

"Hello?"

"Raven gave me this number. Is this her?"

"Yes. Who am I speaking to?"

"This is Harper Nichols. We met at—"

"I know who you are. How have you been?" I took a seat on some empty crates.

"As well as can be expected. I have my moments. Talking with you really brought up all those feelings again. Then I got your message, and I didn't know if I wanted to keep reliving it. A girl has to move on."

"I'm sorry. We should have been more thorough. You mentioned he couldn't start his own group. What did you mean by that?"

After a long pause, Harper finally replied. "Bono couldn't start his own pack because of me. People didn't understand why he chose someone who can't have children. To be blunt, they didn't get why he chose a life mate who was born a man. I'm a woman, but people don't understand it. All Shifters and Chitahs care about is continuing their line—making sure that we don't go extinct. So when one of us mates with even a Vampire or a Mage, you'll get a lot of cold stares. Good packs won't take you in, and going out to eat in a nice place is basically hell. Men like Bono are seen as traitors."

"I'm sorry."

"Aren't we all? Bono was a good man. And yes, he was a good alpha."

I reclined my head against the brick wall. There we had it. Everyone on our list who fit the criteria was either an alpha or a redhead. "The higher authority wants to offer compensation to the families of alphas."

"You don't say?"

A couple ducked into the alley and began making out. His hand was up her shirt; her hand was up his. It smelled like musty old cardboard and vomit. Apparently the perfect spot to romance a woman.

"Do you mind? I'm on the phone," I snapped, irritated by the intrusion. The couple laughed and wandered off. "I'm really sorry, Harper. If it means anything, you'll get the money despite all the bullshit you put up with. I'll see to it."

"Keep the money. Even if Bono had settled with a fertile wolf, there's no guarantee he would have fathered children. He was passionate, affectionate, but very impotent. He didn't climax very often, and I know that's more than you asked for, but I have no secrets. Bono's condition had nothing to do with his desire or mind—it was just how his body was wired. He worried that he wasn't enough. But he was my everything."

"It sounds like he had a good woman. Are you sure you don't want the money? You might change your mind."

"No, honey. If they couldn't accept us when he was alive, I won't take payment for his death. I guess meeting you was the kick in the pants I needed to finally box up the last of his things. It's silly the stuff you keep around when somebody dies. Their razors, an old pair of shoes, their favorite ice cream. I couldn't bring myself to throw it away even though I don't like peppermint. It was the last thing he wanted, so I just held on to it. Anyhow, some of his personal effects I donated to a friend, but I don't know what to do with his medication."

"Toss it."

"It's not the stuff you buy in the store. It's a special heartburn medicine. He got it from someone he knew. Seems like such a waste if it could help someone else. Do you know anyone who needs it?"

I sat forward, suddenly remembering how Andy had mentioned

giving Alisa heartburn medicine before finding her dead. "Who gave it to him?"

"I don't have a clue. He just mentioned it in passing. I think he was trying to find pills that worked for impotency but wound up with these instead. There are only a few left."

"Hold on to those and I'll get back to you. I really appreciate the callback. And why don't you think about the money? I don't want you to feel pressured about making a decision only to regret it. Give it a few days."

"I won't change my mind. But can you donate the money in his name? A good charity."

"What about an orphanage for unwanted children? Or is that… insensitive?"

After a beat, Harper replied, "Bono would have liked that."

"I'll see to it. By the way, you left your cigarette case at the bar. It has an inscription. What's your address?"

"Keep it."

"Are you sure? It looks sentimental."

"I kept what matters. Bono always wanted me to quit anyway."

"I'll hold on to it in case you change your mind."

"You're sweet. Have a nice life, Raven. And if you ever need a boost in the bedroom, you know who to call."

I chuckled softly. "I just might do that." After hanging up, I immediately dialed Wyatt. "Hey, is your ghost still there?"

"A hello would be nice," he replied.

"Wyatt, I need you to ask him something. I don't think this is a natural virus or genetic defect. I think someone's infecting people."

"Now that's a twist I didn't see coming. Hold on."

I paced back and forth between the buildings, rock music thumping in the background. A car horn beeped a few times, some girls cheered, and a beer bottle shattered.

"Welcome to Dialing the Dead. My name is Wyatt Blessing, and I'll be your spirit guide."

"Ask King if he took any medicine for his heartburn. Not the boiling root stuff but real medicine."

Wyatt repeated my question, and then there was a minute of silence. "He had some pills."

"Put me on speaker. Did he get them at the store?"

"No," Wyatt said. "He says human medicine isn't strong enough."

"Does he remember who gave it to him? Was it someone in his pride or did he buy them on the street?"

After a few seconds, Wyatt replied, "His father believed in natural healing and wouldn't have approved, so he got them from a Relic."

I stopped. "Was his name Graham Wiggins?"

"Yes. He wants to know how you knew."

Graham had mentioned how he peddled medicine on the side. Not unusual for a Relic, but why wouldn't he have mentioned treating King? Especially since he didn't work for the Freeman pride? Maybe he didn't want to get in trouble with Sambah for sneaking around behind his back. King must have mentioned how his family didn't approve of Western medicine, but something didn't feel right. In fact, it felt very, very wrong.

"Thanks. That's all I needed."

After hanging up, I sent Blue a quick text message.

> **Raven:** Ask Graham if he prescribed meds to the victims. Be careful.
> **Blue:** Where are you?
> **Raven:** On my way. Don't let him leave.

As soon as Blue hopped out of Raven's truck, she stepped onto the sidewalk and made her way toward the hot dog stand. While she hadn't spent any time in this area of town, she'd flown over it a few times. Young people flitted from one bar to another, but it was also a spot for lovers. Many were presumably on their first or second date, awkwardly holding hands and stealing glances at each other. Human courting rituals were so strange to her. Blue walked beneath the bright lights strung up all around the hot dog stand. The shop was nothing more than a long building with service windows. Most customers took their meals and walked off, but a few sat at the round outdoor tables.

She approached Graham and pulled out a chair. "Raven's having trouble with parking, so she'll be here in a minute."

"Have you been here before?" he asked. "The hot dogs are delicious. Delicious! I took the liberty of ordering for you." Graham handed her a wrapped hot dog from his pile before tackling his fries. "It's on me. Payback for the last meal. That cup is plain soda and the other is grape. You get first choice."

Blue took the plain soda. "Thanks."

The smell of hot dogs and french fries made places like these irresistible to pass by. She hadn't grown up with processed food, and maybe that was why it was so addictive to her. She pulled away the silver wrapping that kept her meal toasty warm.

"I put mustard on it," Graham said. "Hope you're not one of those ketchup people. I can go back and get another if it's not what you want."

"No, this is perfect. I love mustard." She took a big bite and sighed. Sometimes the little things brought her happiness. Blue was also starving since they'd skipped dinner.

Graham wiped his fingers with a paper napkin. "Don't worry about talking out in the open. It's too loud for Vampires, and most Breed don't like busy human streets on a Friday. Too many intoxicated college kids."

Usually people chose isolated areas for privacy. Lakes, underground garages, abandoned warehouses. Not Graham. He needed to be stationed near the food, and Blue was grateful. After finishing her hot dog, she eyed Raven's.

"Might as well," he said, chuckling. By the looks of the wadded-up wrappers, Graham was working on his third wiener. "I'll give her one of mine."

Blue smiled. "Raven likes burgers anyhow."

"Overrated. Just a bunch of mystery meat."

"And this isn't?" She held up her naked hot dog.

"What's the latest update? Your partner said you found something."

Their table was small and intimate, but Blue still lowered her voice. "We found a connection between the victims."

"How so?"

"They were all alphas or redheads."

Graham set down his half-eaten hot dog and picked at the bread. "I don't follow."

"Almost all the men are alphas, and the rest—including all the girls—are redheads. You know as well as I do that a redhead is more likely to produce an alpha, and a strong one." She suddenly belched and sat back, hand on her chest. "Pardon me. Anyhow, we wanted to get your insight. You knew some of these people."

"You two have certainly done your homework. I would have never connected those dots, not without meeting every person. Are you absolutely certain?"

"Without a doubt. We asked everyone to either confirm alpha status or send us a picture. That's more than a coincidence. Most of them were sick right before, so it fits a pattern."

"Your questions must have raised suspicion."

"We had a really good alibi, so you don't have to worry. What do you think?"

"It sounds like what you're suggesting—a virus. The thing most people don't understand about viruses is that they're designed to survive. And sometimes that means mutating and changing their behavior. It's not that different from people except that we acclimate to change while they themselves change. Have you two thought about the consequences of leaking this knowledge?"

Blue cleared her throat. "We've considered it. We thought maybe you might have connections in your world—someone who can do an autopsy on some of the remains and identify the virus. Maybe even find a cure before it strikes more people."

Graham stroked the scruff on his chubby cheek. "Just imagine what the higher authority would do if they thought a virus was spreading among Shifters. They would force you into isolation—away from the general population. People would resist, and there would be violence. So much violence. If it affected all of us, that would be different. But it's just Shifters, and people don't think much of you to begin with. Wouldn't take long before everyone considered you a threat to the Breed population."

"They're more threatened by our numbers than they would be a virus. It could also be a genetic mutation. We're not scientists, so that's why we called for your expertise." She rubbed her chest, wishing she hadn't eaten that second hot dog.

Graham watched a couple walking past their table. He seemed to have a lot on his mind, and Blue could only imagine the heavy weight of deciding the fate of an entire race. "Now that I think about it, I should have noticed the obvious connection. If a person knew enough victims, they'd see it too. But you didn't know them, so how in the world did you connect those dots?"

"Actually, we didn't. We had help."

Graham blanched. "I thought you weren't including any outside help. It could ruin me. Ruin!"

"Calm down. He won't tell anyone because he's dead. You mentioned before that you've heard of the Freeman pride, so I guess you knew King."

Graham stared, blank-faced. "King?"

"Sambah's son. Somehow he followed one of us home, and we have a Gravewalker on our team who spoke to him. He knew several victims, and he's the one who pointed out how many were alphas. More than what we knew. That wasn't a question we bothered to ask, so it got us thinking."

Graham's eyes darted around. "Is he here now?"

Blue chuckled. "How would I know? I doubt it. He's busy haunting our house."

Graham shook the ice in his cup. "Have you found anything else I should know about? Every detail matters."

Blue wasn't sure there was anything additional she could provide, but she also didn't want Graham to run off before Raven had a chance to talk to him. So she stalled. "We can talk through the details when Raven gets here." She reached for her drink to wash down the indigestion.

"I can wait," he said, studying her closely.

A few minutes rolled by, and she watched young people rushing to and fro. One lady actually carried her dog in a purse, and a man walked by, passing out fliers for a local band. Graham had a small pile of hot dogs and was working on another. She didn't know how he could eat so many since they were spicy.

"You have the appetite of a hummingbird," she said.

"Hummingbird? That's a first."

"We didn't have books in my tribe, so everything we learned about animals was passed down from the elders. When I came to the city and learned to read, I found a book on falcons. I wanted to see what people wrote, and then I got caught up reading about all kinds of birds. Hummingbirds eat nearly twice their weight in nectar each day."

Graham put down his hot dog. "Is that what you think I eat?"

"There's nothing wrong with a hearty appetite. That's my point. Hummingbirds are fast and efficient. I bet you're the same. You mentioned you don't sleep much, so your mind must always be going."

He sighed. Relics looked so vulnerable to her. They were closest to humans genetically and even lived as long as them. But their intelligence was unmatched. Keystone was lucky to have Gem, who was born a Relic before becoming a Mage. They didn't have to worry about her getting old and dying. Even Hunter would live longer according to his deceased mother.

"My clients are so demanding," he complained. "They don't appreciate the hours I put into my job. I barely have a social life anymore. Work, work, work."

"That's why I was surprised you didn't have a partner. You don't look strapped for cash unless you have some gambling addiction on the side. Give yourself a break."

"Partnering up isn't as easy as all that. You have to trust them, and that's not easy to do with a stranger. That's why most of them are married."

Blue pulled out her phone when it vibrated. It was a message from Raven. While Graham went on about the dynamics between partners, Blue wrapped up a short exchange with Raven and frowned. Raven wanted her to ask Graham if he'd ever prescribed medication to their victims. Why would she ask that? Then Blue remembered how Andy had given his mate heartburn medication. In fact, several of them had mentioned the same thing. But if they were experiencing heartburn, *of course* they'd reach for medicine.

"Did you prescribe medicine to any of your clients?" she asked, setting her phone on the table.

Graham blinked. "I sell it on the side. That's no secret."

"I meant to the victims."

He wiped his mouth with a napkin. "If they were sick and I had something for it, yes."

"For heartburn?" She tried to read him, but he seemed truly baffled.

"Probably. I'd have to think. Sometimes I give people medicine and they don't take it right away but keep it on hand. I'm not a pharmacy. Nobody gets an entire bottle of medicine. Can you imagine what would happen to my reputation if they overdosed or shared it with others? I only dispense a few pills as needed. Heartburn is a common condition."

"Even Alisa, Andy's mate?"

"Sure. Yeah. I gave her a few pills."

"Why didn't you mention that before?"

"What's to mention? There's nothing unusual about it. All pregnant women have heartburn."

Blue stiffened. "You knew she was pregnant?"

She remembered Graham specifically saying that Teresa didn't have kids. One doesn't skip over the fact that a woman is carrying.

"Nobody knew about her condition except possibly the Packmaster," he insisted, fidgeting with the wrappers on the table. "Alisa hadn't told anyone but me and wanted to get tested because she was having stomach troubles."

So that's what Raven was hinting at. Blue decided to throw out an accusation and see how he reacted. "That seems like relevant information you should have shared. But you didn't want anything tracing back to you. Not directly."

Graham pushed back his chair and stood. "I think we're done here. Hope you enjoyed the free meal."

She couldn't believe her eyes when he turned around and fled. Was he serious? She bolted to her feet and sprinted after him. Halfway across the street, a car nearly struck her before slamming on the brakes. Instead of asking if she was okay, the driver held down his horn. Blue pounded her fists against the hood, but she didn't have time for this joker. When she looked up, Graham had vanished. Despite his size, he was apparently a quick runner.

She jogged in the direction he'd gone and spotted him far ahead, taking a right. Blue dodged into an alleyway and summoned her animal. But as she spread her arms, an emptiness filled her as if a wall had formed, breaking their connection. Confused, she conveyed the urgency, but again, nothing happened.

"What the hell?"

With no time to spare, Blue shot out of the alley and ran nimbly down the busy sidewalk. She turned right, dodging pockets of young people without breaking stride.

Dammit, I can't see!

She felt handicapped on the ground. Was he hiding in a bar? Had he parked on this street and driven off? If only she could shift and get an aerial view. Even though she knew what kind of car he drove, she still looked in the window of every vehicle that rolled by. It didn't seem likely he would have fought his way through crowded doors to hide inside a club—that would only trap him.

Wait a second—this street leads to the subway station.

On a hunch, she headed that way at breakneck speed. She weaved around cars, people, lampposts, every obstacle that blocked her path, all while scanning the street to make sure he wasn't hiding between buildings or among a group of people.

Finally, she spotted him just ahead. He glanced back, his face red and glistening with sweat. It didn't take long to catch up, and when she did, she grabbed the back of his shirt with such force that it ripped.

Panting heavily, Graham leaned against a sedan. "You don't have anything."

"I bet if we asked nicely, some of those people might remember you visiting the victims or giving them drugs. Who knows? Maybe some of the bottles are still lying around."

"Doesn't matter. If it killed the victim, that means they took all the poisoned pills."

She smiled at his admission. "There's always residue."

Graham wiped his face with his hands, finally regaining his composure. "You still can't prove anything. Slander is against the law."

"All we need is a Vampire. I'm sure you'll sing like a bird, you conniving little monster. You poisoned all those people—even children. Why would you do that? How could you hurt a child? For what? So you could sow violence by killing young alphas?"

He scoffed. "Shifters don't need alphas to survive. Not really. Some of the groups might disband, but maybe that's for the best."

"It's not for you to decide."

Rings of sweat had formed on the armpits of his striped shirt. Graham tried to step away from the car, but she shoved him right back in place. When she did, a visceral look crossed his face.

"Alphas are entitled little mutations who do nothing but control people and cause pain and suffering," he spat out.

Her eyebrows popped up. "That's not entirely true. You got a few dark souls out there, but most alphas are decent men."

"Oh? I spent my childhood around packs, tagging along with my parents while they saw clients. I've seen what alphas are capable of."

"So now it's your mission in life to murder them or anyone who can produce them? You're an idiot. *Anyone* can have an alpha. It's not just redheads."

"Anyone can, but not everyone does. Most couples never produce an alpha. Redheads almost always do, and they make the stronger ones who have to be put down. Why do you think I can't have kids? That's a Relic's entire purpose in life—to build knowledge and then have children to pass it down to. This is the time in my life when I should be settling down with a family, but that won't ever happen. An alpha wolf took that away from me when I was twelve. He and his friends thought it would be fun to see how many times they could kick me in the testicles before I lost consciousness. It was part of some initiation thing after the alpha went through his first change. Their little game did irreparable damage."

Blue leaned in, her expression tight. "I'm sorry about your balls, but murder is murder. You're going to jail for a long time."

"Why do you think I have all this knowledge about drugs and poisons? To save Shifters?" He laughed wildly. "This is my destiny. I'm the last of my bloodline, and it all makes sense. It took me years to figure out that this is what I was born to do—it's the will of the fates."

Blue touched her chest and got a sickening feeling. Why was he telling her all this? Criminals didn't just confess their crimes unless they were boasting because they had a backup plan.

Graham sneered, revealing teeth that were slightly yellow. "Why do you think I didn't put any mustard on Raven's hot dog? I know you like mustard because you put it on that chili dog back at the diner. I pay attention. The poison only works on Shifters, so I mixed it in with your condiment."

"You're lying."

"Am I? Remember that gum you so eagerly took from me? That was the first dose. It's a cumulative toxin that doesn't leave your body, and when you get enough of it—death."

"You're not that stupid. It would look suspicious if I suddenly dropped dead."

He smirked. "Not if you two were thinking this was a virus. I *really* like that idea. Very smart." Graham pushed away from the car and dusted off his sleeves. "I gave you the first dose just in case, even though I was certain you wouldn't find anything. But when Raven called and said you had a connection, I knew I had to finish what I started." Graham cockily adjusted his watch, as if proud to finally brag about his plot. "I had to be careful about dosing. Giving someone a single pill that does the job is foolish. If they died after taking it, people would have figured it out. So I divided the toxin into multiple doses and gave them their first one.

The remaining tainted pills in the bottle would only be enough to kill that person and nobody else, just in case they decided to give away or share the medication. Had to be careful I didn't kill the wrong person. Wouldn't want that! Sometimes it was heartburn or indigestion pills, other times vitamins. The ones who weren't my clients, I gave a stick of gum to. When I bumped into them the next time, I'd give them a tainted pack that would finish the job, like I did with that Shifter on the motorcycle."

Blue gripped a sign, trying to steady herself when she got a sudden dizzy spell. "Even if it's true, you're still not getting away with it."

"If you want the antidote, you'll let me walk. And yes, there's an antidote. A smart man doesn't create a poison without also understanding how to reverse it. Once I'm in a safe place, I'll call you with the information."

She fisted his shirt when he tried to walk away.

Graham wrenched free. "What are you going to do, arrest me in front of all these humans? Maybe stab me with a dagger? If you tell people about me, who will believe such an outlandish story without any proof? That a reputable Relic whose family has been working in the community for generations decided to go on a murdering spree? I have a number of Packmasters who would testify on my behalf. I'll convince them it's a virus, and they'll believe me."

"A Vampire works on our team, you nitwit. He can charm the information out of you."

"If your partner comes after me, I'll make this available to everyone. I have a buyer on standby, and all I have to do is send him the formula. How many people do you think would pay good money to launch a massive attack on Shifters? They can sprinkle it in a water source, on food—the possibilities are endless. And it only kills Shifters. I don't think you want that on your conscience," he warned her, holding up his phone as he backed away. "All it takes is one call to destroy your kind. Whose life is more important? Yours or every Shifter on the planet? Don't worry—you still have a few hours. Once I'm safe, I'll call you with the antidote. Follow me, and all will perish, including you."

Graham turned and ran.

Blue started to go after him, but her weakened muscles wouldn't allow it. Instead, she slumped against the car and reached for her phone, but it wasn't in her pocket.

Chapter 27

I RAN IN CIRCLES BEFORE LOCATING the hot dog stand. When I got there, Graham's table was empty, nothing left behind but wadded-up wrappers, drinks, a few hot dogs, and Blue's phone. I spun in a circle and searched the immediate area. "Blue?" I called out.

When no one answered, I grabbed her phone and crashed the neighboring table. "Did you see where my friends went? They were sitting at that table a few minutes ago. Big guy with brown hair and kind of a beard; the girl has long hair and feather earrings."

A blonde sipping her orange drink raised her hand, the baubles on her wrist clattering together. "I did," she replied, her accent so Southern that it was clear she was a tourist. "They went running across the street thataway. Well, he went running, and then she tore after him. Almost got hit by a car. Are they lovers? They didn't look like it."

I dashed across the street and ran down the sidewalk, searching for Blue. There wasn't any sign of commotion going on, just people having a good time. I asked five or six people who looked like they'd been out there a while if they'd seen anything, but it wasn't until I reached a corner that a man directed me to the right. I shoved through crowds of young people pouring in and out of the bars. Finally, away from all the people, I spotted a man hunched over by a brick wall. A familiar pair of boots stuck out from the person sitting in front of him.

Matteo looked over his shoulder at me, a few small braids mingled in his long hair. He was crouched in front of Blue.

"Is she okay?" I asked, out of breath. "Blue, are you hurt? You can shift in the alley. Help me—"

"No," she cut in. "I can't shift."

Matteo gave me a grim look. "The Relic poisoned her."

"What the hell are you even doing here, Chitah?"

He narrowed his eyes. "You don't have to be insulting. I wanted to ensure Blue is safe."

"And where's Graham?"

"He got away," Blue said, her voice barely audible. "I can't shift, and I can't run. I think he gave me twice the dosage. It's not just chest pain and a headache, but my muscles are weak."

I knelt beside her. "What happened?"

"He confessed everything. It's not a virus, Raven. Thank the fates for that. It's just a personal vendetta because of a childhood trauma involving bullies, and he's taking it out on alphas."

"I shouldn't have sent that message. I'm sorry."

"It doesn't matter. He poisoned me as soon as I sat down. He had it all planned. I tried to hold him, but I didn't have the strength. He said if we go after him, he'll give the ingredients to a buyer. They'll use it on every Shifter—not just alphas. I think he has the file on his phone, because he threatened to send it to his contact."

"Then I need to find his ass for the cure."

When I stood, Matteo seized my wrist. "Blue doesn't have to die. If you do nothing, he'll call with the antidote."

I yanked my arm out of his grasp. "*Sure* he will. That's what guys like him do: stay true to their word. He's not a Chitah. His word isn't his bond, and he's already killed countless people—including children. Do you really think he cares what happens to her?"

Matteo locked his fierce eyes on mine. "He'll call. He has to."

I turned my attention to Blue, deciding she needed to make the call. "What do you want me to do?"

Blue sighed and rubbed her chest. "Go after him. He went to the subway."

"You can't." Matteo looked up at me pleadingly. "Then he

won't give her the antidote. Blue will die, and you'll be responsible for what is unleashed."

I pulled a dagger from my belt. "I have an effective way of charming men. No Vampire needed."

"And if you fail, you'll have her blood on your hands."

"He's not going to call. We're not getting a cure sent to us by a messenger boy."

"He stands to lose more if he lets her die."

"I want you to find him," Blue snapped. "No one will care if I die. I don't work for the higher authority—I'm a nobody. But don't let my death be in vain. He's going to murder people regardless, so we need to stop him. You're a Chitah. You can scent his trail."

Matteo flashed his canines. "I'm *not* leaving you to die alone. I won't go!"

I tossed Blue her phone. "Then I will."

Ignoring the law, I flashed toward the subway. Most of the bystanders were drunk and would probably blame the alcohol if they did see anything. I needed to catch up before Graham got on a train. When I reached the station, I bounded down the stairs. A couple blocked me, and I almost slipped when passing them. Then I sprinted down a long tunnel, forced to run human speed since there were people around.

No wonder he wanted to meet in a busy section of town. He knew we wouldn't be able to use our powers or weapons around humans, and that would give him a better chance of escaping if needed. Niko had once told me never to let an enemy choose a meeting place because they would always have the advantage by selecting a familiar location. But I couldn't have imagined that Graham would be the enemy.

The end of the tunnel opened into a mezzanine. People entered from different directions and headed downstairs. Even though Viktor had given us metro cards, I didn't have time to fumble with my wallet, so I jumped the gate. When I reached the lowest level, past the murals, I wound up on the platform. The trains usually came by every fifteen minutes or so, and I hoped it wasn't too late. A homeless man strummed on his guitar, a hat tipped upside down with a few bills inside. I stood behind a pillar and searched both sides of the track.

Gotcha.

On the other side of the tracks, Graham was sitting on a wooden bench, his shirt drenched in sweat and a phone in his hand. His face was beet red, and he was panting heavily.

Dammit. I picked the wrong side to enter.

I needed to cross over, but there was no rush. Even with the tracks between us, it wasn't as if the man could outrun me. He looked ready to keel over, and I also had the advantage of being a Mage.

Instead of a sneak attack, I strutted alongside the track and stopped directly across from him. "How were the hot dogs?" I asked loudly. "I'm a big fan of the cheese dog. Don't bother getting up."

Color drained from Graham's face when he noticed me. Phone clutched in hand, he stood but didn't run. He was too smart for that. And too tired.

"You won't escape," I said, putting my hands in my coat pockets. "No matter what you're thinking of doing, you won't walk away. I'm sure you counted on Blue saving herself, but you don't know what that woman's willing to die for. Are you going to make this easy or hard?"

"One call and everyone dies," he said sharply, finger swiping the face of his phone.

"She told me why you targeted the victims. I don't think you feel that way about everyone. You've spent your entire career helping these people, and nobody wants that much blood on their hands. Not even you. I'm willing to bet you don't even have a buyer."

"I'm calling."

"Great! And then what's your plan?" I jumped onto the track, ignoring the lady who gasped. Carefully stepping over the tracks, uncertain if they would electrocute me, I climbed the wall and dusted off my pants. "Put him on speaker. I'd like to say hello."

Graham hesitated, and I knew immediately it was all a ruse. He thought the only way to keep us off his tail was to spin an elaborate threat that no sane person would risk.

No one ever said I was sane.

"Did you ever get back at the boys who picked on you?"

Graham's eyes became slivers. "Picked on? *Picked on?* My family line is severed because of what they did. *Centuries* of inherited knowledge—gone!"

I could only guess what they had done to him. "You killed a bunch of innocent people. I'm just curious if you ever got the ones who hurt you or if you're just another sadistic serial killer."

"They're all infected with the same evil. That's what it is. Evil."

"You didn't answer my question. Did you ever get back at the ones who did that to you?"

His lips thinned. "I can't. He never liked me, and he won't let me near his territory."

"Coward. You could have used that poison against some of the worst of the worst, but you're too scared to confront the real bullies in this world. Instead, you chose innocent people—vulnerable people."

Graham's eyes darted around, and he glanced at his watch.

"Where's the antidote?" I pressed. "If you save her life, I'll tell the higher authority you cooperated."

"I don't have it on me. We have to go back to my place."

I folded my arms. "I don't believe you."

He approached the edge, searching for the train at the far end of the tunnel.

"Look, we're not going back to your place. Either you're stalling, or you've got some elaborate scheme cooked up, and I'm not playing that game. Tell me where the antidote is, and I won't slice off your toes."

His eyes dragged over to mine.

A smile tugged at the corner of my mouth. "Do you know why they hired me? Because I enjoy doing the dirty work. I'm the monster your bullies have nightmares about. We'll start with all the small appendages—including the one between your legs. Assuming you still have it. Then the tongue."

He blinked, mouth parting as panic and despair washed over his features.

I inched toward him. "Tell me where the antidote is. Unlike you, I don't make empty threats. I'm also not very patient."

From the distant tunnel, I heard the rumble of the oncoming train. Before I could get an answer out of Graham, he jumped onto the tracks.

My eyes widened. There was no way in hell I'd be able to get him out of there by myself. Graham lay there with his eyes slammed shut, waiting for the train to run over him.

Panicked, I leaned over the tracks and waved my arms frantically to get the conductor's attention.

"Stop the train!" someone shouted, also waving their arms. Several people joined in as the train rolled by the platform, the brakes screeching.

"Stop, you idiot! Stop!"

The train neared, a woman screamed, and I turned my head away.

When it stopped, I braced myself for a gruesome sight. How the hell was I going to get the antidote now? I peered over the edge.

Graham sat facing the train, his legs apart and a rivulet of blood dribbling from his scalp. "I can't go to jail," he babbled. "I'd rather be dead. I won't get my food; I won't see anything but bars and walls. Not even television." He swung his gaze up at me, his eyes pleading. "Let me die. You have the power to do it. Just one shock." Graham began sobbing like a little boy.

I'd had plenty of men beg for their freedom or even their lives. But not once had anyone ever begged for death.

"Stay where you are," the conductor said. "We called an ambulance."

This was my case, and I had to make a decision. Turning him

in would open up an investigation, and the higher authority might find out about the kids and what we'd done. I wasn't worried about the paramedics arriving. Even if they took him to the hospital, Graham couldn't escape. Not unless he got himself committed, and imprisonment was what he was trying to avoid.

I took out my phone and made a call. "Viktor? I need to ask for a favor."

Chapter 28

After calling Viktor, Blue sent a text message to Raven, letting her know she was going home. Graham might not have an antidote, and even if he did, he would probably destroy it. What would stop him? A conscience? Apparently he'd lost that a long time ago.

The only place she wanted to be was home. If she was going to die, it wasn't going to be on a street corner, surrounded by strangers.

After explaining the situation, she expected Shepherd to show up in his Jeep. Instead, the black van appeared, Viktor behind the wheel. Both he and Shepherd rushed out the moment they saw her.

"What can we do?" Viktor asked.

Shepherd felt her pulse. "What are your symptoms? What did he give you?"

"Do you want us to call a Relic?" Viktor asked.

She held up her hand. "Hold on with the interrogation. I have chest discomfort—burning and pressure. It feels like bad indigestion. My head hurts, and my muscles are weak. Also, I can't shift."

That shut Viktor right up. He covered his mouth with his hand and stroked his beard, looking to Shepherd to fix the situation.

Shepherd didn't exactly instill confidence. "You said it was poison?"

"He said the toxin had a cumulative effect, so that's how he could give smaller doses over a period of time. He tainted a stick of gum I chewed the other day, and tonight I got a large dose mixed in with mustard. I didn't taste anything different."

"Did you try vomiting?"

She shook her head.

Shepherd opened his medical bag and took out a syringe and bottle. "This works really fast."

After he gave her a shot, Blue started feeling queasy. Not wanting to vomit on the street, she moved to get up. As if reading her mind, Matteo helped her stand and hustled her into an alleyway just seconds before she threw up her meal.

It really didn't get more humiliating than that.

"Let's get her into the van," Viktor said as he hooked his arm around her waist. Her feet dragged beneath her, but Matteo and Viktor all but carried her to the back doors, where a small mattress awaited her.

They lifted her in, and she crawled over the makeshift bed and collapsed. Viktor squeezed her ankle and held it long enough that she looked down and met eyes with him. Seeing his cautious gaze made her heart quicken. For a moment she thought he might say something, but instead, he gave her a curt nod and returned to the driver's seat.

"Feel better?" Shepherd stepped over her and set his bag down. "Still nauseous?"

"No."

Matteo got in, shut the doors, and sat on one of the benches along the side.

Shepherd knelt above her head and offered her a tiny shot glass. "Drink this."

"What is it?"

"Activated carbon with a little juice. If there's any poison left in your stomach, it'll absorb it."

Blue gulped down the inky liquid and handed him the glass.

"Try not to puke that up," he said, no humor in his voice. "I brought a few extra things when you mentioned poison. I ain't gonna lie to you, honey. Poison isn't my area. Unless we know what he gave you, there's not much even an expert can do. Did he tell you anything about it?"

She shook her head. "We think it causes massive clotting and strokes. Wyatt's ghost said that it wasn't just his heart. He got a headache and had trouble breathing."

Shepherd put his rough hand on her forehead, his dark eyes softening. He was such a tough-looking guy with all his muscles and hardened features. Yet something about being a dad had brought out a compassion she'd never seen in him before. "That's good. That's something. When we get back, I'll give you blood thinner, and we'll go from there."

The ride didn't take long, not the way Viktor was driving. Or maybe she had lost her sense of time. Graham had mentioned she had hours, and suddenly, every minute flew away from her like a sparrow. She gave Matteo an impassive smile. He stared down at her as if he were looking at a corpse, and she didn't like it.

She turned away, listening for the voices of her ancestors. Their spirits beckoned her, and never had she felt more detached. She was no longer tethered to the living world and yet was not part of the spirit world. The connection to her falcon was blocked, leaving her terrified. She clung to the memories of her sons, imagining what their final moments must have been like. Neither died with fear in their eyes, but had they felt any peace?

"Maybe the lion should have killed me," she muttered.

Shepherd leaned over. "What?"

"Maybe it was my time." She looked back at Matteo. "Maybe you weren't supposed to save me that night. Maybe we have to follow the order of things."

Matteo glanced at Shepherd. "She's delirious."

Blue smiled. "So what if I am?" It gave her a lot to consider. If it angered the spirits to defy destiny, perhaps there was a reason for death. Maybe her sons were called to a greater purpose.

The ride was quiet aside from Shepherd occasionally asking if she felt any different. It was nice to lie on the soft mattress, listening to the hum of the road beneath the tires. It kept her mind off the pain in her chest, and suddenly, she had to catch her breath every so often.

When the van finally stopped, the back doors flew open. Blue sat up, and Shepherd helped her scoot out into Matteo's arms.

"I can walk," she insisted as he cradled her close.

"Balderdash. You can't even lie convincingly. I can smell your pain, female."

"Pain is life."

Shepherd closed the van doors. "Bring her into the medical room. I'll do what I can."

She handed him her phone. "Take this in case Raven calls."

Viktor appeared in her line of view. "Give her to me."

"I've got her," Matteo said.

Then Viktor did something unexpected. He drew in close and put his arms beneath her. "She is not yours—she is mine."

Blue tried to get down, but the next thing she knew, she was in Viktor's tight embrace. It was then that she relinquished any notion of walking on her own. Resting her head against his shoulder, she could faintly smell his cologne mixed with an earthy scent. Maybe it was his natural smell. Blue stared at his facial hair, always so neatly trimmed except for the scruff on his chin. The silver stubble against his tan skin held her attention.

"I'm sorry," she mumbled. "I'm always getting hurt lately. I don't mean to cause all this trouble."

"Nyet. You are not problem," he said, his broken words trailing off into Russian. She warmed to his soft and comforting tone, the texture of his voice reaching deep into her soul.

Once inside, the smells changed from greenery to the lingering aroma of charred hamburgers. When they entered Shepherd's medical room, she wrinkled her nose at the scent of alcohol and bleach. He kept the room as sterile as a hospital. While Shepherd cleaned something, Viktor set her on the metal table.

"You really need a blanket or a pillow on this thing," she said, trying to lighten the somber mood.

Viktor put his hand on her forehead and stroked her hair back.

Blue rolled toward Viktor when Shepherd approached her with a needle. "Don't you have any pills?"

"You swallowed active carbon, so they won't take. This'll work quicker. It's a blood thinner to prevent clotting. Just don't cut yourself. Let me see your arm."

"Do as he says," Viktor said softly.

"I'm not afraid of needles," she explained. "I just don't like the idea of medicine being forced into my body. The last one made me sick."

Shepherd flicked the syringe. "It was supposed to."

Blue coughed a few times and then let Shepherd give her the injection. After a light prick, he checked her blood pressure and clipped a plastic device on her fingertip.

"How is she?" Christian asked from the doorway.

Shepherd returned to the cabinets and opened them. "I'm working on it. Did you tell Switch to keep Hunter and the kids out?"

"Aye. Claude's helping with that. They won't be disturbing you. How do you feel, lass?"

Blue stared up at the ceiling. "Like I ate a really bad hot dog."

"Raven will find him," Viktor assured her. "She will bring us the remedy."

Blue shut her eyes, unwilling to argue the glaring truth that Graham likely didn't have a cure. Why would a Relic be walking around with both a poison and the antidote? He'd targeted those people with the intent to kill. At least it wasn't a virus, but those poor children.

An unexpected calm swept over her. This wasn't nearly as painful as the lion attack. Yet going out by poison was the cruelest fate. There was no glory in it—no honor. This wasn't a warrior's death.

Overcome with rage, Blue roared and swung her arms. The clip on her finger went flying and struck Christian in the chest before falling to the floor. She forced herself to sit up, unwilling to die on her back.

Shepherd ignored her reaction and checked her pulse again.

Viktor circled the table. "What can I do?"

Blue clutched her chest, the pressure building. It felt like she had swallowed a large bite of something, and it was stuck halfway down. "He promised I had hours," she said bitterly, realizing she was declining rapidly.

Viktor leaned into view. "Can you shift? Try again."

Blue tried but didn't want to waste her energy repeating the effort. "It's not worth it. You know shifting won't help with poison. Where did Matteo go?"

Christian folded his arms. "The pussycat's outside. He doesn't belong in our house without an escort, and he sure as shite isn't invited in here."

Viktor regarded her for a moment. "Do you want him? I can make exceptions."

Blue shook her head before falling back. Viktor caught her, and she rested gently against the table. "I don't want to die in this room. It smells like a hospital or something. Don't let me die in this room."

Viktor collected her in his arms. "We'll be in the gathering room. See if Gem has found anything in her books."

Shepherd briskly marched out like a soldier taking orders. Viktor followed behind but parted ways with Shepherd in the foyer. The lanterns guided the way, and when they reached the dining room, all the candles on the chandelier had been snuffed out.

"Bring a blanket," Viktor said, but not to her.

When they reached the gathering room, he placed her on the sofa and went to the fireplace. She watched him kneel before the massive hearth. It wasn't cold enough for a fire, but it wasn't unusual to find one burning in this room. Candles were insufficient to light up the large space, and they spent a lot of time in here talking, reading, and drinking. She thought about some of those memories and cherished them, realizing she'd taken so much for granted. Viktor had given her a second chance with Keystone in more than one way. This had become her home.

She took a deep breath, and it felt as if her lungs might stop all on their own.

Christian strolled in, wearing all black in true Vampire form. He placed a knitted throw over her feet and dipped into the shadows.

As the wood in the fireplace snapped and hissed, she stared up at the ceiling, trying to recall her sons' faces. Remembering moments helped, but she had forgotten the sound of their voices.

"How is she?" Wyatt asked.

Blue glanced up at Wyatt, who was standing behind Viktor's leather chair.

"She is strong," Viktor answered. "There is hope. She made it through a gruesome attack that no one else would have survived. Blue is a warrior."

Blue blinked up at the impossibly tall ceiling. "I want to see my family."

Wyatt swaggered into view, that floppy hat barely hanging on, his Pac-Man shirt tucked halfway into his jeans. "Maybe we should call them."

"They're dead," she replied.

He put his hands on his hips. "It doesn't work that way when we die. The afterlife isn't a family reunion."

"You said you didn't know where they go."

"That's true. But would you really want to sit in limbo with estranged family members you barely tolerated? No thanks. I have a feeling they go somewhere else, but that's not for the living to know."

Tears stung her eyes at the idea she would never reunite with her sons, not even for a moment. Could the fates be so cruel?

"Shut your gob," Christian barked. "Can't you see you're upsetting the lass?"

Shepherd jogged into the room, out of breath. "Gem can't find anything. She's still looking through a pile of books she separated from the rest."

Viktor turned. "And you called Raven?"

"She got the fucker, but he doesn't have an antidote. He tried to kill himself."

"Didn't try hard enough," Christian added.

Blue had never imagined her death being such a burden on others. It made her want to go outside in the courtyard and die alone like an animal. Viktor left the room, and she stared into the fire for a long while, watching the flames take hold and grow larger. The flickering light became a reel that played out her life, and she reminisced over all the good parts.

When the light went dark, she realized Niko had knelt in front of her. He said nothing, only looked down at her fading light and held her hand.

"You were a good partner," she said to him.

He stroked the top of her hand. "You never treated me differently. You and I are a good match. I just wish I had been there. I might have been able to read his light—see his intentions."

"What's done is done."

"I can't find anything," Gem complained, entering the room and looking around. "Nothing that makes sense." She rushed up to the sofa and threw her arms around Blue, sobbing against her chest. "I'm so sorry. I looked and looked, but I couldn't find anything. I just don't have any books on poisons. I really tried."

Blue patted Gem on the back and then touched Niko's arm. "Please, take her. She doesn't need to be here."

In truth, Blue didn't want to hear any wailing or crying. She didn't want anything tethering her to this world, and hearing someone's heartache made her spirit feel heavier.

Niko hooked his arm around Gem and led her away. Blue took another deep breath, turning on her side as Viktor returned with a guitar in his hand. He dragged a short table in front of her, took a seat, and popped the guitar on his lap.

"But I thought you played violin?" she whispered, knowing it was something he did privately—secretly.

"I come from a musical family." He swung his gaze up for a moment before choosing a slow melody.

As he picked out the notes like a beautiful bouquet, she recognized the tune. She might have expected some old Russian song that was morose, but instead, Viktor played a slow version of "California Dreaming." She smiled and watched as his fingers slid up and down the neck, pressing the strings and changing position. The song was timeless—haunting and reflective. Had anyone else been serenaded so beautifully by death?

Halfway through the song, Blue should have felt herself slipping away. It would have been a perfect moment. But instead, she shot up and clutched her chest. Her heart was beating out of sync and squeezing tightly. The music abruptly stopped.

Shepherd knelt. "Are you feeling worse?"

Grimacing, she nodded. Her long hair curtained her face as her chin touched her chest.

"What can you do?" Viktor hissed.

Shepherd sighed. "Nothing. All I can do is give her something for the pain. My magic won't take it all away. I don't know what's working through her, and even if I did, we can't reverse it."

"That's not entirely true," Christian said from the fireplace. "There's one other option. I've done it before, but I can't make any promises." He looked over his shoulder and gave her a dark stare. "Vampire blood can flush out the poison."

Blue shook her head. She didn't want Vampire magic running through her, dark magic she didn't understand. It might change her, or worse, change her animal.

"I can get an IV bag," Shepherd suggested.

Christian turned on his heel. "Over my rotting corpse. Aside from the offensive nature of drawing blood through a catheter, there's no guarantee it'll work that way. She'll have to ingest it, and better if it's fresh from the vein. Vampire blood loses potency in a glass." He centered his gaze on her. "But she'll have to decide on her own if she wants to live or die. That's not for us to choose."

"I don't want Vampire blood," she snapped back. "I don't want to be a Vampire."

"You won't become a Vampire, lass. Of that I can assure you. There's more involved in making a Vampire than drinking blood. That's a fable for books and movies. This isn't something I offer everyone, you know. You might have your opinions about our blood, but it's sacred. It's a privilege to receive the offer."

Viktor set down his guitar and sat next to her. "You must."

"I can't."

Viktor cradled her neck in his hands. "I understand how you feel—Vampire blood is not natural. But I will ask this one thing of you because I cannot let you go." He leaned in close to her ear, his voice just above a whisper. "What will I do without my Blue? *Ya lyublyu tebya.*"

"I don't understand you." She pulled back to look him in the eyes, but he only looked away. The bend in his voice tugged at her heart. If she refused, would Viktor always see her as someone who gave up? Who failed him? She had a chance at seeing her sons again. Maybe not, but it was a slim chance. Blue felt like a pendulum swinging between here and there, somewhere and nowhere, darkness and light. She'd fought to live during the lion attack, despite the inevitable scarring. This was one fight she couldn't win on her own. If there was any time she could slip out of this painful world, this was it.

"You've captured so many bad men," Viktor went on. "And those children would not be here without you."

Blue had taken the job for money, but she'd also taken it because it made her life endurable. She slept better at night knowing that one less person in the world would suffer as she had suffered.

Viktor's hand fell to her shoulder. "It is your choice. But you have a place here, and that place cannot be filled by anyone."

Christian dipped his chin. "Well, lass? What'll it be? I won't force you to do anything you don't want."

Blue somberly lowered her head. "I'll do it. But if I die anyway with Vampire blood in my mouth, I'm going to haunt you in the afterlife."

Christian chuckled darkly. "I wouldn't expect anything less."

Chapter 29

After the EMTs pulled Graham from the tracks, they sat with him while everyone got on the train and went about their lives. I waited impatiently while they bandaged his head, checked his vitals, and insisted that he go to the hospital. Graham remained taciturn, but he was clearly upset judging by the look on his face. He didn't want to go to the hospital and explained that he'd lost his balance and fell. I corroborated his story—the last thing I needed was to have to bust him out of a psychiatric ward. He could have gone with them to buy some time, but he undoubtedly knew it would only prolong the inevitable. And who wanted to spend their last days of freedom locked up in a human hospital?

Concerned about Blue, I called Shepherd. He sounded grim and said there wasn't anything he could do but give her pain medication and wait. He'd given her blood thinner and something to absorb the poison, but without knowing what Graham had given her, his hands were tied. Before the ambulance arrived, I'd forced Graham to talk by hitting him with small electric shocks until he finally admitted there was no antidote. The poison was made from a substance unknown to man, just part of a collection he'd inherited from his parents, who once ran an apothecary.

Maybe some would sympathize with Graham because of his childhood trauma, but I didn't. Shit happens in life, and if you can't get justice, you don't turn into a comic book villain who uses that pain to destroy the lives of innocent, good people. Graham had bottled all that rage until he got the brilliant notion that it wasn't just those boys who had hurt him—*all* alphas were to blame. He might have seemed normal and highly intelligent, but only a clinically insane person would poison children and pregnant women. As far as I was concerned, he could rot for the rest of his life in a jail cell.

And yet that didn't seem like enough. Three square meals a day and a bed? Graham didn't deserve to get off that easy, even if Breed jails *were* worse than human prisons. That was why I had to call Viktor. Since this was my case, I wanted permission to choose his fate. The higher authority wasn't aware of what we were up to, so turning him in posed a risk. We'd have to break down the details of our case, and they would learn about our mercenary mission. Not to mention the turbulence it might cause among Shifters to reveal someone from the inside had been targeting their alphas. We had already promised them money, and if they discovered it was really a murder spree and we'd lied to them, they would demand a hell of a lot more. No, it seemed far better to send Graham off quietly into the sunset.

Once the paramedics left, I grabbed his arm and helped him up. "Let's go. And don't speak to me."

My blood boiled at the idea that I would never see Blue again, that I'd left her on a street corner to die. That would always be my last memory of a fighter who deserved a better death. Graham panted for breath as we climbed multiple stairs until we finally reached the long tunnel leading out. He didn't ask questions because he knew exactly where he was going.

Or so he thought.

We took a long, long walk back to where I'd parked my truck near the hot dog stand. After he scooted inside, I rounded the truck, half expecting him to make a run for it. But he'd relinquished his last ounce of hope prior to jumping the tracks. His behavior baffled me. Some criminals begged to go to jail even though they didn't want to. They knew there would be a slim chance of escape. But it seemed Graham had no such notions based on his catatonic behavior. His career was over. Even if he could escape, Shifters would put a bounty on his head.

And so the drive was peaceful.

I followed the directions on my phone until I reached a turnoff, and it was at that moment that Graham snapped out of it.

"Why are you bringing me here? What's going on? Aren't we going to the higher authority? Where are the Regulators?"

I turned on the radio, blasting "Kashmir" to drown out his incessant whining. When he reached for the door handle, I gripped his shoulder and gave him a strong blast of energy until he went limp. I had to be careful since Relics were weaker than the other Breeds. Too much juice would do serious damage, and I had special plans.

Though the location was deep in the woods, there were spotlights all around the white mansion.

After parking, I got out of the truck and approached three men. "I'm here to see Sambah. He's expecting me."

My entire body flinched when I caught sight of a massive lion padding toward me from the right. His gait was as fierce as his teeth. I'd seen a lot of lions but none as graceful. None with such a beautiful mane or confident step. I backed up, sharpening my light.

While still in motion, he shifted to human form without breaking stride. One of the men handed him a blue garment, and I averted my eyes while he pulled it over his head. He was a handsome man but very old judging by the steely look in his eyes.

"You must be Raven. I was hoping to see your friend again."

"So am I."

Most people would have ignored the remark, but Sambah was perceptive. He approached me and flicked his eyes between me and the truck. "What has happened?"

"That guy in my truck killed your son. In fact, he murdered a lot of Shifters, including women and children. I think... I think he might have even killed Blue."

Sambah's dark eyes lit up with fire and brimstone. "For what reason would he kill so many?"

"You can ask him that yourself, but it's not an answer you'll like. He used poison. King was taking medicine—maybe you knew about it and maybe you didn't. The medicine was tainted, and that's what caused him to fall down the stairs. The poison killed him, not the fall." When I felt my lower lip quiver, I quickly turned away and stared daggers at Graham. It hadn't really hit me until that moment that Blue might already be dead.

"And why bring him here? Doesn't the higher authority or Shifter Council want him?"

I lowered my voice. "That's what I'm here to talk to you about."

Sambah snapped his fingers, pointed to the truck, and spoke in a language I didn't recognize. The three men surrounded the truck and guarded it.

When I saw they weren't listening, I turned back to Sambah. "For reasons I can't explain, turning him in isn't an option. Hell, even if it was, I'd still be here. I have no sympathy for this man."

"What do you expect I will do with him?"

"Graham once mentioned he wanted to work for you, but he was also afraid of your pride. He said some men killed a lion in your pride and then just… disappeared."

Sambah folded his arms. "And you want to know what we did to them."

"He suggested you ate them."

Sambah threw back his head and laughed. "They were challenged to battle, but we didn't *eat* them. We're not savages." His gaze drifted back to the truck. "I had a taxidermist stuff their animal remains and return them to their pack."

"That's… a little bit extreme. Isn't that illegal?"

Sambah lowered his arms, clasping his hands. "Perhaps that is why they never speak of what happened to their former packmates. They're embarrassed that they're sitting by the fireplace." He smiled grimly. "And that is why you brought my son's killer to me? How do you know that this man killed my child? He doesn't look like much of a warrior."

"He confessed. I wouldn't be here unless I was absolutely certain."

"Why me? You said there are other victims. Why not their fathers and mothers?"

I sighed. "He worked for some of them. If this got out, it would cause a rift between Shifters and Relics."

"Yes, but how is it that you chose *me*?"

I worried my lip and decided to tell him. "Because your son helped us solve the case."

He blinked. "King?"

"One of our people is a Gravewalker. I guess this was King's unfinished business."

Sambah swung his gaze up to the moon and remained quiet for a long while. I could hear Graham rustling around inside the truck, but I'd taken the keys. Finally, Sambah cast his gaze upon me, and I thought for a minute he might go back inside. "Did my son say anything else?"

"I don't know. He helped us with the case. I think he really wanted to do right by you. He offered to help us in exchange of delivering a message to you, but we just caught Graham, and no one has talked to King. Once I get home, I'll have our Gravewalker write down the message."

"I would rather him go to his next life. I don't wish him to linger between worlds."

"I doubt he'll stick around much longer. If he already left, I'll see if he had a message and make sure it gets to you."

"I would very much appreciate that. He must go to his ancestors. I visit his grave each night and speak to him, but I do not want him to be there. This is just my way of coping, you see."

"No offense, but you don't seem upset to find out your son was murdered."

"I have lived many lifetimes and experienced great loss. When an accident takes your child, you blame the gods. When a person takes your child, you spend your life trying to figure out why. No answer is good enough, and sometimes it will only make it worse. Even if they are punished, you always live with that hate. Then you spend your life hating yourself, wondering how you could have prevented it from happening. I no longer let those emotions consume me. They are bad for the spirit."

After a quick nod to his men, they tried to get Graham out of the truck, but he'd locked the doors. When one of the men raised his fist to break my window, I shouted at him and jogged toward the vehicle.

Jingling my keys between two fingers, I went to unlock the door.

Graham was plastered against the driver's door. "Don't feed me to the lions."

"They're not going to eat you. Look, I'm doing you a favor. You don't want to go to Breed jail and face the higher authority's judgment, and I can't let you go free. I don't accept bribes from murderers like you. I've got zero sympathy. But hey, if you *want* to spend the rest of your life in jail, eating slop, I'm more than happy to oblige. Have you ever seen the inside of one of those prisons? Depending on which one you go to, they're pretty bleak. You don't have any rights in there. All you have are walls and bars and a lot of free time. Something else to consider: they might give you the death penalty. I hear they behead you right in front of an audience. Is that what you want?"

Without another word, Graham opened the door and stepped out. He allowed the men to escort him inside, and all things considered, that was probably the bravest thing I'd seen him do. A beheading might have been quicker, but he wouldn't want to chance getting the life sentence. Or maybe he thought he could talk Sambah into letting him choose his method of death—perhaps by poison. Same as his victims.

Either way, Graham was ready to meet his maker.

"Don't tell anyone about this," I said, rejoining Sambah. "We could get in a lot of trouble."

"I will say a prayer for Blue, regardless if she is in this world or the next. Thank you for the gift."

"I don't think he sees himself as a gift."

Sambah tilted his head. "I meant the gift of knowledge. King was stolen before his time, but at least now I know how. Soon I will find out why. Sometimes that's all a parent wants, even if it never lessens the pain."

"I have to go." When I reached the truck, I opened the door and called out, "Sambah?"

"Yes?"

"Just promise me you won't eat him."

All I heard was laughter as he went inside the mansion.

On my drive home, I wondered if Sambah would execute Graham right away. Would he torture him? Or maybe he was the type of man who would offer Graham a last meal and give him a comfy bed to sleep in, drawing out the suspense. Graham might get one last night to think about the innocent lives he impacted with his ruthless behavior. Something told me that despite everything, he would never truly have empathy for the victims. Usually in the end, criminals only regretted what had led to their capture.

It was late, I was tired, and as I reached the mansion, a thin fog hovered over the ground like a soft blanket. The truck rolled alongside the stone walls that bordered our property until I reached the black iron gate. The Roman soldier on the arched keystone gave me a stern look as he always did. I swiped my card, entered the property, and drove to the underground garage. The glossy white floors lit up when the automatic lights came on. There was parking to the left and right with a workbench straight ahead. I did a slow turn to the right and then turned right again to park facing the wall.

Christian was standing in my usual spot, hands in his pockets, one foot propped against the wall behind him.

I got out. "What are you doing in here?"

"I had to escape the wee ones."

"Aren't they asleep?"

He branched away from the wall and then kissed my forehead. "They're giggling, and it echoes in the lower level."

"So go to your room."

He raised his brows lazily and looked more exhausted than usual. "Wyatt's having a private party for one in his bedroom with the pitiful music playing. Unless his ghost friend is keeping him company, but I haven't heard him bickering."

"Ah." Wyatt playing sad music wasn't a good sign. I walked to the back of the truck, tossed my green jacket over the edge, and let down the tailgate. "So… what happened?"

"Not much. We just had a few drinks."

"No, I mean about Blue." I sat on the tailgate, remembering how I left her on the sidewalk without a proper goodbye. "I guess I'm too late. I wanted to tell her about Graham—that I caught him."

"You can tell her tomorrow at the breakfast table."

I snapped my gaze up. "What?"

"She's fine. She'll be sleeping through the morning like a babe, but she'll survive."

"How?"

Christian wedged himself between my legs. "I'm tired, Precious. We can talk about that later."

I nestled against his chest, a burden lifted from my shoulders. "You're never tired."

He stroked my back. "And where's the little shite who's responsible for all this mayhem?"

"I couldn't bring him here with all the kids."

"Aye, and you couldn't turn him in either."

I smiled against his chest. "I gave him to King's father. Since King helped us, it seemed like a just reward."

Christian braced his hands on my shoulders and held me back. "You fed him to the lions?"

"I *gave* him to the lions. I'm not positive they'll eat him." I searched his black eyes, wondering if he thought I was a monster.

Christian leaned in and kissed me passionately, his tongue awakening my arousal. "A woman after my own heart," he said against my lips, his hands unfastening my jeans. The panties and shoes went with them.

He branded me with his kiss, deepening it as he consumed me like a tide. His rough hands were around my waist, under my shirt, on my bare thigh, palming my breast, pinching my nipple, grazing my sex, scooting me closer until I was on the very edge of the tailgate.

His kiss softened but never ceased. It became lazy and rhythmic until I wrapped my legs around his waist.

When he slid his cock inside me, he released a shaky breath. "I could kiss your lips for a thousand years."

And it felt like he did. My body hummed as he kissed the corners of my mouth while gently fucking me. Then his tongue was inside my mouth, and I moaned.

Christian pumped faster, the truck rocking back and forth to his rhythm. "Lie down."

I did as he asked, gripping the edge of the tailgate.

Christian devoured my body in a glance. "Lift up your shirt. Hurry."

I peeled the tank top up to my neck, my breasts fighting against the bra as I rocked against his every thrust.

His fangs punched out. "Touch yourself."

"Like this?" I gently cupped my breast before tugging down the bra.

"Aye," he hissed. "Pinch your nipples."

I felt my orgasm sliding closer as I saw the ravenous look in his eyes. When I turned my head and looked up, I gasped. "Christian, the camera!"

"Aye, love. The camera."

"Someone might be watching." I shouldn't have said that, because he was seconds away from climaxing. "What if Wyatt's recording us?"

He flattened his hands on either side of me and controlled the tempo, reading me like a book as he always did. I forgot the damn camera. I forgot my own name. Pleasure crashed through me as he pumped faster and then made that sexy noise he always made right before coming.

I rode the pulses, clenching on the final one that snuck up on me when he pulled out. Christian kissed my thighs while sliding his pants back up.

"Looks like another car wash is in my future." I sat up and

adjusted my shirt. Then I straightened my legs while Christian dressed me in my panties and jeans. "You really don't care about the cameras?"

Christian chuckled. "Wyatt's on drugs, and if you've ever seen him on those mushrooms, he won't be coming out of his chamber for a good while. He's not allowed to record anything anyhow. Besides, the case is over, we're all tired, and no one gives a shite."

Aside from the cameras, I liked the privacy the garage gave us. "Maybe we should cover them next time."

He arched a brow, clearly titillated by the idea that I'd suggest doing this again. "Perhaps a can of shaving cream?"

"You haven't shaved in a century." I picked my keys up from the floor and grabbed the jacket. "Where did you toss my shoes? The floor is cold."

Christian wrapped his arms around my waist and lifted me high off the ground so that I was looking down at him. I planted a soft kiss on his forehead and pinched his dark beard.

"Someday we'll have a real date," I said. "And maybe romantic sex."

"Romantic? Are you not dazzled by the smell of motor oil? Besides, have you forgotten our rooftop date with burgers?"

I placed my mouth by his ear. "Of course not. I'm just joking."

He walked toward the ramp. "Something I've learned in my long life, Raven, is that women never joke. What you consider a joke is really a veiled threat."

"Is that so? What you know about me could fill a thimble."

Christian tickled my waist and made me wiggle in his arms. "Don't be using my words against me."

These were the moments when everything about us felt normal.

"So how did you save Blue?" I asked.

"I gave her about four pints of my blood."

There went normal.

Chapter 30

THE KIDS THREW OUR SCHEDULE into disarray. Sometimes they ate in the courtyard and other times the dining room. Due to the circumstances, Viktor allowed us to eat where and when we wanted until our guests left. I stayed in my room the next morning. After reading a magazine, I admired the trinkets I'd collected from previous cases, including Harper's cigarette case. Maybe someday she'd want it back. Or not. It made me wonder what I'd hold on to if Christian died. Definitely his ring, but what else? An unwashed shirt? A candy dish? His motorcycle? Maybe it would be too painful to keep my necklace, a constant reminder of his devotion.

Around noon, I put on a tank top and my favorite jeans with all the holes and headed to the dining room, where I heard children chattering.

"Anyone seen Blue?"

Wyatt grabbed a leftover pink donut from a serving table to my right and moseyed back to his booth. "Maybe she had to go flap her wings. If you want a donut, you better hurry and eat the last one before I do. They're still fresh, just cold. Ow!" He lifted his foot and plucked something off his sock. "*Son of a ghost.* Who lost a tooth?"

Shepherd launched out of his seat. "Give it to me!"

"I'll give it to you all right." Wyatt held up his hand as if making a hoop shot. The tiny tooth made an arc, struck the edge of Shepherd's glass, and skittered across the table. "Blast!"

Some of the kids squealed, and one went flying into the gathering room.

Wyatt shuddered as he sat down. "I think I lost my appetite."

Gem leaned back in her chair and snagged my attention. "I saw Blue in the courtyard earlier."

"Thanks."

I made my way down the hall and behind the stairs to the main door that led to the courtyard. Blue was lying against a statue of a winged man. I wasn't sure why she liked such a depressing image. The kneeling man covered his face with one hand as if he'd lost everything. We hadn't mowed in a while, so the grass came above her feet. Her tan cargo pants were rolled up, which wasn't her usual style, but the white tank top caught my attention. Since her attack, Blue had stopped wearing tank tops and chose more conservative shirts. But now the gashes that sliced from her shoulder down her chest were visible, and she didn't seem to care.

I took a seat, watching her spin a wildflower between two fingers. "How are you feeling?"

"Better. Alive."

I leaned back on one hand and tugged at a few blades of grass. "I heard you had drinks with Christian last night."

The yellow flower fell onto her chest, and she gave me a remorseful look. "I suppose *that's* why I've never felt better. I came out here before dawn and couldn't believe how bright the stars were. Christian said because of how much I drank, it might have that effect, but it was like seeing the world for the first time."

"You don't regret it? I know how you feel about Vamps."

She sighed and picked up the flower again. "Maybe there's a reason I'm supposed to be alive. Trust me, it wasn't an easy choice. And he wanted to do it the old-fashioned way."

I laughed.

Her eyebrows drew together. "You aren't jealous?"

"Of course not. The way Christian is about his blood, it was probably more of a nightmare for him than it was for you."

"I doubt it. I mean, his blood tasted strangely pleasant, but it was still blood. Every time I thought about it, I wanted to vomit."

"Good thing you didn't. He doesn't like seeing things go to waste."

Blue rolled to her side and propped her head in her hand. "What happened with Graham? I asked Viktor, but he said I should hear it from you. Did you kill him?"

I bent one knee and played with the hole in my jeans. "Not exactly. He tried to throw himself in front of a train."

"You're kidding."

"No. He jumped at the far end, so the conductor was able to stop in time."

"Buffoon."

"Yeah. It might have been easier that way, but he didn't deserve to choose his death. None of his victims got that luxury. Why should he?"

She tucked her hair behind one ear when it caught in the wind. "So what did you do?"

"I took him to Sambah's."

Blue sat up. "You didn't."

I grinned like the Cheshire cat. "I did. But I don't know what happened. I told Sambah about his son, about the case, and he understands the secrecy. I don't think a man of his position is going to tell our secrets."

"No. He wouldn't want the law getting involved in his affairs. Men like him handle their own business, and that's the way the Councils prefer it."

"I don't think there's any reason to tell the other families what happened. It would cause more pain than it's worth. Graham's gone now, and we'd also have to admit that we lied to them. They'd be looking for someone to blame and hiring bounty hunters to find Graham."

Blue stared at the grass. "Yeah. Some of them probably just got over the loss. They need to move on."

"Do you ever really get over losing someone you love? A son? A father?"

She stood and brushed off her hands. "No. You just reach a point when you stop crying at the drop of a hat. When you can wake up and they're not the first thing that comes to mind. And that fills you with a lot of guilt, but it's how we move on."

I hopped up and squinted from the bright sun. "Why do you think Viktor doesn't let the kids swim in the pool?"

She strolled toward the house. "I suppose he doesn't want them drowning. Imagine fifteen kids in the water all at once."

The thought made me laugh out loud. Poor Switch and Kira would have a heart attack. "Do you feel like doing anything today? I was thinking I might pop over to my dad's house and see how he's getting on with that dog."

"No, I've got something important to do. You should come along."

"Where?"

"Sambah's."

I stopped in my tracks. "What for?"

Blue turned and put her hands in her pockets. "Wyatt said that before King went into the light, he asked us to take the children to his father's house. He wants Sambah to care for them. Wyatt ran a check on his pride and found nothing. In fact, Sambah has high praise in the community and donates to several charities. He's a regular saint. King loved his father, so how could I deny a son his last wish?" Blue stopped near a rosebush. "They won't all fit in the van, and we returned the rental, so I need another driver. Wyatt and Claude drive small cars, so that leaves Shepherd."

"I've got a pickup truck. Sambah doesn't live all that far, and if we take the back roads, I can drive slowly. I'm heading out anyhow."

"Aren't there laws about children in trucks?"

"Are you serious? That's how I grew up. Bouncing around in the back of a pickup truck and on my father's bike. That's how you learn that when things get dangerous, you gotta hold on tight."

"You're the strangest former human I've ever met. So many of them follow the rules."

"Those are the *chosen ones*," I said facetiously, making air quotes. "I live for danger."

"Yes, the Mageri certainly like an obedient Mage. I guess

that's how they make sure they don't wind up with a thousand anarchists."

"One is probably enough." I watched a bee hovering near one of the pink roses. "So Sambah didn't have reservations about adopting fifteen kids?"

She cleared her throat. "I haven't asked him yet. We're paying him a surprise visit."

"You're kidding. He won't agree."

"Is that so? Do you think he'll say no to his dead son's final request?" She plucked a pink petal from the flower and strolled toward the doors. "You already buttered him up by handing over his enemy."

"Maybe you should call him first before landing on his doorstep with fifteen mouths to feed."

"Are you serious? Those sweet faces are my backup plan in case he says no."

"You're cutthroat."

Once inside, we ran into Viktor in the foyer.

"I guess I'm ready if they're done eating lunch," Blue said, slipping on a pair of shoes near the door. "If Sambah has plans for Graham, it won't be until nightfall. Unless he took care of business already."

"Perhaps we should keep the children one more night," Viktor suggested. "Until such violent delights are complete."

Blue shook her head. "They would never let the children watch. Besides, if that is going to be their new home, they're going to have to get used to a new way of life. It's not a wolf pack."

Viktor stroked his beard. "I only wish we could have placed them all with wolves. But so many children." He turned away and clapped his hands. "Come, little ones. It is time to go."

The children came barreling out of the dining room, some still holding their sandwiches.

"Grab your dollies," Viktor went on. "I have a special treat for each of you on your way out."

They trampled each other to get to their rooms down the back hall.

Christian descended the stairs. "Are we ready?"

I glared up at him. "Why are you always the first to know, and I'm the last?"

He gave me a crooked grin. "I'm not the one who overslept."

Switch and Kira looked exhausted, but I saw a wistful look in Switch's eyes. He was used to teaching a pack, and I knew he'd miss them. Gem opened the front door and peered out before swinging the door wide. The van was already waiting.

"I'll get the Jeep," Christian said.

I tucked my hands in my pockets. "Let's give Shepherd a break and take my truck instead. Besides, I think the Jeep has engine trouble, and I don't want it breaking down."

Christian turned on his heel and headed out the door. We kept spare keys in the garage, making it easy if someone needed to borrow a vehicle.

"Don't you dare change the radio station!" I shouted through the open door.

When the kids finally dawdled back into the room, they were clutching stuffed animals, dolls, and the rolled-up clothes they'd arrived in.

Viktor called Kira with the crook of his finger. She handed him a basket filled with wrapped caramels—the fancy kind. He gave each child one piece and a gentle pat on the head before Claude and Gem took turns escorting them outside.

When it came to the last girl, Hunter bounded toward Viktor and snatched the only candy left, clutching it to his chest with his gloved hands.

"Hunter, you need to give that back," Shepherd said sternly.

Hunter walked over to the front door and sulked. The little red-haired girl met up with him.

"I like your shoes," she said, pointing to the butterflies on the side.

Poor kid, I thought. Just when he'd finally made some friends his own age.

He held out his hand to give her the candy, and when she took it, she gave him a quick hug, a kiss on the cheek, and flew out the door.

Shepherd looked flummoxed. "He's only *six*," he growled at Switch, who simply chuckled.

Hunter darted back to the dining room, and Switch followed, calling out, "Time for your lessons, kiddo."

I walked up to Shepherd and clapped him on the shoulder. "Looks like you're going to have a heartbreaker when he gets older."

"Older?" Shepherd put a cigarette in his mouth, hands shaking as he struck a match. "One minute his teeth are falling out, the next he's kissing a girl."

"Jesus. They're only six. It's just a crush. You know, he doesn't have to be friendless. I think it might be nice if he goes to visit them."

Shepherd blew out a breath, calmer now. "If it's all the same to you, I think he needs to make new friends."

"Oh, you mean boys? Then you'll have to worry about him lighting firecrackers in the house and setting trash on fire. Take your pick."

Shepherd shook his head and walked off. "Nobody's got time for that."

I looked at Viktor. "Thanks for giving me this case. I know it was a mess."

"You were very fortunate," he said, and I couldn't tell if it was a flippant remark or he was chastising me. Probably the latter, because Viktor held us to high standards. "Now you realize why you cannot choose which cases we accept. I carefully review each request, and I turn away many."

"You don't feel guilty about that?"

"Keystone is not their last resort. It is their first. That is the reputation we have built. What we turn away, someone else will take. Not every inquiry is worth pursuing. I am not Colombo."

My eyes brightened. "Aha! So you *do* watch television. Do you hide one in your private chamber, or maybe you sneak in Wyatt's room in the wee hours of the morning to watch *Baywatch*?"

He fidgeted with the empty basket he was holding. "I heard this name used before. I know nothing of this show."

I patted his arm before strolling out the door. "*Sure*. I believe you."

Viktor was probably telling the truth. He was an astute listener when it came to pop culture references used in conversation, but it still made me laugh to see how flustered he got.

When I looked up, I saw Christian scowling at me from the driver's seat of my truck. Four girls were bouncing around in the bed, and one sat next to him with her bare feet up on the dash. I don't know why, but I found that visual endearing.

It was a slow drive, and twice I had to stick my head out the window and tell the girls to sit down. They were older and knew better. Blue took the younger ones, and she was driving way below the speed limit since she had a baby and two toddlers on board. The mattress was still in the back, so that was likely where the little ones were since we didn't have car seats lying around. Christian shouted profanities at two cars that zoomed around us, and it was clear he was nervous. Like me, he kept checking on the kids in the back even though the little girl in pigtails between us wanted to tell him all about why Elmo is better than the Cookie Monster.

When we finally arrived, members of the Freeman pride were out front, planting pink flowers by the house. One spotted us and went inside.

"Keep the kids quiet," I said, opening the door. "Don't let them run off."

Christian opened his door, and when he started to get out, the little girl held his hand. He looked at her for a second before lifting her up and setting her in the back of the truck with the others.

I strode up to meet Blue, who was waiting at the door. "Wow. This place is gorgeous in the daytime. Look at all those windows. And you don't see many white mansions in the woods. Usually they're log cabins or—"

The door opened abruptly, and Sambah greeted us with a frown.

Not a good sign.

He studied Blue carefully. "You don't look dead to me."

"I'm… I'm not."

Sambah swung a heated gaze my way. "What is this? Were you lying to me?"

Blue hijacked the conversation. "No, she wasn't. The Relic poisoned me, and I won't bore you with the details on how I was cured."

"Please, bore me. Because I would like to know what could have saved my son."

Blue gave me a sideways glance before giving him a sheepish look. "I drank Vampire blood."

Sambah grimaced as if someone had offered him a glass of urine and he'd caught the smell. "Are you not a woman of integrity?"

"Apparently not."

"To what do I owe this honor? I hope you did not change your mind about the Relic, because he is no longer with us."

Blue clasped her hands together. "King had a message for you."

Sambah shut the door behind him and gave us privacy.

"He said you were a kind and fair man," she went on. "Children in your pride are raised with values and love. That you protect them with your life."

"No one harms our children. What is your point?"

Christian was keeping the kids in the truck preoccupied, so Sambah clearly couldn't see any of them. Knowing him, he was probably passing out candy from his pocket.

Blue pinched her bottom lip. "We have children we need to place. I can't tell you the reason or else it implicates us in something criminal. You understand what I'm saying?"

"Go on."

She turned and motioned for him to walk with her. "These kids are special, and they need to stay together. We think some of them are siblings, but we're not sure, and there's no way for us to find out now."

"Where is their pride?"

"Uh, that's the thing. They're not from a pride. They're wolves."

Sambah stopped at the back of the van. "Why not give them to a pack? There are many—"

"We tried looking into that, but there aren't any with the capacity to take in this many. And fewer that we would trust."

"How many are we talking about?"

She flung open the back doors. "Fifteen."

Sambah craned his neck and peered inside. The children looked warily at him, uncertain of where this trip was taking them, only that they were leaving us. Then he noticed the kids in the back of my truck. "That is a lot of children."

She turned her back to the kids and walked out of their view. "This was King's final request. I wasn't sure at first, but I did a background check on you. Squeaky clean. I wouldn't be here unless you were our only hope of keeping them together. But there's something else you should know," she said quietly. "These kids might grow up with problems due to trauma. They've been through hell, and I don't know what kind of special care they might need."

Sambah straightened his back and looked upward for a moment. "Then they've come to the right place. This is a house of healing. I have more money and more room than a man could dream of."

Blue and I shared a look before she spoke. "You'll take them?"

"You sound surprised. Did you think I would turn away orphans?"

"I wasn't sure you'd want them."

"Why? Because most of them are white?"

"No. Because they're wolves. I don't know how they would fit in with a group of lions, but we don't have any other options. I got a good feeling coming here, and King swore they'd be safe. Can you give me your word that no one in this pride will ever hurt them? That includes you. They need protection."

Sambah held her gaze and rested his hands on her shoulders. "I give you my word on my son's grave that I will never let any harm come to them. When they grow up and choose to leave, they will still be a part of this family."

"If I find out otherwise, I'll gut you like a fish. You know I'll do it."

He stepped back and bowed. "I would expect nothing less." Sambah clapped his hands. "Come, children. Gather round."

Kids poured out of the van and from the back of the truck. Some clung to each other, fear and uncertainty flickering in their eyes.

Sambah bent over and gave them a warm smile. "My name is Sambah Freeman. Can you say that?"

All the kids repeated after him like zombies, and he laughed.

"Yes, but you can call me Father. This is your new home, and I don't want any of you to be afraid. I am going to take care of you from now on. You're a part of a great big family with many traditions. We can decide later if you want to sleep in the same room or spread out. But for now, why don't you join my brother, and he will show you to the kitchen."

"Oh, they just ate," I said.

Sambah slowly pivoted. "And did they have pudding?"

That was enough to stir up their excitement. Some of the kids were practically bouncing like little pogo sticks.

Sambah whistled with two fingers, and Joba emerged from inside. He was dressed in royal blue and looked every bit a prince. It made me wonder if the hierarchy in prides was the same as packs.

Joba gave his brother a loaded glance.

"Meet your new brothers and sisters," Sambah said. "We won't ask them any questions about where they came from, and I know you'll inform everyone else of the same. They are a gift from King, and a new beginning for us all. Please have someone feed them pudding, and I'll be there shortly."

Joba arched his brows, clearly in disbelief, but only laughed when he looked at all the inquisitive faces. "Come, little ones. Who likes chocolate?"

Each one demanded that they liked it more than the last. Two of the older girls carried the babies, and it was the first time I felt like they were going to be okay. They had a lot to figure out, but they would grow up with all the advantages and hopefully receive special care from the best Relics.

"I can't thank you enough," Blue said, closing the van doors. She leaned against the back, her scars on full display beneath the white tank top. "I was losing sleep over it."

Sambah adjusted his brown tunic and directed his attention to me. "You said you would see if my son had a message."

I looked to Blue, who answered for me. "I spoke to Wyatt this morning, and he relayed everything. King said he didn't appreciate you enough, but he hopes that these children will. He really wanted them to come here. He said it was in the fates, and maybe that's why he was compelled to stay behind. He loves his dear father and always will. That's all he said."

Sambah essayed a smile, his eyes glimmering. "If King believes this will strengthen my family and help the children, then we will honor his spirit. Even in death, he was a good man. My heart sings with joy. I think we will celebrate tonight."

Blue gave him a look I couldn't discern. "You just found out your son was murdered, and now he's left this world. How can you look so happy?"

I wondered if he might be insulted by that comment, but Sambah searched her eyes respectfully.

"You can't let the pain of death steal away the memories of life," he explained. "That will take you to dark places you never knew within yourself. Perhaps you know those places already. King is not the only child I've lost. I'm an old man, and I have outlived seven of my children. Four were little and the others grown. It was more painful to lose the small ones. You dwell on the things they'll never experience. But as parents, we must honor their souls as they have rejoined their great ancestors on their next journey. Holding on to pain only allows it to fester. It brings nothing. You close off your heart and won't be able to give back to this world. And what becomes the purpose of your life? You are nothing but a dead tree, struck by lightning but still standing. Hollow inside." He took a deep breath and looked between us. "This is a day for rejoicing. My son has joined his ancestors in the afterlife on their next journey, and he has bestowed us with the greatest gift and responsibility." Sambah shook his head and laughed. "Wolves. King always had a sense of humor. He got that from his mother."

Voices inside the house overlapped in song. The beautiful melody amplified in the quiet space of the woods.

Blue inched toward him. "No offense, but when I first saw this place, I never imagined so much warmth and love would be inside such a cold exterior."

Sambah tilted her chin up with the crook of his finger. "I find that hard to believe." He turned away, heading to the door.

"Mr. Freeman?" I called out. "Would you mind if we brought them a visitor sometime? He made friends with them."

Sambah waved. "Come by anytime, Raven and Blue. You are always welcome here."

Blue gave me a startled look. "Fates. That was easy as hell. I didn't think he'd jump on it so fast."

"King sealed the deal. Did he really say all that? Or was it part of your plan to get on his good side?"

Blue's expression went flat. "I would *never* lie to someone about their dead child."

"Sorry. Didn't mean to suggest you would. Hey, why don't we grab some barbecue?"

"Maybe we should just go home."

"I know for a fact you loved that place we went to with my dad that time."

"Oh, *that* place? Hmm."

I waved at Christian, who was listening from inside the truck. "I still need to meet with Ren and talk to him about all this. He won't want to do it on the phone, so I'll invite him out for lunch."

"Are you going to tell him about Graham?"

I shook my head. "I'm a good liar, but Ren's also a really smart wolf. I need to dance around the truth, but maybe if he gets a few beers in him, he won't notice I'm dancing."

She smiled and headed toward the driver's door. "Let me call Viktor first and tell him how things went. He'll be relieved to know the pride took them in. I think he wants to meet with Sambah to personally thank him and check on the kids."

"Okay then. We'll meet you there."

Blue looked over her shoulder. "Raven? Do me a favor."

"Sure. Anything."

"Don't order any hot dogs."

Chapter 31

WE MET UP AT SKULLS, my father's favorite barbecue smokehouse. Despite being a workaholic, Crush usually took Sundays off, so I invited him to join us. Crush never turned down barbecue. I figured with him there, it would break any tension I might inadvertently create with Ren.

Instead of sitting inside the crowded restaurant, we lounged on the back patio beneath a wooden pergola. Christian and I ordered beers and a large tin of ribs, which he wasn't keen on eating.

"You know you can't leave here without eating," I reminded him. "They have spies. Didn't you learn your lesson from last time?"

"I can't say I'm hungry."

Ren threw him a frosty gaze. "You can't trust a man who doesn't eat."

Christian turned toward him, straddling the bench to my right. "Is that so? Does that mean you don't trust a man who doesn't take a shite? In that case, pass me the potato salad, because I'll have none of that coming out of my arse," he said, gesturing toward the tin of meat.

I spit out my lemonade when Ren dropped the entire tin of potato salad in front of Christian, some of it spattering onto his shirt.

"I'm glad you came," I said to Tank, who bumped shoulders with me.

"Wouldn't miss it."

My father's friends were the closest I had to family. Now that I knew they were Shifters, it cast a new light on them. Some of their rituals made sense, as did their protectiveness and loyalty. Had I never become immortal, they couldn't have kept their secret for long. Not without giving me their anti-aging cream. Even though I'd only invited Ren, when barbecue was involved, it became a family affair. Familiar faces filled the patio space, and kids raced around in a game of tag.

Ren licked sauce off his fingers. "Where's your old man? I thought he was coming."

"He said he'd be here, but there was something he had to do first." I looked across the table at the orange soda and empty plate, suddenly worried. What if something had happened to him?

"I'm in love with this place," Blue said around a mouthful of dinner roll. "We should do this every single week."

"My kind of girl," Ren said. "Raven knows how to pick good friends. Well, mostly." He met eyes with Christian before returning to another conversation.

"Little gobshite," Christian muttered.

I touched my chin against my shoulder and lowered my voice. "Don't start shit with these people. You're out of your league."

"Is that so? I'll have you know I can bend steel."

"And I'll have you know that half of them carry impalement wood and have no problems tossing a fanghole into one of the firepits."

"You come from a twisted family, Miss Black. What do they have against me other than my Breed? Don't they know you're my sweetheart?"

"Yep. But they don't think we'll last."

Without warning, Christian rose to his feet and slowly peeled off his shirt. He stood there in nothing but his black jeans, black boots, and black raven tattoo.

It got quiet.

Real quiet.

Christian sat back down. "That settles that."

Blue snickered from the bench across from him. She seemed different today, and I wasn't sure if it was Christian's blood, the alcohol, or getting a second chance at life. In any case, she was drinking in more than the alcohol.

"Boy, you should have heard what Sambah said to me," she said, eyebrows arched high.

I lurched over the table and lowered my voice. "What? I thought you left right after us."

"I did." Blue reached for a container of baked beans and dipped her spoon in. "But while I was on the phone with Viktor, Sambah came out, thinking something was wrong. We got to talking, and I asked about you-know-who."

She meant Graham, but we weren't going to mention him by name in present company.

I glanced around to make sure no one was listening. "What did he say?"

She finished eating a spoonful of beans, a half grin lingering. "He didn't tell me what they did to him or how he died. All I know is that they buried him on the property."

"That's surprising because?"

"They made his grave a permanent outdoor urinal."

Christian choked on his potato salad.

"I think they put flowers or a bush or something on his grave," she went on, barely bottling her laughter. "So the only way they're allowed to water the flowers is to piss on him."

I had to credit Sambah for his creativity. I sat back in my seat and nibbled the last good meat off the bone before pushing my plate away.

"Are you going to waste that?" Christian asked. "There are starving children in the world, and there's still meat on those bones."

"I don't like fat and gristle."

Ren reached over, took my plate, and stripped the meat clean off the bone, making me grimace.

"*Jaysus, Mary, and Joseph.* Is that your da?"

I turned toward the sound of a motorcycle rumbling on the street to my right. Crush was facing us at the stop sign, and I actually stood to get a better look over the rosebushes. "*Holy shit.* You've got to be kidding me."

"What?" Ren launched to his feet to see what had grabbed everyone's attention. "That motherfucker actually did it. Sorry, Raven. I can't promise what my boys will do to him."

My dad sat on his big Harley, a black bandana tied over his head like a cap and his black shades on. He looked proud as hell, which wasn't unusual whenever he rode his bike around. But what *was* unusual was the sidecar with the dog inside.

Blue sputtered with laughter. "Oh *fates*. Is that dog wearing goggles? What do they call those? Doggles?" She reached for her beer, still laughing.

Crush spotted us and waved as he turned the corner to park out front.

I sat, a stunned feeling sweeping over me. Crush had unwillingly accepted a pet and then taken it to another level.

I patted the table in front of Ren, who had also sat back down. "Does everyone know he has a pet?"

"They do now."

After another minute, Crush sauntered onto the patio and took off his shades. "Everyone, this is Harley. He's my partner."

Someone wolf whistled.

Crush snapped his fingers. "I'll remember that the next time you bring in that piece-of-shit Kawasaki for me to fix again, *Leonard*."

"It's Lenny, you asshole," the man yelled back over all the laughter.

Harley should have been tempted by the smell of delicious meat, but he looked up to Crush with anticipation and seemed to read his body language. Crush didn't give him any commands. Instead, he rounded the table and I stood to give him a hug. It seemed like each time we hugged, it was as if we hadn't seen each other in years. And I loved it.

"How's my Cookie?" he rumbled in my hair.

I jerked back. "A sidecar? You couldn't just leave him at home?"

"Where I go, he goes."

"The years you've spent building a reputation, tarnished in seven seconds. You'll never live it down. You'll always be the guy with the doggie sidecar." I tugged his goatee.

"Don't give me your sass." He passed Christian and patted Blue on the shoulder after rounding the table. "Glad to see you."

She touched his hand before shoveling more beans into her mouth.

Crush couldn't sit quietly. It was always a symphony of grunts, audible sighs, popping knees, and cursing after striking his elbow on the table. He tugged the tray of meat in front of him and filled his plate. Harley circled behind his chair and lay down.

"That's a big-ass dog," Tank remarked. "You better feed it something, or it might eat you up."

"He prefers eating Shifters," Crush fired back, his remark receiving laughter. He sized Christian up. "Do I have to stare at his nipples while I eat?"

Christian folded his arms on the table. "Do you have a problem with fit bodies in supreme condition?"

Crush narrowed his eyes, and when I saw that look on his face, I wasn't sure what would happen next. My father stood up, eyes locked on Christian, and stripped off his Doobie Brothers shirt.

I facepalmed. "Oh Jesus. Make it stop."

"Nobody wants to see that," someone heckled him.

I tapped my dad's plate to get his attention. "At least take the goggles off the dog. People are laughing."

He pulled out his pants pockets before sitting. "I'm all out of fucks to give. They'll have a laugh and get over it. Either that or they'll get a dog bite in the ass."

Ren straightened his back and belched. "Raven, you wanna take a walk while these two make out?"

"Sure." I wiped my mouth and then followed Ren to the short chain-link fence. There were roses on the outside, and we rested our elbows on the fence and leaned forward to look at them.

"So what did you call me here for?" he asked.

"I'm closing the case. You can stop payments."

He cupped a yellow rose in his hand. "What did you find?"

"Nothing. Well, not nothing. Blue and I questioned everyone. We were careful about it."

"Yeah, I heard you're paying for dead alphas."

"It's not what it looks like." I turned to face him, one arm resting on the metal. "We thought it would be a good way to show that the higher authority is trying to work things out with the Shifter community."

He mirrored my position. "Uh-huh. Why just the alphas?"

"We can't afford to pay everyone. Some of the people we spoke to weren't that receptive to our questions. You know how that goes. We had to think on our feet. Alphas are valuable, so we limited it to them. It made our job easier. Don't worry, we have someone paying up."

Ren took his aviators from the collar of his shirt and slid them over his eyes. "What did the Relic have to say?"

"He agreed with our findings. Said he didn't see anything suspicious. I mean, a few of the deaths looked questionable. Most were from natural causes or accidents, and only a handful might have been due to foul play. Probably someone in the family, but we can't pursue those."

"You spoke to him this morning?"

I scratched my neck. "No." I could sense he was parsing my words, so I held my tongue.

Ren looked off toward the road. "Funny. I spoke to someone this morning who said Graham Wiggins went missing. Three packs had an appointment with him last night and today—he never showed. He's not answering. His car's at home, but nobody's there. It's like poof"—Ren snapped his fingers—"he vanished into thin air. You wouldn't know anything about that, would you?"

"Not a thing." I tugged my earlobe and looked at the table. Crush and Christian were playing rock, paper, scissors. Others were laying down bills and betting on them. "I have the name of a bear sleuth who likes chaining up women. Are you interested?"

Ren's jaw clenched. "You sure about that?"

"Yep. They're not in city limits. We freed one woman, but I don't think it was the first time they've done something like that."

"Yeah. Give me a name."

I was relieved he took the offer. Maybe that would distract him enough to stop thinking about the missing Relic. "Franklin. Just do me a favor and leave a man named Ferro alone. He lost a son."

"If he's part of that group, he's part of their dirty crimes."

"Maybe, but all the same, I don't want to see a grieving father slain. Turn him over to the Council."

Ren gave a curt nod. "You got it."

"Sorry I couldn't solve your case."

He fell into stride beside me. "Something tells me you already did, but we're not gonna talk about that, are we?"

"Nothing to talk about."

"That's what I thought. But I think it's worth underscoring that a lot of packs are out a Relic. It's not easy finding a qualified replacement."

"I'll see what I can do to help out with that problem."

He adjusted his glasses. "A problem you don't know anything about."

"Exactly. And Ren? No more side favors. This was a really messy case, and people got hurt. If you ever need help, you'll have to go straight to Viktor."

"Understood."

Harley started barking uncontrollably at the restaurant entryway. Suddenly a few people put their beers down and stood. A tall man lingered in the doorway, a duffel bag slung over his shoulder. This was primarily a Shifter joint, and everyone knew everyone.

No one knew this guy.

But I did.

And so did Blue.

She turned to look. "Matteo? What are you doing here?"

Harley kept barking, drool flinging left and right.

Matteo acknowledged everyone before turning his attention to Blue. "May I speak with you privately?"

"Later," she said. "Not here."

"I'm leaving. I just wanted to say goodbye." He turned his

Chitah gaze to the onlookers and felt their cold reception. "Goodbye, Blue."

Crush patted Harley's side and fed him a hunk of meat as a reward.

I sat down in front of Blue. "You should talk to him before he's gone. He came all this way."

Her eyes swung up to the empty doorway, and a look of regret crossed her expression before she ran after him.

Blue stumbled into the restaurant and rushed toward the front door. It was rowdy in there—a dizzying mixture of laughter, boisterous chatter, and rock music. She accidentally bumped into a woman while rushing outside.

Matteo headed down the concrete walkway.

"Matteo, wait." She strode toward him, wishing she hadn't had all those beers.

He stopped by a rosebush on the corner and turned.

Blue gestured toward the faded wooden bench against the building. "Let's talk."

They sat and waited for a couple to pass them and go inside. A cool breeze stirred up the leaves on the bushes, and Blue was glad that she'd worn the tank top today. And not one that concealed all her scars, but a low-cut shirt that let her enjoy the weather along with everyone else. She didn't give a damn about the stares.

"What changed your mind?" she asked.

He laced his fingers together and leaned back, legs stretched out. "I suppose the thought entered my mind when I helped you rescue the children in the warehouse."

"You shouldn't have been there."

"Where young are concerned, I will always be there to help. It wasn't until then that I realized where I truly belong. You were right. I need to return. Those children need protection to make it safely to the sanctuary, and I'm the only one who knows those woods." Matteo faced her, his voice as soft as the breeze. "Come with me."

"You said you realized where you belonged. It's the same for me. I belong here with Keystone. I figured it out last night when I was dying." She rested her arm on the back of the bench. "After the lion attack, I wasn't the same. I felt guilty for surviving. It didn't seem fair that my sons had to die, and I was still here. Their deaths haunt me, but I've accepted it. I've had enough time to move on. You're still not over the deaths of your mate and child. Everyone heals differently, and I can see your wounds are still fresh."

"Balderdash."

"Really? Last night you should have gone after the Relic. But you just stared at me like you were reliving an old nightmare. You're not as ready for a relationship as you think you are. No one can heal your pain—you have to heal yourself. Going back to West Virginia and working with the sanctuary will be good for you. That's your calling in life. That's what's going to heal you. Not a replacement."

"So I should forego love because I've lost my kindred spirit?"

"No, but what is it you like about *me*? The kiss I gave you was payment, not an invitation. Is it the scars? Do you think because I don't have any prospects that I'll stay by your side? You learned nothing about me back at the cave—not enough to bring you all the way up to Cognito. Tell me what you expect."

"A gentle word. Would you cast me away so hastily? Your scars are a map to your heart, and any man who can't see that is a fool."

Blue sighed and watched a family pile into their car. "Maybe not everyone is meant for love. And that should be okay."

He turned his gaze toward the parking lot. The sun glinted off the windshields and chrome on the bikes. "Have you ever considered paying a Sensor to take away the pain?"

It wasn't unusual for immortals to engage in that type of sensory transaction. Sensors couldn't remove memories, but they could remove all the emotions tied to them. "That pain is what drives me. It's what makes me do what I do. That's what happens when you find a purpose. You learn to channel all that pain into something else, whether it's good or evil. I catch bad guys, and the ass-kicking I do helps me work out all that aggression."

Matteo chuckled softly.

"There was a time I considered it," she admitted, knowing he might be seeking permission. "I once let that pain drag me under, and I thought about it. My boys deserve my tears. But I wouldn't judge anyone for doing it. Sometimes what we suffer through is more than we can endure. I can't imagine what you must be going through with losing your baby and then your kindred spirit. I know kindreds have a bond that's stronger than soul mates. It must have been a crushing loss. If you think removing the pain will help you get on with your life, then maybe you should."

He slowly ran his hand over his mouth. "I'm thinking about it."

"You'll still have all the wonderful memories and feelings for them but without the rest. Time isn't linear. It's a series of lines and loops. The lines are all the ordinary, mundane parts. The loops are the moments that change us—death, birth, tragedy. When we reflect on our life, we get caught in the loops and live in them. We circle back to those moments, replaying them in our head over and over until we drown in the emotions. And when the loop is a tragic one, all you can think about are the things you did wrong. What you didn't say, what you could have done differently, how it could have been prevented, and it consumes you. I lived in the loops for a long, long time." She reclined her head against the wall behind them. "Sometimes, if I'm not careful, I can slip into them. Like I did with you when I told my story. But you know what I found out, Matteo? It's not the loops that matter. It's the lines. It's those ordinary moments that matter more than anything else. The lines are so long, but we waste our lives, caught in the loops."

"You have an interesting mind, female. I would have enjoyed getting to know you more."

"Sorry. I had too many beers."

"I noticed. Your demeanor seems altered."

She shrugged. "I feel reborn in a strange way. It took almost dying to remind me why I wanted to live. As much as I want answers from the afterlife, my job here isn't done."

He reached out and held her hand. "Someday, when this life can give you no more, I'll be waiting. When your heart has been broken by some other male, I'll be there to mend it. When you are alone, I will keep you company. And should you desire children, I will father them and raise them with love. Maybe not in fifty years, maybe not even in a hundred. But life is very long, and it can be so lonely. I know that more than anyone."

"That's because you live in a cabin in the woods." She smiled warmly at him. "Maybe you should move into town. Make some friends, find a routine. It helps to be around people." She shifted to look directly at him but slid her hand out of his grasp. "You're not here because of me. You're here because of a kiss. It made you feel something you haven't felt in a long time, and that had nothing to do with me. Besides, I could never be with someone who knows the pain of losing a child. I can barely manage my own pain, and I don't want to share that same grief with someone. Can you understand that? Losing a child is incomparable to anything else. You know that, and someday you'll understand my reasons. Sometimes it helps to surround yourself with people who *don't* know about your past."

"You don't feel that you're living a lie?"

She gave him a pensive stare. "How many times do you want to repeat your story? Is that even something everyone is entitled to? Being with people who share your tragedy is healing. But being around those who don't is freeing. Maybe it's not that way for everyone, but it is for me."

When Matteo rose to his feet, the light seemed to embrace him. His eyes were as golden as the sun, his hair as dark and wild as the earth. Maybe it was the alcohol talking, but she briefly wondered what her life might look like if she accepted his offer. Could she settle with a man who wasn't her Breed? He was handsome enough, and he'd proven himself noble. But what would she do with herself in a cabin in the woods? Would that be enough?

No. It wouldn't.

He offered her his hand, and she stood up. She got a crick in her neck looking up at him. His clothes were tattered, his dark beard sparse and long. She wanted to tell him that he didn't need to hide under all that hair any more than she needed to cover her scars with shirts and sweaters.

He cupped her nape and gave her a sideways smile. "I hold no judgment against your choice, but I've done my best to prove myself a worthy male."

"And you are worthy."

"Just not worthy enough."

She held his wrist. "Not for me. But someday you'll be worthy enough for yourself."

"Perhaps."

"How will you get home?"

"The same way I got here," he said enigmatically.

"You look like a nomad. You'll never hitch a ride. If you walked, I can pay for a train ticket."

He searched her eyes for a long while before lifting his bag and slinging it over his shoulder. "You should tell him."

"Tell who what?"

"Viktor." He leaned in tight. "Do you think I can't scent your feelings for him, female?"

Blue's words caught in her throat as she looked at him.

Matteo stepped off the porch. "Should he ever be bold enough to court you, he'll be a lucky male." Matteo bowed. "My lady."

Blue gripped a wooden post and watched the mysterious Chitah cross the parking lot and disappear into a blaze of sunshine. Matteo closed the door on a future with him, yet she couldn't help but wonder if he hadn't opened another door… just a crack.

Chapter 32

WE STAYED AT SKULLS FOR hours—well after sundown. The lights wrapped around the pergola created a warm ambience, as did all the beer. I cut myself off early on, knowing I'd be driving. I didn't want to put Crush in an embarrassing situation. It got rowdy, as it usually did with my father's buddies, but we had a good time. Even Christian loosened up and made a few friends. He still kept his shirt off. The whole night.

As did my father, for no other reason than to prove he didn't give a damn what anyone thought about his less-than-perfect physique. Men were shameless.

I straddled the bench next to Christian and nibbled on his shoulder. He turned his head and gave me a heated gaze.

"You're going to have to drive Blue home," I informed him. "She's wasted."

He looked ahead at Blue, who was sitting cross-legged on a table, listening to a woman spinning a tall tale. "Aye, she's a bit langered. But having a good time."

"I don't think I've ever seen her so relaxed."

Christian waggled his brows. "My blood has that effect on people."

"Why are you sitting here all by yourself?"

"No one wanted to arm wrestle."

Our fingers curled and twined as if getting to know each other. I touched the onyx ring I'd given him and grinned like a fool.

Christian lightly smacked my arm. Quicker than a heartbeat,

two angry men hoisted him to his feet, and you could cut the tension with a knife.

Christian held up his palm. "*Jaysus wept.* It was a fecking mosquito."

I rose to my feet. "I think it's time for us to head out. Let the Vamp go. He has permission to kill anything sucking on me."

"Even himself?" a man growled.

That sent me into a fit of laughter.

"Havin' a good time, are ya?" Christian asked me while shaking free from the men's grip.

I found his shirt and tossed it at him. "You better go before you wind up on a spit."

He slid on his shirt and then circled his arms around my waist. "Is that so, Precious? You'd watch them burn me on the fire?"

"I'd make sure they didn't eat you."

He playfully kissed my neck. "Pity. I've heard I'm quite delicious."

"You better get Blue home before someone puts her on the karaoke machine."

Christian sighed dramatically. "It'll be a blessing to not hear the shenanigans of fifteen wee ones. Finally, I'll have some peace and quiet."

"Admit it—you'll miss them."

"Like I miss the plague."

I glanced at a couple dancing by the roses. "I'm thinking of giving my pay to the other victims. Lenore's taking care of the alphas, but I feel guilty about the rest."

Christian frowned. "You can't just be giving away all your money every time you have a job. You need to build your finances. That's the only way to survive."

"I know, but I feel shitty about the whole thing. After talking to Ren, I can't stop thinking about all those people I lied to. Some of them lost children. Maybe they'll accept a compensation package for sharing their stories, and if they don't, I'll donate their share to charity. Don't judge me. I didn't come from money, and I survived just fine. Sometimes it feels like we get paid too much for these jobs. I know I need to save it, and I do, but it feels wrong to keep it all. Even Viktor gives some of his away."

"Fine, Mother Teresa. Just don't come weeping to me in a hundred years because you can't afford a hamburger."

I tapped my foot against his ankle. "I'm a skilled scavenger, remember? I can talk any man out of his onion rings."

His eyes twinkled with the memory of how we met. "You never stood a chance, Precious."

"Not against the Lord of the Onion Rings. I'll meet you back home."

We fell into a deep, passionate kiss. His arm snaked around my lower waist, his hand cradled my neck, and I gave him all of me. Maybe I didn't have much to give, but everything I had was his. My heart, my soul, my family, my friends, my past, my future, my secrets…

Well, maybe not *all* my secrets.

When our kiss simmered to a few lingering pecks, I fell back on my heels. People were staring, mostly women who undoubtedly wished their man would kiss them like that.

He caressed my cheek. "I'll be on my way to take the drunkard home."

"Keep the bed warm."

That put a twinkle in his eye as he hurried off.

I found Crush, who was sitting at the end of a table, Harley at his side.

I patted the dog's head as he licked my elbow. "I'm heading out."

"This early?" a woman said in disbelief.

Crush chuckled. "Sometimes I wonder if she's really mine."

I smacked him on the back of the head.

Ren smiled. "Yeah, she's yours."

We practically dressed alike. Ripped jeans, boots, and usually a tank top or T-shirt. At least I had the good sense to keep my clothes on.

I reached over the table and grabbed his wadded-up shirt. "Put this on."

"Why? Are you ashamed of your daddy?"

"No. But I don't want you to catch pneumonia."

He snatched the shirt from my hand and reluctantly put it on, knowing I would only further embarrass him if he argued with me. In some ways, I mothered him. But Crush needed it. He'd spent his entire life taking care of me, and now it was my turn. Maybe I gave him a little hell, but paybacks were a bitch. This was still the same man who brought his buddies and a bunch of air horns to my sixth-grade spelling bee.

"So what do you think of Crush's dog?" I asked the small group.

Tank chuckled from his spot on top of the table. "We were taking bets on whether he's a horse or a dog."

I patted Harley. "He's a good watchdog," I put out there, knowing Crush would never admit Harley's true function.

Crush cleared his throat. "Yeah, he keeps an eye on my garage when I'm busy working. Makes sure to keep out all the riffraff. Don'tcha, boy?"

Harley leaned into him and cleaned Crush's neck with his tongue. My father wrapped his arm around him, and they looked like old pals.

"I think he's a good dog," Ren declared, and that was all it took to put his pack in line. Those who belonged to neighboring packs respected him enough not to be a jerk.

I was glad for it. Not only glad that I wouldn't have to worry about someone creeping up on my dad's property at night, but also glad that Crush had a companion. One he could talk to, look after, and who would keep him company whenever he felt lonely.

I lifted the dog's goggles off the table. "Daddy, are these really necessary?"

He took them away from me. "Just wait until you see the leather jacket I ordered."

"Goodbye." I turned on my heel, but before I could take a step, Crush gripped my wrist and yanked me backward.

"Hold on, little girl. You don't walk away from your daddy without a hug."

Crush tried to show off by lifting me off the ground. I squirmed like a fish, afraid he would throw out his back. Laughter erupted from behind him.

When I realized Crush wasn't letting go, I asked, "Does he have a little doggie seat belt too?"

Crush dropped me on my feet and glowered.

I kissed his cheek. "Stop pretending like you could ever be mad at me."

When I walked off, I heard him boast, "That's my girl. Did you know she single-handedly took down that fighting ring?"

I rolled my eyes, realizing that man couldn't keep anything secret, let alone tell it straight.

After closing my tab, I left Skulls in the best of moods.

On the drive home, I took my preferred route along side streets and scenic roads. The intoxicating smells and sounds of summertime stole my thoughts. The crickets and frogs sang in harmony the farther away I got from the city. My hair snaked out the breezy open window, and I leaned into the wind, the headlights shining a path down the dark road.

I jerked my head up when a man appeared in front of my truck. I slammed my foot on the brakes, my body lurching forward before coming to an abrupt stop.

Houdini's hands were in his coat pockets, the collar pulled up. The headlights made his hair appear exceptionally white, and he looked more like an apparition than my nemesis. From his spiky hair, black ear studs, and jeans, he seemed desperate to avoid looking like an aristocrat who might have once worn a white wig and breeches. Or maybe a top hat and cane.

I shut off the engine but kept the lights on. Houdini remained motionless, his hazel eyes never breaking contact. His gaze was unnerving—the way his dark eyebrows sloped down, his blank expression.

I got out and searched the dark woods. "What are you doing out here?"

"Taking a walk on a moonlit night."

I closed the distance between us, casting a shadow on him.

Houdini suddenly smiled, taking on that affable personality I'd come to know. But it was odd how he could switch it on and off so quickly. "I've missed my youngling. It seems you've been busy."

"I have a job. And a life. One you're not a part of."

"That remains to be seen."

"Stop pretending like you have claim over me. If you want to talk to me, why don't you come by and ring the bell?"

Houdini bent over and laughed heartily. "That's an asinine idea, but you haven't lost your sense of humor." He inched toward me. "I like privacy. I also like catching you off guard." Houdini winked so quickly that I barely caught it. "You're less likely to be armed."

"If I wanted to kill you, you'd be dead."

"Oh really?" He nodded smugly, suppressing a grin. "Haven't you reached your kill limit for the week?"

Is he baiting me? Does he know what I've been up to? I didn't give him the satisfaction of my surprise.

"Maybe you should focus on your own problems," I suggested, lifting my chin an inch higher. "Don't you have someone else's life to ruin with all your pranks?"

"You think your becoming immortal was a prank?"

"I think you being my maker is the biggest joke of all. I can't tell if you're trying to spark up a relationship with me or get back the key I have in my possession. Someone should teach you how to pick a lock."

"Not knowing my motives really bothers you, doesn't it?" He swung his gaze up to the trees. "Maybe I don't have any motives, Raven. Have you ever considered that?"

"You stopped me in the middle of nowhere to tell me that you don't have an agenda?"

"No, this isn't nowhere. You're always somewhere." Houdini took his hands out of his pockets and clasped them. "Not many people travel this road."

"That's because it leads to a private road, so only people who live out here take this route."

He smiled enigmatically. "Where's your partner?"

I folded my arms. "He's in my bed, waiting for me."

"Are you sure about that?"

I chuckled. "Is that why you're here? To deliver another scolding? I told Christian to leave your club alone, but he has a mind of his own. I didn't tell him you gave me that spiked drink if that's what you're afraid of."

"Of that I'm certain. I'm sure he would have fumbled a murder attempt by now."

"Christian doesn't fumble."

"I do find it curious why, if you are lovers, you don't share that information with him. Don't you believe in honesty?"

"Have you ever been in a relationship? If so, then you'd know that there are two kinds of secrets. The first is deception. You tell a lie or keep a secret in order to protect yourself, or because you think you know better. That's the one that'll get you in the most trouble, because it's usually a lie designed to hurt the other person."

"And the second?"

"That's the one that protects the person you love. I personally don't give a shit that you spiked my drink. I wouldn't expect anything less from someone like you. But if Christian found out, he'd kill you. Whether he succeeds or fails won't matter, because neither outcome is one I want to live with."

Houdini played with the black stud in his earlobe as he paced away from the headlights. "I find that truly fascinating. You know, I never gave much thought about the intricacies of a relationship. So… you believe if a lie is spun that protects the teller, it should be brought to light?"

"Ideally." I glanced back at the empty road. If Houdini was the one who had buried me, I was vulnerable out here.

He kicked a pebble off the road. "If you've kept our little secret to protect Poe, what secrets do you think he's kept from you?"

"None. But if he has any, I trust they're the kind to protect me and not his own mistakes." I backed up a step.

Houdini turned on his heel. "Christian isn't faithful."

"I know your games, and I'm not playing."

Houdini drifted toward me. "Don't you ever wonder where he goes at night? Where he goes for days at a time?"

"If he had another lover, I'd know."

Houdini stood close. Too close. "You can do better than that."

I furrowed my brow, staring at a button on his coat.

"It's not uncommon for Vampires to have bloodslaves," he put out there.

"Christian would never do that."

"Oh?" He turned away and paced a few feet before stopping. "How can you be so sure?"

Though I wanted to argue, I couldn't help but remember how Christian was once addicted to Lenore's blood. How in some ways he was even addicted to mine. Blood was not a necessity to survive among Vampires—it was a drug. Lenore had warned me about Christian's habits, but a bloodslave? That was one secret I had never considered.

Could he?

Would he?

When had his disappearances started? I tried to recall a specific time, but I couldn't. It seemed like it was after Lenore had first shown up. No… no, I was certain it started before that.

"Fuck you," I spat out, returning to my truck. "All you do is stick your nose where it doesn't belong."

I was mad at myself for letting him push my buttons. Messing with my head was one thing, but messing with my love life was another. I yanked the truck door open, and Houdini was there in a flash, gripping it.

"Raven, I'm not here to play games. You clearly stated you think lies should be brought to light if they're only designed to protect the person keeping the secret because they have sinned."

I wanted to ask how Houdini knew about Christian's disappearances, but he would never give a straight answer. He loved riddles. Houdini had shown up on our property more than once, so I guessed his animal flew around this isolated area. Or ran. I'd seen him in more than one animal form, so he was a man of many secrets himself.

He slid his hand over mine and stared at me through the open window that separated us. "If I had a lover, I'd never keep secrets."

I snorted and got inside the truck. "All you do is dance around the truth. You're like the Riverdance of Lies."

"I don't know what that means," he said, gently closing the door, "but I always have your best interest in mind."

"I have nothing to do with this alleged fantasy lover that you may or may not ever have. You're not my type."

A playful smile touched his lips. "Am I not tall and handsome? Would you prefer me with dark hair and a beard?"

"We share the same blood, so it's practically incest."

"Technicalities."

"If you're here to sabotage my relationship, thinking it'll bring us together, think again. I know you don't want to be with me."

He rested his arms on the door. "I do tire of assumptions."

I kept my eyes on his chin. "You don't want me as a lover; you want me as your pet. My dad has a dog. It's loyal, obedient, loves him unconditionally, and does what it's told."

"You know how Shifters feel about pets."

"Yes, and I also know about the human pets some of them keep. Besides, you're not entirely Shifter."

"And you're not entirely Vampire. You will never keep Poe satisfied. Full-blooded Vampires aren't like us, Raven. They have insatiable desires they can't control. We have the best of both worlds because we're not chained to those same desires. Vampires begin immortality with bloodlust. Some of them indulge in those cravings before they're forced to control it. Others suffer in starvation with small victims fed to them until they adjust and learn how to control their desires. But they're always there, beneath the surface. You don't find blood delicious, do you? I'm not speaking of Vampire blood but everyone else's. Neither do I. It's repulsive."

"Now I know what to get you for Christmas. Can I go now? I'm in a celebratory mood, and you're ruining it."

"Should I send a bottle to your house?"

I gave him a mechanical smile. "Please don't. In fact, stop hanging around my house… and the roads that lead to my house."

"All roads lead to you, Butterfly."

Houdini stepped away from the truck as I ran the engine and put it in gear. After passing him, I glanced in the rearview mirror at a white panther standing on top of a grey coat. Every Shifter needed a private place for his animal to roam, but I sure as hell wished it wasn't in my backyard.

It was clear that only death would remove Houdini from my life. Most makers taught their younglings all the ways of being a Vampire before their progeny was ready to go off on their own. But Houdini and I never had a relationship, and now he acted as if he wanted to make up for lost time. Either that or he felt entitled to me.

As I traveled the road home, I reveled in the success of my latest case. Never in a million years had I pictured myself with an organization like Keystone, but they were fast becoming family. Thank God Christian was willing to save Blue, and she was willing to accept. I didn't know much about her past, but I felt connected to her as a person. As a friend. Best of all, I could now sleep at night knowing that my father had someone who would defend his life, even if that someone was a Vampire-hating dog. Not only did we catch a killer, but we saved children in the process. That always counts for something.

And yet… Houdini had planted a seed. I had to decide whether to water it and watch it grow into an invasive vine that threatened to strangle everything good about my relationship with Christian or let it die. I kept my eyes trained on the road because I knew where it led. It was the other road I was uncertain about—the one Houdini had tempted me with. But nothing good ever came from his temptations, so I decided to keep Pandora's box closed.

For now.

Printed in Great Britain
by Amazon